MW01356069
GAMES
OF
TANGLED HEARTS

Ebook ISBN: 979-8-9929282-1-1

Paperback ISBN: 979-8-9929282-0-4

Cover Design by: Kateryna Vitkovskaya at vitkovskaya.art

Editing by: Jessica Booth at Love Notes Editing at lovenotesediting.com

Photography by Kailey at AnnLee Photography at annleephotography.com

For permission requests, write to me at authorkelseywinton@gmail.com

Contents

To myself, for showing up, pushing through, and finishing a lifelong dream.
You fucking did the thing.

"To be wise and love, Exceeds man's might,"

Valentine, Act 1, Scene 1

Two Gentlemen of Verona

William Shakespeare

Content Warnings

Games of Tangled Hearts is a slow-burn gamer romance featuring a plus-size heroine, Sylvie, and a bisexual hero, Valentino. It explores the complexities of human emotion and the line between attachments.

There is on-page use of profanity.

Descriptions of gaslighting.

Depictions of financial, mental & emotional abuse.

There are mentions of internalized fatphobia/body image (FMC).

This novel has explicit sex scenes between consenting partners.

A Note on Piracy

While piracy may be an exciting theme in stories, it's important to support authors by obtaining books through legitimate means.

If you're having trouble accessing a copy of *Games of Tangled Hearts*, or if you find yourself reading a pirated copy, please reach out to me directly at authorkelseywinton@gmail.com. I'm more than happy to assist you in finding the right way to enjoy the book.

Thank you for your support!

Gaming Terminology

Affiliate and Partner Programs: Programs offered by platforms like Twitch and YouTube that allow streamers to earn money from subscriptions, ad revenue and others, provided the streamer meets certain criteria like a minimum number of followers or streaming hours.

AFK: (Away from keyboard) Used to indicate that the player is temporarily not playing or is away from their controls.

Boss: A powerful enemy in a game, usually at the end of a level or as apart of a key story event, that presents a significant challenge.

Co-op: (Cooperative) A mode of gameplay where two or more players work together to complete game objectives, as opposed to competing against one another.

Cozy Games: a genre of games that are designed to be relaxing and feel good. Typically they are non-violent.

DLC: (Downloadable Content) Refers to extra content that can be downloaded for a game separate from the main story.

Donation/Tips: Money given by viewers to support the streamer. This can be facilitated through platforms like PayPal, Patreon, or an integrated service on streaming platforms.

Emotes: Custom icons that subscribers can use in chat. These are unique to each channel and are a way for viewers to express themselves or react during the stream.

Enkin: A broad term used for the enemies one would encounter in Mundo.

Gamertag: a player's in-game screen name. Players often go by their gamertag instead of their real names.

Good Game: what players say to each other after finishing a game/match, sometimes abbreviated as "GG" (phonetically — gee-gees).

Grinding: Performing repetitive tasks in a game to gain experience, level up a character, or acquire specific loot.

Lag: a delay between the input of an action and when the action is completed in game. Commonly, when you are lagging, your character will glitch.

Lobby: an in-game waiting room.

Loot: Items or rewards that players can collect by defeating enemies or completing tasks within the game. These can include weapons, armor, currency, and other useful resources.

MMO: (Mass Multiplayer Online) refers to a type of game in which many people will play together on the same server.

MMORPG: (Mass Multiplayer Online Role-Playing Game) A genre of video games that enables a large number of players to interact with one another in a virtual world. These games often involve character building, questing, and social interaction.

Moderator: An individual who will help a streamer manage their online communities. Sometimes shortened to "Mod".

Non-Player Character: Often shortened to "NPC" these are in-game characters that are not controlled by players, but rather the game's AI. They can provide quests, story progression, or simply populate the game world.

Noob: refers to someone who is new at a game or lacks skills. Often used as an insult.

OBS: (Open Broadcaster Software) A popular, open source software used for live streaming and recording. OBS allows you to capture and mix video and audio, customize scenes, and stream to platforms like Twitch, YouTube, and Facebook.

OP: a shortened form of the word overpowered.

Overlay: Graphics or images that appear on top of the video content during a stream. Overlays can display information like recent subscribers, donations, chat messages, and more, enhancing the viewer's experience.

Player Character: or "PC" a fictional character in a video game or tabletop role-playing game whose actions are controlled by the person playing the game.

PvP: (Player vs. Player) This is a type of game where people play against each other.

Raid: At the end of a stream, a host can "raid" another channel, directing their viewers to another streamer's channel. This helps boost viewer numbers and can introduce fans to similar content creators.

Respawn: When a player or character comes back to life after being defeated or dying in a game. This term can also apply to in-game items or enemies that reappear after a certain amount of time.

RP: (Role-Playing) The act of playing an in-game character within the back-story you've assigned to them.

RPG: (Role-Playing Game) You create a character that you then level up through experiences when playing.

Sandbox: refers to a game that is an open-ended world with non-linear gameplay. It allows freedom for the player to explore however they wish.

Speedrun: The act of completing a game as fast as possible.

Subscribers: Viewers who pay a monthly fee to support the streamer. In return, subscribers usually gain access to exclusive emotes, badges, and other perks.

Troll: a person who posts content online with the aim of harassing, irritating, and/or provoking others.

Twitch: The leading live streaming platform, primarily for gamers, where streamers can broadcast their gameplay and interact with viewers in real-time.

VOD: (Video on Demand) In streaming, this refers to storing a stream on another platform for people to watch after the stream has ended.

Username: a unique name chosen by an individual to uniquely identify them on a network, website, computer etc.

Players, Tags & PCs

In this novel, characters have identities in both the physical and online worlds, including their real names, gamer tags, and player characters. It's typical in online gaming to refer to others by their gamer tags or variations of them. In the game *Mundo*, each player also controls a unique character.

This guide provides all the names linked to each character for reference.

Sylvie Rivera
Gamer Tag: Rheailia
Player Character: Celestina
Race: Dwarf
Class: Two-Handed Warrior
Talent(s): Archeology, Blacksmithing
Faction: Cabbala

Valentino Santos
Gamer Tag: SaintVal
Player Character: Valen
Race: Half-Elf
Class: Dual-Wielding Warrior
Talent(s): Hunting/Fishing, Medicine
Faction: Junta

Preston Hailos
Gamer Tag: PropheticPax

Player Character: Thalarion

Race: Human

Class: Arcane Mage

Talent(s): Alchemy, Enchanting

Faction: Junta

Speed Vittore

Gamer Tag: Amazing69Speed

Player Character: Nix

Race: Half-demon

Class: Bard

Talent(s): Leatherwork, Inscription

Faction: Junta

Xander Lys

Gamer Tag: PixelatedStone

Player Character: Luciento & Krab (wolf companion)

Race: Halfling

Class: Beast Master Ranger

Talent(s): Blacksmithing, Mining

Faction: Junta

Sebastian

Gamer Tag: GenDomna

Player Character: Sebastian

Race: Elf

Class: Druid

Talent(s): Jewel Crafting

Faction: Cabbala

Vyola Jones

Gamer Tag: DualFates

Player Character: Cesario

Race: Half-Elf

Class: Rogue

Talent(s): Enchanting

Faction: Cabbala

Theo Griego

Gamer Tag: TheoDios

Bastian Hawthorne

Gamer Tag: MerchantPrince32

Player Character: Aurelius

Race: Human

Class: Arcane Mage

Talent(s): Enchanting, Alchemy

Faction: Cabbala

Cameron Chase

Gamer Tag: Cam_the_Clever

Player Character: Flickerfoot

Race: Gnome

Class: Theif

Talent(s): Inscription, Tailoring

Faction: Junta

Dominic Wolfe

Gamer Tag: LordDom_TheHunter

Player Character: Maverick

Race: Elf

Class: Archer Ranger

Talent(s): Cooking, Hunting/Fishing

Faction: Machiava

Katerina Minola

Gamer Tag: WildKat

Player Character: Reyna

Race: Human

Class: Sword & Shield Warrior

Talent(s): Blacksmithing, Engineering

Faction: Machiava

Mia Egan

Gamer Tag: TinyTitan

Player Character: Elyndra

Race: Gnome

Class: Cleric

Talent(s): Medicine, Jewel Crafting

Faction: Junta

Chapter 1
Sylvie

I hesitate, my hand hovering above the doorknob. I'm outside my apartment, cringing at the string of expletives spewing from the voice within. My boyfriend, Theo, uses such vulgar language when he's losing in his video game, because his team sucks, or the connection is lagging, or whatever reason he can blame. Either way, angry Theo makes me uncomfortable. He snaps at me for the smallest infractions. But, I can't wait outside forever. He's expecting me home.

You got this Sylvie.

Taking a deep breath and steeling my nerves, I unlock the door and enter the war zone.

Just as I predicted, Theo is at his desk streaming himself playing his favorite game, *Obsidian*. It's a massively multiplayer online first-person shooter. His new LED lights illuminate him in red hues. It reminds me of a demon, if demons played video games for a living.

"Hey, babe," I say, forcing a smile.

Theo furiously pounds on his keyboard while trash-talking into the microphone. This time he's using choice words to describe someone's assumed sexuality and preferred methods of pleasuring their partners.

"My first day of class was great," I say, knowing Theo's not listening. "Since you're streaming, I'll go do some schoolwork."

Still, Theo doesn't acknowledge me.

I retreat down the hallway to my sanctuary: the second bedroom I turned into my office. It's the one place I can get away, relax, and do what I want. The evening light casts a warm glow over the room. I drop my backpack by the desk before the secondhand couch claims me as its own. I lie down, pulling the microfleece blanket around me.

In this room, I can listen to the music he doesn't like, play games he doesn't like, and even listen to my favorite podcast.

Speaking of, my favorite gaming podcaster, Prospero, released a new episode today featuring a streamer I've never heard of. That isn't unusual. Prospero has a talent for giving smaller streamers a spotlight, and then their careers take off.

So, he must see something special in his guest, SaintVal. They're going to talk about my favorite video game: *Mundo.*

My cell phone pings with a text notification, snapping me out of my trance.

Sebastian:

Did you listen?

Vyola:

What he said^^

I smile at my phone. Sebastian and Vyola are my best friends. Vyola, and I worked together at Café Amore before I, before *Theo,* convinced me to quit. He told me that I needed to focus on my studies.

Sylvie:

Just starting it.

Sebastian:

Let us know when you finish!

Sylvie:

I will!

My attention drifts to my backpack where my laptop rests. I *should* start researching local clinics. Next semester I will begin my internship hours needed to complete my master's degree in counseling education.

But checking out SaintVal's social media would be excellent self-care. I bring up my social media apps and search for his name.

I expected to see some guy with short hair, white skin, and a wrinkled anime T-shirt. I wasn't expecting SaintVal to be this gender norms-defying man with long hair reaching his waist, painted nails, a crop top, and a floral tattoo of a rose and an iris on his left forearm.

But that's not what draws me in. It's the genuine smile, the kind that transforms his entire face. It's the aura he exudes even in a group photo. I almost buy it. But, I know better than to be fooled by staged scenes of happiness.

Combing through his socials, I gather that SaintVal is a young IT professional and amateur streamer. His content does feature other games, but he uploads a consistent *Mundo* Let's Play with each weekly update. Besides his gamer content, he also posts about the places he explores in his city.

Wait—I hover over one photo. I know that coffee shop. That's Café Amore. The next photo features him in cosplay outside a convention hall. I know that building too! It's the convention center where the local comic con is held. I've been to that art museum. And to that street fair.

SaintVal must live in Marviewburg, the same as me. He has too many pictures of the city's secret gems to not live here. He likes the same places I do. Have we run into one another before? Unlikely, even if we have the same hobbies, millions of people live here. And I would have remembered that infectious smile.

It's cool that a local streamer is guesting on Prospero's podcast. This opportunity will boost his visibility and take his career to new heights. It would for anyone.

Theo would never admit it, but he desperately wants to guest on the podcast too. He started his career as a streamer after he burst through the door ranting about something that happened at work and throwing his stuff on the table.

Theo jumped into a crowded pool, thinking he would make a splash. Except he didn't.

He didn't do his research into the market or platforms. He didn't plan out his setup. He didn't make a content plan or do any branding. Now, finances are tight and we barely scrape by on his pitiful earnings, our meager savings, and the generosity of his wealthy parents.

If Theo had bothered to ask me before he made this decision for the both of us, I would have said becoming a mainstream streamer was a matter of luck and timing. As in, they made it big because they got into the industry at the right time. Or they have a unique personality, like SaintVal, that attracts people. Theo has none of those things. He's trying to be something like an alpha bro, one of those men who believe they have to be dominant in any situation. The aggression and hyper-masculinity make me sick.

According to him, I have no say in life-altering decisions like his job when we are a single-income household.

I shake my head, tired of that train of thought. Moving to my desk, I set up my laptop. Might as well do some work while I listen to the episode. I open my podcast platform, bring up Prospero's latest episode, and click play.

The catchy four-chord intro music plays, and then Prospero's modulated voice greets his audience. "Hello and welcome to *Tempest Loading*. I'm your host, Prospero. In this episode, I'm talking with SaintVal about Mundo and the long-awaited expansion update."

Energy hums through me. I am ecstatic about Friday's Mundo update. Rhessa Studios releases an update every week to give players a constant stream of new quests. Three days from now, they'll release their revolutionary update that will completely change the way the game is played.

"SaintVal," Prospero's synthetic voice echoes through the monitor. "Thanks for joining me."

"It is my honor, Prospero." I can hear the excitement in SaintVal's response. "But you can call me Val."

He has an intriguing voice, the tone suggesting maturity but tinged with a child-like glee.

"Alright, Val," Prospero says. "Tell us a little about yourself?"

"I grew up military, moving around every two years or so. I kept in contact with my friends by meeting up online to play games together." Val's voice relaxes as he talks about himself. "I discovered *Mundo* when I was in college. My long-distance friends would all play together late at night to catch up."

Well, that's cool. He lives in my city and is around my age. I was a senior in high school when *Mundo* was first released. So far, Val's impressive. Prospero is leading the conversation, sure. But Val strikes me as a knowledgeable passionate gamer.

"And who can forget that scandal?" Prospero comments. "Came out of nowhere."

"It rocked our worlds for sure," Val continues. "Rhessa Akepse, the creator of *Mundo*, sued their long-time best friend, Staric Homer-Wolph, for stealing their intellectual property."

It's a story of friendship and betrayal. Rhessa and Staric were best friends, but creative differences drove them apart.

"Staric made a few changes against Rhessa's wishes and released the best-selling MMO, *Obsidian*," Prospero summarizes.

More like Staric threw away years of friendship for a payday. The day after the two settled their lawsuit, Rhessa announced his new project, *Mundo*. A free RPG game with both local and online multiplayer capabilities.

"Best-selling is subjective," Val counters. "Today, the number of Mundo downloads surpassed the total number of individual *Obsidian* games sold."

"That's an interesting point, Val," Prospero says. "Let's put all that aside and get to the meat of your story. Tell me what keeps you coming back to *Mundo*."

What wouldn't draw them in? *Mundo* is an open-world Japanese-inspired fantasy role-playing game. Imagine walking into a world with the visual beauty of a Studio Ghibli movie. It's breathtaking. And don't get me started on the storytelling.

"The customized playing experience," Val answers. "Before you get into character creation, a player has to join one of three factions. My experience playing with my specific character build in the Junta faction differs from someone playing a similar build in either the Cabbala or Machiava factions."

"What is your build?"

"A half-elf, dual-wielding fighter named Valen. The base build isn't original, but I took medicine as one of his talents, which allows me to gather specific herbs and craft healing potions for cheaper than buying them in the guild. Additionally..." Val pauses, "I'm monologuing."

I laugh imagining him vibrating with energy as he talks about his character. Like me, he's probably been told to cool it before.

Prospero asks, "You ready for Friday?"

"Hell yes! Wait, sorry, heck yes! No more faction boundaries."

"For the first time, players can freely interact with one another. What does that mean for you as a player, Val?"

"New experiences and new challenges. I can explore previously inaccessible lands and interact with new players."

"Do you have any predictions for the update?"

"I think we'll get specific missions encouraging cooperation between players of different factions," Val says.

He breathed life into my fears. Sebastian and Vyola are in the same faction as me, so we can play together. But meeting new people to play with will be hard. Theo bitches at me if I talk to strangers on the internet. But, it's okay for *him* to do it because, according to him, he's just trash-talking.

If I can't play with new people, then I can kiss those rewards goodbye.

"Let's return to the topic we touched on earlier," Prospero says. "The success of *Obsidian* versus the success of *Mundo*. That very question has been a point of contention. So I ask you, which is the more successful game?"

Oh, that's a hard question. Theo and I have had this very debate.

"Success itself is a subjective word." Val pauses, choosing his words carefully. "How do you measure it? In sales? *Obsidian* has a traditional business model. Customers pay sixty dollars for the base game. The game has a small campaign because most players compete online in ten-minute rounds for control of various territories. Then a DLC is released, everyone pays for that, and the cycle repeats."

"Which makes it one of the highest-grossing games of all time," Prospero says. "While *Mundo* is free. So, why don't they charge for the game?"

That was the million-dollar question. Literally. Rhessa could have made bank. But putting it behind a paywall means I wouldn't be able to play. It's available in a way no other game of its size is.

Val continues, "I believe Rhessa wanted to create an accessible experience for all. There is a financial barrier to gaming. Consoles, PCs, laptops, and even smartphones are expensive enough. Rhessa wanted to create a game people enjoyed and could play with their friends at little to no cost."

He took the words right out of my mouth. I'd love nothing more than to play *Mundo* with someone like him who shares the same passion for gaming as me. But it's not like I would ever meet him. There are hundreds of thousands of people in Marviewburg. If I haven't already met Val, I don't think I ever will.

"That's deep, Val. Thank you for joining me today and chatting about Mundo," Prospero starts their sign-off. "Tell the people where they can find you."

"Thank you again for having me, Prospero. I'll be back anytime you want." Val rattles off his social media platforms along with his Twitch platform.

"I might take you up on the offer. To everyone listening, have a magical night."

It felt good to listen to a *Mundo* player like Val. I'm so used to boys like Theo who think women are not real gamers. Or that one must only play first-person shooters to be a *real* gamer.

Fuck that. Women are gamers too. There's nothing wrong with a cozy game.

I open up SaintVal's socials again to follow him. I wouldn't mind seeing more content from him.

Sighing, I close out of my social media accounts, knowing that it's time to be responsible again. I should start looking at these internships to narrow down my choices. I log into the school portal and pull up the list of approved partners. I pass over the usual locations most go to, working with children, families in crisis, behavioral health centers, and even rehab centers.

I know I want to work with children and youth, but beyond that, I haven't given this too much thought.

Then, at the bottom of the list, I see a recent addition–a private practice. I pull up their website. The owner launched it in the last five years. In the About section, he lists how he uses tabletop games and video games as a part of his practice. That would be perfect!

My heart jumps as I hear footsteps coming down the hall. I spin my chair just as Theo bursts in, throwing the door against the wall.

"Babe," he says, then pauses.

I force my body to still, slowing my breathing as I look at my boyfriend.

Most people are taller than me, but Theo towers over my short stature. Now that I'm sitting, his imposing figure looms over me. I don't mind the view. He's handsome, with blonde hair, light blue eyes, and some stubble. One of his viewers said he should grow out his beard, so he did. Nevermind that I've been telling him that for months now.

"What are you doing?" Theo asks, looking over my shoulder.

"Researching internships," I answer, my heart pounding in my chest. "I meet with my advisor on Thursday."

His piercing blue eyes drill into me. I tense. That's not good. I assess his face for his tells, the way his eyebrows pull, how his jaw tenses. He's smug. He thinks he caught me doing something wrong.

"Did you watch my stream?" he asks.

Fuck, I forgot. "I just wanted to focus on my research." It was the first excuse that came to mind.

Theo's gaze flicks to the screen behind me. "Focus while you listen to Prospero's podcast?"

I don't answer. I just close my eyes and pray to whoever's listening that he drops the subject.

Theo's voice lowers, "It pisses me off that you were listening to that fucker when you could have been watching my stream."

"I'm sorry Theo," I say, forlorn. *Please just drop it.*

"I don't know why you listen to that douche," Theo says, moving away from me and pulling out his cell phone before dropping onto the couch.

I want to say that Prospero's not a fool, but that would frustrate Theo more than I already have. And I'm not sure if it's worth my energy.

"I'm not sure why you're even researching. You said you would apply to the clinic around the corner."

I did say that—a while ago. Before Theo quit his job. "I was looking at ones that are paid internships too."

Theo's eyebrows pull together. "Why?" he demands.

"We could use the extra income."

"Are you questioning my ability to take care of us?" Theo stands up, and I shrink into my chair as he approaches.

"No, I just—"

"Then don't worry about it." When I say nothing, Theo raises his hand to cup my face. He's won, and he knows it. "Trust me, baby."

"Okay," I force my best fake smile. He loves me, he wants the best for us, right?

"That's my girl," Theo says, leaning to press a lingering kiss to my mouth. It lasts longer than I'd like.

He leaves not long after that. I take a minute, breathing deeply to calm my racing heart. I just need to hang on for a couple more months. Two more semesters and I will graduate and can get a job. Then everything will go back to being normal.

Chapter 2
Valentino

Prospero's fancy sign-off music plays and the episode is over. The pressure fades and I feel like I can relax. the episode over, I close the laptop and turn around to face the crowd that erupts with applause. Several people come to pat me on the back.

One of my close friends, Xander, comes up to me. His strong, scarred hands clasp my own. "Congrats, Val," he says.

His service dog, Pixel, looks up at me, too. She's sitting on Xander's left foot, with her tongue hanging out of her mouth. I want nothing more than to take her face in my hands and tell Pixel she is the best girl in the whole world. But she's working and I know better than to distract her.

Several others come up to congratulate me for guesting on *Tempest Loading*. It's an amazing opportunity. When I started streaming, I never thought I'd be a guest on the Prospero's podcast. Then again, I never imagined my subscriber count would ever be more than ten people. And all those people want to watch me play video games—mostly *Mundo*.

I stream for fun. IT professional by day and an amateur streamer by night. I love the community I've built and my subscribers are the best. They make me custom emotes and help moderate my chats. I owe everything to them.

Someone's arm hooks around my neck and my head jerks to the side. I see my friend Speed's unruly curls in my peripheral. "Don't thou forget thy poor pauper friends, whence thou art rolling in thy sweet sponsorship money."

Speed is not his real name, but it is his preferred nickname among his friends. He only uses his government name at work.

Wielding his unwavering charisma, Speed commands the crowd to silence like a maestro conducts their orchestra. "The honorable Preston," Speed gestures to my best friend with his other hand. "Hath prepared us a speech."

This screening party is courtesy of my best friend, Preston Hailos. He steps in front of me, looking like a prince. If princes casually dress in fitted jeans and a dark grey t-shirt. He looks delicious.

We're at our usual hangout spot and Marviewburg's premier gaming cafe. 2Game is an oasis for nerds, geeks, and otakus alike. For a generous daily rate, you get access to all new-gen gaming consoles and games, PCs for gaming, a ramen and boba bar, an imported snack cafe, tabletop gaming areas, collectibles, and a private streaming room. Which is where we are celebrating.

"Valentino Santos," Preston begins, his voice caressing each letter. "When you first told me Prospero had reached out to you, I thought you a lying scoundrel." He pauses, anticipating the crowd's laughs.

I laugh too. When Prospero first contacted me, I couldn't believe it either. I thought it was a spam email.

"But here you are," Preston says, extending his hand to me. "Just like I said you'd be. It's awesome Prospero featured you on his podcast. But Val-" his vibrant blue eyes turn to capture my gaze. "It's only the beginning for you."

Preston does that thing with his mouth where one corner lifts. It makes the tingles crawl up my back and my heart jumps into my throat.

"Raise your soda, to SaintVal, the next big *Mundo* streamer," Preston finishes. He raises his Mt. Dew and tips it back. I watch his throat bob with the pull of soda.

"Speech! Speech!" the crowd demands, snapping me out of my thoughts.

Reluctantly, I calm the room down. Where do I start? "I want to thank everyone for coming out tonight." That feels like a good start. They're here because they're supporting me. *Just be yourself, Val.* "It means the world to me to celebrate with those who were there before all this. I also want to extend my thanks to Theseus, the owner of this fine establishment."

A rugged-looking man with a well-kept beard nods at me from the back of the room. "The pleasure is mine Val," he says.

I continue, "As I said in the podcast, I moved around a lot. Making friends was easy, but keeping them was harder. Video games were a way I kept in contact. I found my passion with *Mundo* and wanted to share that passion with others."

I find Preston's familiar gaze and hold it. "It is through my passion that I found my people."

Preston winks. I smile and continue, "Enough of my rambling. Let's go play some video games!"

There's another round of cheers and the people scatter around the store. My closest friends, Preston, Speed, and Xander with Pixel, wait for most of the crowd to leave.

"Care to grind out a mission for some experience points before we call it a night?" Xander asks.

"Hell yes!" I say. "I need some experience points to level up by Friday."

"What else is there to do on a Tuesday night?" Speed asks.

"Exactly." I give Speed a fist bump.

"Theseus reserved our usual spot," Xander says, nodding to the space.

As if anyone would take our spot. But I'm still going to thank Theseus for that, and for so much more.

I take my usual seat. It's the interior computer in a quad against one of the interior walls. Preston sits at one next to me and Speed takes the computer directly across from me, while Xander claims the one next to him so Pixel will be comfortable lying at his feet.

"What were they like?" Speed asks as we boot up the computers and log into our *Mundo* accounts.

I know he means Prospero. The podcaster is a mystery. "We had a video call about a week ago, but they never turned on their camera and used a modulated voice."

"I wonder why?" Xander deadpans the rhetorical question. Nobody knows why.

Whoever Prospero is, they created this mysterious persona. They drift through the gamer community, working their magic, and shifting the tides. In a way, that's the best part about them. Prospero worked hard to establish themselves as a knowledgeable and credible voice in the community.

Mundo's main menu appears on the computer screen. I enter my login information to bring up my profile, put on my headset, and launch the game. Since we are in a quad, Xander, Speed, Preston, and I don't use the mics, but we do use the headsets to keep the noise down.

The opening music lilts in soft and airy, like a butterfly's wings. It crescendos until, at the peak, the full orchestra begins. The vibrant melody sweeps along with the familiar graphics and opening credits. The camera pans over rolling hills filled with monsters, then a dense forest of mist and secrets, before arriving outside the gates of Anorev, home to the Junta faction. My player character, Valen, loads on the screen next to the bronze and purple Junta emblem; two ravens on a field of purple with interconnected diamond shapes.

I chose the Junta faction because of its emphasis on team building and cooperation. Since I like to play with friends, I might as well get rewarded for it. For example, if I complete a quest with a group, the chances of rare loot drops increase, and I'd get additional experience points.

I choose the multiplayer option and then press start. The gates on the screen open, and the camera moves into the city, then the screen changes. Valen appears in the Junta Faction headquarters, a tavern in Anorev proper. It serves as a home base for us. We can get our daily quests, team up with our friends, and buy supplies we will need for adventuring.

Other player characters bustle around Valen, their names floating like halos above their avatar's head.

Pres_the_Paragon wants to join your party.

I accept Preston's request and say, "Have I ever told you how pretentious your username is?"

"Have I told you I don't care?" Preston says as he laughs.

His avatar, a human wizard he named Proteus, enters my screen. Proteus sports a purple wizard's robe with bronze accents. As the official colors of the Junta faction, purple items are prestigious and difficult to find. Preston and I worked hard to get him that robe.

Amazing69Speed wants to join your party.

I spot Speed's avatar, a half-demon bard, Nix, sitting at the bar. He put all his points in Charisma-based skills, earning him a smooth tongue and getting them out of more than one sticky situation.

Preston leans over, his shoulder touching mine. "You think my username is pretentious?"

I laugh deep in my chest. My next inhale is full of Preston. He smells of spiced toffee.

Xander's gnome beast-master ranger, Luciento, and his wolf companion, Krab, appear on the screen.

PixelatedStone wants to join your party.

I accept Xander's invitation. Our group is ready to go.

This quad is the best. We have a fluid synergy and a balanced party.

"So Val, what do you want to do tonight?" Speed asks.

"Grind out some XP," I answer. One more mission will get me those sweet experience points to get me to the next level. When I do, I get an additional item slot. I want that to happen before the update on Friday.

"Let's grab one of the daily missions," Xander says. He navigates his avatar, Luciento, to the bulletin board on the wall to the right of the bar.

A nest of Beastkin made a nest in the forest bordering my farm. They're ruining crops and attacking my livestock. It's dangerous for me and my family. I may not have much, but if you can clear the nest, it's yours.

We won't take any money from the farmer. Maybe some resources for crafting potions if he has some. "Let's go," I say.

Quest Accepted: Clear the Enkin Threat for Famer Eldwin

We navigate our avatars out of the tavern, out of Anorev, and into the countryside.

As we travel, Speed asks me, "Did you check your number of followers?"

"No," I admit.

"Why not?"

"I'll see a bigger number if I check in the morning." If I was being honest, I'd say I was scared to look. I don't have a goal number in my head, but I can't help but imagine a scenario where I open my platforms and see that the numbers haven't changed.

Right now, all I want to do is play my favorite game with my favorite people. Because at this moment all is right with the world.

"Regardless of the number of followers," Speed says. "I'm excited to go live on Friday."

"Speaking of, what time on Friday?" We plan to meet up here, at 2Game. Theseus is keeping the store open late for a members-exclusive event.

Preston audibly exhales beside me. His hands tremble on his keyboard. That's not the reaction I was expecting. "You okay, man?" I ask.

He lifts his shaking hands from his keyboard, and his avatar, Proteus, stops moving in the game. "Not now, Val." Preston's voice trembles over the words.

Xander, Speed, and I all stop moving our avatars. Preston's gaze doesn't meet mine. He only does this when he's sitting on bad news. And I'd bet money I won't like what he's going to say.

I lean back in my chair, dropping my headphones around my neck. My heart sinks. "Preston, what's going on Friday?"

"Please Val," Preston's weak voice pleads, "Not now."

"Oh no, please do this now," Speed says, stretching his arms out behind his head.

Xander remains silent but sits upright, his headphones around his neck. He reaches down to pet Pixel, whose golden head is raised, sensing the emotionally charged moment.

He's ditching me. I see Preston's guilt in the way he puts his head in his hands. The awkward silence tells me more than he dares to. "You're not coming to the release party," I say, because it's not a question.

"Something came up," Preston admits.

Disappointment, anger, and a dozen other emotions build inside. I shove them down and appeal to my logic. Preston wouldn't ditch me if it wasn't something serious. Maybe something with his family. "Did something happen with your dads?" I ask.

He shakes his head. "Nothing like that."

Well, that's good at least. "Then what?"

Because if whatever came up doesn't involve his family, then what could be so important? What is more important than something he's had planned with us, with me, for months?

I study him. Preston drags his hands down his face until it comes to rest in front of his mouth. He's still not looking at me.

"Dude, just tell me."

I'm not prepared for his answer. "I have a date."

Chapter 3
Valentino

Preston is a supportive friend. He would give me anything I needed, no questions asked. Hell, he's the one who threw me this party.

But Preston is also a hopeless romantic. He believes in "love at first sight"—in committing yourself entirely to one person, with no room for exceptions. And, he would drop everything for love, including his friends.

"Out of all days you could schedule a date..." I struggle to find the words, "You pick this Friday? What the hell?"

Preston gets defensive, "I didn't have a choice—"

I cut him off. "Because you have no control over your schedule." Ice coats every word.

What love has Preston found that is more important than his plans, more important than me?

"The date is with Julianna," Preston says.

My stomach drops.

"Sinclair?" I ask.

Preston nods.

Defeat washes over me. Fuck.

Julianna Sinclair is a beauty and wellness influencer based in our city. Some would call her classically pretty with natural golden blonde hair and large, grey doe eyes. Others would say she's no different from the dozens of other beauty influencers. But Preston has worshiped the ground she walks on since they went to that expensive private high school together.

As the legend goes, Julianna was a grade behind Preston in high school. He insists she was never interested in him because he was a hideous teenager. I can't imagine a world in which Preston was ever hideous. But to him, Julianna is the girl who got away. He follows her on every platform and is one of her biggest supporters. Now, after years of pining, he's finally got her attention.

"Congratulations, Pres," Xander says, breaking the awkward tension. I notice Xander's right hand reaching down to rest on Pixel's head. The tension melts from his shoulders as he does.

Preston's face glows in response. "Thanks, man."

"How did you land her?" Speed asks, his voice a touch too casual. He leans forward, hands resting in front of him, mouth pulled into a firm line. I know that look. Speed, the lawyer, analyzes Preston like he would a witness.

"She did a fundraiser for her favorite charity. Since I donated to the highest tier, I was entered into a lottery for the chance to win a one-hour virtual date with her."

I doubt there was an honest lottery system, not with social media. But Preston probably sees this as the chance he never had to tell her how he feels.

"When did you find out?" Speed asks.

"Yesterday," Preston admits, his smile falling when he looks at me. "I didn't say anything because today was supposed to be about you." He looks at me and I see the sincerity in his eyes. Dammit, I believe him. He did everything in his power to make today great. Other than my mom, he's been my biggest supporter.

But it still hurts to know Preston was keeping this from me. I would have rather known yesterday, even with this party today. But I don't say any of that. "It's fine."

Speed smirks, "And when was our goatish varlet going to tell us?"

"Save your grilling for deposition." Preston snaps

That's a deflection. My eyes flick to Speed's. After a moment, Speed's head drops and he puts his hands up. "Apologies my guy."

"Just be happy for me. I'm finally going to get the girl," Preston says.

"You don't know this girl." I don't stop the venom in my voice.

"I've known her since high school," he argues.

"Because people's personalities are totally cemented in high school."

"I know who she is in her core."

"Pres," Xander says gently. "She's an internet personality."

Speed is not so gentle. "You've fallen for a parasocial relationship."

We fall into another silence. Because there's nothing more I can say. We've had this conversation often enough that Preston's responses are rote. This girl is the love of his life and nothing will convince him otherwise.

"Say something, Val," Preston pleads.

"Like what?" He said he'd be there, and now he's not because of this girl.

Preston's voice drops, "I had every intention of being right there with you. It's just-"

"Julianna Sinclair," Speed tosses his shoulder-length hair from side to side as he bats his eyelashes at Preston.

"You've never had a one-on-one with her. Maybe this is your lucky break." Xander says. Always the optimist.

"I have a good feeling about this, you know?" Preston gives a nod and a small smile.

I can't believe my best friend is choosing the chance to date a girl who doesn't know he exists over the people who care about him most. But then again, it's typical Preston.

With this conversation at an end, Xander tentatively asks, "Are we good to finish this mission? I have a client at eight a.m. tomorrow."

Part of me wants to call it a night and go home. I could cuddle up with my cat and try to forget about Preston. But that's not how I want to end this night. I want to get those experience points to level up.

"Yeah," I say, forcing a smile.

We turn our attention back to our computers, slide the headphones over our ears, and dive back into the world of *Mundo.*

I pan my camera over the rolling hills of the countryside outside of the city proper. The landscape is dotted with lush vineyards, olive groves, and quaint villages with stone buildings. Clusters of trees are scattered around and line the winding road. In the distance, I can see the mountains where Emor is located.

We follow the in-game navigation to the farmer's land. He, like many others, has a small stone house.

Farmer Eldwin tells us he saw the Enkin—the game's overarching term for monsters— run off into the forest.

There are three subtypes of Enkin: Grasskin, Stonekin, and Waterkin. Each subtype has three different species, giving *Mundo* players nine different types of enemies.

"Some type of Grasskin," Xander reasons.

Grasskin are the most common subtype of Enkin around Anerov. Now we need to figure out which species of Grasskin we're dealing with.

I use the mouse to move my camera and look around the property. "Nothing is burned. So it's not a Firekin." They're chimera-like creatures with a feline bodies, large sweeping horns, goat hooves, and scales that sweep down their spines and into their tails. They leave a trail of fire wherever they go. With no evidence of burns on the farm, that leaves Beastkin and Forrestkin, the two other Grasskin species as options.

Preston's gaze drifts to mine. He winks at me. The same wink he gave me when we sat down next to one another in English 101. He was an accounting major, and I was a computer science major. We clicked immediately over *Mundo* and *Naruto.* We chatted so much that the professor had to separate us.

I knew I was bisexual by the time we met in college. When I realized he was too, I thought, maybe, I'd found my person. While we flirted, those intense stares, the small touches, the sexually charged compliments, they weren't only for me. Preston and I have never been anything more than friends. There were plenty of times when we could have had something more, but the timing never worked out. We didn't want to compromise our friendship, or whatever lie we told ourselves.

“Val,” Speed barks.

“What?”

A Cheshire cat's smile spreads across his smug face. He caught me daydreaming. “We were asking your thoughts on Xander's plan?”

Xander's our tactician. His eyebrows are pulled together, lips pursed. He’s looking at me, but I know his mind is turning over various scenarios. “So we are probably looking at some Beastkin.”

“You okay?” Preston leans into my space to whisper.

“Yeah, I'm fine. Just thinking.”

“About me, right?”

Of course, I'm thinking about him. “The podcast,” I lie.

Xander continues his plan. “I'm thinking we send Nix in to distract them. Then we can ambush them from the back.”

“Does Nix have any say in being the bait?” Speed asks, referring to his avatar in the third person.

“No,” Preston, Xander, and I say in unison.

"Well, aren't you all a bunch of foul and pestilent congregation of vapors?” Speed says with a huge grin on his face.

“Shut up, you love being the distraction,” I retort.

“So, what will you be doing while I risk my neck?” Speed asks.

“I'll keep the big guy busy,” I say. Valen is the strongest out of our four characters. Therefore, it's my job to engage the strongest Enkin.

“It's a good plan,” Xander agrees. Then turns and nods to Speed. “Do your thing, Nix.”

Speed navigates his avatar into the cluster of trees farmer Eldwin indicated. The rest of us follow at a distance. Nix pulls out a lute and begins to play as he walks. It takes thirty seconds for the playful adventuring music to switch to the short staccatos of battle. There are three Beastkins in total.

"Here we go," Xander says. He moves his avatar, Luciento, to mount his animal companion, Krab, and rides off to the right. He fires an arrow towards the Beastkin charging straight at Nix.

These enemies are a monstrous combination of a badger and raccoon, but as big as a bear and with a thick hide. I've seen them slice down an avatar with one claw attack. It's best to attack them at a distance. One Beastkin is dangerous. When they start to surround you, run.

I command Valen to run forward. The largest Beastkin charges towards Nix. I try to attack it before it hits Nix. I get a good swipe in, but because this is the leader, my swords don't do as much damage as they would to a normal Beastkin. The leader has an additional, magical armor barrier so Valen's attack damage is halved. I get two more hits in before the Beastkin hits me, taking one-third of Valen's health bar with a single slash. A second slash and Valen is down, a third and is knocked prone. One more hit and Valen will be dead.

Suddenly the head Beastkin is blasted back. A stream of powerful purple magic whizzes by my avatar. "Thank you, Proteus," I say to Preston.

Nix helps me up and uses a low-level healing spell to raise my HP.

The lead Beastkin rears up on its hind legs, aiming for another strike. It never comes. Our MVP Luciento makes a critical hit right through the Beastkin's head.

"Nix was supposed to be the distraction, not you." Xander jokes with me.

I give a half-hearted laugh. "Everything worked out in the end."

We loot the Beastkin, gaining some claws, fangs, and heartstrings that I can use to make a powerful potion. Afterward, we return to Farmer Eldwin with our report that the threat has been eliminated. He offers a few gold coins as a reward. I politely refuse the monetary compensation in favor of some herbs I can use to make a healing salve.

Mission Complete
1500 XP Gained

Both Luciento and Valen level up. I received the new item slot and immediately equip a ring, giving me a ten percent higher defense. Now, I'm ready for Friday.

But even with the update looming on the horizon, I can't find it in me to celebrate.

Mission complete, we shut down our computers and gather our things. I thank Theseus again for his generosity in hosting us tonight. Then Speed and Xander bid their goodbyes, walking in the opposite direction towards their cars.

I go to walk towards mine, but Peston grabs my arm. "*Mundo* will be around after this weekend." His hand is warm, and while I want those arms around me, I pull away.

Preston means well, but I can't stop hearing *you'll be around after this weekend*. It is as if he expects me to wait patiently at his door when he returns with his heart in pieces. Preston and I have danced around each other for a while, but I refuse to be his second choice. If I choose to be with someone, I want to know that I'm their first choice.

"I wish you the best of luck," I say. "I'm just going to adventure without you."

Preston's expression changes, his mouth pulling down at the corners. "Someday, I hope you'll understand. You'll find a partner who is worthy of you."

"I don't need a partner to be happy," I say, probably with more malice than he deserves.

"If you say so, Val." Preston's pearly whites shine as he laughs and gets into his Uber. I watch him ride off into the distance, as I sulk in my disappointment.

I walk down the street to the lot where I parked my car, reflecting on everything that happened today. How many conversations have I had with my mother about "settling down with a nice partner?" I'm just not interested. Maybe eventually I'll shack up with someone, but I'm still young. With my streaming career taking off, I shouldn't be focusing on dating.

I don't even know where to find someone who likes the same things. I like to think I have a broad range of interests—coding, anime, comic books, video games, baseball, fitness, and travel. Finding a girl who likes the same games, or even watches anime, seems to be hard enough. And unfortunately, the few gamer boys I've tried to talk to are chauvinistic and homophobic.

I slide into my car and start driving to my apartment. As I drive off, I find the resolve I need to get through this weekend.

I'll let Preston pine away after a girl. I'll move on to bigger and better things, even if it means leaving my friend behind.

Chapter 4
Sylvie

I love Thursday nights. My first date with Theo, the start of what I believed would be an epic love story, was on a Thursday. Over the next six years of dating, moving in together, of combining our incomes, Theo and I always (with a few exceptions) took Thursdays as time for each other.

Today that means no extra school work, no streaming, just the two of us. I say extra because, unfortunately, this semester I have classes on Tuesday and Thursday nights. I promised Theo I'd come straight home. I'm looking forward to having my boyfriend all to myself. We need this time together now more than ever.

Before I can go home, I have class. And before class, I have a meeting with my advisor. Time seems to crawl as I wait. I glance down and notice a spaghetti sauce stain on my white shirt. Just my luck.

The door opens, and another student walks out of the office, followed by Dr. Hermione Winters. "Sylvie," she smiles warmly. "Come in. I'm excited to hear your thoughts on your internship."

Slinging my backpack over my shoulder, I step into the office as Dr. Winters holds the door open. I take a seat in the designated guest chair and wait for her to settle behind her desk. "I have your file here. You're on track to graduate summa cum laude. You must be very proud." Her ice-blue eyes glitter like diamonds scattered across fresh snow.

"Thank you. I'm enjoying my time in the program." I am proud of the work that I've done, balancing my Graduate Assistant position and my school work. It pays for my tuition. When she acknowledges it too, my heart jumps at the praise. But that warmth is quickly smothered by the cold, familiar pang of longing. My mother would be proud if she were alive. My father might be too, if he'd bother to text me other than on my birthday and Christmas. My two half-siblings are the same.

"Wonderful," Dr. Winters exclaims. She leans forward, eyes sparkling with curiosity. "Have you looked over your options?"

Flipping through the Notes app on my phone I find my list. "My first choice is Yorke Behavioral Clinic."

"A good choice," Dr. Winters' eyebrows furrow. A wrinkle creases between her brows as she regards me. "They offer unpaid internships. Last time we spoke, you expressed interest in paid internships. Are you still wanting to pursue any?"

My thoughts flash back to Theo looming above me, his anger coming off of him in waves at my suggestion of a paid internship. I shake with chills. He can't set his pride aside to see how much a paid internship would help us. I take a breath, quelling my frustration with him.

My gaze connects with Dr. Winters', and a knowing smile tugs at the corner of her mouth. "Tell me which ones captured your interest," she presses.

Sometimes I feel like those sparkling blue eyes grant her superpowers. Dr. Winters can read me like a book. Where Theo sows doubt in my head, Dr. Winters shows me the sun.

I push back the self-doubt clawing at me. "Arino Family Practice," I say.

The world seemed to slow, waiting for something, anything to happen. "I was hoping someone would be interested," Dr. Winters starts. "However, Sal Arino will be selective when choosing his intern."

Oh. Figures. I try to stomp down the hope blooming in my chest. "I read his research about self-discovery and self-exploration through board games and tabletop RPGs. That's exactly the type of work I want to do."

"I think you should apply." Dr. Winters' words shock me.

"Really?" I lean forward in my chair, then pause. If I get accepted, I'd have to get a bus or subway pass to get to the practice. And Theo might not help me with those extra "unnecessary" expenses.

"You have concerns." Dr. Winters purses her lips. Her intense gaze isn't uncomfortable but it still feels like she's peeling back my layers. She folds her hands on her desk.

I wrap my arms around the curves of my midsection. "The commute. I live on the east side in Yorke, the commute would be forty-five minutes to the Umberwoods." Shameful heat rises in my neck and cheeks.

Dr. Winters drums her fingers on her desk before she spins in her chair to rummage through her desk drawers. She produces a single sheet of paper and slides it toward me. "The university provides some scholarships for internship assistance. It's not a huge sum, but it can cover expenses like personal attire, transportation, even temporary housing costs."

A hesitant smile touches my lips as I scan the paper. Hope blazes in my chest again, as I scan the list. A scholarship for a bus pass alone would be a big help. Maybe, just maybe, I could get Theo to agree to this if I had financial assistance.

"Let's meet again in mid-September to go over your application and personal statement before they're due." Dr. Winters stands and I follow suit. She ushers me to the door. "I'll be in touch."

I tuck the paper safely into my backpack. "Thank you, professor," I say.

Leaving her office, I'm filled with a renewed sense of confidence. This isn't just an internship, it was a chance to grow, to become the professional I dream of being. And, for the first time, I truly believe I can do it.

My heart buzzes at the thought of more uninterrupted time with Theo as I rush to the bus stop to catch an earlier ride home. Hopefully, Theo sees I'll be home earlier since I have my location shared with him. I send him a text just in case.

He doesn't text back.

The bus ride is uneventful. I get off and speed walk to my apartment.

Opening the door I call out, "Hey babe!" and remove my shoes by the door.

There's no response. I look over to his setup. Theo's face is illuminated by the glow of his computer screen. He doesn't turn to acknowledge me. A tiny knot of unease—or maybe disappointment—tightens in my stomach.

He is fully engrossed in his game, fingers flying across the keyboard, eyes glued to the screen. The voice in my head, an echo of his past complaints, reminds me that he needs to consistently stream to build his audience. Why shouldn't he play when I'm not home? But I am home now, and here he is, ignoring me once again.

Sighing, I turn my back on him and head down the hall. I put my backpack in my office and then slip into the bathroom—any tension I was holding within falls away with my bra to the floor. I crank the hot water and let it burn away the day's stress. Showers never last long enough. Afterward, I pull on a worn pair of leggings and my favorite anime shirt. *Romeo x Juliet* is a loose adaptation of the Shakespeare play but in a fantasy setting and with a better ending.

Now that I'm clean and changed, I venture back to the living room. Hopefully, Theo has finished up his stream, and date night can finally start.

"Do you want me to get started on dinner?" I ask.

"Shut up, I'm busy," Theo growls, eyes fixed to the screen. He's either oblivious or doesn't care.

I open my mouth to tell him off, but hesitate. If I interrupt him, Theo won't listen to me. I can imagine him saying how I ruined his stream by telling him to watch his mouth, that I would ruin his reputation. Even though nobody is falling for his alpha-male persona. I roll my eyes and head to the kitchen. I'm hungry, even if he isn't.

Yesterday, I stuffed shells and assembled them in a dish for tonight's dinner. All I need to do is cook it at three hundred and fifty degrees for thirty minutes. As I open the refrigerator, the cool air soothes away the warmth from my shower. I reach down to the shelf for the pan...and it's not there. My stuffed shells and sausage casserole is gone.

"Babe," I call, my eyes darting around to various kitchen surfaces. It's not on the counter, or the sink, or the catch-all table. I check the fridge again, but nope, still not there. Microwave? Nope. Did I put it in the oven before I left? Nope, not in there either.

I stop to think. I was already in my office, bedroom, and bathroom and saw no casserole dish. That only leaves one place.

Sure enough, the shredded remains of pasta, ricotta cheese, and red sauce sit in a dish on the floor—next to Theo.

Chapter 5
Sylvie

My pulse quickens as hot anger floods through my veins. The entire pan, what should have been three or four meals, is gone.

Now, I don't care that he's streaming.

"Theo!" I yell, loudly and suddenly enough, that his head snaps in my direction. My eyes burn with righteous fury as I stare down my boyfriend.

At first, he gives me a wide-eyed look, as if he's shocked I'd speak to him in such a tone. Then he rolls his eyes and turns back to his mic. "That's my woman, she's begging for my monster dick." Theo laughs and signs off.

The temperature in the room seems to cool as he turns his chair to face me. He leans forward, placing his elbows on his knees. "Please tell me," He starts slowly. But I know better than to trust his icy tone. "What the fuck is so important that you need to interrupt my stream?"

"Are you kidding me?" I cry, throwing my arms out horizontally. He realizes it's Thursday, right? That he's supposed to spend time with me, his girlfriend?

Theo doesn't move. The silence begins to beat at my anger-forged armor.

Does he want a reason? I'll give him the list. "Streaming when you said you'd be ready to spend time together when I got home. Sexualizing me to your followers. Brushing off my feelings." I hold up a finger for each offense and raise my voice for my final point: "Eating the entire dinner meant for us to share!"

Theo shrugs. "I was hungry." He leans back in his chair and pulls out his phone.

That's all the explanation he's giving? I pinch the bridge of my nose. "I made you other lunches."

"I tossed that shit after one bite," he snaps, still not looking at me. Then he finally turns his gaze on me. "You know Sylvie, it's pathetic you can't make a sandwich right."

His words pierce my heart. I consider myself a good cook. Cooking is a type of creative expression. Right now, I can't always make fancy meals. Theo knows we're on a budget, so sometimes that means I have to make a ham and cheese sandwich.

"That's bullshit."

"So now I'm a liar?" Theo says, his voice low and menacingly. He stands up, closing the distance between us.

What? How did he jump to that conclusion? "I—"

Theo cuts me off. "What do you want from me, Sylvie? It's like nothing I do is ever good enough for you."

"I didn't say that Theo." Concern and worry replace my anger. I walk around the kitchen counter to put my hand on his chest, his heart. "You know I love you."

Because as foolish as he may be, I love this man. We've been together for six years. He tells me that I taught him how to love, but he's the one who saved me—freed me from a loveless household.

He pulls away from me to pace the living room. I watch as he runs his hand through his short dirty blonde hair. "You're always nagging me about this or that or needing to spend my money."

"I'm trying to budget," I argue. "So the money lasts longer."

"Speaking of budgets," Theo pauses and rubs his chin. He's going to give me bad news.

I cross my arms, holding each elbow, and raise a brow.

"I canceled your anime streaming service."

"Wait what?" I ask, my mouth hanging open a little. "But you just bought a new gaming chair. You said you got a new sponsor." He was always doing this to me, canceling my little luxuries while splurging his.

Theo's mouth pulls into a hard line. "Are you questioning what I do with my money?" He speaks softly, whispering but the words are anything but loving.

Oh, shit. I swallow, my throat suddenly dry. I made a mistake, I crossed a line. Moving forward, I need to choose my words carefully. Theo will explode, only registering the tone of my voice instead of my words.

"No, I—" I try, but he cuts me off.

"Sounds like it. You don't want to support me."

Cautiously, I take his hands in mine and keep my voice calm and sweet. "Theo, I never said that."

"Then why are you getting upset at me over a streaming service? You showed me how to pirate that shit."

His anger is simmering beneath the surface. I'm playing with fire. I look down, trying to calm myself. Getting angry won't solve any of our problems. He supports me so I can pursue my dreams. My gaze falls to his new gaming chair, and then to the empty pan.

The dish that's empty because he ate what was supposed to be *our* dinner. Because he didn't like the lunch I made him. And he was prioritizing streaming over spending time with me.

I release his hands and school my features. How did this conversation get so twisted around? I feel acid rise in my throat and I'm fighting back tears as I say, "So my feelings mean nothing?"

"I think about you all the fucking time."

"Like when you ate my dinner or made derogatory comments about me to your stream?"

"It was a joke!" Theo pinches the bridge of his nose. "You know I just say that stuff for the stream."

"It's only a joke when both parties laugh," I say, folding my arms across my chest. And I'm not laughing.

But that was the wrong thing to say. Theo explodes, "The fuck are you talking about Sylvie? Why are you like this? You never laugh anymore. It's always serious. Where did my adventurous, spontaneous girlfriend go? Maybe you should take a break from school so you can have fun again."

Tears threaten to burst from my eyes. But this time, I'm not sure if he's worth my tears. "Just," I begin with a deep breath, "go back to your games and leave me alone." I turn, leaving the living room and retreating to my sanctuary.

Theo calls after me, "You can't say I don't spend time with you when you're the one walking away."

I slam the door to my office in response. I turn my back against the cool wood and collapse, biting my lip and squeezing my eyes shut. Our argument plays in my head in a loop. I can't make sense of Theo's logic. He wonders what happened to me? I wonder what happened to the gallant man who whisked me away and promised me a happily ever after.

We had a picture-perfect romance. We'd nerd out together playing video games or watching Marvel movies. He's supposed to be my person. Theo's supported me through undergraduate and graduate school. He's given me a roof over my head and kept me fed. But now I just feel like a burden to him. A box he's checked off. Where did our passion go? Is our love truly gone? If so, what does that mean for my future?

All questions I don't have the brain capacity to answer right at this moment. Luckily, there's still one place I can go to escape reality.

Chapter 6

Sylvie

I open my laptop and boot up *Mundo*. The familiar music soothes my soul, chasing away the tears. Not for the first time, I thank Rhessa Studios for making *Mundo* free. That way Theo can't take it away from me with his budget cuts.

Pulling my microfleece blanket around me, I settle into my chair and log in. The start menu appears, and I enter my username, Rheailia.

With a few clicks of my mouse, all thoughts of my ungrateful boyfriend are banished and I'm focused solely on the immersive world of *Mundo*.

During the opening sequence, the camera pans over open fields with low foliage, beautiful beaches with endless oceans, and finally zoom in on a city of white stone and blue roofs built on a cliff: Nalim, the home of the Cabala faction.

Statistically, it's the least popular faction with players. Machiava values power, which entices the trigger-happy. Other players, like SaintVal, join Junta to receive bonuses when playing with friends. I chose Cabala because it values intrigue, intellect, and the arts. Cabala players create characters with broad sets of skills rather than maxing out one. A "jack of all trades, a master of none" feel.

There's also a collective sense of "down-with-the-man" in our faction—a sentiment that resonated with my nineteen-year-old self who battled my ice queen of a stepmother every day.

The loading screen shows my avatar, Celestina, standing beneath a banner featuring a pearlescent octopus on a field of vibrant blue. Celestina is a female-presenting, dwarven, two-handed warrior. I started playing *Mundo* when I was a senior in high school and never made another character. She's very good at hitting things. Which makes her a valuable teammate in a faction of intellectuals.

Most often, I play with my two best friends.

I ran into Sebastian while playing *Mundo*. His avatar was severely wounded after a boss battle. Low-level mages are fragile, so I offered him a healing potion and we've been friends ever since. Although, he's never offered me his real name—Sebastian is the name of his avatar. His username is GenDomna. If I were to guess, his real name is probably something like Gene or Gianni.

I send him a quick text.

Sylvie:

Hey handsome. What are you up to?

He immediately replies.

Sebastian:

What are you doing texting me? It's Thursday.

Sylvie:

Theo's being a dick. I'm going to play some *Mundo*. Wanna team up?

The next text message is in the group chat with Sebastian, myself, and Vyola.

Sebastian:

What did he do this time?

Vyola:

Who do I need to maim?

I bite my bottom lip. It was so like Sebastian to move the conversation to include Vyola. I know he's right though. Vyola's been there since the inception of our friendship. I still remember the day she stood behind me, reading the first message Theo sent me on that dating app.

Glancing at my friend's list in *Mundo* I see she's online. Her username is DualFates. Briefly, I wonder where she is. Vyola does a lot of traveling for her sales associate job and playing together is a way we keep in touch. Her avatar is a male human rogue named Cesario.

Sylvie:

Snitch.

Sebastian:

Sylvie's asking to play *Mundo* on a Thursday.

Vyola:

I can, but WTF did the asshole do this time?

With a heavy sigh, I type out a response about the stuffed shells, then delete it. Maybe I am making too big of a deal about things. Eating too much and canceling a subscription service—those things don't ruin relationships.

Sylvie:

Just stupid stuff. I'm probably overreacting.

Vyola:

A lot of stupid stuff seems to happen lately.

Sylvie:

We're just stressed.

Vyola:

Is Theo meeting your needs?

Sylvie:

We've both been working hard.

I'm honestly tired of talking about Theo. It seems like every day something happens, but there are a lot of good moments too, like when he stood up to his mom for me.

Sylvie:

Listen, I'm trying to put this behind me and play some *Mundo*.

There's a pause in our conversation. *Are they angry with me now?* I wonder. A single second turns into dozens as my heart pounds louder in my chest, waiting for a response.

Finally, one comes through.

Sebastian:

Will you do us a favor?

Sylvie:

Of course.

Vyola:

Make a list in your journal. On one side, list what Theo brings to your relationship. Not what he's done for you in the past, or the stuff with your dad and stepmom. What does he do for you currently? On the other side, make a list of all this so-called petty stuff.

Sylvie:

Okay. Will do.

Sebastian:

We're team Sylvie. All day, every day.

Vyola:

Meet you in the guild hall.

I know that. Sometimes they are more team Sylvie than I am. And I appreciate them for it—more than they will ever know. My friends mean well, but they don't know Theo like I do. Still, if they want me to make a list then I'll make a list. Even if it's just to say I did it.

But right now, I just want to lose myself in *Mundo*.

Celestina loads inside the Cabala guild hall, beneath the city's theatre located at the pinnacle of Nalim. The light from the sconces bounces off the white stone, giving the room a warm glow. A diverse cast of Cabala faction members bustle around, talking to various NPCs.

In this virtual realm, I embrace my powerful dwarven warrior, who is free from the frustrations of my real-life problems.

DualFates wants to join your party

I click accept and put on my headphones.

"Hey girl," Vyola says. "What did you want to do?

"The daily quests. Maybe get to the next level before tomorrow."

"Heard."

We head to the job board and accept the daily quest:

Quest Accepted: Deal with the Reptikin

Reptikin are a bipedal turtle-like creature with a concave depression atop their head. They are part of the Waterkin subclass, but prefer freshwater to saltwater, unlike their ocean-loving Wavekin cousins.

We follow the quest marker out of the tavern and into Nalim proper. The city stretches out before me, its white stone buildings and breathtaking ocean views capturing my attention.

"This way," Vyola says. I follow Cesario, Vyola's avatar, out of the city.

As we near the marker, we slow down and crouch behind sparse foliage by the lake. Peeking out from our hiding place, I can see the creatures splashing around the water's edge.

"How do you want to deal with them?" Vyola asks.

"Good question."

Part of the fun of being in the Cabbala faction is that there are always multiple ways to complete a mission. Plus, we get bonus experience points for solving problems creatively. In this case, option one would be to fight the Reptikin, but they're not an easy opponent like Beastkin. Reptikin have naturally high defense levels because of their shell and have a poisonous bite. Most annoyingly, they regenerate hit points as long as there is water in their head.

Option two could be to try and bargain with them. Reptikin are mischievous, childlike creatures who enjoy making deals with players.

"How about I distract them and you hit them from behind?" I offer.

I can hear Vyola's smile as she says, "I like this plan."

Gods, I love this game. In *Mundo*, I have control over my destiny, far removed from the disappointments and frustrations of my relationship. This is a much-needed escape, a place where I can find solace and reclaim a sense of agency in my life. As I immerse myself deeper into the game, all my troubles with Theo, money, and school fade into background noise.

Chapter 7

Valentino

I send Preston a quick good luck message. Even though I may not understand Preston's crush, I still want the best for my friend. I still haven't heard back from him.

After the fallout with Preston, I texted both Speed and Xander, telling them I want to play alone. They understood.

I'd be lying if I said I'm not hurt, but none of that matters right now.

I put my phone on silent and set it aside. Time to focus on *Mundo*.

I've gathered everything I need for the stream. My fridge is stocked with beer, water, energy drinks, and sports drinks. Various snacks are piled on my desk, including chips, energy drinks, and various synthetic cheese products. All off camera of course.

I'm all set to stream my first play of the *Mundo* update. I'm also recording my gameplay and commentary to upload on YouTube.

When seven p.m. hits, I start the stream and log into *Mundo*. I leave my screen on Valen standing beneath the Junta banner.

"Hey everyone." My heart threatens to beat out of my chest when I see the number of people in the chat. "Whoa, hold up—am I reading this right?" On a good night, before Prospero's interview, I'd have over three hundred people watching me stream. Tonight, over one thousand viewers are taking the time out of their day to watch me play.

I blink, thinking maybe I'm seeing things. I look at the count again, and it's gone up another fifty viewers. "Looks like this stream will be one for the records. I'm honored to have so many new people joining me tonight."

Seriously, where did they all come from? Am I going to need more stream moderators?

Usually, I take the first fifteen minutes of my stream to relax and interact with my viewers. They ask me questions to get to know me more. But with the way my heart's pounding, I'll need more than fifteen minutes to calm myself.

I settle in my chair, take a breath, and look at the camera. "Tonight I'm playing the long-awaited update of Mundo. Y'all know I'm excited to play, so I'll only take a few questions."

The chat immediately lights up with questions. Thankfully both my moderators are ready. They pick one and send it to me. I make a mental note to send them a gift card or something for putting up with the frenzy of tonight.

"Does pineapple belong on pizza?" I read aloud. "Hey, pizza's a personal journey. I'm not going to tell someone what to put on pizza. Or tell pineapples they don't belong somewhere. My pizza is a pineapple-free zone, but you do you!"

My viewers fill the chat with emotes of my avatar, Valen's head, either crying to show their disagreement, or thrusting his sword in the air like Thor in agreement. This pattern continues with other questions.

"What animal would you choose as your animal companion? Easy—my cat Annie. What kind of superpower would I want to have? The power to stop time— so I can catch up on all my work and get a full night's sleep."

My fifteen-minute timer goes off. "Alright Saints, you know I love these questions, but it's time to play this update. Let's get questing." The intro music starts, setting the stage for my adventure.

Valen spawns in the Junta guild tavern in Anorev. There is an NPC character in the middle of the usually empty space. A chat bubble appears over his head beckoning me over. On the screen, an older gentleman with white hair and dark skin appears. He's simply referred to as "The Duke", and he's in charge of every town.

"The Duke appears at the beginning of the game when a new player starts. He also goes over any tutorials," I say to my stream. "He's probably here to go over the update. Let's see what he says."

The Duke is dressed in Anorev colors, royal purple pants paired with black boots and a gold and purple jacket.

"Greetings and salutations, Valen," he says.

My mouth drops open in surprise—full on cartoon, open jaw, would be on the floor if that were possible. I recover a second later and say what I'm thinking aloud. "Never in *Mundo*'s history has an NPC addressed the player directly like The Duke just did. You all heard that right?" I ask the stream. "The producers didn't say anything about character recognition for NPCs when they were describing the update. It makes me wonder what other surprises I'll find in the game tonight."

I resume the game and the Duke continues, "Today is an auspicious day! I'm pleased to announce the summit has been a success. There is to be free trade and travel across the known realm." He declares the city of Anorev is now open for visitors and that its denizens can traverse the land but to be cautious when traveling.

"Okay Duke, get to the good stuff."

He holds out a rolled piece of parchment, which the game identifies as "Map of the Known Realm."

"Our cartographers have returned with an updated map," the Duke says.

I press the key to interact with the item, watching as Valen reaches out to take the map from the Duke. He opens it up and looks at it. The map fills my screen and a smaller picture of the Duke appears in the bottom left corner.

"As you see, our realm has expanded," the Duke says.

"That's an understatement," I say. "This map is easily triple the size of the previous one."

Examining the map, I notice landmarks like rivers, forests, lakes, and mountains. However, there are no specific details about what lies in between. Additionally, in what seems like the center of the map, there is a large section that is blacked out so the player cannot identify what is there.

"I don't even know where to begin. But I don't see either Nalim or Emor on the map. What's up with that?"

"That star location is the central point between the three major cities: Anorev, Emor, and Nalim." The Duke explains. "Cartographers noted mystical regional phenomena around the area, but were too afraid to venture further."

The Duke points to a glowing blue marker on the map next to Anerov. "As you explore you will find these waypoints. Activating one will allow the user to return to that particular point at any time. They are much faster than horses!"

"Rhessa Studios did announce they were adding fast travel to the game with the map expansion," I muse aloud to my stream. "I'm still wondering why there are no other locations marked on the map. Do I have to go and find it?"

"There is one more thing I need to give you, Valen," the Duke says. He holds out what looks to be an earring. I am prompted to interact with it.

Valen takes the item and clips it onto his ear. "It looks like a small quartz stone set in gold," I say to my stream.

"This is a communication device," the Duke explains. "It will allow you to directly communicate with new acquaintances you meet across our realm. I implore you to try it with some of our townspeople in Anorev before venturing forth."

"Wait, hold up," I stammer. Energy is boiling under my skin. "We can already freely communicate with other player characters. So is this to communicate verbally with NPCs?"

The Duke continues, "If you choose to use it, you will need but a moment to calibrate it to your voice."

Another window pops up with more information. I read the information aloud,

"This communicator is an optional setting that allows players to talk to NPCs. Oh, video game gods, what is this?"

I rock back and forth in my chair. I stand up. I sit back down. I reach for a beverage, change my mind, and choose another. "I can talk to NPCs," I repeat the information.

The chat is encouraging me to try out the feature. "Hell yes, I'm going to try it!"

I accept the prompt to use the new feature. The vocal calibration takes time. The Duke informs me that voice recognition will get better the more it's used.

When it's done, I test the feature by addressing the Duke, "Thank you for the information, m'lord."

The Duke smiles, "The pleasure is all mine, Valen. Now go forth and bring glory to Anerov!"

With this natural pause in gameplay, I turn to the chat. "I had no idea this was going to happen. This feature alone could revolutionize how the game is played."

I get a message from Speed in our chat feature.

Amazing69Speed: Popping in to say hi Saints

"Everyone say hello to Speed, he's on his adventure right now." Speed's sparkly purple guitar emote fills the chat.

"The Duke said to talk to some townsfolk in Anorev before going to explore. So let's head to the adventurer's guild."

The chat floods with messages suggesting that I go directly to the starred area. "There is plenty of time to go check that out later," I answer, "I want to take my time to test this new feature."

I figure most players will go directly to the star, which means the area will be crowded. The moderator has to jump in to calm my viewers.

Mod: Chill out everyone. If SaintVal wants our input, he'll poll.

"Thank you," I offer. "Let's give some hype to our moderators for all their hard work in this awesome community."

The positivity fills the chat for them per my request.

"There is plenty of time to check out the star later. I want to follow the Duke's suggestion and test this new feature. I have a feeling that there is a reason why the voice input feature fosters a deeper sense of immersion."

I bring up the map. "We know we're meant to explore different areas and find these two cities, find new people. But why not mark the new cities on the map? At least the major geographical features are marked. Since the entire map isn't blacked out, I have a feeling I can gather more information about the area before heading out."

The Adventurer's Guild is next to the museum, which stores various rare collectibles the guild earns as its members level up. It takes a little navigation through Anorev before we get there. The building is unassuming, built with the same red stone and architectural style as any other in the city.

Entering the guild hall, I walk up to the large map of the world that's on one wall. I'm silent for a while, as I examine the map, processing the information. As I do, the Guild Master, Caemo, walks up to me. "Are there any questions I can answer for you?"

After a moment of consideration, I ask, "Is there anything pressing we should look into?"

"Great question. Establishing contacts with the guilds in either Emor or Nalim is the most pressing matter for the Anorev Guild. However, we also don't know what treasures are out there. Adventurers who return with rarities will be rewarded."

"I like the sound of that," I say.

"Then I wish you the best of luck on your adventures. If you do find something of interest, be sure to let me know," Caemo says, turning to leave.

I take that as my sign to leave.

"Talking to the Guild Master paid off. And it seems like the game is driving us to collaboration rather than exploration. So I think I'm going to head toward either Emor or Nalim. I'll put up a quick poll for you to vote as I navigate out of town."

With a new plan in place and the poll in progress, I leave the guild building to stock up and resupply with Shylock, the town's purveyor of goods and adventuring gear. Based on the player's crafts, talents, and stock, his inventory is constantly changing. When I'm satisfied with my inventory, I head west, hopefully moving toward Nalim. Unfortunately, nobody has returned with rare items yet or crafted anything with new material, which means there is no new gear for Valen just yet.

Two minutes later, I have the results. Forty-nine percent of my viewers want me to travel to Emor, while fifty-one percent indicate Nalim.

"Nalim it is," I say.

I orient Valen west and begin moving. Meanwhile, I speak to my audience. "We have no idea what's out there, and I'm flying solo with Valen tonight. I think it might be best to explore the areas between the two cities. Maybe I can find a fast travel location in case I need to jump back and resupply."

"You're the boss," someone types in the chat.

I have to laugh at that. "I should not be the boss of anything. Adulting is too hard."

"You have the big sword," another viewer comments.

"That," I smile, filling my voice with innuendo, "I do have."

Anorev is built in a lush valley between two mountain ranges. I travel the main road, heading west. With my visibility on, I can see other players moving around too. The majority are going toward the center waypoint. I pass a few other players and continue in my westward direction.

Every so often I stray from the path, exploring the regions and gathering herbs for potions and other crafting materials. But I never stray too far. I want to find another fast travel waypoint before I engage too much with the Enkin around me. If I die, I don't want to spawn back in Anorev and lose my exploration progress.

I use the downtime while Valen travels to respond to more comments in the chat and provide commentary on the game.

"Are you going to team up with anyone new?" a subscriber asks.

"Sure! If I see someone."

I hadn't encountered any players from different guilds yet. It was possible that they weren't visible, but it still didn't sit right with me that I was just clearing out some Grasskin and gathering resources after streaming for two hours.

"Something should have happened by now," I comment. "What am I missing?"

Suddenly, a shadow passed over the land like a rolling storm. I pan the camera in a circle as the shadow grows. I missed the chat encouraging me to look up at the sky. If I had, I would have been prepared for the giant bird creature that swoops in to take Valen in its claws.

Mundo's combat music plays as the ground shrinks below my camera. "Windkin?" I read off my screen. "A type of Skykin? Is this a new subclass of Enkin?"

Even twisting the camera I can't get a good look at the creature. "Oh no, oh shit," I verbalize my stream of consciousness.

A large beak clamps down on my avatar, taking a third of my health. Then the flies into the air before spitting Valen out like spoiled food. All I could do was watch as Valen plummets. His impact on the ground takes another half of my health.

"The fuck!" I exclaim, bouncing in my seat. "That one attack took my health bar almost to zero." If I hadn't leveled up on Wednesday, I would be dead.

My health bar flashes red in a warning. I pop a healing potion that only brings me to half health. I can only take three more hits before I'm out of potions—if I'm being generous.

The Windkin lands in front of Valen on my screen, and I see the creature for all its horrible glory. It's gargantuan. There's no way I can outrun it.

"Well, this isn't how I expected this play to go," I say to my chat, preparing for a fight I know I'll lose. "But I'm going down swinging."

But to my surprise, the blow never comes. Instead, I see a request:

Rheailia would like to join your party.

A dwarven woman, wielding a great axe, rushes the Windkin. I never hit the accept button so fast in my life.

My chat explodes with questions about if I know the avatar or if this is someone new. "I don't know. But I'm happy they came to my rescue."

Her weapon sparkles with radiant energy. I know that weapon. "Starwrath. It's one of the rarest weapons in the game. Less than ten percent of all players have it. It has a special attack that—"

The dwarven woman brings the axe crashing down on the Windkin's head, demolishing half its health in one hit. A special attack that does exactly *that*, a devastating blow that leaves the wielder open and vulnerable.

I will remember the words that flashed across my screen for the rest of my life:

Rheailia: Get your ass up and help!

Chapter 8
Sylvie

It's finally Friday, the day of the update. I spend the day working on my schoolwork, trying to be responsible. But the moment I'm done, I log into *Mundo.*

Celestina loads in the guild, and the Duke is there to give me a rundown of the new features. This update is overwhelming—in the best kind of way. The map has tripled in size with new geographical features. As much as I would like to, I don't use the voice sync. Speaking aloud might cause Theo to come to ask questions. And I'm still avoiding him after yesterday's date night fiasco.

I quickly visit Kleo, our guild master. Her office is on the top floor of the theatre, giving her the best view of the city. Like the first time I met her, Kleo sits behind her desk. Her blue-black hair is styled into a short bob. Her pearlescent scholar's robes are accented with pieces of chain mail. The key to the Nalim Guild's secret archives hangs around her neck.

"Welcome Celestina," she greets. "To what do I owe this pleasure?"

Usually, dialog options would appear. However, this time a text box pops up. That's cool. I can customize the dialog even if I'm not using the voice feature.

Rheailia: Have you looked over the Duke's map?

"Yes, I have." Kleo doesn't elaborate. I realize I have to word my questions deliberately to get the answers I seek. I'm not surprised. Our faction values intrigue and intellect.

Rheailia: What insights did you uncover from your analysis?

Kleo gracefully rises and moves to the framed map on the wall. As she does, I press the appropriate keys to move Celestina next to Kleo.

"This starred area is of interest." Kleo raises an arm to point. "It's in the delta between Nalim and Emor. Go there if you wish."

There's such an obvious emphasis on this area that I feel like the game designers at Rhessa Studios are dangling it out in front of everyone. Not that there wouldn't be something there. Rather, I think it's a diversion from a richer secret.

Rheailia: The area feels like a distraction.

"Clever deduction, Celestina," Kleo smiles. "Our cartographers have unveiled new horizons. Our world has expanded substantially. I question what else is out there."

Rheailia: I think I'm going to find out.

I can't wait to explore that starred area, but I'll move toward the less populated regions first.

Kleo turns her head and smiles. "Ensure you peruse the map carefully and diligently. Our faction knows well enough what secrets can lie within the details."

Rheailia: Thank you.

"May fortune favor your journey, Celestina."

After speaking with Kleo, I visit the merchant Shylock to sell him an artifact I recently found. As I level up Celestina, I put talent points into Archaeology. I'm one of the five percent of players to do so. I understand why others choose other talents such as Alchemy, Enchanting, or Medicine. They're all enticing and have immediate buffs. Archaeology takes a while to build up but it's the most lucrative talent. Celestina can find, restore, and sell rare relics. The more points I put into the talent, the more rare objects I find and the more gold I earn after selling them. Combining Archaeology with the Blacksmith talent means I can find and restore rare weapons.

My eyes drift to the greataxe in Celestina's hands, and have her swing it just for fun. Starwrath is one of the rarest weapons in the game.

It has a special ability that allows its wielder to empower one attack, producing triple the normal damage output with radiant damage. But that attack causes a temporary exhaustion, leaving the wielder unable to move for two rounds of combat. I only use the attack when I know I can knock out the enemy or when I play with my friends so they can cover me.

With my errands done, I maneuver Celestina through the descending streets and out of Nalim proper. Just as I cross the threshold, I get a notification and Vyola's gamer tag pops up.

DualFates: I found a waypoint.

Vyola sends me coordinates in another message. I use them to drop a marker on the map. This waypoint is northwest, while Anorev is northeast.

Rheailia: Wanna team up?
DualFates: No sorry. Early flight.
Rheailia: Travel safe. Any other tips?
DualFates: A new subclass called Skykin. A new one of them is flying around, terrorizing travelers.

Noted, avoid big flying things.

According to the map, a main road follows a river north. If I travel that way, I can get halfway to the waypoint with fewer distractions. Staying on a main road means fewer enemies, but also less loot. Since I'm playing alone, I want to conserve as much health as possible before I get to this waypoint. If Celestina dies before then, she'll respawn at the guildhall. I'd have to take the time to do all that exploring over again.

As I move Celestina north, the expansive virtual landscape changes from grassy dunes to flatlands littered with rocky outcroppings. The few paltry Enkin I encounter, I easily dispatch with a few clicks of my mouse. I stop every so often to move the camera and scan the sky. I don't expect to see this new Skykin until closer to the waypoint. As I travel, the number of players I see dwindles, especially after the main road to Anorev curves east, crossing a bridge.

Two hours into gameplay, I reach the crossroads where the main road curves east to cross the river and head towards Anorev. That's not my path today. Instead, I push Celestina forward, into *Mundo*'s new wilderness.

I'm about five minutes of travel away from the waypoint when my screen dims. The effect is like clouds blocking the sun. Is this the Skykin? I hit the keystroke to have Celestina crouch and move her behind an outcropping of rocks. Then, I point the camera to the sky, looking for the creature.

It doesn't take me long to find it.

Vyola didn't do the size and scale of the Skykin justice. She said it's a large bird, but this? This bird could swallow Celestina and still have room for others.

It does a wide circle, then plummets down to the ground. It's hunting for something—or someone else. Thank the gods, I wouldn't want to be the focus of that thing's attention. Still, curiosity calls me. What or who is it hunting? Slowly, I move Celestina's avatar out from under her cover, creeping until I see the bird fly back up with another player's avatar in its claws. The beat of its wings sends powerful gusts of wind, destroying the surrounding terrain.

I target the bird, and the new species' name appears, ***Windkin.***

I hover my cursor over the avatar. The name "Valen" pops up. Sounds familiar, I think. Maybe because it's a play on the word valor? It's better than some who use a name like *BigDick*.

The Windkin tosses Valen into the air, catching him in its beak. After a few good shakes, the bird releases its prey like a toy, letting it fall to the ground. Valen lands with a thud and I wince. I watch as the player's avatar stands on shaking legs. They must be a high-level player to have enough health to survive that fall.

Celestina moves forward. Wait, what am I doing? Running into save this guy? I know Celestina will probably die if I do. Despite knowing that, I'm running to aid this player I've never met and fight a new species of Enkin. If I don't take care of this Windkin in one or two swings, Celestina is going to be its next meal.

I rarely invite internet randos to play with me, but this is the only way he and I have a chance at survival. I click on Valen, scanning the player information to find the "Join Party" button. There's no time to wait and see if he accepts.

The combat music plays and my battle with the Windkin begins. Now that I'm up close, I can appreciate the artistry in the design. The Windkin is a strange abomination of prehistoric might and mythical elegance. Its skin resembles the tough, textured hide of a dinosaur, yet it has feathers interspersed over its chest, arms, and elongated neck. The Windkin's wings are akin to a bat's, but with the additional distinction of supporting membranes stretching over elongated fingers. Its eyes pierce me with predatory dominance, like I'm the scum of the earth for intruding on its domain.

The claw at the end of the Windkin's wing slashes towards Celestina. She dodges and rolls out of the way. A gust of wind swooshes toward, from where Celestina stood before I dodged the attack. That was too close.

A notification pops up that Valen's player accepted my request. Relief washes through me, if only for a moment. I'm happy we can fight this Windkin together now. And after this attack, I'm going to need his help. I press the combo of keys needed to activate Starwrath's special attack, then dash towards the enemy.

The Windkin tracks Celestina with its raptorial gaze, cocks its head back, and readies to lurch forward and snap her up in its beak. I wait for the Windkin to strike and command her to roll out of the bird's way again. The brief second the creature has its neck extended, I click to attack.

Celestina brings her greataxe down on the Windkin's neck. On contact, golden bursts of radiant light shoot off like fireworks. The creature spasms, releasing an ear-piercing squeal. I revel in every inch the Windkin's health bar decreases. It was a good hit. A little over half of its health is gone.

The whole thing was epic. I wish I would have recorded it.

But then Celestina freezes. The side effect of Starwrath's special ability takes hold.

The Windkin beats those giant wings and I'm helpless to do anything as Celestina tumbles backward, crashing into the rocks. I'll need a health potion or healing soon.

My heartbeat rises as the Windkin stalks towards my helpless Celestina lying unmoving on the ground. And I can't do anything. In those brief moments, before the creature attacks me, I bring up the chat with Valen's player.

Rheailia: Get your ass up and help!

It's only then when I'm staring at the username, that I realize who I helped.

SaintVal: I got your back

Chapter 9
Sylvie

There have been a few times in my life when I've felt like a computer that crashed and needed a reboot. But staring at his username causes an all-systems shutdown.

I blink and the name is still the same.

I do it again. Nothing changes.

It's the guy Prospero just interviewed on his podcast two days ago. I mentally hit myself in the forehead. That's why his character's name looks familiar.

SaintVal: Take this healing potion. I'll lead him away.

Ten seconds later, Celestina is free to move. I command her to stand and look at the ongoing battle. Valen keeps his distance, dodging attacks and shooting arrows. I remember from the podcast, that SaintVal built Valen to be a melee fighter. His ranged attacks barely do any damage.

The Windkin is airborne, focused on Valen on the other side of the battle-field. It dives, trying to recapture him in its talons. SaintVal uses the rocks and trees as protection from our enemy's powerful wind attacks. He has moved the creature as far away from me as possible, not just for my protection, but I can tell he's also creating a diversion. It won't be enough to bring the Windkin down, it's too strong. It only takes two hits to take one of us out.

I have to get the Windkin on the ground. Opening my inventory, I have Celestina drink the health potion SaintVal gave me. Back to full health, I position Celestina so I have a direct path to the Windkin. When it dives again, Celestina charges towards the gargantuan creature. If I wasn't so nervous about dying in this fight, I would find the humor in the size difference between my dwarven avatar and the Windkin.

Unfortunately, I can't do another special attack yet. Instead, I have Celestina unleash a series of relentless attacks at the Windkin's soft underbelly and spindly legs. The Windkin screeches again, moving and beating its wings. One hits Celestina and sends her rolling away on the ground.

She'd be dead with the damage she took if not for the health potion SaintVal gave her. Though death might still be a possibility with the Windkin's attention now on her. It retracts its neck, preparing to eat Celestina.

But it doesn't. The creature lets out another piercing screech, and I watch the light die in its eyes. As it falls to the ground, I stare transfixed at Valen, standing on the back of the defeated creature, both of his swords embedded in the creature's back.

The combat music fades away, and it takes a couple of breaths to stop my heart from beating out of my chest. I stare speechless at Valen. I put a hand on my chest as all the tension leaves my body. We did it. Two strangers just took on a powerful monster, and we beat it.

A notification pops up in the corner of my screen. I pull up the chat log. He sent me a message.

SaintVal: OMG

I agree, *oh my god*. The odds were against us in that battle. We're two close combat builds, who have never played together before, fighting a never-before-seen aerial Enkin. We both should have died. I cannot stop smiling.

He sends another message.

SaintVal: Chat?

Aren't we already chatting? Then, I realize he means voice chatting. He wants to *talk* to me. That feeling of weightlessness vanishes as I sink into my chair. A Theo-sounding voice in my mind tells me I shouldn't. Theo doesn't like it when I talk to other guys online. I look over my shoulder at the closed door, then back to SaintVal's message.

A third message pops up.

SaintVal: ??

Would it be worth the fight if Theo caught me? I stare at the SaintVal's half-elf avatar. Of all the people I could have run into, today of all days, I ran into him. Maybe the universe is telling me something.

Screw it. A calming warmth spreads through me, and a smile forms on my lips. Yes, this is right. The universe gave me this chance and I will take it.

Rheailia: Can't talk. Is DM ok?

It's difficult to quiet that voice, but I push thoughts of Theo aside. I want to chat. SaintVal shares my passion for *Mundo* in a way that Theo doesn't. And we shared this unbelievable moment. It's worth it to take this chance.

SaintVal: You DM and I chat?

Wait, he still wants to talk to me even if I can only message him? Wouldn't that be annoying for him? But if he is okay with it, I'm thrilled.

It's not just my fear of Theo that keeps me from talking to him. I also don't want to make a fool of myself. I've never chatted with a famous person. Not that SaintVal is an A-list celebrity, but he has a spotlight on him. I don't want to go all fangirl on him.

Get it together, Sylvie, I tell myself. Just treat him like any other guy.

Rheailia: Ok!

I heard his voice on the podcast, but hearing the same beautiful, silvery tenor in my headphones sends shivers down my spine. His voice feels like a caress. "Interesting gamer tag," he says. "Rheailia, is that a nod to the mother of Romulus and Remus?"

I'm impressed he got that. My mother named me Sylvie as a variation of Silvia. She wanted to name me Rhea, but my father disagreed.

Rheailia: Yes! Not many get that.

I hear the chuckle in his voice as SaintVal says, "Well, I'm not most people."

Rheailia: Big words for a damsel in distress.

"Guilty," SaintVal says. "So, where are you headed, if you don't mind sharing?"

Out of the corner of my screen, the Windkin's head falls to the side. A reminder that we're not done with it yet.

Rheailia: Loot first

"Oh shit," SaintVal says, "You're so right."

We move around the carcass of the Windkin. We harvest its teeth and claws, some feathers, and an extract from the bone of its beak.

Rheailia: What is it?

"Medicine is one of Valen's talents," he says. I knew that. He said as much during his interview on Prospero's podcast. But he doesn't know I listened, and

I won't mention that now. Thankfully, SaintVal continues without a second thought, "But I'm not picking up on any medicinal properties."

Rheailia: Alchemy?

I suggest it because I don't know what else to say. I haven't talked like this to a new person since I met Sebastian.

"Must be," SaintVal says. "I guess we'll have to find out together."

My heart stops. Did I hear that right? He wants to do what now? With me? More importantly, how can he drop a line like that so casually?

"If you're open to teaming up together again?" He follows up when I don't respond.

As much as I want to jump at the opportunity to play with him again, I don't know if he's saying that to be nice. Like when you meet someone who says "Sure we'll play again" but never hear from them again. The last thing I want to do is get my hopes up.

Rheailia: Sure. But why me?

"You're an awesome player and we kicked ass on our first meet." The excitement in his voice reminds me of the way he spoke during the podcast. Like he's vibrating with so much energy he can't sit still. Except this time he's that excited at the thought of playing with *me* again. I'm not used to feeling valued. "We made a great team. Anyone who has a weapon like Starwrath must be as passionate as I am about *Mundo.*"

I feel flutters in my stomach and a warmth in my chest, the kind you get when your first date asks you for a second.

Rheailia: You know about Starwrath?

"Oh, I know it. And I know the only way you can get that weapon is by paying the astronomical price, or with the archeology talent." I hear the smirk as he adds, "I'd put some gold on the second."

Rheailia: Archeology for the win!

"Yes!" He exclaims. "You hear that Saints?! I guessed right."

Saints? Wait—Has he been streaming our conversations this entire time?

I mentally kick myself. How could I be so naïve? Of course, he's streaming. How many people are watching? Or worse, what if Theo finds out? My username is out there for everyone to see. It would have flashed in the notification when I asked to join his party.

Anxiety grips my throat and squeezes. With shaky hands, I type.

Rheailia: Are you streaming? I'm not sure I'm comfortable with that.

A private message pops up.

SaintVal: I get that. Please, just hang on one second.

I shouldn't read into the message too deeply, but I sense a tone of desperation.

"Alright Saints," Val says. "In the spirit of this update, I'm ending the stream here. Thanks so much for joining me these past couple of hours. Now go play some *Mundo* and make yourself a new friend!"

Rheailia: Did you just end your stream?

"Yeah! I get being uncomfortable being on a stream. I'm lucky I came across someone like you. So yeah, I'd like to travel with you and learn more about your character build and how you got Starwrath."

I'm speechless. SaintVal would rather play *Mundo* with me, someone he just met, than continue his stream for his fans? I bite my lower lip to keep myself from crying. When was the last time someone prioritized me like that?

Rheailia: I'd like to keep playing with you too

In a world full of gamers like Theo, it's nice to meet someone like SaintVal. He streams to connect with others who love the same game, not because he wants to be famous.

I can't stop the smile that overtakes my face as I type.

Rheailia: Do I have to rescue you again?

I typed it out before I thought better. It's a joke, but I cover my face with my hands and groan. Of all things to say to him, why did my brain think *that* was a good idea? I want to be myself, but I don't want to come across as an asshole either.

SaintVal surprises me. Instead of being offended, he laughs. "Of course! The valiant knight escorts the damsel to safety."

Relief washes through me.

Rheailia: Then follow me.

SaintVal follows me north towards the waypoint. I told him a friend gave me the coordinates. As we travel, SaintVal asks me non-stop questions about Celestina's character build, how long I've been playing *Mundo*, my experiences with the update, the Cabbala faction, and more. I have to type so much that I'm forced to stop our travel just to message him. SaintVal doesn't seem to mind our slow progress.

"I've never met someone who has a character build like yours," he says.

I want to tell him that I've never met someone like him either, but refrain.

We crest another hill and are greeted by a small village called Crestview. It's a quaint village nestled among the rolling hills with a small winding creek. Ancient trees are scattered among ivy-clad cottages. As we walk through the cobblestone streets, we're greeted by villagers bustling between market stalls. The waypoint is at the Oakshade Inn and Tavern.

When we activate the glowing sigil on the side of the building, the waypoint appears on our maps as a fast travel point. Now, I can travel here with a click of my mouse.

"Do you have to go, or would you be up for a small quest?" SaintVal asks.

I glance at the clock. It's almost midnight. I have to do some chores before Theo streams. He doesn't like the noise in the background.

Rheailia: Idk if I can stay up much longer.

"Oh," he says. He sounds sad, or regretful maybe. It's late though. I'm tired and probably delusional. "How about tomorrow?"

SaintVal is persistent if nothing else. He narrows in on what he wants and goes after it. I want to say yes. I'm having such a good time with him. I could log in and play while Theo streams.

That little voice reminds me I'm playing with fire. What if Theo finds out?

Then, a familiar voice I haven't heard in a while, asks, *How could he? Theo doesn't watch Mundo streamers. Just do it. I know you want to.*

"I promise not to stream," SaintVal adds when I don't answer him right away.

It's the vulnerability in his voice that catches me. His usual bubbly tone is gone, replaced by something somber.

Rheailia: You would do that?

"One hundred percent," he says with conviction.

Rheailia: But that doesn't make sense for your platform.

"Streaming is something I do for fun and to connect with like-minded people, but it doesn't replace real interactions like this." He pauses, probably gathering his thoughts. "I realize the irony. I don't know who you are behind a screen, but I had a lot of fun playing with you. And if teaming up again means not streaming, then the choice is easy."

Before I lose my nerve, my shaking fingers move across the keyboard.

Rheailia: Okay, tomorrow then. :)

He sends me a friend request which I happily accept.

"Before you go, what name would you like me to use?"

Rheailia: My username is fine.

"That's too long," he stops to think. "How about Rhea? Like the earth titaness?"

I think that's a little silly. But the more I think about it, the more it makes me smile. I don't think I've ever had an affectionate nickname before.

Rheailia: lol okay. Nice meeting you SaintVal.

"It's just Val," he says. Then adds, "Sweet dreams, Rhea."

Chapter 10
Valentino

The damn clock is taunting me. Every time I look at it, next to no time seems to have passed. I've been doing everything I can to keep myself busy. Clean the house—check. Go to the gym—check. Now I'm editing the video footage of my stream yesterday and it's not even noon.

There are still two hours to fill before I play with Rhea again. I can't stop myself from opening up the *Mundo* dashboard and sending her a message. At least, based on her username and character, I think Rhea identifies as a woman. I could be very wrong though. Plenty of people play as feminine characters.

I make a note to ask them about their pronouns when we play.

SaintVal: Still good to play today?

I stare at the chat, waiting for an immediate reply. Logic tells me they're busy and not sitting at their computer so they won't message me back in—I look at the clock at the bottom of my computer—ten seconds. But there's a chance, right?

Annie jumps up to her new spot where a scratch-pad laptop I bought rests. As a pseudo-functioning adult with disposable income, I spoil my cat. She eats better than I do most days. She puts her brown and black striped paws out and dramatically stretches in a downward-facing dog position. Annie looks at me and then at her screen.

I can hear her thoughts, *Get back to work.*

"Fine," I tell her, reaching over to pet her head. "I'll go back to editing my footage."

Good, I can practically hear her say. Then she claws the scratch pad before settling down.

Since I stream my gameplay, I upload my recording to my Twitch channel. I'll have to blur Rhea's gamer tag but that's no problem. Once that's done, I'll make a twenty-minute highlight video for my YouTube platform. It takes a couple of hours to sift through the b-roll, cutting out the extensive travel times. But it's part of the grind.

Yep, I have all that to do and, so far, I've only watched one clip on repeat: Rhea executing Starwrath's special attack on that Windkin.

My computer is silent but my phone sounds with an incoming text. Preston, maybe? I look at my phone and let out a long exhale.

Nope, it's my mother.

Mama:

Why are you avoiding me, mijo?

My mom is the best, but also dramatic. It was easier to tell her about my sexuality than my ambitions to become a streamer. Mama likes to tell me she knew all of that before I did. She says she named me Valentino because she wanted me surrounded by love. When I told her I am bisexual, she took my hand and said: *I don't care who you love, as long as they love you and treat you well.*

But video games? While Mama supports my gaming hobbies, she doesn't understand how one plays video games to earn money. She thinks I should stick to my day job and stop laundering money before the police catch on.

Valentino:

I'm not avoiding you, Mama. Lunch soon?

Mama:

Next weekend, Bardwich Café.

I shake my head. Mama knew exactly what she wanted before she texted me. I set my phone down and turn back to editing, further examining Rhea and my fight with the Windkin.

I can't stop admiring how much thought Rhea put into their character build. Celestina is a statistical anomaly. She's from the least populated guild. Very few Cabbala players focus on strength builds, but Rhea did. They also chose an unpopular talent, but the combination works.

I could have talked to them for hours.

At 1:46, I get a notification on my *Mundo* dashboard. They messaged me back!

Rheailia: Ready. Are you sure you're okay with not streaming?

For a moment I thought about recording. Not streaming, Rhea set that boundary and I would respect it. But just recording our gameplay in case I got some cool footage of Valen I could use for social media. That still feels deceitful and wrong, though. I don't want to lie to Rhea like that.

SaintVal: Absolutely! I've been waiting all day to play with you.
Rheailia: Logging in. :D

I do the same. This time, instead of loading into the guild hall, Valen is in Crestview, at the Oakshade Inn and Tavern. Celestina stands next to him. I send a request to join my party.

Rheailia has joined your party

Turning on voice chat, I say, "Hey! You cool with me talking again?"

Rheailia: Yeah, if you are.

"Of course. You're typing again?" I ask. A part of me was hoping that was just last night. It's fine, but something inside me sinks.

Rheailia: I'm using the voice-to-text feature.

"Don't want to talk to me just yet?" I jest.

Rheailia: I've watched too many true crime dramas not to be suspicious.

I laugh out loud. Since they're using voice-to-text, I can get a feel for their voice, better than if they are just using the game's shortened text.

"My apologies, benevolent Titaness, Mother of Rome." I put all my dramatic flare into my response. "I will cease my serial killer vibes immediately."

Rheailia: Now that's my kind of title lol. Make that my nickname.

If they can keep up that level of wit, this is the start of a great friendship. "I am at your service. Now, what mission do you want to do?"

The village's quest board has two requests for help. One from a gentleman farmer whose cattle have gone missing. The other is a request to deliver a letter.

Rheailia: The letter intrigues me.

"Same," I agree.

Rheailia: Let's do it!

The quest says to find a young woman called Elara. We ask the tavern keeper where we can find her. Rhea lets me do most of the interaction to test the new voice-activated features. We learn that you can't talk with everyone, but you can with certain NPCs like quest givers, barkeeps, and shop owners.

If AI doesn't recognize what you are asking, you get a standard answer: "I'm not quite sure. Are there any other questions I can answer for you?"

We find Elara outside a cottage tending to a small herd of goats. She's young, but it's hard to determine age with the NPCs. I click on Elara and say, "Hi, we're looking for Elara. We're here about the job request."

"Oh! I didn't think anyone would take my request," she says. "Give me one moment to fetch the letter." She disappears inside the cozy cottage.

Rheailia: Why doesn't she deliver the letter herself?

"Good question. Maybe she can't for some reason?"

Rheailia: Ask her?

When Elara returns with the wax-sealed letter, I ask "Who should we look for?"

Elara casts her eyes to the side as a tint of blush colors her cheeks. "His name is Gavriel, the blacksmith's apprentice. He lives in Stonebrook, a village north of us."

Stonebrook has been added to your map.

Rheailia: It's a love letter! Should we bring a letter back?

"We'll ask if he wants us to bring something back to you," I echo Rhea's thoughts.

"I'd like that," Elara says.

I thank her, and then Rhea and I start our journey towards Stonebrook. The digital landscape doesn't change much while we travel further north. I didn't expect it to. If anything, there are more clusters of trees. After my near-death experiences yesterday, I don't spend extra time looking at the local flora. I'm more worried I might have missed something.

"Hey Rhea, do you mind if we take a look for some herbs?"

Rheailia: Sure. Medicine is one of your talents, right?

My brows furrow. Rhea and I talked a lot yesterday. Mostly about them and Celestina's build. "I don't remember telling you that. "

They pause before they answer.

Rheailia: You said so on Prospero's podcast.

"You listened to me on the podcast?! Why didn't you tell me earlier?"

Rheailia: I didn't want to come off as a fangirl.

I get that. "If anything, I fangirled over you."

Rheailia: True story.

The mention of fangirling reminds me to ask about their pronouns. "Quick question. What are your preferred pronouns?"

Rheailia: I use she/her. You?

"He/him," I say.

The trip to Stonebrook would have taken fifteen minutes at most if I hadn't taken so much time looking at every plant. Most of the flora is similar to what we have in Anorev, but some of it I've never seen before. Thankfully, Rhea is patient with me, telling me what she knows about the foreign plants. Around forty minutes later, we see Stonebrook in the distance.

The village could be a cookie-cutter copy of Crestview, except the architecture consists of rocks. There's also no waypoint here. But the blacksmith's shop is in the same spot. A young man of undeterminable age tends the forge, hammering away at a piece of steel.

"Gavriel?" I ask.

"That'd be me," he answers, putting his hammer down. He looks at us and asks, "What can I do for ya?"

"We have a letter for you from Elara."

The man's eyes go wide and he looks around his forge. Is he afraid someone will listen in?

"Let's talk back here." He motions to a location deeper in the blacksmith's shop.

Rheailia: He looks paranoid.

She's right. It's like he doesn't want to be caught. "Do you not want the letter?"

"Thanks for bringing her letter," Gavriel answers. His response is not a perfect match to my question, but the context comes across the same. "I didn't think she'd remember me."

Rheailia: Is she making the first move?

Seems like it to me. "How did you two meet?"

"Crestview's smith was feeling under the weather. I helped out for a while," Gavriel says. "One look at Elara and I fell in love.

I click away from Gavriel to say, "Sounds like a Romeo and Juliet situation."

Rheailia: Hopefully, this one ends better.

"The Baz Luhrmann version is the best."

Rheailia: The anime is better.

Well, that's a throwback. I think I watched *Romeo x Juliet* it in high school to discuss alternative adaptations of the play, but haven't thought about it since.

"You like anime?" I ask, hopeful.

Rheailia: Love it. Better storytelling than most Western shows.

"Got that right," I say. Dozens of different questions fly through my head. Shoujo anime like *Romeo x Juliet* aren't typically my thing. Does she like Shonens? We could have something else to talk about then. Maybe we could watch some shows together. But Rhea sends another message pulling me out of my daydream.

Rheailia: Back to Gavriel?

Oh, right. We are in the middle of a mission. We can talk about anime later. I resume the game. Gavriel opens the letter, and reads it. His cheeks turn red as he folds the letter and puts it away.

"Would you like to respond?"

"I'd like nothin' more. But I'm no good with those romantic words," Gavriel answers. "Could you help me?"

Rheailia: I believe the term "bless his heart" is applicable here.

I pause the game. "Are you up for it?"

Rheailia: Fancy yourself a bard?

I clear my throat before I launch into the first romantic thing I think of. "Elara, thou art the muse who doth inspire a love both deep and true, a sonnet waiting to be sung. In anticipation, I linger, in wait to hear thy voice again."

Rheailia: You can do better than that.

"Come on, that would have made Shakespeare proud."

Rheailia: But it doesn't sound like Gavriel.

"Okay, your turn."

Rheailia: Elara, thank you for your letter. I will cherish this one as much as the others. They make me feel closer to you despite the distance between us.

Oh damn, that's good. I might joke around in Shakespearean with my friends, but I'm no poet. She's showing me up. And I can't look bad in front of my new friend.

"Okay, that's a good start," I begin. "In truth, you are the part of the day I look forward to most. These letters are a gateway to see the world through your eyes. I long for the day when I can hear your voice, your laugh."

Rheailia: Val that's beautiful.

Happiness swirls in my chest. "Now we need an ending?"

Rheailia: Thank you for reaching out, for being you, and for bringing so much light into my days.

"I will be your sun if you want," I say. Then add, "Until we meet again."

I let Rhea type the response in a chat box. Gavriel pulls a pen and paper from—I don't know where—and writes everything down. He signs the letter and hands it to us with his gratitude.

The trip back to Crestview is much faster since I'm not preoccupied with gathering herbs. Rhea and I continue our conversation about anime, and then delve into TV shows. It's nice to connect with her on something other than *Mundo*. Rhea seems well-watched, except for things that aired in the last six to twelve months.

Rheailia: I got busy with my master's program.

If I were to guess, Rhea is nervous telling me this much about herself. I understand why women are cautious on the internet.

"What are you studying?"

Rheailia: Counseling program at a local college.

"I bet you're wicked smart. Why did you choose counseling?"

Rheailia: I want to help kids.

I can understand that. Not that I would have admitted it then, but I wish I had someone to talk to whenever my family relocated every time my dad was stationed somewhere new.

We went straight to Elara with Gavriel's letter. She loved it, reading it immediately and hugging it to her chest when she was done. We collect the small reward of gold and head back towards the inn.

"Do you want to do the other job request?" It's been two hours since we started playing together. I'd gladly play more, but I want to be respectful of her time.

There's a pause before her message comes through,

Rheailia: Unfortunately, I have some homework I need to do.

That's a bummer. "Gotcha. Go help those kids," I say, and try not to let too much disappointment come through.

Rheailia: Thanks for playing with me.

"Anytime," I say. "Let me know when you're free to play again."

Rheailia: Okay. I'll message you.

She logs off and I lean back in my chair, disturbing Annie from her slumber. She looks at me, yawns, and snuggles back into her spot. I lean over to give her some quick pets.

Today was so much fun. It's been a while since I just sat back and played a video game with a stranger. I'm usually focused on streaming and keeping up with this newfound popularity. Even if Rhea heard me on Prospero's podcast, she didn't treat me any differently. I'm truly lucky to run into someone like her.

My phone chimes, another text message. I have several missed messages from the guys' group chat. Preston's date with Julianna went well. They met in person at a coffee shop and he's taking her out for dinner tonight.

My first instinct is to ignore his texts. The dark part of my heart wants to make him feel as abandoned as I do. But after a great session with Rhea, that bitterness is fading. She leaves such a warmth in my heart. I try to be happy for my friend.

Valentino: Sounds cool. Congrats.

I spend the rest of the evening editing footage and uploading it to my various platforms. That night, my dreams are filled with dwarves, letters, and big axes.

Chapter 11
Sylvie

I fiddle with my bracelet as I'm squished between Theo and his mother, Jennifer, on the restaurant's waiting pew, trying not to choke on the stench of her perfume. It's the weekly post-Sunday church service lunch at Jennifer's favorite bistro. Daniel and Jennifer Griego own our apartment, and let us live there at a fraction of the rent they charge others in the building. So when Jennifer invites us to join them, we don't have any other option but to go.

Theo grabs my wrist, halting my fidgeting. "Stop," he hisses, a little too loudly. I glance towards Jennifer, her mouth pulls into a thin line. Did she hear her son? Or is she annoyed at the wait for a table?

I rearrange Theo's grip so we are holding hands. "Your mother is watching," I whisper.

He grunts, but straightens his posture, and does not let go of my hand. I suffer Theo's balmy palm and Jennifer's stink for the next fifteen minutes until our party is seated.

Our server greets us and leaves with our drink order. "Isn't this nice? I had lunch with Michelle Baptista here on Tuesday," Jennifer says. She looks directly at me when she adds, "Their Greek avocado and quinoa salad is organic and non-GMO."

Theo squeezes my hand once. Reminding me he's here, and that his mother means well. Her words are too similar to my stepmother's. Melissa would make my half-sister, Randy, weigh food portions every day. If that wasn't enough, Melissa compared Miranda to me. "You don't want to end up like Sylvie, right darling?" I'll never forget the day Theo told her off at a family dinner. Then, he excused both of us, took me back to his apartment and ordered pizza.

Not that Jennifer knows that history. I give her my best fake smile. "Good to know."

Jennifer is the type of woman who flits between favorites. Brands, restaurants, diet plans, fashion trends. She uses the forced proximity of our Sunday lunches to prattle on. It's probably because Daniel is fixated on whatever game is on the television.

I know Jennifer is just trying to connect with us, but it all feels incredibly shallow. I'm not the type of woman to care about what's in fashion or on-brand. Appearances don't bother me as much as they do her.

Still, Jennifer needs to fill every silence with chatter, including when we're trying to peruse the menu. "Sylvie, what do you think the thread count is for these napkins?"

Who cares? I want to ask. Instead, I settle for saying, "Three hundred." I fail to put any inflection in my voice. Which, somehow, only encourages her to continue her small talk.

Theo leans over to whisper, "Order whatever you want."

I turn my face to look at him. I usually order some small soup or salad when we go out with Jennifer to help keep our bill down. Does he truly mean that? I search his face. Theo's mouth curves into a soft smile, a reminder of the Theo I fell in love with.

"What are you ordering?" I ask. He might tell me to get whatever I want, but I don't want my meal to be more expensive than his.

"Don't worry about that," Theo urges, nudging my shoulder playfully. "Order what you want."

This time, my smile touches my ears as I whisper, "Thank you," and reach for Theo's hand under the table. He intertwines his fingers with mine, squeezing gently.

When the server returns to take our orders, I happily order loaded nachos, fajitas, and fries. Jennifer purses her lips, then frowns. I glance at Theo out of the corner of my eyes. We both try not to laugh as Jennifer orders her salad.

"That's certainly a lot of food," Jennifer comments. Although her smile returns, her eyes remain hard.

"I'm a lot of woman," I shrug.

Jennifer is thin and blonde, two things I'll never be. And that's okay. I'm not ashamed of my body. It's big, strong, and beautiful.

"Yes, you are," Theo says, his voice laced with innuendo. Before Jennifer can say anything, Theo winks at his mother, puts his arm around me, and kisses my temple.

Daniel, Theo's father, drags his attention away from the game on the television to cough at his son's behavior. "Finally making money off of this streaming business are you?"

Theo bristles but doesn't bend under his father's scrutiny. "I'm on the edge of a big break," Theo says. "I can feel it."

My smile falters. He's said similar things before, and I'm still waiting for them to be true. Nevertheless, I enjoy every last bite of my nachos, fajitas, and fries.

An hour later, we are back at the apartment. I shed my coat and flop down on the coach. "I don't remember the last time I was so stuffed!" I say.

Theo laughs, tosses his jacket on the floor, and crosses the space to me. "I have something else for you," he says.

"More surprises?" I ask, sitting up with a playful smile on my lips.

Theo sits beside me on the couch and hands me a small, flat, rectangular box. "One I'm sure you'll like."

"So sure of yourself," I quip back as I eagerly slide the inner compartment from the external case. Inside is a *Mundo* gift card.

Theo's voice caresses my skin as he says, "That is a year's worth of the first subscription tier. It's not my favorite game, but I know it's yours."

I stare at the fifteen-dollar gift card. It may not be that much money, but the gesture means a lot to me. "What's this for?" I dare ask.

"A way to show you how sorry I am," Theo admits, pulling me closer to him. "You've been working so hard. Making sacrifices just like I am."

I don't deny it.

The corner of his mouth twitches, but he continues, "Forgive me?"

"I'll consider it," I tease, and take the gift card.

Theo gently grabs me by the chin, lifting my face to meet his. "Come on baby, I love you more than anything. Say you'll forgive me?"

This is the Theo I fell in love with. The one who whisked me away, who took me on adventures. The one who doesn't want to spend a day without me. The Theo who takes his time kissing me.

"Okay," I say, placing the card back on the coffee table. "Thank you for this, babe."

Theo pulls me into his lap, burying his face into my neck.

"You deserve so much more," Theo murmurs as he kisses and licks at my neck. "When I hit it big, I'm going to buy a new state-of-the-art computer for you to just play *Mundo*."

It's a pleasant dream, but I've learned not to count Theo's fantasies in my future plans. I will finish graduate school. Then I will get a job and make damn sure I never have to depend on someone financially again.

Someday, I'll buy *myself* a computer to play *Mundo* on.

"You are the light of my life, Sylvie," Theo purrs. His lips graze the curve of my neck, the stubble of his facial hair contrasting with the softness of his mouth. I close my eyes, letting my head roll to the side to give him more access.

With painstaking slowness, Theo kisses up my neck to behind my ear. "Let me take care of you," he whispers as he runs one hand up my leg, to my mid-section, and then closes around one of my breasts.

Well, when he asks like that, who am I to deny him?

I take a deep breath and try to relax into Theo's touch.

He kneels in front of me, pushes up my dress, then pulls down my leggings and underwear clumsily. Theo slides his arms under my legs and yanks me to the edge of the couch. He leans down, the tip of his tongue dancing over my core, slowly circling my clit. I lean back, enjoying the building sensation—until he stops too soon. He reaches into the side table for a condom, fumbles with his zipper, then rolls it on. I wrap my hands around his shoulders.

Theo fucks me hard and fast. I send a thank you out to whoever invented lubricated rubbers. It's the kind of sex where more is said skin-to-skin than with words. I reach down to rub my clit, giving myself that extra boost, trying to make myself come before Theo. I'm right on the edge of my release again, when suddenly, Theo slows, pulsing twice, then a third time and finishes.

I sigh and sink into the cushions as I watch Theo walk away to clean himself up. He gets a paper towel for me on his way back. I've told him I hate using paper towels to clean up. It grates on my sensitive skin. But I take it because I know he means well, then stand and head towards the bathroom.

"I'll be right back," I say.

"Okay," Theo whispers, pressing a kiss to my temple. "We'll watch something together then."

The sex may have been disappointing, but my heart warms that he wants to spend some quality time together, especially since we didn't get to on Thursday.

Retreating to the bathroom, I use the soft toilet paper to clean myself. *Is this what sex is going to be like from now on?* I wonder. *This empty kind of carnal connection. Get in and off as quick as possible to get back to streaming?* The last couple of times have been like this. I can't remember when I last got off without a toy. But I shouldn't let this spoil what has been a generally good day for us.

I return to the living room, Theo's sitting on the couch, his favorite movie queued up. My shoulders drop as I let out a heavy sigh. I have to remember to pick my battles. Today he treated me to a great meal and gave me a thoughtful gift.

I should meet him halfway on this. So I sit on the opposite end of the couch and pull out my phone.

"What are you doing?" Theo asks.

"I'm going to load the gift card onto my account."

His eyes narrow briefly before his attention turns back to the movie. "Just be quick. This is one of our favorites."

One of *his* favorites maybe. I've seen it dozens of times.

"I'm still watching," I try to assure him. I open the app and begin typing the letters and numbers on the gift card.

My phone buzzes with a text.

Sebastian:

Wanna play some *Mundo*?

Sylvie:

Sorry. Spending time with Theo.

Sebastian:

NP. Was Jennifer civil to you?

Sylvie:

Civil is one way to put it. But Theo let me splurge on lunch. He also bought me a year's subscription to tier one of *Mundo*'s subscriptions as an "I'm sorry for being a dick" gift.

I watch as the three dots indicate Sebastian is composing his response. He stops, starts, and then stops again.

Sebastian:

That's nice of him...

The ellipses tells me he's got something more he wants to say. But he wants me to prompt him.

Sylvie:

U ok?

Sebastian:

I'm worried about you.

Sylvie:

Me? Why?

Sebastian:

It doesn't sit right with me when one partner "lets" the other do something. Like they have to ask permission.

I start to respond that Theo isn't like that, but the proof is in my earlier text. I used that exact word.

"Babe," Theo's voice makes me jump.

"What?"

Theo nods towards the TV. "You're missing the best part. Put your phone down."

"Sorry," I say, then wonder *what am I apologizing for?*

Theo closes the space between us, takes the phone from my hand, and places it on the side table. Before I can object, he kisses my lips and rests his head on my lap.

But I can't focus on the movie with Sebastian's words echoing through my mind. How much do I *let* Theo dictate my life?

Chapter 12
Valentino

Preston:

Meet me at 2Game after work.

I let out a sigh, doing my best to hide my irritation. This is such a typical Preston move. He ghosts me all weekend then expects me to be at 2Game just because he asks.

So where do I go after work on Monday? Yes, I'm at 2Game. Sitting in my usual seat with Xander, Pixel, and Speed, because, despite everything, I care about Preston.

I scan the length of the space, trying not to stare at the front door. Theseus stands behind the front desk attending to customers. Some mingle around the cafe, while others sit on the couch playing *Super Smash Brothers*. My foot bounces as I watch yet another person who is not Preston walk through the door. He's late.

"Glare a little harder Val," Speed says.

I flip him off. "Lecherous rogue," I say, my voice tight.

"Val," Xander warns, nodding towards Theseus behind the front desk.

Speed disregards Xander's warning, firing an insult back at me, "Goatish knave."

"Santos, Vittore," Theseus raises his voice like my dad would when I'm in trouble. "Shakespearean curses still count as curses."

Speed holds up his hands as if he's an innocent man. "What?" he asks.

I kick Speed in the back of the leg. "Our sincerest apologies," I tell him.

Theseus grunts and returns to his work.

The next moment, Preston bursts through the doors. From the shit-eating grin and the euphoric aura, I'd say he's more than courted Julianna Sinclair.

Xander, Speed, and I stand to greet our friend. Xander gives him a simple congratulations while Speed laughs and says, "Just look at this fool's grin," Speed grabs Preston's face. "He's in love."

I step closer to embrace Preston, inhaling that spicy cologne that is so uniquely his. For a moment, I can't be angry with him. But all too soon he pulls away. It's then I notice his outfit. He's wearing warm layers—a sweater over a button-up and dress jeans. But it's all wrinkled. He never dresses like that when he comes to hang out with us.

"Date must have gone very well," I joke, pulling away from him to sit back down.

Preston grins and takes his usual spot. "I didn't want it to end. So I asked her out. And she said yes! We met up for coffee—" Preston launches into a recap of his whirlwind romantic weekend with Julianna. Complete with coffee, an arcade date, dinner, a movie date on Sunday, and—as noted by his rumbled clothing— a sleepover.

I brace myself for the wave of jealousy to hit, the one that always comes when I hear how happy Preston is romancing someone else. But today, I don't feel it. Instead, my thoughts drift back to the love letter mission I did with Rhea. How easily we fell into a rhythm. She's so smart and easy to talk to. Looking at my group of friends, I imagine her sitting with us. She'd be able to keep up with Speed's quick wit. She's in grad school like Xander. I imagine her sitting and laughing with us.

"Val," Preston says, breaking me out of my thoughts. "You okay?"

He's looking at me with those soulful blue eyes. In the past, I would have interpreted his expression as caring. I momentarily debate telling him about Rhea, but then I remember that he hasn't once asked me about my stream, or really about how any of us are doing? It makes me question how much he really cares. Or are we just friends of convenience? The truth tastes bitter in my mouth.

"Yeah, I'm fine," I say, then turn my eyes away. Speed catches my gaze. His eyes narrow at the corners. Then the man dares to smirk at me.

He turns his attention to Preston. "Glad to hear breaking the bro code worked out for you."

"Don't be like that," Preston groans. "Jules is the real deal."

Speed rolls his eyes and I hide my laugh. Instead, I do my best impression of a gentleman straightening a necktie. "I dare say Julianna Sinclair is the finest young lady of the season."

Xander and Speed burst out laughing. Even Preston cracks a smile.

"If you had someone—"

An email notification cuts Preston off—probably for the best. I pull my phone out of my pocket and see a new email to my streamer account.

"What is it?" Preston asks.

"Someone named Paula from BGN," I read off the email.

"BGN as in Big Gaming Network?" Xander asks, eyebrows raised.

My first thought is that it's a marketing email. BGN is one of the largest gaming-influencing cross-media companies out there. They produce a bunch of content, "Let's Plays," tutorial videos, and more.

I open the email and read over the contents, "Mr. Santos, please contact me at your earliest convenience to discuss a possible..." My eyes go wide at the next word.

"Don't leave us hanging," Speed says.

"...Partnership," I finish.

Speed, Xander, and Preston all go wide-eyed. A partnership with a company like BGN would change my life. It would elevate me to an entirely different level of notoriety. I might even be able to stream full-time—if that's what I decide I want.

The cautious part of my brain flashes warning signals, just like when Prospero emailed me and I thought it was a scam. But she's not asking me to download anything or click on any links. Paula signs the email with her title: Creative Content Director at Big Gaming Network. And her email doesn't suggest any phishing scams.

"I think this is legit," I say, passing my phone around for the others to look at.

"Call her," Xander says.

"Now?"

"You got something else going on?" Speed asks.

He has a point. We're not in the middle of a mission or anything. Preston hands me the phone and I call the number listed.

Two rings and I'm greeted by a feminine voice, "Hello, this is Paula."

"Hello, um" I stammer, suddenly nervous. "I'm Valentino Santos. I got your email."

"Yes, thank you for calling me so quickly." She speaks fast, her voice full of confidence. "As stated in my email, my name is Paula and I work for Big Gaming Network. Have you heard of us?"

"Of course." I stand and start pacing. My breaths come fast, and shallow. This is not a drill. I'm on the phone with BGN. "I mean yes. I've been a long-time consumer of your content."

"I'm thrilled to hear that, Mr. Santos," Paula says.

"Please call me Val," I say.

"Okay Val, do you have time to discuss a business proposition?"

"Yeah, I'm free." Are my palms usually this sweaty? I glance around at my friends whose eyes are trained on me. Even Pixel lifts her head to stare, ears up and forward. She probably senses my nerves.

Paula clears her throat. "We listened to your recent guest appearance on Prospero's podcast, and we watched your latest *Mundo* stream. We're impressed with your enthusiasm and passion."

"Thank you," I say, not knowing how else to respond.

"Of course. Rhessa Studios reached out to us. They are planning an exclusive *Mundo* exhibition event in the upcoming months. They're calling it The Guildmaster's Odyssey.

We haven't been given much more information than that, but BGN has been invited to take part. We are tasked with curating a four-person team to participate in the exhibition, and we'd like you to join our team."

I've never had my body freeze, or my brain shut down as suddenly as it does in that moment. All software shuts down, and any applications cease to work. This mainstream gaming network wants me, a small-time streamer, to join their team? This isn't a dream. An exclusive Rhessa Studios exhibition is going to be broadcast internationally.

"Mr. Santos?" Paula prompts

"Yes, sorry, I mean I'm still here," I stumble.

Thankfully, Paula doesn't comment. "What do you think about our offer? Are you interested? You will be competitively compensated—"

"I'm in," I cut her off. I don't care about any compensation.

"Wonderful. Our HR department will reach out with the paperwork. Do you have an agent representing you?"

My eyes go wide and I look at Speed. He understands whatever fear he sees is in my face and nods, offering his fist for a silent bump. He's got my back. Speed may be a family and divorce lawyer, but he's still a lawyer.

"No, but I do have a lawyer if that works," I say and rattle off Speed's work email. "Copy him on any emails you send to me."

"Wonderful. Once all the paperwork is in order, I'll be in contact again."

I don't know how to end a phone call like this. "Thank you for the opportunity."

"BGN is looking forward to this partnership, Val. We'll talk again soon." She ends the conversation like my entire life didn't change in the span of a two-minute phone call.

"Dude, don't keep us in suspense," Xander says.

"I'm not sure if you just won the lottery or someone died." Speed adds.

I feel so light I could float away. I'm not sure why, but I begin laughing. "That was Paula from BGN."

"We got that much," Preston says. "They had a proposition, and they said..." he trails off, waving his hands in small circles, encouraging me to continue.

"She said Rhessa Studios is holding an invite-only exhibition event. And they want me to join the team."

Speed launches from his seat, and wraps his arms around me in an enormous hug. "I told you, man. I told you! Prospero was just the beginning."

"Rounds of boba on me," Xander says as he makes his way to the café, Pixel dutifully following him.

At some point, Theseus left his desk because he is there too, shaking my hand. "Congratulations Val," he smiles. "You deserve this. We're here to support you."

I smile and nod at the man, appreciative of his aid.

Then there's Preston. I can't read his expression. His posture is stiff in contrast with the bright smile on his face that doesn't quite reach his eyes. "Congrats man," he says.

My eyebrows pull together. That didn't feel sincere. There was no handshake or hug. Something feels stuck in the back of my throat. What was going on in his head? He was the one who threw the podcast party for me. Why is celebrating that okay, but this isn't? Or is it that he thinks I stole his spotlight from his extended weekend with Julianna? Irritation returns, but for an entirely different reason. Why can't he be happy for me?

Xander returns and hands out a drink to each one of us. Once everyone has their boba, Xander raises his, "To SaintVal," he cheers.

We all take a drink. I savor the mango flavor with tapioca pearls before sitting down again. "Alright let's play some *Mundo*."

As I log in, my cursor hovers over Rhea's contact. Would she be happy for me? What would she think of The Guildmaster's Odyssey? I decide to ask.

SaintVal: You'll never guess what just happened!

To my surprise, her response is immediate.

Rheailia: You wrote a better love letter?

SaintVal: Haha no, but this is almost as good.

Oh wait, I shouldn't be telling too many people.

SaintVal: But you have to promise not to tell anyone else.

Rheailia: I'm not sure if I'm ready for that pressure.

SaintVal: Insert puppy dog eyes.

Rheailia: Lol sure. My lips are sealed.

I summarize the conversation I had with Paula, trying not to sound like I'm bragging too much.

Rheailia: DUDE THAT'S AWESOME!!

Rheailia: Seriously congratulations! This is such a big deal. I don't know if it means much, but I'm proud of you.

That one statement brings a smile to my face. I can feel her genuine happiness for me through the screen. It's funny, she could be thousands of miles away and her words warm my heart in a way that Preston's didn't.

Chapter 13
Sylvie

I'm in my Tuesday night class, paying attention to my professor's lecture and simultaneously working on my professional statement revisions. It's part of the application to my first internship choice, the Arino Family Practice. I decided to apply. Dr. Winters believes in me, and she thinks my chances of getting accepted there are good. Theo's not going to bully me this time. I won't have to rely on him if I'm awarded some of that scholarship money. Just in case, I'm also applying to Yorke Behavioral Clinic as a backup.

When I finish the statement, I email it to Dr. Winters. I have a good feeling about this. Like the universe is telling me this is the path I'm meant to walk.

Speaking of the universe, I get a message notification from Val.

It's been over a week since Val told me his good news. Of course I was excited for him. I've known him for just under two weeks—if talking to someone virtually can count as knowing them—but he seems like a genuinely good guy. I'm honored that he would toe the line of any NDA he might have signed to tell me.

SaintVal: What do you think of this?

Attached is a promotional image of him and his character, Valen, for BGN and The Guildmaster's Odyssey.

Rhessa Studios officially announced the exclusive, invite-only exhibition. Each participating organization will have its own four-man team. During each of the three Odysseys, teams must complete some mission, with ranking determining the winners who will receive a mysterious prize.

I flick my eyes up to the student giving the first presentation of the class, then over to my professor. Nobody's paying attention to me. I open Val's attachment. The graphic was professionally done with a waist-up shot of Valentino with his character, Valen, behind him. Junta colors, purple and bronze, fill the background. Val's arms are crossed and he has a serious look on his face. I purse my lips and run my hand over my mouth, holding in a laugh. Val looks so unnatural with—whatever that expression was trying to be. BGN's logos and information about Valentino and his socials are on the right side of the graphic.

Rheailia: You could have smiled or something.
SaintVal: The photographer said I look more intimidating this way.
Rheailia: If by intimidating he meant constipated, then sure.
SaintVal: Lol. Keep me humble, Rhea.

There's something about that nickname that makes me smile and my stomach flutter. Theo calls me babe or baby, but he's never called me something special like this.

Rheailia: They'd be better off advertising your beautiful smile.

Beautiful smile? What the heck is that Sylvie? Red hot embarrassment flames my cheeks. I look down at my traitorous fingers mentally asking them, *you just had to type that, didn't you?*

SaintVal: A beautiful smile eh? ;D

Did he take that as flirting? Oh gods.

Rheailia: I'm going to disappear now.

Val doesn't know about Theo. Not that I'm keeping the information from him. I don't volunteer much information about myself. Sometimes I let things slip when we talk. There's just something special about our—friendship. I feel at ease with him like I used to with Theo.

My attention returns to the lecture, as I try to convince myself I didn't just ruin things with Val. Five minutes later, Val messages me again.

SaintVal: Want to team up tonight?

That calms my beating heart. Val messages me every day asking when we can play together. Unfortunately, I need to prioritize my coursework, so I don't play with him as often as either of us would like. Val's attention is flattering.

Wow, I don't think I've ever thought of another person's attention as flattering, not since I've been with Theo. The admission makes me feel lighter though, when I know it shouldn't.

Leaving Val on read isn't ideal, but I don't have the emotional capacity to deal with those thoughts. I leave the chat to focus on my professor.

When class is over, I pull up the message again. As much as I want to play, maybe it's a good idea to put some distance between us. I don't want to give Val the wrong idea about me. Especially after that message. With a heavy heart, I type.

Rheailia: Sorry, I have plans.
SaintVal: Damn it. I wanted to team up... and possibly meet a friend of m ine.

My eyebrows shoot up in shock. This man keeps surprising me.

Rheailia: Meeting the friends already?
SaintVal: What can I say? I know what I want.

Is that flirting? I can't seem to tell anymore. But he didn't use any emojis. I'm probably reading too much into it. Yeah, that's it. He's just the friendly type who is nice and people perceive it as flirting. The type of nice that makes my heart flutter. It's so easy to fall into playful banter with him.

Val told me a little about his friend group.

Rheailia: Which friend, Preston?
SaintVal: No. It'd be my friend, Speed.
SaintVal: Speed isn't his real name.
SaintVal: Maybe my friend Xander too.

I'm a bit surprised by this. I heard about these guys, but it seemed like Val was closest to Preston. Maybe he's just busy or something. Speed sounds like he's—I'm not sure if fun or interesting would be a better descriptor.

Unfortunately, I can't keep talking. I need to leave now to make the bus on time. I send a quick message.

Rheailia: I'll see what I can do.

Then I slide everything into my backpack, pack my headphones, and take off across campus. I'm the last person to board the bus, sinking into a seat between two strangers. I pull out my phone and check my texts. Or lack thereof.

Theo hasn't texted me all day. I know he's streaming, but how much time does it take to send an "I'm thinking of you" text? I've known Val for a fraction of the time and he messages me every day. Granted, that's to play *Mundo* together, but he does ask how my day is going and how my classes went. For the first time, I think about giving Val my phone number. Just as quickly, I decide that's a bad idea. Theo would check my phone, see the name, and start asking questions. I could say that Val is short for Valerie, a girl from class.

Wait, I stop my thoughts. Why do I have to lie? Sebastian's words echo in my mind. *How much do you let Theo dictate your life?*

Why do I let Theo control who I talk to? I shouldn't need his permission to be friends with someone.

I take a drink from my water bottle when I get off the bus and head toward the apartment. Once again, my hand hovers over the doorknob and I catch myself schooling my features, like I'm preparing for battle.

With a deep breath, I turn the knob, entering to an onslaught of curses—again. "Fuck you, you little bitch. Your mother should have swallowed. Go make me a sandwich."

I freeze, scowling at Theo, fighting the urge to rip his head off. Then I notice he's facing his computer, smashing a series of buttons.

He hasn't noticed me. Or rather, he doesn't even acknowledge that I walked in the door. I clench and release my fists, going to the kitchen to make myself a quick meal. Maybe I'm feeling a bit vindictive, but I'm purposefully loud. Rummaging through the pots and pans, closing cabinets harder than I usually would, and slamming the fridge door.

Nothing. He's either completely oblivious to me being here, or he's ignoring me on purpose. I'm not sure which feels worse. I sit at the small table picking at my meal.

"You punk ass bitch!" Theo yells.

This time, I take out my phone and record him. After a few more choice colorful phrases, I send it to Sebastian and Vyola.

Sylvie:

If I ever start playing *Obsidian*, I'm going to use Shakespearian insults.

Vyola:

Your mother was a hamster and your father smelled of elderberries!

Sebastian:

That's not Shakespeare

Sylvie:

But it's still British.

I laugh at my own joke.

Sebastian:

I'm assuming that's Theo?

Have I never sent Sebastian a photo of him before? Sebastian knows plenty about Theo, knows how we met, but Theo and I don't take many photos together anymore. So I guess I've never sent him one.

Vyola:

The one and only.

Sebastian:

He looks like my ex-boyfriend.

Vyola:

An ex for a reason?

Sebastian:

You know it.

I don't know what to add to the conversation, considering Theo is still my boyfriend. So I compliment my friend.

Sylvie:

Their loss.

Sebastian:

Ikr? Since your roommate is busy, are you up for an adventure?

My roommate? Is he talking about Theo? My eyes flick to my boyfriend, who is starting yet another round. How many evenings have we spent like this? Barely talking? Are we any better than roommates at this point?

I purse my lips, trying to keep the anger simmering inside me at bay as I clean up my dinner and retreat to my office. I relax into the comforting embrace of my couch.

If I'm going to escape into *Mundo*, technically Val asked me first.

Sylvie:

Sorry, someone else asked me to play first.

Vyola:

Who???

Sebastian:

Did you meet someone new and not tell us?

I feel guilty for a moment. It's true, I didn't tell them about Val. But it wasn't on purpose. It just never came up. Whatever this thing is with Val is still new, and I'm still figuring it out. A part of me is still waiting for him to tire of me, and stop asking me to play.

Sebastian:

WHOOOO??????

Drama king.

Sylvie:

Just a guy I met when I played the update last Friday.

Vyola:

A GUY?

Sylvie:

It's not like that.

Sebastian:

Then don't keep us waiting.

I don't get a chance to respond as Theo rips my phone out of my hand.

"What the—" I cry, sitting up.

Theo crashes his mouth to mine in a bruising kiss. Day-old facial hair irritates my skin as he kisses me like he's sucking the life out of me. When he releases me, he gives me a single-word order, "Come."

He grabs my wrist and pulls me to my feet. "What are you doing?" I ask, pulling against his grip. If he just talked to me, he wouldn't have to manhandle me.

"I need a shower and a good fuck. We'll save time, water, and money by doing it in the shower."

"I'm not in the mood," I argue, pulling against his hold. "Let go, you're hurting me."

Theo's eyes flick down to where his hand encircles my wrist. His shoulders tense. He releases me like I'm poison.

"Whatever," he mumbles and stalks off to the bathroom.

Moments pass as I stand there for a moment, trying to process what just happened. Once I hear the shower going, I force my shaking body to close the door. Then, I pick up my discarded phone, wrap myself in my blanket, and retreat to the furthest corner of my couch.

I've endured an angry Theo before. He's got a short temper, but he's never put his hands on me in anger.

Sebastian:

Sylvie? You okay?

Vyola:

You don't have to tell us anything you don't want to.

Great, now I made them worry because I didn't respond right away.

Sylvie:

I'm fine. Just talking to Theo.

Sebastian:

Is everything alright?

I type out a response, then delete it. I'm not entirely sure what to make of his behavior tonight. Was he upset at his game and just grabbed my wrist a little too hard? I don't want to tell them about that. It would make them worry more. And it's not like Theo's ever hit me.

Sylvie:

Everything's fine. I'm going to solo *Mundo* while I watch him stream.

I don't wait for a response, locking my phone and setting it aside. I might not be spending time with Theo, but I could message Val back. Talking with him will make me smile. Well *texting* with him. Although I've been considering actually talking to him. When Theo's not around of course.

I open up the chat we have. Val sent another message.

SaintVal: So? Can you play?

SaintVal: Don't think too hard. They're good guys I promise.

Then I remember he wants me to play with his friends.

I decide tonight isn't the best night to meet new people.

Rheailia: Tonight's not a good night.

SaintVal: Okay, another night then?

I feel guilty turning him down when he seems so excited to play. After my interaction with Theo, I just don't think I can fake being happy for other people. Does that mean I'm faking being happy more than I realize? Before I think about it too hard, I grab my journal and a pen and write everything down, letting it all out. Including my tears.

Chapter 14
Valentino

Saturday, at two p.m. sharp, Speed bangs twice on my apartment door, then strolls in like he owns the place. He has a coffee in one hand and a folder in the other. I'm sitting on one of two barstools at my kitchen counter.

"Ready to go over some offers?" he asks, dropping the folder before me and taking the other seat. I sit my coffee aside and pull the folder closer.

Since that first phone call with Paula, Speed has become my manager-slash-lawyer. My subscriber count was already doubling from my interview with Prospero. When BGN announced their handpicked team, I jumped to hundreds of thousands of subscribers. My new visibility also came with sponsorship opportunities.

I flip through the different offers in the folder.

"How are you feeling?" Speed asks.

That's a great question. I pull my hair into a messy bun, then run my fingers over my undercut. I should probably get it cut again soon. "It feels surreal," I admit.

I know I'm not dreaming. My routine is the same: gym, work, streaming, and cuddles with Annie. But the moment I go online, I have hundreds of likes, comments, new subscribers, and messages. I can barely keep up with it. It's exhilarating, but overwhelming at the same time.

"It's real my dude," Speed says. "First Odyssey is two weeks away."

"Yeah," I nod. I got a boost of subscribers after Prospero's podcast. That number tripled in the first twelve hours after BGN announced their team for The Guildmaster's Odyssey.

"Speaking of *Mundo*..." Speed pauses for dramatic effect. "Is Rhea joining us tonight?"

"You just want to meet her," I laugh, getting up to put my coffee mug in the sink. I'll wash it later.

"Hell yes I want to meet Valentino's secret girlfriend." Speed doesn't bother to hide his shit-eating grin.

"It's not like that man."

"Sure it's not," Speed says. "You just don't tell us about this mysterious new girl you've met."

"Rhea is a good person."

"Good. You deserve someone who sees your heart." His words take me aback, along with the sincerity in his eyes.

"I thought you didn't believe in true love?" I ask.

"I don't believe in marrying someone for love," Speed corrects me. "Love doesn't save people from divorce."

It's a bleak outlook on life, but I don't blame Speed for his opinion. He works in family law and mediates nasty divorces weekly. At this point, I'm surprised he believes in love at all.

I should probably change the subject, "Rhea's finishing a paper and said she'd let me know when she's done. I have to stream anyway."

And Rhea doesn't want to be on camera. I wish she felt differently. The only thing I can do is show her that not everyone on the internet is an asshole.

Speed gets up and leaves the kitchen area, walking to my living room where Annie lounges on the couch. "What's her username again?" he asks while giving Annie a few pets.

"I'm not telling you." I know what he's up to. "You'll message her and scare her away."

Speed crosses his arms over his chest. With a pointed stare, he says, "Either you can tell me, or I can watch the stream again and get it."

I freeze as the reality of his words sinks in. When Rhea and I met, I was streaming live. Her username did pop up on stream once when she sent the friend request. I blurred out her username on the video I recorded, but I couldn't do that to the live video. I haven't told Rhea yet, and that guilt sits like a void in my stomach. I know how she is about her privacy.

Only people who want to know would go looking for it— people like my best friend who is currently threatening me. I know Speed isn't bluffing. The sly rogue probably took a screenshot of the name.

"Fine, I'll message her," I say reluctantly.

"Glad we're on the same page."

I flip him off as I leave the kitchen to sit at my computer. I work and game from the same base setup. Three screens, with the left one turned vertically to see the chat. I set the LEDs to purple for Junta colors. I log into *Mundo* and message Rhea.

SaintVal: Speed and I are good to play if you're done with your paper.

Speed takes a seat on the couch and pulls out his laptop. He's joining my gameplay today.

I try not to think about any new obligations. All I want is to enjoy this moment with my friend, and over ten—my eyes flick to my subscriber count—ten thousand followers. Oh gods. This is more people than I ever thought would want to watch me.

I turn to my camera, start recording, and start my stream. I spend the next five minutes bantering, then another ten taking questions from the chat. A lot of questions are about the Odyssey. I feel bad that I can't give them the answers they want—I don't like disappointing my subscribers. But either I can't tell them because of legal contracts or I don't have the answers.

For the next two hours, Speed and I continue the main questline. We return to Anorev and venture into the unexplored land on our maps. The chat fills with purple lute emotes for him and a new emote of my face with a big smile that another one of my moderators designed for me. We finish clearing a nest of Beastkin when Rhea messages me.

Rheailia: Ready when you are done with your stream. :)

My heart beats loudly in my chest. She's going to be joining us soon. Oh gods, she's going to meet Speed.

"Val?" Speed says from behind me. "You okay? You spaced out for a second."

"Sorry," I stammer.

"Rhea responded?" Mischief shines through his eyes and it makes me nervous.

I move him out of my camera's view.

We have to tie up a few things before I can end my stream. An easy ten minutes later and I'm signing off. I bring up my messages to respond.

SaintVal: Meet you at Crestview!

A nervous energy works through me. I stand and walk to the kitchen, stretching my legs. I drink a glass of water and feed Annie before returning to my computer.

I turn in my chair to my friend. "I swear if you embarrass me—"

"No worries," he says. "I've got your back."

Something tells me I shouldn't believe him.

I have to let it go because I want Rhea to meet my friends. I feel like she'd fit right in with them. Speed and I pull up our maps and select the waypoint in Crestview to fast-travel. Our avatars appear at the inn and Celestina is ready and waiting for us.

Rheailia wants to join your party

I accept her request. "Good evening Rhea."

Then the most beautiful voice comes through my headphones, "Thanks for the invite."

My body freezes, words catching in my throat. Her voice is warm, expressive, and captivating.

"Val?" the angel prompts.

The best I can do is stammer out, "Your voice."

"Are you star-struck?" I hear the playful lilt of a gentle tease followed by a vibrant laugh.

I still can't believe this is Rhea's voice. I've thought about how her voice would sound since we met. This voice is richer and more decadent than I'd imagined. And her laugh draws me in. She sounds like she's laughing with her whole body.

I wish she would have given me a heads-up. Now I'm stammering like a fool in front of her and Speed—who won't let me forget this for a long time.

"He's bewitched m'lady," Speed says, eyes sparkling with mischief.

"I don't think I've seen Val at a loss for words," Rhea comments. "You must be Speed."

"So you've heard of me?" Speed grins. I get a sinking feeling in the pit of my stomach. "My pronouns are he/him and I'm single."

"Pronouns noted and relationship status disregarded," Rhea says.

"You wound me, madam," Speed laments. He clutches at his heart dramatically for my benefit.

I laugh. "Rhea, feel free to hit him with your axe."

"Rude," Speed feigns offense. "I'm just trying to talk to your mysterious friend."

I need to redirect this conversation. "So Rhea, do you want to continue with—" I start.

Speed cuts me off. "If I'm not your type, who is? Someone like Val?"

The fuck? I stare open-mouthed at my friend. Speed smiles and gives me a thumbs-up like he's doing me a favor instead of being a pain in my ass. I know

Speed is blunt, but I didn't think he would be brave enough, or *stupid* enough, to ask a question like that to a stranger.

I shake my head, hands pulling at the roots of my hair, messing up my bun. "I already regret introducing you two."

"It's fine," Rhea says. "I expected an interrogation. Are you done with your questions or can we play?" She doesn't sound upset or angry, just eager to play.

"Absolutely," I say. Anything to keep Speed from his absurd line of questioning.

"Great! I found something I want to show you." Celestina leads us out of the village, to an unexplored area next to a cliff.

"Cheating on me?" I joke once we clear the village proper. Rhea told me she normally plays with two friends.

"If anything, I'm cheating on them with you," she quips.

"Any room in this new relationship for me?" Speed asks.

Heat rises in my cheeks. I'm about to tell Speed off, but Rhea speaks up. "To be determined, I don't share well."

Be still my beating heart. That sounds like she's claiming me—and I don't think she's joking.

Speed makes eye contact with me. That spark of mischief says *you're welcome*. "You should see Val blushing, Rhea. It's adorable."

"Lies!" I cry out, knowing it's the truth because my cheeks. I feel like I'm making a fool of myself and Speed is eating up every moment. I wouldn't be surprised if he pulled out his phone to record all of this.

"I'm sure he is," Rhea says. "But this is the spot." We've arrived at a singular rock half buried in the ground. It looks like it was dislodged from the cliff. There seems to be a cave entrance not too far from the spot.

"A cave?" Speed asks.

"Watch this," Rhea says, and Celestina targets something in the distance. The mouth of the cave? I don't see any enemies around, so what exactly is she targeting? Maybe there's an Enkin just inside the cave and she's going to attack them.

"Hello? Is anyone there?" Rhea asks.

A moment later, a distressed middle-aged woman runs out of the cave. "Oh thank goodness, I need your help!"

"What's wrong?" Rhea responds.

"Enkin kidnapped my daughter! She was helping me forage for food and they ambushed us! Please help me get her back."

"Of course, we'll help. Which way did they go?"

The lady points back to the cave. "In there! Please save my daughter!"

"We'll do our best! Go back home and wait for us," Rhea says.

As Rhea talks, I stare at my screen. My gaze flicks over to Speed, whose eyes are wide, and mouth slightly ajar. His expression matches how I'm feeling.

"Was that-" Speed starts.

Rhea cuts him off. "Yep."

"Quests can have verbal triggers," I summarize.

"Cool isn't it? I wish I could see your faces." I can hear the laughter in her voice.

"This is amazing!" I say. "You're amazing, Rhea."

"Thanks," her rich tone drops in pitch. Hearing her voice is a gift. It makes me wish I could see her face to read the emotions there.

"Did you complete this quest?" I ask Rhea.

"No, we found it completely by coincidence and didn't explore further." she says. Then her voice drops to a whisper. "I thought—maybe this could be our next adventure together, Val."

Her hesitation is adorable and my heart feels full. She found this quest, and thought of me. She wants to do this quest with me. Nothing could make me happier.

I don't get the chance to answer her. There's a noise, like a door slamming, on her end of the connection. Rhea mumbles something I don't catch. It sounds like her mouth is away from the mic.

"Rhea? Everything okay?" I ask.

She doesn't answer, but I hear mumbling from a new voice. It's not Rhea's melodic one. This one is masculine and crass. Whoever they are, I can hear the anger in their tone. A roommate? I certainly hope it isn't a partner talking to her like that.

"Rhea," I call out again, this time a little louder.

A notification pops up on our screens.

Rheailia has left the party

I look to Speed as if there's something he can do to bring her back. A moment of silence passes as Speed and I process Rhea's sudden departure. I get a sinking feeling. Something is not right.

"Is that usual for her?" he asks.

"Not like this." She's signed off quickly before. That felt like leaving because she forgot food in the oven, or she remembered something she had to do.

I have a bad feeling about that guy. He sounded angry at Rhea, and that doesn't sit right with me. That's not the tone you take with someone you care for.

"What name did she say?" Speed asks.

"I didn't catch it."

"Let's look at the video." Speed suggests.

"What video?"

"You never stopped recording after your stream," he explains.

I check my computer screen. He's right, I'm still recording. I must have forgotten after I got Rhea's message.

"You're a genius," I tell him, then stop the recording and begin exporting the footage.

"I know," he says, coming to peer over my shoulder.

The progress bar creeps along what feels like a millimeter per hour. My mind drifts back to how cautious and private Rhea is about her personal information. I respect her wishes, but I can't help but feel like I've failed her. I didn't record her on purpose. I honestly forgot.

"You're thinking too hard," Speed says.

I chuckle under my breath. "I feel like I'm invading her privacy," I say, turning my chair to face him.

Speed nods his head in understanding. "What would you do if she was Preston?"

What wouldn't I do for my friends? When Preston first told me about Julianna, I researched her extensively. I needed to make sure she wouldn't hurt him.

Speed's question implies I see Rhea on the same level as Preston, but I don't think I'm crushing on Rhea like I have on Preston for years. I would consider her a friend. I'm trying to get her to play *Mundo* with my closest friends.

I care about her.

A notification pops up that the video is ready.

"I'd make sure he's okay," I answer. I want to make sure Rhea's okay, too.

I hover the cursor over the button and click play.

Chapter 15
Sylvie

I didn't expect Theo to get home this early. He was supposed to be helping his parents with something. So I'm talking to Val with my headphones on and don't hear his footsteps until he barges into my office.

I whirl around in my chair and time seems to slow as understanding passes over his face. Theo knows I'm talking to someone and he lunges.

"Theo don't!" I tried to stop him, but I'm not fast enough.

He reaches for me, his fingers curling around the headset and into my hair. Instinctively, I reach up to stop him from pulling the hair from my head. I can't save the headset though, and Theo throws it to the side like garbage. It smashes against the wall.

"Ouch, Theo!" I yell at him.

"Who. The fuck. Are you talking to?" he demands, body vibrating with anger.

My heart beats as fast as a hummingbird's wings. Even though I'm shaking, I keep my voice calm and steady as I answer, "An NPC."

It's a half-truth.

"Don't lie to me," Theo punctuates each word like the stab of a knife. His tone is dark and dangerous. His eyes lock onto my face, searching for any sign of weakness.

"We can do that in *Mundo* now," I say. "Remember?"

Slowly, so I don't disturb a feral creature before me, I reach behind me to shut the laptop.

Theo doesn't say anything. He does extend his hand to me, palm up. I know what he wants. I pull my cell phone out of my back pocket, unlock it, and hand it over.

"I've got nothing to hide from you," I say.

He goes through my text messages, my social media, and my emails. He goes through my photos checking for sexy pics or screenshots.

I think he's going to give me my phone back when my phone sounds and Theo's mouth twists like the villain who finally caught the hero. My bad luck continues.

"Who's SaintVal?" He asks, turning the phone around to show me the message. He opens the group chat I have with Sebastian and Vyola.

My heart aches thinking about how I cut out of our game without warning. What is he thinking right now?

What can I say that will help control the Theo bomb? I can't tell him that we've been playing *Mundo* together. How can I explain why I've been talking to my friends about him?

"He guested on Prospero's podcast." Again, not a lie.

"You're lying," Theo argues. "I bet you're messaging him behind my back."

He cannot be serious. "You just went through my phone. I don't talk to him," I rationalize.

Why is it so hard for him to believe me? I'm his partner. When did our relationship become like this? *How much do I let Theo control my life?*—the words come floating back. I'm doing it again now. My body coils with tension as anger replaces fear. I'm trying to placate him when he's the one accusing me of something I did not do. Yes, I chatted with Val, but I'm not cheating on Theo with him.

"You could have deleted it," Theo says.

I start to answer him, but hesitate. Time stops and I can see this argument unfold in my mind. Theo's insecurities play like a broken record. There are creeps on the internet. They could be anyone. I'm talking to other guys behind his back. I shouldn't be gaming when I'm supposed to be doing housework or focusing on school. If I truly loved him, then I wouldn't need to talk to anyone else.

But Val isn't a stalker. He's not hiding behind a screen. He respects me. He's made time for me in what is probably a busy schedule.

Theo doesn't do that.

The realization feels like the Fates cutting the last cord. This is the end.

I'm done.

"So fucking what, Theo?" I explode, throwing my arms out wide, letting my anger, my irritation bleed out of every word.

He's taken aback by my anger, leaning away from me. After all this time, I rarely fight back anymore.

"You're so stupid, Sylvie," he seethes.

"No. I'm not stupid, Theo. And SaintVal is a real friend. He cares."

"*He* cares?" Theo draws out the pronoun.

"Stop. I'm so over your jealousy and paranoia. I'm not doing anything wrong. *Mundo* is supposed to be a collaborative game."

"After everything I've done for you? You betray me like this?" Theo accuses. "You'd be homeless if I broke up with you right now."

I open my mouth to defend myself, but I stop. Theo's not listening to me. He doesn't care about what I say. He doesn't give me his time. He refuses to connect with me or to even try to understand my heart. Yet he makes a big deal about me hanging out with anyone other than him and his family.

This isn't about me talking to strangers on the internet. It's about control. Theo doesn't like me talking to people he doesn't know because he can't control them. But he knew he could manipulate me.

No more.

"You know what, Theo? I'm done."

"What does that even mean?"

"I'm tired of this. Tired of you keeping me locked up in this apartment like your personal servant."

"You're no maid. A maid would make money."

"You wanna have that fight again too? It's just like you, to try to change the subject."

"You-"

I don't let him continue. "You told me you would support me if I quit my job to focus on school. You told me if I take care of the house, cook, and clean, then you would pay the bills. I agreed to that. But I did not consent to being made to feel like a worthless burden."

Theo's anger turns his skin red. "I didn't think you would be like this."

"Like what?" My words are like arrows, daring him to say what is truly on his mind.

"You're so needy and clingy! You're always begging for attention. Bugging me to spend time with you when you know I'm trying to build an empire!"

I close my eyes, trying to calm the storm of emotions inside. I need to get away from him. I move to leave the room without looking at him.

We are not sleeping in the same room tonight. I'll grab my pillow and — I pause at the door. This is my home as much as it is his. Why do *I* have to leave? He's the one fucking up our relationship, not me.

"You should sleep someplace else tonight," I say.

"And where am I supposed to go?"

"I don't fucking care," I tell him truthfully and walk away.

I retreat into the bedroom, locking the door. From behind the safety of my closed door, I can hear Theo rummaging around the apartment. I hear the jingle of keys and the thud of his boots.

"Don't bother calling me!" Theo yells.

I focus on my breathing. Inhale, count to four, exhale, count to four.

Still, I jump as he slams the door on his way out.

"Wasn't going to," I whisper, placing a hand over my heart. I fight for control as my nerves slowly come down from the adrenaline high.

A stillness settles over the empty apartment. I don't breathe deeply until I'm sure he's not coming back.

I move to the bed, curling up against the headboard. I wrap my arms around a pillow and tuck my legs under me. The impact of what I just did settles over me.

I've never kicked Theo out of the apartment before. I didn't know if it would work. If I need space, I'm usually the one who leaves. He's the one who pays rent. And he's not entirely wrong. If Theo kicks me out, I have nowhere to go. My father lives on the other side of the country with my evil stepmother and their perfect family. I have no one in this city except for Theo.

Oh gods, what if I made a mistake? I should have told him the truth about Val. Maybe he would have been fine once he saw our messages. We're just friends.

No. A voice long forgotten echoes in my mind. I can't think like that. I didn't do anything wrong.

My mind wanders to other scenes like this. What else did I concede to? What else did I let him tell me?

I squeeze my eyes shut, refusing to cry.

Not for him. Not anymore.

Inhale, hold for four seconds. Exhale, hold for four seconds. Repeat.

When I feel emotionally stable, I leave the bedroom to draw myself a bath. I rummage in the cabinet under the sink for the rarely-used bath oils and epsom salts, the ones I save for that one occasion that never comes. For the next half hour, I sink into a space of serenity. One where candlelight, music, and warm water melt away any remaining tension.

After the water goes cold, I return to my room, dressing in comfortable clothes and settling into the middle of the bed. My mind drifts back to Val, and how I left our game suddenly. I grab my laptop from my office and bring it into the bedroom. Something I never would have done with Theo in the house.

Opening up *Mundo*, I see an unread message from SaintVal.

SaintVal: Hope you are ok. Wanna team up tomorrow?

My heart squeezes inside my chest. He's such a good guy.

Still, that traitorous voice inside my head echoes what Theo would say to me. No guy is this nice for no reason. Especially a good-looking man like Valentino Santos.

I banish that voice deciding that I don't care. I am a grown woman. Talking with Val is refreshing. He's quick-witted and exudes positive energy. He's the rarest gem from what I can tell so far—a genuinely good man.

Rheailia: You are relentless. XP

SaintVal: I knew you might say that. I've developed a three-point argument to defend my honor.

Rheailia: I'm listening.

SaintVal: First, we should explore your cave together.

Rheailia: Is that a euphemism? ;P

My thumb hits the send button before I realize what I typed. That was flirting. And I sent that message without thinking twice.

I lock and drop my phone, pulling the covers around me.

Is this the type of woman am I? Flirting with another man just because my partner and I are fighting.

At this moment? Yes. Every wound Theo inflicted on my heart is begging for affection.

Also, Val seems to have his own nice, flirtatious nature and I want to know if he's doing it on purpose.

The notification sounds and I grab my phone again.

SaintVal: I didn't mean it like that.

Well—that wasn't very reassuring. Then again, Val would never be interested in someone like me.

Stupid butterflies go away.

I type out a quick *LOL* response then pull up his social media. Val is always smiling in his photos.

I notice the shape of his jaw, the depths of his eyes, the shine of his hair which is so much longer than my own. For a moment, I imagined what would happen if I sank my hands into his hair. Would that smile give way to something else?

Stop it, I tell myself. It's one thing to innocently flirt to make myself feel better. It's another thing to be lusting after another man when I—

The thought of Theo turns my heart cold. Am I even happy with him anymore?

My phone pings again.

SaintVal: Normally, I'd make a flirty comment back, but I don't wanna be creepy. You're my friend.

SaintVal: But, if you do want to hear my cheesy lines, here's my number. Text me anytime.

SaintVal: Or you can just tell me to fuck off. That's fine too.

A friend. I don't have many of those. I deserve a friend who cares about me.

I type the number into my phone.

Sylvie:

It's Rhea. How cheesy are we talking?

Chapter 16
Valentino

The next day I meet up with Preston at the Bardwich Café. It's a small café a short walk from Preston's work, with half a dozen booths lining one wall and tables scattered around. The polished hardwood floors, minimalist art from local vendors on the walls, and —my personal favorite— the vintage pendant lights create a warm and inviting atmosphere. It's the perfect place to eat and read for lunch.

Preston is dressed casually in a polo and slacks. The host greets us by name and takes us to our favorite booth.

When the server approaches the table, they drop off two glasses of water with lemon. "The usual boys? Or are we changing it up today?"

We don't. Preston's usual is a Cuban panini with fries. I prefer the crispy chicken Caesar wrap with sweet potato fries. The server laughs and takes our unopened menus.

"How's your latest project?" I ask. Preston is a project manager for an IT company.

"I'm tired of meetings that could be emails," Preston groans. He reaches into his pocket and pulls out his phone. "Xander sent me this article from BGN."

"Oh yeah?" I know exactly which article he's talking about. The one where BGN announces their full team for The Guildmaster's Odyssey.

But Xander sent him the article, and apparently Preston's got the time of day to text him, but not me. It doesn't even seem like he cares about my new opportunity.

Preston continues to read, "Big Gaming Network headhunts young talent for Odyssey team. LordDom_TheHunter joins Cam_the_Clever, Merchant-Prince, and SaintVal."

Yep, that's my gamertag in a news headline. It's just the next piece in a never ending news cycle. My name is in headlines, news articles, YouTube videos, and more. Emails continue to flood my inbox with requests for interviews, guest appearances, and brand collaborations.

"You reading up on me?" I try to make a joke.

Try because Preston doesn't laugh. He leans back in the booth, appraising me. I feast on my wrap. "You seem so unphased by all this," he says.

That's because I try not to think about it. If I did, I'd be overwhelmed.

I glance up from my wrap to see Preston's tongue sweep over his upper lip, catching a renegade drop of sauce. In the past, I might have focused on that tongue, on how the sauce would taste on his lips. A lightning strike of desire might have shot through me.

Instead, my mind keeps turning over the events of last night.

Rhea's voice, her sudden departure, and her contact info I saved in my phone after she texted me last night. I gave her my number on a whim, preparing myself for the rejection. At first, I was stunned she texted me, especially when I saw the Marviewburg area code.

Now, I know that doesn't necessarily mean anything. Someone could have that area code and live four hours away on the West Coast, but now I have a phone number and the name of her roommate-slash-possible partner, Theo. Speed says it's enough for his contacts to do some research.

"Val," Preston prompts me.

"I'm trying not to let it go to my head," I answer. Stay humble as Mama would say. "Speed is helping me manage it."

"Julianna said something about needing help too," Preston adds.

I don't try and stop my eye roll. Preston always brings Julianna up in his conversations, lately. It's like nothing exists outside of her.

"Hey," Preston takes a serious tone, his voice dropping. "We're okay, right?"

"Sure," I answer, not knowing if it's the truth. I don't want to get into our baggage in a café during his lunch hour. I want to take the focus off of me. "How are things with Julianna?" I ask.

Preston chews on a fry before he answers. "Good."

That's code for he has something on his mind. I wait to see if he'll elaborate.

After another french fry, he continues, "Her high school ex texted her last night. She showed me the messages."

I've never met the guy. But Preston has told me enough about his high school experience that I get the picture. "Let me guess, he misses her and wants to meet up to chat and catch up?"

Preston nods. "She didn't go, and I appreciate her telling me."

"But?" I urge him to continue.

"I'm paranoid."

I nod. His insecurities are written in the worry lines on his face. Preston's got a history of people leaving him. His mother left his father in the middle of the night. Then a toxic college boyfriend decided Preston wasn't enough and found love with someone else's dick.

"Dude's a debauched varlet. Token jock, controlling asshole," Preston continues.

I swallow the last of my lunch. "Can't take no for an answer?"

"Exactly!" Preston exclaims before nibbling on his sandwich. We sit in silence for a moment. "What if he doesn't stop—"

Preston doesn't get to finish. The door swings open, bouncing off the door stop, and Speed charges in, his hair windblown. He halts at the hostess stand, scanning the café for us. When he spots me, he gives me a wide smile. He clutches a paper in his right hand.

"I got the list," Speed says, sliding into the booth beside me. Simultaneously he hands me the paper and steals a sweet potato fry.

I scan over the Theodores, Theobald, Theophilus, and even a few Theodoras.

"More names than I thought," I admit. I'm still grateful. "One of them has to be Rhea's partner."

"Who's Rhea?" Preston asks.

Speed and I both freeze. *Shit.* I never told Preston about Rhea.

Preston leans back in his booth, crossing his arms over his chest. "Either of you rogues want to fill me in?"

"Val does," Speed answers. He's looking down, fascinated by the number of fries I have left in my basket.

Traitor, I want to say. My eyes flick back to Preston. His jaw is set in a look I know all too well.

"Rhea—short for Rheailia—is the friend I met during the *Mundo* update."

"You'd like her," Speed shoves another fry in his mouth. "She's quick-witted."

"She?" Preston looks like he's been sucker punched— twice. "You've been talking to a girl?"

"Kind of?" I answer carefully. Rhea talked to me for the first time last night. Not that Preston will care about technicalities.

"And you met her?" Preston asks Speed.

"Last night, online," he clarifies.

The silence that follows is telling. The three of us are in a pocket dimension, locked away from the rest of the bustling café. Preston blinks several times as if he's dreaming and needs to wake up. Speed and I remain silent. I wait, my heart in my throat, for whatever chamber Preston's emotional roulette will land on.

He curls forward resting his elbows on the table with his head in his hands. With a pained expression, Preston finally asks, "Why did you keep this from me?"

I answer with a not-so-simple truth. "You've been busy."

It's not my intention to add more guilt for ditching us to be with Julianna, but I'm not going to lie to him either. He's been gallivanting off and we haven't seen as much of each other. Communication goes both ways. I'm sure I would have told him about Rhea—eventually.

"She must have a magic pussy to come between you and your best friend," Preston says.

The fuck? That was uncalled for. My first instinct is to rise to his petty behavior. I almost mention how he's ditched me for Julianna or how Rhea isn't some piece of meat or flavor of the week. But Preston wants to put me on the defensive.

I choose my words carefully, "Say something like that again and I will walk out of this restaurant."

Preston's eyes narrow. "You *like* her."

Not this again. I fall back against the booth. Shaking my head. "It's not like that."

"It's totally like that," Speed chooses that moment to open his mouth, "You should have heard them yesterday."

"Goatish villain," I curse at him.

"Self-deceived dreamer," Speed fires back.

"Lies and slander-" Why does he keep insisting I'm denying some boyish infatuation with Rhea?

"Stop acting like you don't think about her all the time," Speed says. "I'm not blaming you. She's cool. It's like the perfect meet-cute for you. But I'm not going to feed into that lie you tell yourself."

My eyes drop down to my abandoned lunch. I'm not lying to myself—am I? No, Rhea hasn't shown any interest in me beyond friendship. We're being friendly and Speed is reading our dynamic wrong.

Changing the subject, Preston asks, "So, what's with the paper?"

I take a deep breath. Preston's already being an ass, and I'm sure he'll have more opinions about this. He's still my best friend, and I want to talk to him about the important people in my life.

"We think she's in trouble," I say as calmly as I can.

"How is that any of your business?" Preston asks.

His question makes me stop. He has a point—it's not any of my business. But last night I claimed Rhea as my friend, and I'm the type of man who looks out for my friends.

"I'd do the same if I thought you were in trouble," I say.

"Is this like legal trouble?" Preston asks.

Speed and I exchange a glance. "Like abusive partner trouble," Speed clarifies.

I see the judgment pass on Preston's face. "You're crushing on someone else's girlfriend?"

Now I'm irritated. Is no one listening to me? "I said, it's not like that," I growl.

"Speed thinks it's like that," Preston argues.

"Speed knows it's like that," the man reaches over to take one of Preston's fries now that he's eaten all of mine.

"If I'm understanding this correctly," Preston starts, "You're trying to find this mysterious online girl that you met to do what? Even if you find this Rhea, her relationship is not your responsibility."

"You don't know anything," I snap. The table goes silent. Normally, I might agree with Preston on this point. But, he wasn't there, he didn't hear the fear in Rhea's voice. I can't sit back and do nothing.

I run a hand through my hair, taking a moment to collect my thoughts. "Listen, she randomly dropped off the mic in the middle of the game. We heard an angry male voice on her end of the connection, then she just cut out."

A deeper part of me wonders if her partner's anger is my fault. The first time I got to hear her angelic voice—then this happened.

"There are other ways to help without inserting yourself into someone else's relationship. You have your image to worry about," Preston reminds me.

"What?" My brows pull together.

"You're a public figure now. The last thing you want is a scandal."

I want to protest that I'm hardly that, but my current number of subscribers suggests otherwise. My newfound visibility shouldn't matter if a friend of mine is in trouble.

"Children, stop," Speed says. "Val, Preston does have a point. You don't want to go down the bad press route. But Preston, you can't tell Val who he can or cannot care about."

An alarm goes off on Preston's phone. A reminder that we have jobs and lives beyond this lunch hour. Preston stands, then pulls a few dollar bills out of his wallet to toss on the table for our server's tip.

Before he leaves, Preston shoves his hands in his pockets. "I'm happy for you Val. You have a life-changing opportunity, I don't want to see you blow it on some nobody you met online."

I search his features, noting the steady eye contact, his pursed lips, and the subtle tilt of his head. It all tells me he's voicing an honest concern. But there's something else in the tension of his jaw, his sullen look, and the anger he spewed earlier. What is all this about?

"I know. Thanks, Preston."

Preston nods and leaves the café. Speed bids me farewell as he leaves after Preston. I'm left to go home with just the company of my thoughts.

My Theo research begins as soon as I get home. Do I have deadlines? Sure. But I'm less worried about those.

I *am* concerned about Rhea.

First, I type the list of names Speed gave me into a document. Next, I try to recall the little details that Rhea let slip. I know she's writing papers for a master's program. She's on a scholarship working as a grad assistant. She never mentioned a time difference when we were playing. I'm sure she's in my area between time zones and her area code.

It's not a lot, but it's enough to start. For the next hour, I research each name on Speed's list. I make note of their socials and their city, skipping any that aren't in my time zone for now. And then I find TheoDios or Theodore Griego, a Marviewburg native.

He's attractive, light skin, blonde hair, blue eyes, with a sharp jawline, and a beard stubble. Not my type of man. Not as handsome as Preston. And his content makes my skin crawl. TheoDios primarily streams *Obsidian*. His short-form videos are laced with offensive language. It seems like he's had some videos removed for violating community guidelines.

Could he be any more stereotypical? Or maybe toxic is the better word. He seems exactly like the type of guy who would control his girlfriend. From his online profiles, I find his social media and dive deeper. TheoDios doesn't post regularly. Mostly life updates and upgrades to his streaming setup. Looks like he quit his job to stream full-time.

I keep going further back into his history. I have a feeling that I'm on the right track, I just need to find something concrete.

Then I see a picture of the Bardwich Café.

Wait, is it the same one I was just at? A quick internet search reveals there is only one Bardwich Café. Maybe he just visited Marviewburg once and posted about it. I keep scrolling.

The next picture stops my heart.

It's a profile of a woman with mountains behind her. She has warm skin and curly brown hair that is pulled into a loose topknot. The caption reads: *Shout out to my loving, amazing girlfriend for getting accepted into her graduate program!*

My soul knows this is my Rhea. This bright, vibrant woman, with a smile of sunshine and smoke-colored eyes.

There is no link to the woman's profile, but it is clear as I continue scrolling that Theo is in a relationship with her. There are photos of them together, going on dates, hiking, gaming together in an apartment, moving into that apartment together.

I spy a candid picture of the woman sitting on the couch engrossed in something on her laptop. The caption reads: *Rheailia in her natural habitat, playing Mundo.*

Energy buzzes through me as my heart races. This is her. I found Rhea.

And she lives in Marviewburg.

Chapter 17
Sylvie

Theo didn't come home Saturday night, Sunday, or Monday. He hasn't called or texted since storming out of the apartment. I'm assuming he's staying with a friend or his parents.

I don't care where he sleeps, as long as he's not around me. These past couple of days have been the best. I walk around in my underwear without fear of being caught on stream. I gorge myself on my favorite meals and snacks and watch anime.

My first class on Tuesday isn't until the afternoon, but I still leave the apartment early in case he comes home. And that's the crushing epiphany I'm still wrestling with: I don't want my boyfriend to come home. I don't want his apologies or his "I'm sorry" gifts. They don't make me happy.

Theo doesn't make me happy.

I meditate on the reality of my relationship as I wait in line at the bustling campus coffee shop. The truth has hit me like a lightning bolt, fusing the pieces of my broken heart. I'm holding onto the memory of the Theo I fell in love with instead of seeing the Theo who is in front of me now. When we first met, I thought of him as a protective knight. He gave me refuge from my stepmother. He supported my dreams.

As the rose-tinted glasses fall away, I see that Theo is not the knight in shining armor who fights my battles alongside me, supporting me. His protectiveness is a disguise for his possessive and controlling behavior.

I convinced myself that things would return to normal when I graduate. That was a fool's dream. Our problems are deeper than monetary fixes.

The university coffee shop's chalkboard menu is handwritten in chalk paint with the school's colors. Pumpkin spice season is here, and I salivate at the thought of a savory latte. When I reach the cashier, I order a pumpkin chai. When they ask if I'd like anything else, I add a chocolate scone to my order.

I deserve to treat myself.

The coffee shop is cozy. The ample natural light and soft ambient light combine to create a warm glow. There are several seating options from sturdy wooden tables and high tops, to cozy armchairs and inviting sofas. I choose a high top next to the exposed brick wall decorated with student artwork. I am pulling my laptop from my bag, plugging it into the wall when the barista calls my name.

I take my cup carefully, wary of the beverage filled to the brim. The first sip is divine. Totally worth any angry words Theo will have about me spending unnecessary money. Not that I care anymore. If he can go to the bar for drinks, I can have a latte.

I make myself comfortable on the high top, pulling up the guidelines for my latest assignment. My hands shake and my foot bounces up and down on the rung of the chair. Try as I might, I can't focus.

I pull up my group chat with Sebastian and Vyola. Trembles radiate from my hands through my body. It's been a long time since I've been vulnerable with someone other than Theo.

Now that I'm thinking about it, it's been a long time since I've truly been vulnerable with Theo too.

Sylvie:

Hey queens, do you have a moment?

To my surprise, they answer right away.

Sebastian:

Sure, what's up?

Vyola:

Everything okay?

I wasn't expecting immediate answers. I was hoping they would give me time to think about what I want to say. With a deep breath, I type out a message—then decide it's stupid and delete it. I type a new message —then delete that one too.

Finally, I settle on what to say.

Sylvie:

Theo and I fought Saturday night. Something in me snapped. I broke up with him. I can't be with someone who doesn't value and support me.

Sebastian:

Oh, honey! Sending hugs, babe. Are you okay? <3

I start to text, *Yeah, I'm fine*, but that's a lie. I'm not fine and I'm done making excuses for him.

Sylvie:

He ripped my headphones off my head and threw them against a wall.

Vyola:

I'm asking this because I love you.

I brace myself.

Vyola:

Did he hit you? Or otherwise, lay a hand on you?

Oh, that is a direct question. But she's only asking because she cares.

Sylvie:

He did not hit me. But he broke my headphones.

Sylvie:

He found our texts talking about Val and got angry and accused me of cheating.

I still remember the look on his face. I don't want to make them think it's their fault, but I do want to be honest with them. They can't control how Theo chooses to react.

Sebastian:

It sounds like things have been escalating for you. How long have you two been together?

That makes me think. Theo didn't acquire negative traits overnight. This has been a long time coming. A gradual relinquishing of my agency.

I rub my palm on my jeans as I take three deep breaths.

Sylvie:

7ish years now.

My heart hurts texting that. I've been with Theo for seven years. My major life milestones and he was there, interwoven into the tapestry of my life. For seven years, I settled for this treatment. I blink my eyes rapidly, fighting to keep the tears back.

Sylvie:

Yes, I'm settling for a memory of happiness instead of being happy.

Vyola:

I'm so proud of you Sylvie. This decision takes so much strength.

Sebastian:

So proud. What are your next steps?

That's a great question because I still have one big problem. I need to figure out my living situation. I have years of things accumulated in the apartment.

Sylvie:

I need to figure out the money situation. I'm financially dependent on him. I don't have a job, money, or a place to live.

He's controlling me by controlling my access to money. Without money, I can't do—well anything.

Sebastian:

Financial abuse is real.

Vyola:

You can sleep on my couch.

She's so sweet. I know her couch is always open to me. But it's further away from campus than where I am now.

Sylvie:

Thanks. But it's further from school, and leaving Theo means I'm still cut off from money.

Vyola:

You know I can spot you.

I could never ask that of her. Letting me crash on her couch would be more than enough help. I cannot ask for more. I know Vyola isn't Theo, but in my head, it feels like I'd be moving from the generosity of one person to another.

Sylvie:

It won't solve the bigger problem of money.

Sebastian:

What about an emergency shelter?

I've thought about it. Short-term shelter for a month, maybe two.

Sylvie:

Theo hasn't hit me or anything. Those rooms should go to someone who needs them.

Sylvie:

I've thought about waiting out this semester. I've endured him this long. I can sleep in the spare room.

Vyola:

I don't love this. But it sounds like you have a plan.

I do. Last night I looked at the numbers. Between the paid internship and the scholarship money, I might be able to afford a small one-bedroom. I can even get a part-time job for some extra cash if need be.

Sylvie:

If I get the scholarship and the paid internship, and get a job now to hold me over, I should be fine.

My phone is silent long enough for me to finish my pastry and half of my latte.

Vyola:

And you'll call me if this doesn't work out.

Sebastian:

And promise you'll consider the emergency shelter if he gets violent.

Sylvie:

I promise.

Sebastian:

Do you want to earn money now?

Sylvie:

I'm open to it. Depending on the job.

Most jobs have a direct deposit. For that, I'd need a bank account. Which I don't have. I closed mine when Theo and I combined finances. And I'm not able to open a new one without money to deposit—which I also don't have. I refuse to take money from Theo. A latte is one thing, but I don't want any part of Theo in this new life I'm forging.

Sebastian:

I have an influencer friend who could use a digital personal assistant. Would you be interested?

Sylvie:

What would I be doing?

Vyola:

Usually, those jobs involve administrative tasks, like scheduling appointments, social media, and managing emails.

Sebastian:

Yep basically what Vy said. It's a remote job too.

For a brief moment, I wonder if this friend is Val. He mentioned Speed was helping him manage some things. But Sebastian and Vyola have already said they don't know Val—and yes, they looked him up online.

I could be a virtual assistant. If I can get a master's degree, I can manage someone's emails and calendar.

Sylvie:

I'm interested. Can you give them my contact information?

Sebastian:

Of course! She'll reach out soon.

Sebastian:

Her name is Julia BTW.

Vyola:

I'm seriously proud of you. This is a big step. You deserve to be happy.

I don't know what to say.

Sylvie:

Thank you.

Sebastian:

Anytime Queen.

I make a list in my notebook of the things I need to separate from Theo, organizing them by their estimated cost, and order of importance. A bank account, a new phone plan with a new number. Oh, I should probably change passwords to everything too.

And then, finally, at the bottom of the list, I write: "To never again let another person treat me as less again."

Chapter 18
Valentino

It's the Wednesday night before The first Guildmaster's Odyssey and Paula scheduled a virtual meeting with my new BGN team to go over the logistics of the day. Looking at my screen, I see my new teammates, Bastian, Dominic, and Cameron along with Paula in their video windows. I'm settled in my home office with Annie lounging next to me.

"Thank you for joining me. I won't keep you long," Paula begins. Her voice holds authority without being bossy.

From her window, I see Paula's rich brown hair is braided back from her face, her hazel eyes are complimented with minimal makeup. Her warm skin is glowing. I can tell by her build she's athletic even in her tailored suit jacket. Paula wears her signature red lipstick that makes it almost impossible to look away from her mouth when she speaks.

Valentino:

Do people wear lipstick so we stare at their mouths?

Rhea:

100%

"First, we think it would be best if you refrain from playing together as a group before the first Odyssey," Paula says.

"By 'we' do you mean BGN?" Bastian asks. I'm not sure where he's at, probably one of his family's many office buildings. I am sure he's wearing an Armani suit, one of the many perks of being a Hawthorne I guess. His styled blonde hair swoops to one side, not a five o'clock shadow in sight. And what's worse? The trust fund rich boy is *nice*.

Rhea says nobody can be kind, rich, and handsome. It's too boring. Normally, I'd agree but I have evidence to the contrary sitting virtually in front of me.

He has the largest following out of all of us and is by far the biggest pull. Bastian's username is MerchantPrince and he streams almost daily. From the little I saw, he has a very active chat.

"You would be correct. The four of you are not to play until the event," Paula says.

From a business perspective, I get BGN's decision. Seeing us play together for the first time will be part of the allure. It feels strange to be beholden to BGN and their whims. I'm used to doing things on my own. Still, they're elevating me to a level I never think I'd make it to on my own.

"Well, that sucks," Dominic scoffs. He always has a comment to make.

"I curated this team specifically for you to have a cohesive playstyle," Paula says. "Are you suggesting that will be an issue, Mr. Wolfe?"

A muscle ticks in Dominic's chiseled jaw. His simple black t-shirt stretches across his chest as he leans back in his chair. Piercing green eyes shoot towards Paula. "No ma'am"

From his streams, it's easy to see that Dominic Wolfe, or LordDom_The-Hunter, is the type that likes to push people's buttons for fun. The challenge authority type. *Mundo* isn't the main game he streams, but when he does play, his avatar is Maverick, the Elven Ranger.

While expressed poorly, I get what Dominic is saying. We won't get to work out the kinks of our group dynamics until the day of the Odyssey. The entire world is going to see us make decisions, resolve conflicts, and either succeed or fail—in real time. I shudder at the thought of embarrassing myself. Watching each other play isn't the same. We have this amazing opportunity and I don't want it to tank because we can't get our shit together as a team.

Talk about pressure.

Valentino:

She doesn't want us playing together.

Rhea:

Rude.

"Anything else we should know?" I ask.

"Three hours before the start of the event, you will be emailed a code and a link to join a new server," Paula says. "Your characters have been recreated in that server. I don't think I need to emphasize that you are not to share this information with anyone. The link and code will expire once you enter the server. So do not lose it. You won't be able to get back in."

"Man, this is locked down tighter than a nun's—" Cameron Chase, or Cam_the_Clever, starts.

Thankfully, Bastian cuts him off. "Thank you, Paula. We appreciate the information."

"Mr. Chase," Paula addresses Cameron. "Do I need to remind you of BGN's expectation of professionalism?"

"It was something I said, wasn't it?" Cameron asks.

"More like what Bas stopped you from saying," Dominic quips.

"Don't make me have a conversation with HR. Do I make myself clear?"

"Yes ma'am," Bastian answers.

"So what if," Cameron continues, tying his long black locks back from his face. "We play together in groups of twos."

If I compare my new teammates to my friends, Bastian will probably take a natural leadership role like Preston. While Dominic will likely be the logical and strategic one like Xander. Cameron—he's pure chaos, like Speed. It makes me feel like playing with a new team will work out well.

"No," Paula states. Yet there's a hint of a smile on her lips.

If Cameron's half the charmer as his gnome rogue, Flickerfoot, is in *Mundo*, we'll do just fine.

I'm also low-key jealous of his hair. Deep brown, shoulder-length, wild, and curly. It would make the perfect man bun.

"What marketing do you want us to do?" Bastian asks.

"I've uploaded marketing materials to our channel. Use them and show support for one another. Val, you're streaming tonight?"

"With my usual group," I answer.

"I'd love to see at least one of you in his chat supporting him." Paula says with emphasis on the '*at least*' like it's not a request.

"I'll jump on in an hour Val," Bastian says. Given his office background, he has to leave one penthouse for another before he logs on.

"I'll be there," Cameron adds.

"Awesome! I'll let my mods know," I say, picking up my phone to message them.

"Any more questions?" She says, "Good," before Cameron can open his mouth again. Then Paula signs off with little more than a thank you.

That leaves me with half an hour before I'm supposed to start my stream.

I get up from my chair, disturbing Annie, who glares at me until she realizes I'm going to feed her. As the microwave warms up one of my prepped dinners, I shoot off a text to Rhea,

Valentino:

Are you still good to play with Speed, Xander, and me on Friday?

Rhea:

About that...

My heart skips, she's going to cancel on me. I watch my screen impatiently, jumping a little when the microwave beeps. After removing my food, my phone chimes.

Rhea:

Do you mind if a friend of mine joins?

Oh. She's not trying to cancel. My heart settles. Rhea wants me to meet her friend. I cannot help my smile as I respond.

Valentino:

Depends, do I have competition to be your favorite? :0

Rhea:

Threatened much? :)

Yes.

Valentino:

I plead the 5th.

Rhea:

Well they did come first.

In my head I want to type out "I'll make you come first," but then stop myself. Where did that come from? I must be feeling flirty tonight.

Valentino:

Is this one of your other *Mundo* friends?

Rhea:

Sebastian, yeah.

Rhea:

I promise he'll fit in nicely.

The faintest ping of jealousy zings through me. Then I remember Rhea is in a relationship with TheoDios, not Sebastian.

Valentino:

Of course they're welcome.

And because I'm feeling flirty I add,

Valentino:

Anything to see that gorgeous smile ;)

I put my phone to the side and start my stream.

"Good evening. How's everyone doing tonight? I just got off a call with our team manager at BGN. Watch out, some of my Odyssey teammates might end up in chat to say hello. Tonight, I'm running with Nix and Laurence."

The chat fills with emotes of a purple guitar for Speed and a wolf for Xander.

"Who's all planning on tuning in Saturday, October sixth for the Exhibition?" I ask.

The chat fills with affirmatives. So many yeses and mes, and hands-up emojis.

"It means a lot that you'll be there!" My heart swells with the support I see. I've come so far in the year or so I've been streaming. And even more so now with BGN—I should probably plug them. I quickly discovered that plugging sponsors is not my favorite. I especially dislike doing it in the middle of other content, but it's part of my contract. So I smile and say, "For those new or out of the know, BGN is sponsoring me on a Guildmaster's Odyssey team along with MerchantPrince32, LordDom_TheHunter, and Cam-the-Clever."

I get a private message from one of my mods asking what I want to do about the influx of people asking about Preston's character, Proteus, in the chat.

I want to tell them to delete it. Like I want to wipe the memory of Preston's behavior yesterday. I can't believe he said those things about Rhea. Oh *fuck*.

My mind feels like it crashed into a brick wall.

"Hey Saints, I'm going to take a quick break. Be back in five," I say, turning off my camera.

I grab my phone, pulling up the text thread I have with Rhea.

My last message is left on read.

Anything to see that gorgeous smile.

And that's when I realized my mistake. I'm not supposed to know what she looks like. Rhea also doesn't know that I found her. Or at least she didn't. That careless text message just might have given my secret away.

Fuck.

Chapter 19

Sylvie

On Thursday I'm sitting in the one place I never thought I'd spend extensive amounts of time: a table in the middle of the campus quad.

My leg bounces as I scan the passing people. The campus isn't busy in the evening, but there are more people than I thought there would be. Usually, I just come to campus and then leave. Maybe I'm just hyper-aware. Or paranoid.

I take a deep breath, telling myself that people are not staring at me. That Theo didn't follow me to campus to catch me meeting my possible new employer.

Technically, I'm still early. Julia said to meet at five this evening. From the few emails we exchanged, she seems straightforward and efficient. I wouldn't be surprised if she was punctual and showed up early.

I've done my research on Julia. She's a lifestyle vlogger and influencer. She built and grew her brand to over two hundred and fifty thousand followers, and she's only in her twenties.

On-screen Julia gives off an authentic vibe. She advocates for women's rights, and volunteers at domestic abuse shelters. She's open about the fact her that mother had to use one when Julia was a toddler.

Still, I wonder how much of the woman in her videos is the woman I'm waiting to meet.

This job handles her social media. Which doesn't seem hard, but I have my concerns. Social media marketing differs from personal social media. Julia has a brand. One off-brand message and all her hard work could go to shit.

I glance around the quad again. No signs of Julia. I hope she isn't lost.

My phone is in my hand again, and I'm pulling up my messages—again.

Val:

Anything to see that gorgeous smile.

He sent me that yesterday and we haven't spoken since. It feels strange since we've spoken every day since the day we met. We're supposed to be gaming together tomorrow. Sebastian is joining us.

I should text him soon, there's just—something that doesn't feel right about that text. Nor with his continued silence.

Val doesn't give compliments lightly. He's not backtracking or pretending he texted the wrong person. It tells me he meant what he said, and he meant to send it to me.

This leads me to my second suspicion—Val figured out who I am. Otherwise, how does he know what my smile looks like?

My stomach twists thinking about it. Some annoying voice in my head tells me that it's only fair he knows who I am because I know who he is. I banish that voice as I see a stunning blonde looking around the quad like she's lost. Julia.

She's dressed in elevated staple pieces, dark wash skinny jeans, pointed-toe flats, and a white tunic under a black blazer. Her blonde hair is styled in loose waves.

I take a deep breath, forcing thoughts of Val from my mind. Julia sees me when I stand and wave. She smiles and returns the wave.

"Thank you for meeting me," Julia says, walking over to me. She reaches out her hand to shake mine. "When Sebastian told me you were interested, I was over the moon."

I just thought Julia across the quad was stunning. Up close, the styled blonde hair, the sparkling hazel eyes, and her warm smile are dazzling. After a few seconds, I realize I'm still shaking her hand. And I should stop, and probably say something back.

"Thanks—wait—I should say that to you." I withdraw my hand and stumble over the words. "I mean, I should be thanking you for meeting me."

Julia smiles, then laughs so deeply that the sound resonates around us. Then she snorts—a nasal, abrupt, and uncontrolled burst of air through her nose.

Her face contorts in horror and embarrassment. Hazel eyes connect with mine. Moments pass awkwardly. Considering I also made a fool of myself, I just smile at her.

And we both divulge into a small fit of laughter.

"I'm so sorry!" Julia says. She moves to sit at the table. I follow, returning to my spot.

"No need to apologize," I tell her. "I'm going to assume you did that on purpose to break the ice."

"You're feeling awkward?"

I nod. "It's not every day I meet a pseudo-famous influencer."

Julia purses her lips. "Sebastian talks about you all the time. I feel like I know you already."

Oh, that's... surprising. Sebastian doesn't talk about her. I wouldn't have guessed he knew her at all. But I also don't want to tell her that.

"Thank you," I say, the end of the word lilting up as if in question.

A safe and simple answer. This is still an interview.

Julia flashes that brilliant smile. "Anyway, the job can be done virtually, but I like to meet anyone I'm working with face to face. Get a feel for a person's energy."

I'm not sure if I believe in energy reading, but I also won't admit that.

"What's my energy say?"

"I'm getting a gamer, garden goddess energy. Also, you have the type of ambition that means you will go after your goal, even if you have to forge the path yourself."

"Sebastian told you a lot."

"Not enough about your goals in life," Julia says. She rests her head in her hands and looks at me. "Tell me about yourself."

I hate this question. What should I say? My mom died when I was a girl. My wicked stepmother parentified me while my dad did nothing to stop it. I miss my brother and sister, but they're on the other side of the country.

Nah, that all seems like too much. She mentioned life goals, so I'll go with that. "I'm in grad school, set to graduate in three semesters. I've applied to my dream internship. I want to use tabletop gaming in combination with counseling to help troubled teens. The practice is in the Umberwoods, so I'm trying to move down there—by myself." I add the last part for emphasis.

"That's amazing Sylvie," she says, taking my hand and squeezing it. "Listen, the job is simple. There's just one of me, and I can't do everything, so I need help with the administrative things. Managing emails, scheduling appointments, responding to inquiries generated from my social media, and maintaining my email campaigns."

"Do I have to manage your social?" I ask.

"Not at first," Julia answers. "I'm very particular about my brand and self-image. As I get to know you, and as you get to know the brand, I'll hand more of it over."

"That makes sense."

"I tried researching you on social media. You don't have a large presence. Social media doesn't seem to be your thing. That's fine with me as long as you can help me with the other tasks. I can't give you full-time work, but I'll give you as many hours as your schedule and part-time working laws allow."

"That's fine. I still have to focus on school."

"Does all of this sound doable?" Julia asks.

"Yeah, what's the pay like?"

"Fifteen dollars an hour okay with you?"

More than okay. I was thinking it'd be minimum wage. "Where do I sign?"

"Great!" Julia claps her hands together. She reaches into her bag and pulls out a folder. "Here's the paperwork."

She hands me the tax paperwork and the NDAs about any brands she's working with. There are some other legal documents, and a direct deposit form.

"I don't have my own bank account," I tell her, choosing my words carefully. I have access to the joint account, but I don't want this money going into an account Theo can access.

Julia goes silent for a moment, her bubbly demeanor shifting to something more serious, but still light. "Well, I guess we'll have to change that."

My eyes go wide.

"Or, if you don't want to do it now, then I understand. We can meet another time."

"I um," I start, trying to rack my brain for any reason, any lie why right now wouldn't be a good time. Then I stop myself. It's time to stop making excuses for myself. For him. Small steps.

"I don't have access to the cash needed to open one," I tell the truth, letting the weight of the statement hang between us.

Julia nods and gives me a small smile. I'm not sure how much Sebastian told her about my life. He's one of my closest friends so I hope he wouldn't spill my personal business.

She understands and she's not making it awkward. "I could give you an advance," she suggests.

I shake my head. "I couldn't ask that—"

"You're not asking," Julia interrupts me. "I'm offering. Or if you'd prefer let's do a mini photo shoot around the campus. Then I can pay you in cash. That should be enough to open an account."

Why is she so nice? I have no doubt Julia understands where I'm coming from. She's offering a way for me to earn the money without me feeling indebted to her.

"Okay," I agree.

"Great!" Julia beams, her smile lighting up. She gets up, and assesses the quad. "Sunset is a great time to take photos. The lighting is softer, but you have to make sure you're lit from the right angles. My right side photographs better than my left."

Julia continues talking and walking while I try to keep up.

Two hours and a bazillion photos later, we are driving to the local credit union to open up my new checking and savings account. The gentleman who helps us is patient as he explains all the options to me. They even print my card on-site.

Julia sits in the waiting room the whole time without complaint. Back in the car, Julia shows me how to upload the card to my virtual wallet, so I don't have to carry it around.

Which brings on the, "where do I hide the information from Theo" worry. And the fear of what would happen if Theo found out.

I have to stop and realize that I fear my soon-to-be ex-roommate/former boyfriend. How long have I felt this way? Scratch that thought. I don't need to know specifics because the answer is "too long."

How could I stay in a relationship for so long feeling like this?

"Do you want me to drop you off back at the college?" Julia asks.

"The bus stop near it would be great." I've already missed my class. I hope my professor doesn't punish me for missing work."

"Thank you for your help today," I tell her as she parks.

Julia's brilliant smile lifts her eyes, "Of course."

"You didn't have to."

"We have enough forces working against us in the world. Women need to support one another."

I smile and reach for her hand, squeezing it in a silent thank you.

"I won't pry, but I've seen other women in similar situations. I hope you're not offended by this but I must ask. Do you feel unsafe going back to your apartment?" Julia chooses her words carefully.

"I'm not offended. And I feel safe."

Julia nods. She then looks down at my phone. "You've been staring at your phone for a while," Julia comments with a knowing smirk. "Waiting for someone to text you, or thinking about what to text them?"

It's on the tip of my tongue to deny it. But I don't. "I don't know what to text them."

"You know, a woman can be long over a relationship before she decides it's time to walk away from it."

"True story," I agree.

"Building new relationships, of any kind, is important. We need to permit ourselves to forge the life we want. Take you for example. New job, new bank account, a new path forward."

"This feels different."

Julia shrugs, "There's only one way to find out."

Chapter 20
Sylvie

When I arrive home, Theo is deep into his video games. He acknowledges me while I ignore him and go straight into my office, locking the door. Theo came home yesterday—unfortunately. I think he said something about staying with his parents. I wasn't paying attention.

I just don't care about him anymore.

After showering, I grab a quick bite to eat, ignoring Theo's paltry attempts at small talk. I flop down on the day bed and wrap myself in my favorite blanket. Only then do I pull out my phone to text Val. How do I start this conversation? How do I ask a guy "Hey, did you mean to call me beautiful?" or "Did you social stalk me?"

There's a soft knock at my door.

"Sylvie?" Theo asks.

I make a grunting sound.

"Sleep well," he tries.

I don't respond.

"You know you're welcome back in our room anytime." I imagine Theo on the other side, head resting against the door, blonde locks falling in his blue eyes. After moments of silence, he mumbles something like "goodnight" or "stuck-up bitch" and the bedroom door shuts.

I pull up the text thread with Val. *Anything to see that gorgeous smile.*

Heat rises in my cheek as my stomach flutters. Val has a way of making me feel comfortable and off balance at the same time.

Which brings me back to my current conundrum.

With a deep breath, and not knowing what else to say, I text him.

Sylvie:

Hey, how's your day?

Boring, yes. But non-threatening. It also lets him know I'm not mad. He responds instantly

Val:

Hey Rhea! It was good. It's good to hear from you. I thought you were ghosting me. ⊠

He's right. A part of me would rather do that than have this conversation.

Sylvie:

:(Guilty

Val:

It was my text, wasn't it?

I drop the phone like it's on fire and curl my knees up to my chest. Well, as close as I can with boobs. My head hits my knees, and if it hurts I won't know until I see a bruise.

With a single text, he confirmed all my worst fears. Valentino Santos figured out who I am. The questions begin to flood my mind to the point I have to focus on my breathing to calm myself down. I feel violated—but also hurt, betrayed, nervous angry, confused, relieved, and a bit curious.

No matter how I feel, I still need answers. And I'm not going to get them unless I talk to Val.

I look at my phone again, he's sent a few more messages.

Val:

Rhea?

Val:

You there?

Val:

Please don't ghost me again.

He's stuck on the ghosting thing. What's up with that?

Val:

My father was military. Sometimes we wouldn't hear from him for a while.

Sylvie:

That sounds tough for a kid.

Val:

Yeah

Now part of me feels guilty for not texting him back sooner. He's been stewing in anxiety for as long as I have.

I need to put myself first. And what I need is time to collect my thoughts before having this conversation. Deep breaths, Sylvie. You can do this.

Sylvie:

I didn't text because I didn't know how to respond.

Val:

Rhea, I know I messed up. I'll answer whatever questions you have.

He's respected my boundaries until now. I appreciate his willingness to answer my questions. He's making an effort to be honest with me to repair my trust. My cheeks warm while my heart races at the thought.

I shake my head. Focus Sylvie. This is about you, not him.

Sylvie:

Do you know who I am?

Val:

Sort of. I don't know your name, but I know what you look like.

My stomach turns. You already guessed this Sylvie.

Sylvie:

How?

Val:

I found Theo's profile.

The next message is a screenshot from Theo's social profile. It's me alright. Theo rarely posts about me on his social media anymore. Val had to look far back. How many profiles did he look at to do that? How did he even get Theo's name? Now I have so many more questions.

Sylvie:

How?

Valentino:

Can I call you? It'll be easier to explain.

My heart skips right into my throat with that single text. At the thought of hearing his voice again. I love that he's putting my comfort first. He's leaving the decision up to me. I can say no.

Sylvie:

Give me one minute.

I put my phone down, roll off my bed and quietly pad to the door. Placing my ear on the door, I close my eyes and listen.

Theo doesn't believe I've broken up with him. He says I'm just mad, that I'll get over myself, that he'll forgive me when I come to my senses. It's like he's indulging me in a rebellious stage, as if I'm a petulant teenager.

Oh so carefully, I unlock the door and crack it slightly, listening for Theo's snores. Despite what Theo thinks, we are broken up. But I still need him to let me live here until I get that scholarship and move out.

When I'm satisfied by Theo's steady snores, I lock the door again and return to the bed.

Am I really doing this? I've spoken to him before—on *Mundo*. But this feels different. More intimate.

Is that my heart pounding? No—I shake my head. Can't be. I can talk to boys.

I pick up the phone, and pull up Val's contact number, pressing the call button. It rings twice before I hear Val's voice.

"Hello?"

Oh shit. Be cool, Sylvie.

"Hey." Nailed it.

"Thanks for calling me," Val says.

"You said it'd be easier on the phone?" I don't know why I say it like a question. I don't know why my heart is pounding or why my hands are sweating.

"So," Val starts. I get the image of him pacing around his apartment. "You remember that night when you suddenly dropped off?"

The night that changed my life? The night when I decided enough was enough and I was done with Theo? "Yes."

"That terrified me," Val admits. "I was terrified for you."

Likewise, I want to say. But I don't. "Why?"

"Theo was angry. I thought it was my fault." He pauses, like he's collecting his thoughts. "You're my friend Rhea, and I protect my friends. I couldn't stand the thought of you being in trouble and me not being able to help. "

"But how does that give you the right to look into me?"

There's silence at the other end of the line. "It doesn't," Val admits. "I violated your trust and I'll be forever sorry."

I feel a "*but*" coming.

"I'm not saying this is the case, but if something, or someone, is hurting you, I want to help you. And that started with finding out who you are. Or rather, I found more on your—"

"Ex," I finish for him. "Theo is my ex."

I don't know why, but it's important to me that he knows.

Val is silent on the other end of the line for a moment. "I found more on him than you," he continues.

Not surprising. Theo doesn't like me posting on social media because "I don't know who's online." I have social media but it's private.

"How did you find Theo?" I ask.

There is another pause. "Speed and I heard you call his name before you cut out. Between that and your phone number, we made a list—"

"We?"

"Speed helped."

Of course, he did. Val said Preston is his best friend, but from what I see, he and Speed seem to be closer. His relationship with Preston must be as complicated as ours. "Continue."

"Speed came up with a list of names. Social media and time did the rest."

As it usually does. I release the breath I didn't know I was holding and set my phone down. For the next minute, I focus on steadying my breath and calming my racing heart. Over the last couple of days, my mind went to every worst-case scenario. Most of them were malicious, things Theo would do.

But Val's story originates from a place of concern and care. From what I know of him, the story makes sense. Do I believe it though? The alternative is that this is all an elaborate lie that Speed would back up if I asked him. Val wouldn't do that.

I roll my shoulders, releasing the tension. Then I hear Val's voice.

"On a scale of one to ten, how mad are you?" he asks, his voice rich with a touch of humor.

"Solid six."

"I can recover from a six," Val jokes. A giggle escapes me. "I promise I had no ill intent."

I believe him. But I still have questions. "Who did you show my picture to?"

"Speed, Xander, and Annie."

Annie? Oh, his cat. "What did Annie say?" I ask, genuinely curious.

"She looked up at me with big eyes then curled into me and began purring." Val's voice perks up when discussing his cat. I imagine him petting her as he talks about her.

"What else did you learn about me?"

"You play video games."

"That's not new information."

"You love the outdoors."

That is true. I don't get out as much anymore with grad school. There's a park close by I spend some time at before going home if it is nice out. It doesn't have wi-fi though.

"And we live in the same city," Val stammers.

I start to say "duh" but stop. I never revealed I knew that bit of information. But Val's being upfront and honest with me. In the spirit of transparency, I should be honest too.

"I know," I say.

"Shut the front door!" Val exclaims. "You've known we're in the same city all this time?"

"I recognized the places you tagged in your socials," I admit.

I heard the distinct sound of a palm smacking a forehead. "Duh Val," he says. "Why didn't you say something?"

"Why would I?"

"Hypothetically, we could meet up in person."

Shivers run through me. We're just taking steps to reconcile. I don't think we're ready for that step. "I don't think I'm comfortable meeting just yet."

"I said hypothetically," Val defends himself. "I respect your boundaries and I want to earn back your trust."

I exhale more stress and send a silent thank you to his Mama for teaching him manners and boundaries. Even if I am a level-six mad, I still feel safe with Val.

"Thank you," I say. "For being honest with me."

Val is silent for a beat. "I'll only ever be honest with you Rhea."

The intensity of his statement, of his voice, sends jitters down my spine and to my fingers and toes.

"Thanks again for the call."

"Can we talk again another time? Tomorrow maybe?"

I can't help but laugh. "We're playing *Mundo* together."

"I guess that counts."

"Goodnight, Val."

"Goodnight, Rhea," he says softly, his voice caressing my ear and throat.

After we hang up, I bask in the warm fuzzies. Val knows exactly what to say to put a smile on my face. I also appreciate how he owned up to his mistake. I feel like Val's apology was genuine.

I stare at my phone, waiting for him to text me something—anything. Does he feel this too? We just got off the phone, but I don't want to stop talking to him. Is that why he asks to play *Mundo* with me so much?

What if he's waiting for me to reach out to him? He could be giving me space after that conversation.

I might regret this later, but my heart wins the battle. I text him.

Sylvie:

Also, thank you.

Sylvie:

For being concerned.

Val:

Of course, I look out for my friends.

Is that what we are? Just friends? Because it feels like we're dancing along the line of something more.

Maybe I could try flirting with him? See how he responds?

How do you flirt again? I haven't had to do that for—a while.

Maybe I can joke with him about what he said in his text. That way he knows I'm putting the past behind us.

Sylvie:

So...You think I'm pretty? ⊠

Val:

I believe I said beautiful. ⊠

That word freezes my brain. Beautiful. He called me beautiful. I never thought I was ugly, but rather a perfectly average mid-sized woman. My exercise routine involves typing on a keyboard or clicking a mouse.

Val:

I'm not the type of man who frivolously calls a woman beautiful.

Val:

I mean it when I say you are the Titaness Rhea reincarnated.

What is it about this man that leaves me speechless?

With nothing else to say I reply:

Sylvie:

<3

Chapter 21
Valentino

The first Guildmaster's Odyssey event is finally here. Excitement and stress flood my body as I set up. I'm playing in the comfort of my home with just Annie as my support. Theseus offered me his private room for the Odyssey, but I politely declined, deciding I'd feel less nervous in my own space.

My stomach is in knots and my appetite is nonexistent, but I'm forcing myself to drink water. I should probably stop that soon. The last thing I want is to have to pee in the middle of the game.

My phone pings. It's Preston. He sent a selfie of, Speed, Xander, Pixel and him at 2Game. Theseus is live streaming the Odyssey and hosting an after-party. I'll see my friends there, but I can't shake the tiny voice that says I should be there with them, that I'm not good enough to stream for the entire world to see.

Annie jumps onto her laptop next to my desk and looks at me, then at the computer.

"It's time," I agree, reaching over to give her some quick pets. It's half an hour before the event. I start my camera, not to stream, but to capture what is going on. Then I login with the exclusive, single-use link BGN gave me. I enter the private server. Paula made it very clear not to share the link—not that I would. But also the moment we log on, BGN's stream will start.

I'm surprised to find my hands shaking. I've got this. I stream on the internet all the time.

My avatar, Valen, loads into the holding area, which looks like the inside of a double-wide cargo container. There are already dozens of people in the server. Teams are clustered in groups of four, names floating above their heads. Bastian finds me before I see him.

MerchantPrince wants you to join their party.

The rest of my team appears in video windows on my right monitor. We're all wearing the custom BGN Guildmaster's Odyssey t-shirt Paula had designed for us. It shows our unity as a team even though we've never played together.

For a moment, I wonder how different it would be if I were playing with my friends.

"Two million people are already tuned in," Cameron, aka Flickerfoot, the gnome thief says. While I put my hair up in a bun, Cameron let his long dark locks down, his headset doubling as a headband.

My heart pounds in my ears. *Two million people.* All of *Mundo*, and most of the video game world, will have their eyes on this event. And all the social media clips that will follow.

I may have been downplaying my nerves. Pressing a hand to my chest, I try to steady my breathing. Inhale. Exhale.

"No pressure," I say to Annie more than anyone else. Still, the guys heard me. Annie yawns and looks at me with her big green eyes.

Big green eyes that remind me of Rhea's. I think about her and wonder where she's watching.

"How are you feeling, Val?" Bastian asks. He's playing his human Arcane Mage, Aurelius. On camera, he looks exactly like he did the other night. Blonde hair styled to the side, filling out the t-shirt with those biceps. I can't help but admire the clean cut of his jawline.

"I'm stoked, man," I answer. "How about you?"

"Fighting the nerves too," Bastian says, rubbing the back of his neck.

"Speak for yourself," Dominic mumbles. His Elven archer, Maverick, stands in the corner. Dominic looks like he just rolled out of bed, but there's not a wrinkle to be seen on his shirt.

Five minutes until eight, my phone pings again, and I smile at the text. It's like the thought of Rhea summons her.

Rhea:

You got this!

Rhea:

Be yourself. Make new friends.

I laugh.

Valentino:

As opposed to? ;D

Rhea:

Being a smart ass XD

As the clock turns to eight p.m., I send a quick message thanking her, and tell her that I'll text her when it's over.

It's time. There's no turning back now—not that I would want to. The next couple of hours will be the highlight of my life or the downfall of my short-lived gaming career.

A booming, disembodied voice fills my headphones. "Welcome adventurers to Rhessa Studio's first *Mundo* Exhibition. Over the next three hours, you will explore never-before-seen areas of the *Mundo* world."

Oh my god, that's Rhessa's voice. So cool they got them to record the message.

The voice continues, "Your objective is to find a lost object and return it to its owner."

My mind works through the implications. The objective is vague enough that we can complete it in different ways. *Return an object to its owner*, I think. An owner implies a person. We will need to find a town or some band of traveling merchants.

The voice speaks again, this time with music swelling in the background. "I'm excited to see what you will do in," the music reaches its peak, "the Guildmaster's Odyssey."

The cargo hold waiting room dissolves into the digital realm in pieces of pixelated confetti. With the world open to me, I move my camera around, taking in the panoramic view of our new surroundings.

We're in a vast expanse of flatlands, stretching out until it collides with a mountain on the horizon to the north. A mosaic of green grasses, blue shrubs, red and orange clusters of rock, and yellow patches of sandy soil surround us. Small animals scurry away at the appearance of all the players.

It's unlike anything I've seen in *Mundo* before. My brain can't process anything else but the beauty before me. "What do we do?" I ask.

I close my eyes and bite my tongue. Damnit, I sound like a noob.

"I thought we'd get more direction," Cameron agrees, thankfully.

There are no signs of a road or a town. The mini-map in the upper left corner of my screen usually shows us our surroundings, but it's ominously black, only revealing the area we're currently in.

"We need to find people," Bastian says, reaffirming my earlier thought.

Yet we stand still. One by one, teams peel away from our cluster. They move in different directions. My foot bounces under my desk.

Teams continue to move in different directions. I feel the pressure of our team's indecision. We're not exactly fighting, but nobody is deciding. Thankfully, we don't have a stream chat to call us out on the dysfunctionality. Still, we don't need this right now, not while the world is watching.

With a deep breath, I settle into that space inside my mind where I can solve problems. Yes, we need to find people, but moreover, we are going to need to find the object. Lost objects are found where? I press the key to turn my camera again. No temples, no cities, so no buildings or vaults. Where else could an object be hidden? My eyes narrow in on the mountains. And the idea clicks.

"Let's head towards the mountain," I suggest.

"Why?" Dominic's question strikes me as aggressive. I don't know him well enough to know if he means it that way.

"In my experience, if I'm sent to retrieve something, it's usually underground or in a cave."

"Makes sense to me," Cameron says. "Maybe we'll find a town."

Dominic grunts in agreement. "As long as we get moving in a direction. I don't want to be the last group standing around." I notice that only two other groups are standing with us.

Bastian nods his head. "Lead the way."

I press down on the key to navigate Valen —and the rest of our party —forward. As we travel, Dominic asks to stop and look at the surrounding flora. His avatar, Maverick, is a ranger: plants and animals are his specialty.

Since Valen also has medicine as a talent, I also take quick breaks to identify plant. But we don't linger. My teammates' stiff postures tells me that, while they're letting us explore, they're becoming increasingly impatient.

But, a lifetime of playing video games has taught me to be observant, break all the pots, and collect all the things. We might either need them later, or we can sell them.

"You finished?" Bastian asks pointedly. I see his hard smile. It's the first time I've noticed clear signs of irritation.

I get it. There are too many unknowns in this Odyssey. Sure, we have a direction, but we don't know what we're going to find—if we encounter anything. Besides we only have three-hours to complete the task.

"We're good," I say before Dominic can snip back. The man in question simply grunts, his preferred form of communication.

Cameron changes the subject. "What's that?" He asks and his avatar, Flickerfoot, takes a few steps to the east. Far in the distance, I see something akin to a signpost.

"Directions, hopefully," Dominic says. Then addresses Cameron, "Lead on."

We follow Flickerfoot to the very real signpost next to the faintest trace of a road. The left arrow points to some place called Stonehaven. The other points to the Shadow Mines.

"Sounds sinister. Ten dollars says we'll have to go there," I say.

"Shadow Mines *totally* don't sound bad," Cameron comments sarcastically.

"To Stonehaven?" Bastian asks.

The group agrees, and we're off racing again. I'm feeling good about this new plan, even if there are no other teams around us. That just means either they have a head start, or we're doing something unique.

I cannot wait to see the gameplay of the other groups' adventures tomorrow.

We travel along the road to this mysterious Stonehaven. My leg bounces under my desk again, the nervous energy working itself out. It's the silence that is getting to me. If I were gaming with my friends, we'd be chatting away. But what do I say to guys I barely know that won't embarrass us on the internet?

Unsurprisingly, it's Cameron who breaks the quiet asking those get-to-know-you questions, the safe kind that are meant to get you talking. What's our favorite food?—empanadas. Why did we get into streaming?—to connect with a like-minded community. Do we have any pets? I pan my camera to Annie, who lifts her head to my hand for some friendly pets.

To my surprise, Dominic has a free-range rabbit who tries to take a bite of the camera. Cameron just lost his dog and Bastian has a salt-water fish tank—because, of course, he does. Those are expensive to maintain.

The banter makes the time pass quickly, and it's almost like we've been playing together for more than thirty minutes when we arrive at Stonehaven.

If drought were a town, it would be Stonehaven. Buildings intertwine with the natural hills and cliffs at the base of the mountain. The structures are built with rough-hewn stone, timber, and corrugated metal roofs. Broken mine carts mark the entrances of collapsed tunnels, along with piles of excavated rocks and dirt. There's a single well in the center of the town.

"There's a tavern," Dominic says, moving Maverick in that direction.

The Rusty Pickaxe. Good name.

"Taverns always have quests," Cameron says.

We push through the swinging doors of the Rusty Pickaxe. The room is lit with low-hanging, wrought-iron lanterns that cast a warm glow over the aged, stained wooden tables. Most of the furniture has seen better days. The seating provides a mix of private booths and communal tables. In the corner, there is a mini-display of minerals and gemstones—presumably found in the local mines. I make a note to examine those if there's time.

A human barkeep with heavy boots, denim overalls, and a thick red beard calls out to us. "Hullo travelers. Sit anywhere." We do just that, interacting with the table closest to the door.

He pours a few mugs of ale and then brings them to us. "Haven't seen yins 'round here before," he says as she sets the mugs down with a clank. As Valen takes a drink, I raise my water bottle to my teammates. They all do the same and we drink. I swear I see Dominic crack a genuine smile at our antics.

Sitting my drink down, I notice the voice-activated interaction. Call me impatient, or excited, but I don't wait for my teammates. I lock onto the barkeep. "Hello sir, my name is Valen, hailing from the city of Nalim."

"Hank Stoneforge," he grunts. "Ain't never met someone from Nalim."

"I'm Maverick, hailing from Emor." Dominic says, following my lead.

"Emor," Hank repeats. "Don't get many city folk here. What can we humble mining folk do for yins?"

So we're close to Emor. That would make sense with the mountains. Emor is nestled among a scary-looking mountain range.

Bastian clears his throat. "Good sir, we would like to lend our aid to anyone who might need help recovering a lost, or even stolen, item."

"The help board is over yonder," Hank waves his hand towards the front wall. "But I think my one barmaid was saying she lost something."

This is great. Even in this middle-of-nowhere village, we have choices. Before I go to ask the group what they want to do Cameron says, "Fantastic! Can we speak with her?"

I bite my tongue and swallow my irritation. He could have at least asked us, but a lost item is a lost item. We're forty-five minutes into the Odyssey and we still don't have a mission.

Hank calls out, "Lucetta!"

A young woman with fiery red hair approaches, a serving tray in her hands. "You hollered?"

"You gave your grandmother's ring to that boy who ran off, right?" Hank summarizes.

Lucetta's gaze drops to the floor. "Yes, Stephan wore my grandmother's ring on a chain while he worked in the Shadow Mines," her voice wavers. "One day he ain't never come back. The mines are dangerous. Something evil lives down there. Would you brave adventurers return my grandmother's ring?"

Text flashes across the screen:

Quest: A Shadowy Retrieval.

Then the options:

Accept

Refuse

I disconnect from the conversation with Hank and Lucetta to ask my team, "Any objections?"

"None here," Bastian says. Dominic agrees. We all chose to accept.

Quest Accepted: A Shadowy Retrieval

Lucetta puts her hand on her chest, closes her eyes, and gives us a deep nod in thanks. "Thank you. Please take this." she hands us a lantern that she pulls from—somewhere. Video game magic I guess.

"You'll need this in the shadow mines." Lucetta continues. "To chase away the darkness." Bastian takes the lantern while I thank Hank and Lucetta again.

"What is the danger?" Dominic asks.

"No one knows," Hank says. "After Stephan died, the mayor said nobody else is supposed to go down there. Adventurers never come back.

He's just saying that, I think. And I hope Cameron didn't accidentally choose the harder of two missions.

"Thank you," Bastian says. "We'll be back."

We leave the Rusty Pickaxe without looking at the rocks and forgoing checking out the general store.

"I'd rather just get going," Dominic says. We have a little over two hours left.

That makes me uncomfortable. I'm usually the player who talks to everyone in the town. But I also understand Dominic's rush.

"To the mines." Bastian navigates his avatar out of Stonehaven proper back the way we came, passing the signpost and moving toward the Shadow mines.

Cameron plays his questions game. "Is a hotdog a sandwich?"

"Absolutely not," Bastian is adamant and will not hear any other answer.

I laugh and glance at my phone. Maybe playing with new people isn't so bad.

Chapter 22
Valentino

We reach the gaping entrance to the Shadow Mine with two hours left in The Guildmaster's Odyssey. A wooden frame supports the entrance. Deeper into the mine shaft, darkness lingers like a predator in wait. I can't see more than thirty feet in front of me. Thank you, Lucetta for the lantern. We'd be lost without it.

"Looks like we'll have to move in single file," Dominic says. His avatar, Maverick, holds Lucetta's lantern. "It looks like a really long shaft—"

It's immature, but the words cause me to burst into laughter. This breaks Cameron, who joins in with a series of snorts. I glance at Bastian, who would have us think he is above an unintentional dick joke, but a faint smile tugs at the corner of his mouth. I think our team needs this moment of levity.

But Dominic continues without acknowledging the innuendo. "It starts wide but gets narrow fast." I can tell by the tone of his voice and the purse of his lips that he isn't amused.

Cameron recovers and asks, "Is it cliché to say I have a bad feeling?"

"No," I say. This would be the perfect spot for some sort of Enkin encounter.

There are three distinct parts to *Mundo*'s gameplay: world exploration, social interactions, and combat. We've done the first two. It looks like combat is coming our way.

"About that," Bastian says. "Anyone else notice that Lucetta seemed more concerned about the retrieval of the ring than her lover's body?"

We all freeze. Not that we were doing much but standing in front of the entrance to the mine... shaft.

Fuck. He's right. Hank even said something happened to—oh, what's his name? Stephan? But Lucetta was only concerned about her grandmother's ring.

"Any chance that's a developer error?" Cameron asks.

"No," Bastian, Dominic, and I all say at the same time. Cameron puts up his hands like he's innocent.

"You think he's dead?" I ask.

"Probably," Bastian says.

"Then we're going to fight the Enkin that killed him," I summarize. "I'd put money on Stonekin."

Of the three Stonekin subspecies, I'd least like to fight the Giantkin. Something about their brightly painted, humanoid, corpse-like appearance freaks me out. They are also wicked strong or have devastating magic. Thankfully, they like to live above ground, not deep below it. Same with Stormkin, the second subspecies. Their canine forms are fucking adorable, but the wind, thunder, and lightning they can summon in a flash are not.

"Rockkin thrive in underground tunnels," Dominic verbalizes my next thought.

They will present a unique set of challenges. I think Rockkin look strangely cool. They are like bipedal praying mantises with hardened exoskeletons and can phase in and out of stone, making nests in carved-out sections of the wall. We'd never know one is there until we knock down the wall or move the stone with magic.

All of this also means the ring could be hidden behind a stone wall—and we don't know the structural integrity of the mine. We can't just go around knocking down walls. I close my eyes and take a breath. *You got this Val,* I tell myself. *Don't freak out*. I just wish we had a natural magic mage on our team. They could use their magic to manipulate the stone without damage.

I look at Bastian in his chat window, "Does Aurelius have any magic that stops or slows time?"

"One slow spell," Bastian looks away from the camera, probably consulting his spellbook on another screen.

"We'll need it if Rockkin appear," Dominic adds, unnecessarily. "The best way to fight them is to freeze or slow them as they come out of the rock."

I glance at the clock. "We need to get moving." I urge. "Under two hours left."

"I'll stay in the front and be our guide. Flickerfoot you next, watch the right side, Valen goes next, watch the left side, and Aurelius in the back." Dominic orders.

I could question the formation, but I don't. We need to get moving. It's as good a plan as any.

The narrow tunnel descends into the bowels of the earth, the rough-hewn walls glistening with moisture that seeps from countless fissures. The path is dimly lit by Lucetta's lantern.

I'm on edge. Not just because I'm preparing myself for the Rockkin to jump out of the earth and attack us, but because of the silence. I know my teammates are focused, but if I were playing with my friends, we'd still find a way to chit-chat or joke to make light of what is happening. Playing with near strangers who have not developed comfortable banter, creates tension. The mere sound of a water drop makes my heart rate spike.

A sense of dread lingers as I lean back in my chair. I feel like we didn't prepare enough for this. We should have asked more questions about Stephan, about Lucetta, about the Shadow Mines.

We continue to descend into the mines, taking several ladders. My foot bounces under the table as our avatars descend. With each level, nothing jumps out of the walls, no enemies attack us. The lack of enemies makes me worry about what we are going to find at the bottom.

After several minutes of navigating the maze of ladders, and tunnels, the space opens into a vast cavern so large our light cannot reach the ceiling. The ground is covered in stalagmites, stones, abandoned mining tools, and—are those bones laying next to some gold coins?

"What is that?" Dominic asks as he moves Maverick closer to a large boulder in the center of the room. It looks different, darker than the stalagmites scattered around the space.

To quote Cameron, I have a bad feeling about this.

Something's off, I just can't figure out what it is. Maverick creeps closer to the rock as I assess our surroundings. There's something we're missing here. We're in an enormous cavern at the bottom of a mine. There are no other Enkin in the area and bones and gold are littered along the floor.

"Guys," Dominic whispers. The light shines over the rock, revealing a texture that looks like interlocking teardrops, where each pointed tip aligns perfectly with the curve of the next rock. It's rendered in a blue so deep it looks black. In my experience, the rocks in video games never look the way this one does.

Then the rock inhales.

My heart beats in my throat as my eyes widen.

Maverick moves close enough to illuminate a wedge-shaped snout adorned with rows of sharp, black ridges. The rock exhales wisps of smoke that curl into the air.

"Oh fuck," Bastian curses as we all back away so the not-rock is bathed in darkness once again.

That's not a rock or series of rocks.

Those are scales.

And that—

"I know everyone is thinking it, so I'm just going to say it," Cameron says. "That's a dragon."

"Fuck," I run my hands over my head—as best I can with my bun.

"I think we found what killed the others," Cameron adds.

Hence the bones scattered around.

"Let's fight it," Dominic says. I shouldn't be surprised that's his first thought.

Nobody talks. Are we supposed to fight it? How? And it's sleeping, which makes it even more strange. There has never been a dragon type Enkin in the history of *Mundo*. When Paula told us there would be never-before-seen content, she wasn't lying. Overcoming these feelings of fear and of dread, has to be part of the Odyssey. We must use what we learned as players to figure out these new situations. Even then, that knowledge won't be helpful if we can't learn to work together.

I fight the urge to blame Cameron. Shove down the thought that if we only went to the quest board, we wouldn't be here, woefully unprepared, in front of a dragon.

Focus Val. I analyze my past gameplay, looking for any ideas and strategies.

Fighting this thing would be like fighting the Windkin, as I had with Rhea, but on a much larger scale. And the only reason Rhea and I beat the Windkin was Starwrath's special ability.

My thoughts drift to Rhea, and everything we've done together in *Mundo*, how much she's shown me.

Wait—an idea pops into my head. "Maybe we don't have to fight it," I say, more to myself than to my team. "Can I have that light?"

In the game, Maverick hands the light to Valen. Then, I ease Valen towards the slumbering mountain of a creature once again. As I move, I shift my camera around, moving my focus over different objects, seeing what I can interact with. My cursor snaps to an auto-lock on the dragon itself, but it's not meant for combat. It's verbally activated, as we saw with the cave quest Rhea showed me two weeks ago.

"What are you thinking, Val?" Bastian asks. His voice pulls up at the end of the question.

"I'm going to talk to it," I say.

"That's stupid," Dominic spurts. "We should attack it now while it's sleeping. We can get a surprise round on it."

I can think of a dozen reasons that would be a bad idea. Just like I'm sure Dominic can think of an equal number of arguments for why my idea is equally idiotic.

"Think of it as a distraction," I offer. "And if it attacks me, then ambush it."

I watch on my screen as my teammates shift in their seats, their eyes bouncing between video windows. Eventually, I see Cameron give a subtle nod.

Then Bastian finally says, "Do your thing."

I position Valen so I'm looking at the creature's head, but give myself plenty of space to react if it wakes up and attacks.

Here goes nothing—live in front of thousands of people.

Adjusting the microphone on my headset, I take a breath and begin. "Oh great and mighty wyrm. I am Valen, a humble adventurer who comes seeking an audience with your fearsome...ness." I command Valen to crouch. My avatar looks like it's about to shit, which frankly, feels appropriate right now. This is mortifying.

A second passes in what feels like an hour. My mouth is dry. I hope the camera doesn't pick up my sweat. I don't think I can take another moment of this stress.

My team, however, is trying—and failing—to hide their laughter. I don't blame them. Tomorrow maybe I'll laugh at myself too.

Next Odyssey, I'll let them embarrass themselves.

But then the dragon lifts its head, sapphire eyes flicking in my direction. "Are you here to kill me, too?" he asks. His voice is low and flat. It almost sounds like he's been crying.

I'm not sure what I expected the dragon to say. Part of me is still prepared for the worst-case, fight-the-thing scenario.

But having a weeping dragon ask me if I'm here to kill it—as if *I'd* be putting it out of its misery, throws me off balance.

Off-screen, Annie reaches out her paw and hits my headphones. The action snaps me out of my momentary freeze.

How do people not like cats?

"No! Your...wickedness," I sputter.

"I. Am Not. Wicked!" The dragon roars. The creature stands, revealing its full size. Light bursts forth from previously unseen sconces on the walls of the cavern. Must be part of the dragon's magic to control its lair.

Now I can see the creature standing in all its glory. It's easily as big as two Windkins. His body is covered in those blue-black scales. His tail stretches well behind him with a sharp spike on the tip. The front limbs are slightly shorter than his hind legs and end with massive claws that could easily shred Valen. Its wings stretch wide, the membrane taut between long, powerful fingers. They shimmer with a hint of iridescence against the new light.

"You dare insult me with your lies?" The dragon snarls.

Fuck, I've insulted it.

"We never came up with a go word," Dominic notes. Go-word is the agreed-upon phrase that kicks us into action.

True. I don't need them rushing in before I get the chance to talk to the dragon, but this conversation did not start off the way I wanted. If I don't get it under control, we're going to have to fight the dragon.

I don't want to fight the dragon.

I whisper to my team, "No need to rally forthright."

The dragon said, "Repeat your statement, human."

"My deepest apologies." I stop my attempts at honorifics. "Please tell me how I should address you?"

The dragon's lumbering head moves closer, sniffing the air surrounding Valen. Not sure what it's sniffing for and my every sense is on alert, but I still don't move Valen from his position.

After possibly the longest moment of my life, the dragon says, "You may address me as Stephangor the Drakin."

An information tag appeared above Stephangor's head:

Stephangor the Drakin.

I take a moment to revel in the fact I could be the first person talking to the first dragon in *Mundo*. The thought energizes me. I'm sitting on the edge of my seat as adrenaline pumps through me. This is both the coolest and the most nerve-racking experience of my streaming career.

"Thank you, great Stephangor," I say, commanding Valan to stand. "We come here on a quest to find a lost artifact."

"We?" Stephangor asks.

"Val," Cameron whispers, "introduce us."

Right, good idea.

"Please allow me to introduce my companions, Aurelius, Maverick, and Flickerfoot." My teammates move their avatars forward, as I name them. They too crouch briefly before rising.

"As my companion was saying, a woman asked us to retrieve her grandmother's ring from these mines," Dominic says. Typical of him to want to regain control.

"Who is this woman?" Stephangor's voice drops into a deep timbre of curiosity.

"Lucetta from Stonehaven," I explain. "She claims she gave a ring to her lover as a token of her affection and he did not return from the mines. The ring had once belonged to the woman's grandmother and she would like it back."

"I know she would," Stephangor huffed. "But she gave it to me and I do not wish to return it."

There is a moment of collective silence.

"Wait," Cameron says. "You're Stephan?"

"That is the name I give when I am in my human form," Stephangor explains.

Huh. A dragon who fell in love with a human. Who would have thought?

"So, you have this ring?" Dominic asks, stubbornly. His tone suggests he's bored with this conversation.

Stephangor snorts smoke again. "The ring is mine. Lucetta gave me the ring as a token of her love. A love that was quickly forgotten when I revealed my true form to her."

I don't move so I don't trigger any more dialog. "Rally forthright," I say, employing the phrase I suggested earlier. My team understands and stops moving so we can chat.

Cameron speaks first. "Let me get this straight. Lucetta rejected the dragon and then sent us down here to get her ring so she doesn't have to deal with her ex? That's a little...lame."

I let out a breath, nod my head, and fall back in my chair. I rub my temples. This crap belongs in a badly written romance novel.

"Looks like our options are one, fight the dragon for the ring," Bastian says. I watch him hold up one finger in his video window. He holds up a second finger. "Or two, convince him to give it up by talking it through?."

Both seem like equally daunting tasks. I wish Speed was here. His character, Nyx, is built for charisma.

"Let's just fight the thing and be done with it," Dominic groans.

"We'll get crushed," Cameron returns.

"We're not Stephan's therapists," Dominic says, a little more snap in his voice.

"This Drakin is the largest Enkin I've ever seen," Bastian says. "Maybe we can trade something for the ring?"

"He loves her," Cameron says. "He's not giving up the ring."

Dominic laughs. "That's not love. That's possessiveness."

"We need to get that ring back to Lucetta to complete the mission," Bastian reminds us.

And here we are, fighting again. I exhale as I lean forward, my elbows on the table, head in my hands.

I can't help but empathize with Stephangor. This situation with Lucetta feels like a parallel to my feelings for Preston. To love someone who doesn't love you back, to look at a ring like that every day and be reminded of it? When they won't even come and visit me—.

"Wait a minute," I say as an idea forms in my head.

I raise my head and look at my teammates. From the looks on their faces, I must have interrupted them.

"If we can't bring the ring to Lucetta, let's bring Lucetta to the ring."

"And how do you propose we do that?" Dominic challenges.

Good question. Before I can answer, Cameron suggests, "We could tell her the truth."

Dominic just shakes his head. "She knows the truth, and she wants nothing to do with him."

There's a saying about truths,- how there are two sides to every story. The way Stephangor spoke about Lucetta—how she freaked out the moment he revealed himself and didn't allow him to speak—makes me wonder.

"Whose truth?" I ask.

"What do you mean?"

"Does she know Stephangor's truth?" I clarify. "If we can get Stephangor to—I don't know." I rack my brain for the first thing that comes to mind. I suddenly remember helping Gavriel write a love letter to Elara. "Write her a letter, explaining himself. Then maybe she'll come visit him."

My team is uncomfortably quiet as I watch their eyes shift on my screen. They don't know what to think. I'd bet this is the weirdest game any of us have ever played.

"Fine," Bastian relents. "Let's do it."

With little over an hour left in the Odyssey, we resume our gameplay and relay the plan to Stephangor. Before we can react, dense gold swirls of magic conceal the dragon's form. As quickly as they come, they leave, revealing a burly human man with a mop of curly black hair and blue eyes.

This must be Stephangor's human form. It's entirely—normal-looking. Which, I guess, is the point if a dragon is trying to blend in.

"Give me parchment and I will write this letter," he demands.

Aurelius hands over some paper and a quill. Stephangor takes it, closes his eyes, and squiggles the pen over the parchment. Words magically appear.

He hands the letter back. "If this does not work, I will burn the town to the ground to get to her."

Well, that's not extreme or anything. "I hope he didn't write that in his letter," I say.

Aurelius nods, pockets the letter, and then we all retreat as Stephan morphs back into a dragon.

Despite Stephangor's threat, hope blooms in my chest. With less than an hour left, I feel like we can accomplish our mission.

"Not bad, Val," Cameron admits begrudgingly when we're on our way back to Stonehaven. "How did you figure that out? "

I think of Rhea as I smile. "Just something I learned while adventuring with someone."

I note that Cameron's expression has changed and that he's peering intently at my video screen.

"Someone, huh? Sounds like a special someone."

"Yeah, I guess she is," I admit, in front of millions of viewers.

Chapter 23
Sylvie

I get to watch Val's brilliant gameplay on the living room TV. Theo went out again for the night, so I have the house to myself.

Which is fine because Val just about gave me a mini panic attack. That's why my heart is beating so fast.

He just had to agree with Cameron's comment about this mysterious "she" being someone special.

Someone who showed him the same things I did. I'm the only girl Val plays with—to my knowledge, anyway. But I can't be his someone special. Sure, Val flirts, but he's like that with everyone. Right?

As my heart settles from that not-so-small revelation, Val's team returns to Stonehaven to give the letter to Lucetta. I watch as her eyes dart across the page and her blush rises. She agrees to go with them. When they return to the lair, Lucetta runs across the cavern and into Stephangor's human arms.

With six minutes left in the game, Stephangor returns the ring.

Mission Complete. Val's first Odyssey is a success.

I pick up my phone to text him.

Sylvie:

I want to know what was in that letter.

Sylvie:

You did okay too

I switch the stream from BGN and watch Rhessa Studios'. They invite Val's team back to participate in the second Odyssey. Teams that did not complete their mission, end their journey here. I don't recall that rule. Did Val know they'd be eliminated if they didn't complete the mission? Did BGN?

My phone sounds.

Val:

I'll tell you if you come to my after party.

I smile at my phone. This man is relentless. There's no way I'm emotionally and mentally prepared for that. I haven't met him, let alone anyone else who will be at his party.

Sylvie:

Thanks, but no. Too many people.

Val:

I get it.

A moment passes then another text pops up.

Val:

Will he not let you?

At the not-so-subtle allusion to my ex-boyfriend, the little voice pops back into my head. The one that tells me to forgive Theo before he finds another girl he wants to bring home and kicks me out of the apartment for good.

I shake my head, attempting to rid myself of that voice. I have a plan for that scenario. I'd go to a temporary shelter for women.

Sylvie:

I'm not under duress. He went out with friends. I'm home alone.

Two seconds later, Val's contact info flashes on my screen. Holy shit, he's calling me. I exhale my nerves as I swipe to answer and bring my phone to my ear.

"Hello?" I answer like I don't know who's calling—or why.

"Hey Rhea," Val's smooth tenor voice comes through. "How are you?"

"Fine." I don't know what else to say. Is my voice shaking? I hope Val can't tell. "You did great in the Odyssey."

"Thanks. I'm glad you watched. But hey about the afterparty—"

I cut him off. "I appreciate the invite. But I'm settled in for the night and don't feel like peopling."

"How about we meet up, then?" Val suggests. "Just you and me."

"Wait, what? Now?" I ask as I get up off the couch to pace. I need to get some of this nervous energy out of my body. "Don't you have a party to get to?"

Nerves race from my heart to my stomach, toes, fingers, and tongue.

"Why not?" Val laughs. "It's my party. I'm allowed to be late."

I'm not sure what his motive is here. Why would he want to be late to his own party just to meet me? But this is such a Val thing to do, suggesting a compromise to spend time with me.

Meeting him in real life is just a step beyond playing *Mundo* together. Right?

"Please Rhea," Val says. "Let's meet up. You can even pick the place."

It's the genuine plea in his voice that hits me in the gut.

Is this happening? Am I going to agree to meet Val?

"Fine," I say. "But just for a bit. To celebrate your big win." Then I give him the name of the park that's close by.

"Sweet!" Val says. I imagine him pumping his fist into the air. "Is fifteen minutes enough time?"

"Fifteen minutes is fine."

"Can't wait to meet you," Val says, then hangs up.

I stop pacing and stare at my phone. What did I just agree to? Meeting Val in person for the first time.

The voice returns, reminding me that Theo could drive past the park and see me with another man. That would most certainly start an argument.

Wait, why do I care? Theo and I are not together. I tell him almost every day when he asks when I'm going to stop being mad at him. He's probably out at the bar trying to pick up another girl one that would get on her knees and worship his god-tier ego.

I'm allowed to meet a boy—a friend, without needing Theo's permission.

But I should tell someone what I'm doing. Just to be safe. I open my messages to pull up the group chat with Vyola and Sebastian. But something makes me hesitate. They'll have more questions that I don't have time to answer.

Like why I agreed to meet him in—I look at the time on my phone—twelve minutes.

With a deep breath, I pull up Julia's number. She knows about Val, gave me advice about him when we met in person. She'll be happy for me and want me to be safe.

Sylvie:

Going to meet Val. Letting you know in case I go missing.

She replies immediately

Julia:

GET IT GIRL!

I'm in yoga pants and a graphic t-shirt. Not much I can do about that now. I pull on some socks, slide on my boots, and grab my coat, dropping my phone into my pocket.

Stepping outside to lock the door—it finally hits me, I'm going to meet Val.

This is real. He's going to be a real person. Not that he wasn't before, but we have only communicated digitally.

Are those butterflies in my stomach?

I'm the first one to arrive at the park. The last remainders of light linger but the street lamps cast enough glow to chase away the darkness. I take a seat on the empty swing set, the material cold against my butt.

My phone sounds.

Val:

Almost there.

Why is my heart racing so much? Why is my stomach doing somersaults?

Gods, I feel like I'm going to be sick. This is a bad idea.

It's too late.

When I look up, I see a figure turn the corner and walk into the park—walk towards me.

My heart stops. His social media pales in comparison to how handsome Valentino Santos is in person.

I can tell the moment he sees me because that brilliant smile becomes a beacon brighter than the street lights.

"Rhea?" he asks when he's in range.

On shaking legs, I rise from the swing and he approaches me.

"Val?" I ask stupidly. I already know it's him. Granted, he knows what I look like too.

He spreads his arms out, "Can I hug you? We're kind of past the handshake phase right?" I love that he asks my permission.

In that moment, there's nothing I want more than his hug. I nod my head and step into his embrace.

"I can't believe you're here," he says, as his arms engulf me in a hug. And of course, it's the best hug, with the perfect amount of pressure. I would be lying if I didn't admit there's something more here. He's taller than I expected, and leaner. My arms wrap around him easily. His long hair creates a curtain to shield us from the world.

"Afraid I wouldn't show?" I tease, turning my head so I don't speak into his chest.

I feel the rumble of his laugh as he says, "Goddesses rarely bless mortals with their true form."

He lets me go, but I still feel this energy simmering between us, like we're two magnets drawn toward one another. Heat rises in my cheeks as my heart continues its pounding rhythm. Does this man just not understand how words like that can affect a person?

Attempting to put some distance between us, I sit back down on a swing and motion for Val to sit next to me, twisting towards him so we can look at each other better.

"Meeting you feels more epic than the game I just played, but still, what did you think of the Odyssey?" he asks.

"Talking to the dragon was brilliant. There was no guarantee you would have come out of that alive."

"I have you to thank for that."

My curiosity gets the better of me. "So ...the thing you said."

"That you're someone special to me? You are." Val nods and gives me that gorgeous smile again.

How many butterflies can fit in my stomach? And I thought it was supposed to get colder as the sun sets? But I'm a pool of heat. "You're just trying to flatter me."

"Always," Val admits. "But that doesn't mean it's not true."

If I thought Val was flirty online, I have no defense for him in person. The blush returns to my cheeks.

A few seconds of comfortable silence pass between us. "Can I ask a question?" Val asks.

"Depends on what it is."

Val laughs, then his mouth pulls down and he looks at me. Looks at me like he's seeing into my soul. "How are things with Theo?"

Well, that's a loaded question. I purse my lips and look to the ground, watching my toes dance beneath the swing. "We're done," I say softly. "I broke things off two weeks ago. I'm just stuck living in the same space with him until I figure things out."

Val says nothing, but maneuvers his swing closer to mine, putting an arm around me. "I'm sorry."

Instinctively, I turn my face into him, so my cheek rests against his arm. "Don't be. It's not your fault. I'm the one who let things go on too long."

"Hey," Val takes my chin between his thumb and forefinger, lifting my head to look at him. "It's not your fault either. You deserve to be happy Rhea."

My eyes drop to his mouth, then look up into his warm brown eyes. Something inside me bursts like I can't hold back the dam anymore.

I didn't know how much I needed to hear that. But as my tears begin to fall, Val pulls me back into another hug—as best he can while we sit on two swings.

"I kept trying to tell myself things would get better once I graduated, but I was fooling myself." I mumble against his chest. "I have a plan to get out. It's just awkward until then."

"Your internship?" Val asks.

I nod.

"Did you hear anything?"

I shake my head. "Not yet. I'm hoping to soon though. Definitely by the end of the month."

Val doesn't press for any more information. He just holds me as I cry like a fool in front of him.

"This is not how I wanted our first meeting to go," I blubber through my tears, angling my body to put some distance between us. I need to regain my composure.

Val laughs and lets me go, but still hangs onto the chain of my swing so he stays close.

"You can stay at my place," he offers. I open my mouth to say something but he continues, "But I know that's not what you want to bounce between men."

He's right. And it's refreshing to hear from him. He understands me and respects what I want. He's not trying to be a knight coming to my rescue. He's supporting me as I try to stand on my own.

"I want to be financially independent, but I do appreciate you offering your home to a stranger."

"You're not a stranger. We've known each other for over a month now."

He gazes at me intently. That crackling energy lingers between us, drawing me to him.

Distance, Sylvie! Get your shit together.

"How are things with Preston?" I ask, trying to change the subject.

We're side by side, each of us hanging onto the chain of the other's swing.

Val shrugs. "He's making more of an effort."

"But?"

"I can't shake this feeling he's hanging on tighter because ..."

"Because what?"

Val purses his lips like he's choosing his words carefully. "I think that Preston is afraid I've replaced him with you."

Oh.

I wasn't expecting that.

"How does that make you feel?"

"Like he doesn't know me at all," Val answers, looking out into the barren playground. "And I still can't help but feel like we're drifting apart."

"Seems like we're both losing a relationship," I say, then mentally kick myself. That was insensitive of me. I didn't realize what I said until the words were between us.

A cool breeze blows through, contributing to the now-broken spell between us.

"You should get back inside," Val says. "It's cold."

I nod, understanding. He has someplace he needs to be, too. "And you have a party to get to."

Val stands, releasing my swing, and I drift away from him. But he stops, turns, and offers me his hand. I place mine in his, relishing the feeling of his warm skin. He probably won't want to see me again after my comment. He helps me up, pulling me towards him, and steadies me with his other hand on my waist. "Are you sure you don't want to come with me?"

"I don't think that's a good idea." He just announced to the entire world that he has someone special. If I go with him, it could give people the wrong idea.

"I disagree, but I respect your decision."

He pulls me into another tight hug and I wonder how many hours I could spend in his arms.

"Thank you," I say, and mean it. Theo doesn't always respect my "no." He complains until I give in and do what he wants.

When he releases me, his hand lingers on my waist. His other hand tucks a loose piece of hair behind my ear. His fingers trace a line up my cheek and down my jaw.

Oh gods, is he going to kiss me?

I don't think I'm ready for that.

"Have a good night, Rhea," he whispers to me.

"Sylvie," I blurt out. When I see the confused look on his face I add, "My name is Sylvie."

"Sylvie," he repeats as if my name on his lips is a magic spellbinding us together. I watch his eyes drift down to my mouth, then back up to my eyes. "I'm glad I got to meet you."

He lifts one of my hands to his mouth, placing a kiss on the back of it, maintaining eye contact with me the whole time. His lips are soft and I didn't know my hand was so sensitive. My jaw is probably on the floor. There is no way this man doesn't know what he's doing. Does that mean he's intentionally flirting with me?

I still feel the ghost of sensation when the kiss ends.

"Enjoy your party," I whisper. Because I don't know what else to say.

"I'll text you," he says, giving me a smile and a wink.

I return the smile. "I might respond."

As he walks away, he shoves his hands in his pants and I can't help but admire the way they hug his perfectly formed ass.

Better to check him out than to think about how much I wanted him to kiss me.

Chapter 24
Valentino

I should turn this car back around, go back to the park, and kiss her. But the chances of her still waiting for me are slim.

The sight of Rhea...no—*Sylvie*, looking up at me, with her big brown eyes and luscious lips, consumes my mind as I drive to my afterparty at 2Game.

Hard to believe just hours ago I played in the exclusive Guildmaster's Odyssey. Or that Paula, from BGN, has three interviews for us scheduled tomorrow.

None of it seems to matter right now. All I want is to spend more time alone in the park with Sylvie. I could call her and beg her to come with me to the party again, but I don't want to push it. She's always been a little skittish with me. I remember she wouldn't verbally talk to me online for the longest time. With an ex like Theo, I understand why.

I don't want to push her too hard, too fast. That's the only reason I'm not calling her to ask her out right now.

When did I start thinking of Sylvie romantically? When I found out she lived close by? When I first heard her voice? In the end, it doesn't matter. She walked into my heart when I wasn't looking and made herself comfortable.

Monday, I resolve. I'll ask her out on Monday.

I park my car near 2Game and let out a sigh. I'm already thirty minutes late to the party. I have text messages from Speed and Xander asking me if everything is okay and where I am. I send a quick text.

Valentino:

Parking now.

Then to Sylvie, I text.

Valentino:

Goodnight beautiful.

I get out of the car, lock it, and head toward the store.

As I enter 2Game, I'm shocked to see that the place has been decorated. Simple decorations like purple and yellow streamers and my BGN team photo with Valen blown up on the wall. It is more than was here for my podcast party. There's food too. Pizza, sodas, and other shareables are spread out on a folding table.

Speed launches himself at me, wrapping his arms around me. "Congrats, man!" He releases all but a wrist and raises my arm into the air. "The man himself has arrived!" he hollers across the room.

The crowd chants, "SaintVal!, SaintVal!, SaintVal!"

Xander approaches, offering me a hand, then pulls me in for a classic bro hug. Pixel sits dutifully at his side. I have to remind myself not to acknowledge Pixel while she's working.

One by one, other friends come up to congratulate me on a job well done. If I'm honest, I don't know everyone very well. Some I recognize as members of 2Game, but we've rarely talked beyond a general acknowledgment.

Although, there are more people here tonight than at my podcast release party. I remember how I thought that was a big deal—and now here I am. It makes me wonder what's next for me.

Hopefully, a date with Sylvie.

Feeling thirsty, I head to the food table to grab a drink. Preston intercepts me, putting an arm around my shoulders.

"Everything okay?" he asks. "It's not like you to be late." He's wearing the perfume. The one I like—used to like—so much.

I should be honest with my best friend and tell him I met Sylvie for the first time, and that I have feelings for this girl. The thought makes me pause and question if he is my best friend anymore. His disapproving comments pop into my head, and I can see the conversation before it happens. I don't feel like arguing with him or telling him Sylvie's no longer with her boyfriend.

"I was journaling," I explain. Not an entire lie. I spent some time jotting down my thoughts until I called Sylvie and we met up. "Bas told us to write our thoughts down to prep for interviews tomorrow."

"When's your first one?" Preston asks.

"Three," Then another at five, and a third at eight.

Preston nods his head but asks no more questions. Instead, he says, "I'd like to introduce you to someone."

There's only one person I can think of who Preston would want me to meet so badly that he'd have the audacity to bring them to my party. He motions to the wall across from the food where a thin blonde woman stands. She's dressed casually in leggings and an oversized purple tunic. Supporting Junta, I guess.

"Val this is—"

I interrupt him. "Julianna Sinclair." I put on my best smile and thrust my hand out to her. "I've heard so much about you."

"Only good things I hope," she laughs, looking over to Preston. I can see the genuine affection in her eyes and the tension in her shoulders. She's nervous. She wants this interaction to go well.

"Oh, he swoons at the thought of you," I say.

Julianna laughs. "He does not!"

I take a drink from the cup I'm holding. "He absolutely does."

"Dude, you're supposed to make me look manly and stuff in front of my girl," Preston elbows me in the side.

"You brought her to the wrong party then, my man," I say, still smiling at him, but also letting him know exactly what I think about his move.

"Well," Julianna hooks her arm in mine. "I'd love to hear all the embarrassing swooning stories after you tell me how you thought to talk to the dragon."

Out of the corner of my vision I catch Speed dramatically rolling his eyes, and I crack a smile. He cocks an eyebrow, probably wondering how I'm doing with Julianna here.

The thing is, I feel nothing. No jealousy, no anger. Not that Julianna deserves my ire. She's done nothing but follow her heart.

And if I'm being honest with myself, my lack of feeling means I've finally moved on.

Chapter 25

Valentino

The weekend is a whirlwind of parties and interviews. Prospero hails our team as one of the best to watch. The other team he praises is called The Outlaws. They are an independent gaming group, so a gaming network like BGN does not sponsor them. They found Stonehaven too, but they took a quest from the board instead of finding the dragon.

As much as I bask in the accolades, I'm relieved when Monday rolls around and I have a normal day at work.

I can't stop thinking about Sylvie, about what I should have done—kiss her. But I didn't want to push her too far, too fast.

We text throughout the weekend. I tell her how happy I am to have met her, that it's the highlight of my weekend.

I wake up Monday unwavering in my decision. Today, I'm going to ask her out.

Well, I have to go to work first. When my lunch hour comes, I leave my desk, walk past Annie sunbathing on the couch, and go to my kitchen, putting my pre-prepared meal in the microwave.

While I wait, I pull up Sylvie's text thread.

It's time to ask this girl out. You got this, Val. You've rehearsed what you want to say. All you have to do is—*ask her out*.

Valentino:

Happy Monday.

Well, that was stupid. Why did I text that? Just trying to open up the conversation, I guess.

Thankfully, Sylvie texts back immediately.

Rhea:

Lol, happy Monday. Ready for your next interview today?

Paula arranged yet another interview tonight. Then it's back to our regularly scheduled streaming. The thought makes me nervous. With so many new followers, I'm afraid the vibe of the channel has changed. I should probably put a call out for more moderators too.

Focus, Val.

Valentino:

I think so.

By the third interview, they were all asking the same questions.

Valentino:

Are you going to watch this one too?

Rhea:

Of course.

Rhea:

Remind Dominic to smile.

I bark out a laugh, scaring Annie into looking up at me. Once she determines that this is just my usual insanity, she goes back to sleep.

Dominic doesn't interview well. He has what Cameron calls "Resting Asshole Face." He looks like he wants to fight someone all the time—unless you get him talking about his rabbit, then he's all smiles.

Not the point.

Focus Val. Ask the girl out.

The microwave beeps, signaling my food is warm. I take it out and set it on the counter to cool, then return to texting Sylvie.

This is it. My hands shake causing a couple of typing errors, but I manage to send it.

Valentino:

Do you mind if I call?

I set my phone down on the counter, then take a couple of deep breaths as I pace back and forth.

I've asked plenty of people out before—why am I this nervous?

Rhea:

Sure, let me step out of the library.

Rhea:

Is everything okay?

She's spending a lot of time on campus. Probably to get away from Theo. She's only told me a little about what happened. I have a feeling that's only the surface.

Valentino:

Yeah, just want to talk about something.

I don't want to be that person who asks her out over text.

Rhea:

Ready when you are.

I shake the nerves out of my hands before I pick up the phone and press the call button. With another deep breath, I raise the phone to my ear.

My stomach is doing somersaults and I haven't eaten anything yet.

Sylvie picks up on the first ring. "Hey you," she says. For a moment, I'm mesmerized by her voice again.

"Hey Rhea," I use her nickname. I still have her in my phone as Rhea.

Sylvie laughs, but then the line goes quiet.

Oh, she's waiting for me to say something. I'm the one who asked to talk.

"How's your day going?" Damnit, that's not what I want to ask. I've rehearsed this, why is it so hard to stick to my script?

"Fine now," she says. I catch a bit of flirtation in her voice. Then she says, "Theo was bitching about me not making him food anymore."

I don't want to talk about Theo, but I opened the door by asking about her day. "What did you say?"

"That I'm not his girlfriend and I'm not making him food."

Her blunt delivery of the line makes me laugh again. "Sorry, it's just the way you said it."

"I get it," she says.

I feel like I'm kicking myself. This interaction is not starting how I want. I was supposed to be charming and have her laughing and reminiscing on how awesome it was to hang out on Saturday.

"I don't think I asked you about your after party?"

"Preston bought his girlfriend."

"How was she?"

Again, how did we get on a topic I didn't want to talk about? "She was nice. We didn't talk for long."

Strangely, the small talk calms my nerves.

There's another lull in the conversation before Sylvie asks, "There's something you wanted to talk about?"

This is it. This is your moment, Val.

But then a voice that sounds a lot like Preston creeps into my head. It says that dating Sylvie would be messy. She's so fresh out of a relationship that she is still living with the guy. Hell, it sounds like Theo still thinks they are in a relationship.

I shut down the voice fast. I never told Preston how I felt about him, and I know why now. The connection I have with Sylvie is unlike anything I've felt before—including what I've felt for Preston.

Okay, here it goes.

"Sylvie, I can't stop thinking about Saturday night," I begin. "I know we get along online, but I didn't expect that electric chemistry between us. I've never felt so connected to another human. I want to take you out. I want to see you again. I want to spend more time with you, get to know everything about you."

The words roll off my tongue. There, my truth is out in the world.

I wait for her response.

And wait.

And wait.

There's nothing but silence and I fear I've said too much, too soon. Oh shit, I scared her off before I could sweep her off her feet.

"Please say something," I plead.

"I think this is what it feels like to get dusted by Thanos," she says.

I don't know if that's good or bad.

"Sylvie?"

"I thought it was just me."

"What?" I ask, holding onto a sliver of hope.

"The chemistry. I felt it too. But I thought it was just me. You're flirty by nature, so I thought you were just being you."

My heart stops, then does backflips. Sylvie feels the same way as I do.

"Let me take you out, and I'll show you flirty."

"Where would we go?" Sylvie asks.

"Let me worry about that."

I can hear her hesitation. "Come on Sylvie. Just one date. Give me the chance to impress you."

There's another moment of silence that seems to stretch on before she says the one word that would change my life.

"Yes."

Chapter 26
Sylvie

I stare at my laptop, trying to comprehend the placement email from Dr. Winters. I blink. Blink again and read, *"Your placement will be Arino Family Practice."*

I got accepted to my dream internship.

I'M ACCEPTED.

My fingers automatically type out a thank you note. Then I'm on my feet, pacing the room. I feel like I could fly from happiness. This is the internship that uses tabletop role-play games in their practice.

Gods, I want to share this good news. Where's my phone? Well, I guess I don't need to text Val. I can tell him on our date. But I should text Vyola and Sebastian.

I'm still on high about my internship, so I don't hear Theo open the door.

"What's going on?" he asks from the doorway.

When I don't answer him, he crosses the room to read my email. I rush to shut my laptop, but I'm too late. Theo's seen enough.

"I thought you decided to do your internship at Yorke Behavioral Clinic?"

He decided. Not me. But I don't answer out loud. There's no arguing with narcissists. But I stand my ground, maintaining eye contact.

"How the hell do you think you'll get to the Umberwoods?"

But, again, I don't answer.

I grab my phone from beside my laptop and push past him, moving out to the living room.

"I won't pay the bus fare," Theo threatens, following me.

"Okay."

"And I'm not giving you extra money."

I dread the day that Theo follows through on that threat. If I start buying things, Theo could catch on that I have an income.

I've been working as many hours for Julia as I can. We have an unspoken agreement that she'll give me as much work as I can handle as a part-time employee without it impacting my schoolwork.

With Theo still fronting my daily living expenses, I've saved up several hundred dollars. I know the amount is tiny compared to what I'll need for an apartment, which is why I need that scholarship. Now that I have my placement email from Dr. Winters, I should hear about the scholarship soon.

"Sylvie," Theo growls.

"Hm," I grunt.

"What's wrong with you? Why can't you be my reasonable girlfriend again?" "You've become such a spiteful bitch."

I cringe and bite my tongue, willing myself not to snap out a "fuck you." He wants my attention. For me to acknowledge him and see that his words have some effect on me.

I cannot, will not, give him that satisfaction.

Right now, I don't want to be in the apartment with him. Good thing I put on my favorite graphic t-shirt and a pair of jeans before Theo burst into my office. I slip on my denim jacket and my favorite pair of ankle boots. It will have to do.

"Where do you think you're going?"

It's so very satisfying to slam the door in Theo's face. Though I dread what he will say when I return. No time to worry about that right now.

As I walk away from the apartment and into the sunshine, all thoughts of Theo are banished from my mind. Because I have a date with Valentino Santos.

I pass the playground and pause. A few young families are playing, but the two swings where Val and I sat remain vacant.

After arriving at the bus stop, I pull out my cell phone and shoot a text off to the Vyola/Sebastian group chat.

Sylvie:

I got the internship!!!

Vyola:

That's awesome!

Sebastian:

CONGRATULATIONS

I can feel their genuine happiness through the text. It makes me smile.

Sylvie:

Thanks. :D

Vyola:

Step one in the get-the-fuck-away-from-Theo plan.

The bus pulls up and I take my seat near the front.

I think about what Val has planned for us as I stare absent-mindedly out the bus window. It's mid-October and warm in the sunshine, but we could get chilly if we're outside too late. He didn't tell me to wear anything specific, so we're not doing anything too athletic—thankfully. Theo took me hiking for our first date. I don't want a repeat.

But Val would also know I don't want to be around large groups of people. It would make me uncomfortable. And someone could recognize Val.

The more I think about Val, the more I worry if I'm enough. Am I dressed okay? Despite my rush to get out of the apartment, I'm a little more put together than I would normally be for class. But not enough to cause Theo to be suspicious.

Maybe I shouldn't call it a date. Things may be over with Theo, but they are still complicated. I shouldn't be dragging Val into my disaster of a life.

But I *want* it to be a date.

As the bus rolls to a halt, I spot Val leaning against the building behind the bus stop, leg bent, foot against the brick wall behind him.

He's dressed casually, like me, in a pullover sweater and dark-wash jeans. I watch as tendrils of his inky black hair dance in the wind.

I exit the bus and Val's face lights up as we make eye contact. His smile is so wide it almost touches his ears.

In this moment, he makes me feel like I am the sun, lighting up his life.

I *absolutely* want this to be a date.

"Hey Rhea." He offers his hand as I make the single perilous step from the street to the sidewalk.

"Such a gentleman," I tease, giving him a smile.

"Mama raised me right."

"But no flowers?" I ask, mostly as a joke.

He shook his head. "I'm not picking you up. If I bought them now, you'd be carrying them around and I'd just end up holding them."

Val tucks my arm into his elbow and leads me down the sidewalk.

"So, what do you give someone on a first date?" I ask. Hoping he's not going to contradict me saying 'it's not a date'.

Val leans in close enough that his temple touches mine. "Something to remember me by," he whispers.

His voice sends shivers through me.

"Which is?" I ask.

He shakes his head. "Not yet, my Titaness."

"Rude," I say with a laugh.

Let him keep his secrets.

He leads me on a short walk two blocks off the main street. We stop outside an old brick townhouse. Above the door is a hand-painted sign that reads Potions and Pages.

"A townhouse turned part tea shop, part book store?" I ask.

"An adventure," Val says and opens the door for me.

Entering the shop is like stepping into another world. I marvel at the sight. Natural light filters through the bay windows in the front. There's a small coffee bar in the front room with handwritten chalkboard menus. Comfortable armchairs and couches are tucked away in nooks, creating cozy spaces.

And books. So many books, precariously stacked on the shelves that line and weave through the building. I approach one shelf, looking at its inhabitants. Each book is slightly worn, with folded pages or cracked spines. This is their second home.

And what a home. The whole place is warm and welcoming and the most magical place I've ever been.

I turn to look at Val, lights in my eyes and dozens of questions on my tongue. How did I not know about this place? How does Val know about it?

The barista appears. They're shorter, about my height, with a blonde pixie cut and bright purple eyeshadow. "Welcome to Potions and Pages," they say.

My questions can wait until later. I give Val a small smile and turn to face the barista.

When we make eye contact, they continue, "The brew of the day is black tea infused with roses."

"That sounds lovely," I say. And it does. I've never had roses in tea before. But even if it's a cup of tea, it's a luxury I don't need, no matter how much I want it.

Val says, "I'll take one as well."

I panic for a moment. I didn't think my compliment meant I ordered.

But Val slides his credit card to the barista, who confirms the two beverages before swiping.

He gives me a look that says he knows I'm a strong, independent woman who can buy her own tea. "Let me treat you."

I blush and I suspect it won't be the last time.

Turning my attention away from the man making my heart shoot off fireworks, I ask the barista, "Are you the owner?"

"Oh no," they say, the light catching their lip ring. "My uncle is. I just work here part-time."

"It's magical in here."

"It is," they agree, and continue to prepare the tea. I watch their hands methodically add the dry leaves and zest ingredients before finally adding the rose petals on top. Then they pour hot water over the mixture and let it steep.

"My uncle says there is magic in books," the barista continues. "You have to go on a journey to find it. I think that's why he started this store."

"Sounds like a smart man," Val says.

He moves next to me, and I feel feather-light touches on the small of my back. My blush is back, or it never left.

The barista laughs, "Occasionally." They hand the two cups of tea over.

Val and I each take one, thanking them for their efforts.

"Enjoy, browse, get lost in something magical," they say before disappearing into what I think is the kitchen.

Faced with the rows of books, I ask Val, "What do you like to read?"

He shrugs. "I don't read as much as I should."

"Yet you brought me to a bookstore. Do you want to go someplace else?"

Val shakes his head and leads me into the next room. Floor to ceiling bookshelves cover each wall and a few smaller ones in the center. "I brought you here because I thought you would like it."

I catch his gaze moving down to my mouth, then back up to look me in the eye.

Oh shit, the heat in my cheeks spreads. Does he want to kiss me? There was a moment I thought he might have wanted to on the night we met.

"Sylvie?"

"Hm?"

"I asked you what you like to read?"

He did? I take a drink of the tea. "Fantasy. Manga too."

"What's your favorite manga?"

I purse my lips. How nerdy do I want to get here? Well, I need to be honest with him. "It's a shojo, *Romeo x Juliet*."

"Are you a thespian?"

"My brother is," I answer. It's the first time I've talked about my family in a while.

"Do you have any other siblings?"

"A sister." I take out my phone and show him the photo of us at my high school graduation. It's the last photo I have of all of us together.

"I have a younger sister," Val says.

"What's her name?"

"Rosalind, Rosa, or Rose, depending on my mother's mood." He says it so casually I cannot help but laugh. I'm imagining what his home life was like.

I feel like I'm always laughing with Val. It feels good. I continue to peruse the books, my fingers dancing along the spines.

A voice in my head says I'm taking too long looking at books I know I won't buy. But when I look back at Val, he's happily watching me, a smile on his face. He's giving me space to explore, content to observe me.

We continue to make small talk as we traverse the sections. There are three levels, and each level has floor-to-ceiling bookshelves.

Best sellers, children, and middle-grade books on the first floor. Young adult novels, classic literature, and self-help are on the second. I wondered if that grouping is on purpose or a happy accident. Science fiction and fantasy dominate the third floor.

While exploring the second floor, I remember to tell Val my news. "I got my placement," I say, my voice shaking. Is it possible to be both nervous and excited?

"It's Arino, isn't it?" Val says with a smile.

My jaw drops. "How did you know?"

Val picks me up in a big hug. If this were a fairytale, he would have swung me around. But we're in a bookstore, so that's probably a bad idea.

He sets me back down. "If even half your passion came through in your application, you'd be the obvious choice."

"I'm so excited Val. I feel like my life is starting over."

New job and, hopefully, a new apartment.

Maybe even a new man.

"You deserve this," he validates me, his brown eyes shining with pride.

It's been a long time since someone has looked at me like that. I can't maintain eye contact with him. Nervously, I purse my lips and look at whatever book is closest to me.

We continue exploring and I climb the third-floor stairs to the fantasy section. At the top, I see a beautiful stained glass window separating the two sections with a chaise and coffee table. The glass depicts a single rose growing in a garden.

Just then, the sunlight hits the window and dozens of multicolor patches of light dance across the wooden floor. I dare to look back at Val and freeze.

I've always known Val is a handsome man, but with this rainbow of color painted on his skin, he looks breathtaking.

"Rhea," he says.

I love that he still calls me that. He thinks of me as the Titaness, that I have this primordial strength and power.

If I am Rhea, then he's Ra—the heavens with all the sun and light they contain.

I feel more towards him during this one date than I felt towards Theo in the past year.

Val steps closer, tucking a loose strand of hair behind my ear, then trailing his finger down my cheek.

"Want to know a secret?" he asks.

More than anything. "Yes."

"Every time I close my eyes, I see that moment, back at the park, when I should have pulled you in close and kissed your perfect mouth."

If that sentence wasn't enough to stop my heart, he takes my chin between his thumb and forefinger, tilting my head up to look at him.

My heart feels like it's racing out of my chest as heat floods my body. I'm sure I'm as bright as a tomato.

"You good?" he asks.

I nod. "Do you still want to kiss me?"

Val leans down, closing the space between us. "If you'll let me," he whispers against my lips.

"Yes." I want to feel his full lips on my own.

I close the distance between us, and we collide together among the multi-colored splashes of light.

Valentino's lips move softly against mine in slow waves of pressure. It isn't gentle, but sensual. The tip of his tongue grazes the seam of my lips but he doesn't force himself in.

Too quickly, he withdraws. I know then that one kiss will never be enough. Valentino Santos lit an inferno inside me with that kiss.

He leans back just enough to look me in the eye. A question lingers in his gaze.

Yes, I feel it too.

Yes, I want more.

I wrap my arms around his neck, pulling him back down to me.

Our second kiss is deeper than the first. He slips one hand into my hair, the second around my waist. We fall into a passionate rhythm. This time, when his tongue teases the seam of my mouth, I let him in.

And I happily lose myself in Valentino Santos.

Chapter 27
Valentino

Over the next week, Sylvie and I talk every day. Twice I brought her dinner on campus and hung out in the study room with her.

But it's been more difficult than I had thought to balance work, my streaming schedule, my friends, and now spending time with Sylvie. Unfortunately, with BGN as a sponsor, I can't just drop everything in the middle of a stream to privately play with her.

Thankfully, Sylvie is supportive and understands.

One week after our first date, we're back at Potions and Pages, lounging together on a chaise on the third floor.

We could get lost in this bookstore. It gives us a sense of privacy we don't normally have together. I can't come over to her place because of her stupid ex-boyfriend, and she doesn't feel comfortable coming over to mine yet.

So, here we are with our half-drunk cups of tea and a stack of books.

Sylvie rests against me, her back to my front. She's reading some novel about fairies aloud while I caress her arm with the tips of my fingers.

I'm only half paying attention. Not that the book is boring. Rather, the cadence of her voice soothes me.

I'm noticing subtle changes in her the more time we spend together. It's like she's coming back to life. There's a sparkle in her eyes and her skin glows with a new warmth. And there's this moment when she lets go of her worries and sinks into me. It's like she puts down the burden she's carrying around.

I'll happily be that foundation for her.

As she reads, my mind drifts to the question I want to ask her. So far, we've kept our relationship between us. I think Speed's figured it out with his superhuman powers of deduction. If he has, he's said nothing to me. Xander will be happy for me as long as I'm happy.

Then there's Preston. He's going to be so mad that I've kept this secret from him. That's the thing, though. I don't want Sylvie to be my secret. I don't want her to be the girl I sneak around with, or see in the dark.

Sure, things are moving fast now, but we started this relationship as friends. Things have developed since then. Preston has to understand that. If he doesn't, hopefully, Julianna will knock some sense into him.

Which brings me back to the question I don't know how to ask her.

"Val?" Sylvie asks, turning her head to look up at me.

"Hm?" I ask, pausing my caress.

She purses her lips. "I thought that was a spicy scene. You're not phased. How experienced are you?"

I freeze. Oh shit. She caught me not paying attention. Think Val. Isn't "spice" a code word for sexy times in the book community? "I'm just in shock an author would write that," I bullshit.

Sylvie cracks up laughing, sitting up out of my arms. I reach for her, pulling her back to me. "I'm guessing there was no spicy scene," I murmur into her hair.

"No," Sylvie says through her adorable giggles. "But the look on your face was priceless."

I laugh at her, laughing at me. When we calm ourselves down, she asks, "So, where was that beautiful mind of yours during my fabulous narration?"

Well, I guess this is my chance to ask my burning question. I take a deep breath and tuck her hair behind her ear. "There's a little over two weeks until the second Odyssey," I begin.

"Are you nervous?"

I shrug. "I wouldn't say nervous. Rather, some mixture of excitement, terror, and confidence. It all feels like one knot in my stomach." Like the question, I want to ask her.

Sylvie nods, "Theseus is holding a live stream and a party again?"

"That's right," I agree, then pause. "Would you consider being there with me?"

"For the second Odyssey? Or the after-party?"

"Both."

There, it's out in the open. I'm asking her out on a public date.

Sylvie goes eerily still, her brown eyes blown wide. A few seconds of silence pass and she stands and starts pacing around the space. I don't say anything, giving her the time to process.

Finally, she speaks. "Won't Annie be jealous?"

I catch the way her voice quakes. She's using humor to deflect. But I give a small laugh. "Give her a few pets and she'll be your new best friend."

Sylvie paces again, bringing her hands to rub at her face.

Something is wrong, and I think I know what.

"Is it Theo?" I ask.

Her pathetic excuse of an ex-boyfriend is a thorn in my side. I wish I could erase him from existence. He's a spoiled fuck boy playing at being an *Obsidian* streamer. She hasn't told me everything, but I know an abusive relationship when I see it.

I'm the one who sees Sylvie for the cosmic power she is. She is every pearl in the sea, every precious gemstone, and every drop of ambrosia.

She stops and looks at me, then down at the floor. "That Saturday is...his birthday," she confesses. "We usually go out with his parents."

"And they pay your rent," I finish for her. Hoping it isn't true.

She nods.

Even though I suspected it, I can't say I'm not heartbroken to see it confirmed. I understand. If doing this one thing with him will make her life easier while she saves up money, then I get it. She needs to do what's best for her.

"I'm sorry, Val."

"Hey," I say standing and crossing to her. I cup her cheek to lift her face to mine. "None of that now."

She leans into my touch. I love it. "My life's a mess," she cries.

I pull her into my arms. "It's only temporary," I say, pressing a kiss to the top of her head.

Sylvie pulls back and studies my face for a moment. Then she stands on her tiptoes to kiss me.

I could kiss this woman every day for the rest of my life.

Her lips are supple and full.

She should model lipstick or something.

"You *really* want me there?" she asks when she pulls away.

"Of course," I whisper as I trace her bottom lip with my thumb. "I only figured out that dragon thing because of you. Imagine what I can do if you are in the room with me."

"You're amazing all on your own."

My confidence swells. She believes in me, even when I doubt myself.

Sylvie looks down, then looks back up at me. "Would I have to go to the after-party too?"

The worried look on her face breaks my heart.

"Hey," I put my hands on either side of her face. "Would I like you there? Yes, but, Sylvie, I'm never going to make you do something you don't want to do."

She takes a deep breath and purses her lips. "I'll be there with you."

Did I hear that right? I capture her mouth in another kiss. "Are you serious?"

She pulls away briefly, gives me a hesitant look, but ultimately nods. "I'm not promising the after party yet."

"Is it because you don't know anyone?" An idea pops into my head. "What if I arrange a day for you to meet the guys before the Odyssey?"

My mind is racing to see how I could facilitate this for her.

I could even ask Preston to bring Julia again.

"Technically," she held up a finger. "I've already met them."

"Online," I specify.

Sylvie gives me a stare that threatens bodily harm. Or a verbal tongue-lashing. I'm not sure which one is worse. "I wouldn't mind meeting them in person," Sylvie allows.

I sense a "but" coming.

"But," she continues. "I'm still not sure about the party."

I have a feeling there's a deeper fear going on in that big beautiful brain of hers. One that makes her hesitate to hold my hand on campus, or walk too close to me. "You're not comfortable with me in public yet, are you?"

"Don't say it like that," Sylvie says.

Running my hands through my hair, I take a seat on the couch again.

"Val," she says and sits next to me. "I just don't want someone to use me against you."

I don't know who in their right mind would put this angel in the crosshairs of internet gamer drama just to get at me.

"Who would do that?"

"I don't know," Sylvie says. "Preston?"

Well, that's a name I didn't expect to hear. Sylvie grabs my hand.

"I'm sorry," she starts. "It's just, from everything you've said, Preston doesn't have the best opinion of us."

Unfortunately, she's not wrong. But as salty as Preston might be, I can't see him purposefully sabotaging me like that. After all, he's supposed to be my best friend.

"Don't worry about him," I say, even though I know it won't stop her from worrying. "Preston's just very—"

"Jealous."

Well, that's an interesting word choice. "I was going to say protective. But now I'm more interested in why you say jealous."

Sylvie leans back and crosses her arms over her stomach. "It's more like a feeling. I can't explain it."

She's picking up on the threads of my past with Preston. Since she's being honest and vulnerable with me, I should also tell her about the mess that is Preston and me. I'm not ashamed of my sexuality, but I also know not everyone would be comfortable with it. She wouldn't be the first to walk away because I'm bisexual.

I take a deep breath and say, "I have to tell you something. About me."

"I'm listening," Sylvie says, giving me her full attention.

"There have been times, in the past, where Preston and I could have been something—more." I struggle to find the right words. "But the timing was never there. The feelings remained, though. At least, until recently."

My confession takes a few seconds to truly sink in. I can tell the exact moment it does. Sylvie makes an O shape with her mouth. "You're bi?"

"Does that bother you?" I ask, tensing, preparing for the worst.

Sylvie shakes her head. "Not at all. I'm honored you told me."

Relief washes through me. "I don't want you to worry about Preston," I say. "The connection I have with you is nothing like the connection I had with him. He's in my past, as are my feelings for him."

She lets go of my hands. "I don't think I have any right to worry."

I grip her chin between my thumb and forefinger, turning her face towards me. "What do you mean?"

"I'm still living with my ex-boyfriend. My life is complicated and messy right now. If Preston showed up and declared his undying love for you, I wouldn't stop you if you wanted to be with him."

Tears are shining in her eyes. I pull her back to me, tucking her safely against my chest. "That won't happen," I state firmly.

"You can't know that."

I cup her face, bringing my lips to her own, and kiss her with every ounce of myself. When I'm out of breath, I break the kiss and whisper against her lips, "I'm not going anywhere, Rhea. No matter how long it takes, or how messy it is. I want to be with you."

Sylvie's smile dominates her face. And gods, she is beautiful.

Is it too soon to say I love her? Maybe. If it's not love, I don't know what else to call it. What I do know is that I can't imagine my life without her.

Chapter 28
Sylvie

Valentino:

Ready to meet my friends tonight?

I feel like I need to drink a bottle of wine and throw up at the same time. Especially after the news I received today. The scholarship came through, and I didn't get as much as I wanted.

But I can't think about it too much right now. Tonight, I'm meeting Val's friends— and whatever Preston is.

Val and I have been seeing each other when we can over the last two weeks. Our schedules don't allow for a lot of time to connect. So I'll take this opportunity to see Val, even if that means meeting his friends too.

Sylvie:

I think so.

I'm spreading myself thin between school, my work with Julia, the demands from Theo's weaponized incompetence, and trying to spend time with Val.

I have a midterm paper due in two days, and I've barely started the research. I'll be up half the night working on it.

But seeing Val is worth the lack of sleep.

And I know meeting his friends will mean a lot to him. I'm hoping that it will make me more comfortable with the idea of going to the afterparty.

I also need the distraction.

My phone sounds.

Valentino:

5 mins away.

Sylvie:

Leaving soon.

He's picking me up at the same park where we met for the first time. In my mind, I think of it as our park. It's a safe enough distance away from the apartment that Theo won't see Val and Val won't see Theo.

I slip my laptop into my backpack and leave the safety of my room.

Moving out to the living room, I notice all the stuff lying around. Dirty dishes in the sink, dirty laundry on the living room couch, and trash on every surface. Theo leaves it all out. I have to spend more time cleaning the apartment which means he gets to spend more time around me.

All the more reason I need to get out of here.

"Going somewhere?" Theo stops doing whatever he's doing on his computer. I hesitate at his tone. He's not being pugnacious or antagonistic. He's just simply asking.

Whatever cool boy act he's giving me, I don't trust it.

"Going to campus to work on my paper," I lie.

Theo stands and walks towards me, hands in his pockets. "How long will you be gone?"

"No idea," I say, putting on my jacket.

"Okay, just be safe," he says as he leans against the counter. "Call me if you need anything."

I shoot him a skeptical look. Why is he being so nice?

"Come on, Sylvie," Theo rolls his eyes. "I love you. Of course, I want to know if you're going to be safe. Why is that so hard for you to believe?"

Because you don't treat someone you love the way Theo treats me. But, I don't respond. Instead, I slip on my shoes and walk out the door, letting it slam shut behind me.

It's six o'clock in the evening when I arrive at the park. Val's already there, leaning against the side of his car. When he sees me, he holds out his arms.

Folding myself into him, I bury my face into his chest and inhale the scent of citrus and sandalwood. He leans down, kissing the top of my head.

"Everything okay?" he asks.

No, but it has nothing to do with meeting his friends. "I got some bad news today."

After another tight squeeze, he releases me and opens the car door. "Here, you can tell me on the way, Rhea."

I blush at the nickname and slide into the passenger's seat. Val rounds the front of the car and enters from the driver's side. He starts the car and we're off to 2Game.

Despite my nerves about meeting his friends, I'm excited to see this place Val talks so much about.

He takes my hand in his and raises it to his mouth, pressing a kiss to the sensitive skin on the back. "So what's going on?"

"I heard about the scholarship today."

"And?"

"I was awarded enough for an annual subway pass, and a little more, but not enough to cover the cost of the deposit and first month's rent for a decent apartment."

Val grabs my hand and brings it to his mouth for a kiss. "I'm sorry Sylvie. I know you were hoping to get more. But the subway is faster than taking the bus. We will look again and see if there's an apartment in your price range.

With the amount I have saved up? I'll be lucky to find something. But I don't want to sour the evening more than I already have.

"I'm sorry."

"Stop that," Val orders, turning his head briefly to look at me. "I'm glad you told me. I wish you'd let me do more for you."

Val's offered to loan me money, but I won't take it. I can't be indebted to another person.

As he speaks, my eyes are drawn to his irresistibly tempting mouth. *Look away, Sylvie. A forearm, sure that works.* I see the fine tendons in his arms move. Damn, I didn't know forearms could be so sexy.

I try to shove thoughts of the scholarship behind me. Tonight I have something else to focus on. Something like the crackling energy between us and the milestone we're driving towards.

It's been a long time since I've tried to make friends with someone. These guys already have a strong dynamic together. How am I going to fit into that?

"What are you thinking?" Val asks.

How is our relationship going to work? How much longer am I going to have to live with Theo? Can I keep up with all my responsibilities? How am I going to fit in with your friends? That your forearms are sexy.

Except I can't verbalize any of that.

Instead, I ask, "Did you talk to Preston?" Val said he'd talk to Preston about us at their weekly Monday lunch.

"I did," he says.

Silence hangs in the air. He must have bad news, too. Suddenly I feel bad for monopolizing the conversation with my problems. "And?"

"Preston's hurt. He feels like I kept secrets from him." He squeezes the steering wheel. "And I see his point."

Val must be feeling guilty. I've never seen someone take away his smile. "To be fair, you said Preston hasn't been around," I offer.

"Communication works two ways."

"That goes for Preston too."

Val looks at me for a moment and gives me a small smile. "You're right." His gaze returns to the road and he purses his lips. "But I'm afraid he might take his feelings out on you tonight."

"Valentino Santos, are you nervous for me?" I say in jest, masking my own anxieties.

He laughs. "Me nervous? My girlfriend is meeting my closest friends. Shouldn't she be the nervous one?"

Wait.

Did he just say girlfriend?

Heat rushes through me. Val and I haven't talked about labels yet. Any nerves I had about meeting Val's friends fade away with each beat of my heart.

"Girlfriend?" I ask.

"If you want to be," he offers.

Yes. Yes. YES! A part of me screams on the inside.

Another part of me hesitates. My messy situation doesn't fit with the squeaky-clean image BGN wants for their Odyssey players. And, somehow, Theo still thinks we're going to get back together, even though I've told him dozens of times we're not.

Val and Speed found me with such little information. Someone else could do it as well. A little digging into me would reveal a lot of gossip and bad press for him. *Does it matter?* Val knows my situation, and he still wants me.

And I *want* to be his girlfriend.

"Are you sure?" I ask him. "I don't want to be the reason you lose your sponsorship."

"What are they going to say?" Val asks. "You're broken up with Theo."

"But I still live with him," I argue.

"Not for long."

"They don't know that." We don't know that.

"Sylvie," Val says in his deep velvet voice. "Stop worrying and say you'll be my girlfriend."

I can't resist that look he's giving me, all big brown eyes and a sexy smile.

"Well then," I say. "My boyfriend should keep his eyes on the road."

Val smiles as bright as the sun and kisses my hand again.

Chapter 29
Sylvie

Val finds a parking spot as we approach the storefront. He jumps out and rounds the hood to open the door for me. As soon as I get out of the car, he cups my face with both his hands and kisses me deeply.

"You're going to do great. They're going to love you," he says.

I don't know what else to say, so I smile and nod. He takes my hand, leading me into the store.

A handsome, bearded man greets us. "Hey Val, the crew's already here."

I assume this is Theseus. Now, I'm not usually into older guys, but after seeing Theseus, I think I'd make an exception. He's the ambiguous type of forty-something man who ages like fine wine.

Of course, I'd be single in this hypothetical situation. Which, as of five minutes ago, I'm not. I feel the blush rise to my cheeks.

"Thanks, man, but I'd like to introduce you to someone," Val puts his hand on my lower back. "Theseus, this is my girlfriend, Sylvie."

That's me. I'm Valentino Santos' girlfriend.

I can't stop my smile.

My worries about not getting enough scholarship money to cover my dream apartment are temporarily banished.

"Hello," I say, hoping it doesn't come out as a squeak.

"Welcome to 2Game, Sylvie," Theseus says. "We're happy to have you."

I look around, taking in the board games, and tables for RPGs, consoles, and PCs. Val was right. 2Game is an oasis for gamers. "This is amazing," I say. "May I have a guest pass, please?

Theseus holds up a hand and shakes his head. "No need. Val took care of it. Here's your guest login information." Theseus hands me a slip of paper.

I look at Val, and he gives me a smirk and a shrug. It feels good to be taken care of instead of always taking care of my partner.

"Thank you," I say to Val. Then to Theseus, "It's nice to meet you."

Theseus nods, then goes back to doing something on his computer.

"Ready?" Val asks, turning me towards a group of PCs where three men are sitting and staring at us.

No, but here goes nothing. Please, don't let me fuck this up.

"Sure."

Val keeps his hand on my lower back as we approach. The three figures stand when they see us heading in their direction.

The man, wearing a Metallica band t-shirt with dark-wash jeans, steps forward. "See, I told you, saucy varlets. She is real. Hi Sylvie!"

Ah, that's Speed. I recognize his voice from the times we played together. A man who boisterously oozes charm and charisma. "Speed, I'm assuming? It's nice to meet you."

"The one and only." He extends his hand to me. I shake it. "And I'm still single," he adds.

"Give it a rest," a man with a dog at his side pushes Speed behind him. Xander and Pixel. He's the tallest of the four men, with broad shoulders, a toned build, and perfect posture. He has a military vibe about him, although his hair is a little longer than a military cut.

He shakes my hand with a firm grip. "I'm Xander, it's a pleasure to meet you."

Out of the corner of my vision, I see Pixel look up at me with enormous eyes and her tongue hanging out of her mouth. Now, I understand what Val means when he says it's hard to resist grabbing the sides of her pretty face and scratching behind her ears.

"Sylvie," I say. "It's nice to meet you too."

"We know who you are," the third figure grumbles. There's venom in his words.

Preston.

I can see why Val would be attracted to him. Preston's handsome and well-dressed. He must put a lot of energy into his appearance and how he presents himself.

"He means Val won't shut up about you," Speed says, slinging an arm around Preston's shoulders. Preston shrugs him off. I appreciate his effort to cut the tension Preston creates.

I look back at Val and see a faint blush rise in his cheeks. He's not denying it.

"Val's told me a lot about you." I approach Preston with my hand out.

"Funny," Preston shakes my hand, then quickly releases it. "He hasn't told me much about you."

His vitriol hits me in the gut. What is with this guy? It's like he's determined not to like me on some unfounded principle.

Then Preston gives me a once over. "You look familiar. Have we met before?"

I shake my head. "I don't think so. But I get that a lot. Short girl with brown hair, brown eyes and all."

Preston grunts and shakes his head. "No, I know you. But you don't have to tell me. I'll figure it out."

Something about his tone makes it sound like a threat. His attitude is throwing me off balance. All my previous insecurities come back. I have a feeling there's nothing I can do to get this man to like me.

"Preston," Val snaps. He steps to my side and puts an arm around me. The two make eye contact in the way friends do when they're having a silent conversation.

I can only imagine what they're saying.

Eventually, Preston scoffs and returns to his seat.

Preston is Val's best friend. I don't want to be the reason they're fighting.

Maybe I shouldn't have come.

Speed puts his arm around my shoulders. "Don't mind Preston. He's mad he was kept out of the loop. That's what happens when he spends all his time with his new girlfriend."

At least Speed seems to like me, even if that was an insult to Preston. I don't disagree with what he said. Val's told me a little about how Preston's been absent from their group because of a new girlfriend.

I never got her name. Maybe I could ask, and that would loosen Preston up.

"Ready to play?" Xander asks. "Do some side quests? Fight some Enkin?"

I'll ask questions about the girlfriend later. "You mean kick some ass," I say.

Xander and Speed laugh.

I get warm and welcoming vibes from these two. I could see myself having a beer at a bar or sitting down and gaming on a Friday night with them.

Like clockwork, the boys all take their normal seats at the quad of computers, leaving no seats for me.

Val notices the problem and stands back up. "We can sit at the other computers," he motions to the second quad of computers behind him.

"It's okay," I say, not wanting to disturb their usual routine. "I brought my laptop. I just need the Wi-Fi—"

Preston interrupts me. "That won't work. Your connection will be slower than ours. Just sit behind Val."

Well, I definitely won't be asking him any personal questions with that attitude. I take a seat at the computer behind Val. I guess it doesn't matter if I'm sitting alone because we'll all be playing the same game together, anyway.

"Fuck that." Speed gets up from his spot next to Xander, rounds the computers, and takes a seat next to me, behind Preston. I don't miss the elbow he jabs in Preston's side.

"Here, I'll show you how to log in." Not that it's hard, but I appreciate how Speed is making me feel welcome.

Val also gets up from his spot and moves to the computer opposite from me. Preston gives him a forlorn look, his eyes lingering on Val.

After using the login information, I log into my *Mundo* account. In five minutes, Celestina is loaded and waiting to meet up with the boys.

I have to admit, it's a nice setup between the computers, monitors, and the headset.

Val leans forward between our computers. "You okay?" he whispers.

"Yeah," I say. Then add, "Thank you for bringing me here tonight."

He looks at me like I'm the stars in the sky. "Anything for you."

"Dad, they're flirting," Speed calls back to Xander.

Everyone but Preston laughs.

Chapter 30
Valentino

The sun had long since set when I pull my car into the park's lot. I cut the engine and turn towards Sylvie, reaching over to play with a renegade curl.

I don't want her to open that door. I don't want to let her go.

"You did great tonight," I say.

She smiles and leans into my touch. "Your friends are good people."

Two of them were. Preston took his anger at me out on her. I could swear even Pixel gave Preston a disappointed stare.

"I'm sorry Preston was such a dick."

"Hey," she takes my hand and squeezes it. "It's not your job to apologize for his destructive behavior."

She's right. Still, I make a mental note to kick Preston's ass later. I've got better things to focus on.

Like this goddess who agreed to be my girlfriend. I tug her to me—as close as I can in the car—my hand cupping her jaw as I bring my mouth down to capture hers.

Sylvie relaxes into me, opening up and giving me access, giving herself over to me. It's so easy to kiss her. I can't get enough of it.

"Come home with me," I say against her lips.

Sylvie groans and pulls away from me. "I can't."

I follow her, kissing along her neck. "What if I sleep on the couch?"

That makes her laugh. "No, you wouldn't."

She's right. It'd be torture for me to sleep in a different room knowing she's in my bed. Of course I'd respect her boundaries, but I can't say I wouldn't end up on the floor outside the door.

I lean back and place a hand in fake offense over my heart. "Excuse me ma'am. I'm an honest gentleman."

Sylvie laughs, then leans in to kiss me again. I gladly welcome her affection. She deepens the kiss by digging her hand into my hair.

I can't get enough of this girl.

As much as I want to kiss her forever, there's something hanging between us we need to talk about. The reason she hesitated when I asked her to be my girlfriend.

"Sylvie?"

"Yes?"

"Why aren't you comfortable with us going public?" She has reservations, but I don't want to hide our relationship. I'm not ashamed or embarrassed to be with her. Sylvie's a survivor and such a strong woman.

She groans as her head falls to my chest. I trace lazy circles on her back. After a deep breath, she says, "I can't be the reason you lose your sponsorship with BGN."

That's it? How could she cause me to lose my sponsorship?

"I doubt BGN cares about who I'm dating or how we met."

Hell, we met playing *Mundo*—if anything, it's a great PR story.

"I don't know when I'm going to get out from under Theo's thumb," she says. "Especially since the scholarship didn't come through."

"What if I spot you the money for the deposit?" I suggest. I have a surplus of income from sponsorships this past month.

Sylvie shakes her head and falls back into her seat. "You know that's not what I want."

I know it's not. Sylvie's stuck in a situation where she depends financially on Theo—or rather, his parents. Now she's trying to build a future where she doesn't have to be financially beholden to anyone else.

"I don't want to keep us a secret," I tell her. I want the world to know this amazing woman is mine.

Sylvie reaches over to run her hand through my hair. "You are the kindest man I have ever met, Valentino Santos. You barely know me and yet you'd be willing to take me under your roof. I could explore all corners of the internet and never find someone as kind and gorgeous as you."

Her words mean a lot. I want to show her that there are good men out there, too. Yet her pause makes me feel like there's a "but" coming.

"But I need to do this on my own," Sylvie says. "And I need you to respect that."

This is her boundary. Pushing her further is only going to cause friction. With a deep breath, I nod my head. "Okay, fine, but just tell me you know my home is a safe place and is open to you at any time?"

"I know," she says, then leans over to kiss me.

"And answer me one more thing."

"Anything," she says, smiling again. I love it when she smiles.

"Do you think I'm pretty?" I ask, teasing her.

"I believe I said gorgeous," she teases back.

I kiss her again, climbing over the center console to get closer to her. When I tease the seam of her mouth with my tongue she opens for me. Greedily, I drink ambrosia from her mouth. My hands run from the side of her head, down her arm, and hesitate at the swell of her breasts.

Sylvie and I have done little more than make out, but there's been an growing energy between us that's getting harder to ignore.

We break our kiss but not our eye contact. A question mingles in the space between us.

My pulse pounds in my ears and my breath trembles, waiting for her answer. She nods enthusiastically and tension releases from my shoulders.

I take her generous breasts in my hands, kneading the supple mounds, focusing on one, then the other. Sylvie lets out a small breathy moan. She maintains eye contact with me as my hand travels further down, over her luscious, soft stomach, to the hem of her shirt.

Damn, my woman has curves in all the right places.

"We can stop at any time," I remind her, my hand slipping under her shirt.

"Don't stop," Sylvie says.

"Lean your seat back."

Sylvie reaches down next to her seat and pulls the lever, leaning the seat back as low as it can go. I move to position my knee between her legs so I can get better leverage. Then, I kiss her again, bracing one hand on the seat while the other returns to her luscious body.

This time, when I reach the hem of her shirt, I ask, "Can I lift this?"

Sylvie nods.

I raise the shirt until her bra is exposed. Then I lean down and pepper kisses over the swell of her breasts. Her tits are lush and smooth as I work my mouth and tongue over them.

"Here." She reaches up and pulls down her bra.

All my blood rushes south. But tonight's not about me. I'll take care of it later. I just need to not blow my load like an inexperienced teenager.

I greedily take in the sight before leaning down to capture a hardened, dusky pink nipple in my mouth. I swirl my tongue around the peak, teasing her. My hand squeezes her other breast, rolling the nipple between my thumb and forefinger.

Sylvie sinks her hands in my hair, and I feel the gentle pull on my scalp. "Val," she breathes heavily.

Her small reactions are everything to me. It makes me wonder what else I can do to cause those noises.

Sex is out of the question. I don't think we're there yet. I also don't want our first time to be in a car. But there are other ways I can make her feel good with my hands.

Hovering over her, knee braced between her legs, I arch my back towards the roof of the car to make room between our bodies so my hand can reach down towards the hem of her leggings. I brace one hand next to her head for balance, trying to keep my weight off of her. My muscles burn, holding the position. But it's worth it.

As my fingers dance under her waistline. "Is this okay?"

Sylvie nods. "Yes please, Val. Make me feel good."

Her words stir me. I kiss my way up her breast and neck to her ear. "I want to see how wet you are for me, Rhea," I whisper. "To run my fingers through your perfect pussy until I give you an orgasm."

"Oh, gods." She turns her face into my neck. I feel her warm breath as she says, "I want that too."

No gods here. Just me. And I'll give her what she wants.

I push my hand into her leggings, dragging my knuckles against her core. Just her damp panties between us. "So wet for me."

That makes me harder than I already am, knowing that I can turn her on so easily.

"Just for you," she says, face still buried in my neck.

I push her panties aside so I can run my index finger through her folds.

For a moment, I regret starting this in the car. This is my first time pleasuring her and I have to get this right. I listen for her reactions as I experiment with pressure and rhythm to find out exactly what she likes.

Sylvie gives a sharp inhale when I find her clit.

"Harder or softer?" I ask her.

"Softer," she breathes.

I ease up and make small circles around her clit, then back down her slit, dipping my finger into her warm channel. Then I repeat the pattern.

"How does that feel?"

"Perfect," Sylvie cups my face. "You're perfect, Val."

She brings me down for another searing kiss. I can taste every bit of her need for me. Her need to be touched, and her need to be seen.

I slip my middle finger into her while my thumb works her clit. Sylvie squirms, breaking the kiss. Her head falls back as she moves. She's getting close.

"Val... please."

My arm burns from supporting my weight but I don't dare stop. "Let go, Rhea," I whisper into her ear, giving it a little nibble. "Give me your orgasm."

I rub her clit once, twice and on the third pass, she does. Her release rolls over her in waves. I lean down to take her mouth, kissing her through the experience.

But I don't stop my slow circles around her clit until she pleads, "No more. Too sensitive."

I pull my hand out of her pants and fall back into the driver's seat, watching as a post-orgasm, glowing Sylvie rights her clothing.

She adjusts her seat and rolls on her side to look at me. "That was amazing."

I smile, glad I could please her. "Just wait until I get you in my bed."

Sylvie laughs, then reaches over, stroking my erection through my pants. "What about you?"

I take her hand, bringing it to my mouth for a kiss. I can smell her sweet musk on my fingers. "Tonight is about you."

"You're always taking care of me."

"I get pleasure from taking care of you."

She pulls her eyebrows together, intensely looking at me, wondering if I'm telling her the truth. I hate that she doubts me. A result of the abuse she's suffered. "I'll take care of myself later. I did that because I wanted to. Not because I expected anything back."

She smiles and nods, accepting my explanation, then leans over, and kisses me.

We stay like that for a while more until I see guilt flash in her eyes. "Val."

"You have to go," I finish.

Together, we exit the car. The night is colder now that the sun's set. Sylvie has a jacket but I wonder if she'll be okay walking home.

I catch some shadows moving—probably just some small animals running away from us. I turn to look at Sylvie. She runs her hands through her wild hair before throwing it up in a messy bun. Afterward, I hold my arms out to her, and she snuggles into me. "Goodnight. Rhea." I kiss her forehead, then her mouth.

"Goodnight, Val," she whispers against my lips.

Reluctantly, she withdraws and walks away through the park and is swallowed by the darkness.

Chapter 31
Valentino

When I return home, Annie greets me as soon as I walk through the door. I run my hand along her back. She bumps my hand with her head, then trots over to her food bowl, demanding her dinner.

"Yes, I know," I say, putting my keys in the bowl.

I open a can of wet food for her and Annie pushes my hand out of the way to devour her dinner. I dispose of the can and move to my living room, flopping down on the couch. Pulling out my phone, I see a message from Sylvie.

Rhea:

Home safe. Thanks for tonight. <3

Valentino:

Imagine what I can do with a bed. ;)

Rhea:

OMG I can't believe you just said that. I was talking about taking me to 2Game.

Valentino:

Sure you were.

Rhea:

Goodnight Val. <3

Valentino:

Goodnight Rhea. <3

I take a deep breath and let my head fall back on the couch. Tonight was such a big step for us. I know Rhea was hesitant to say yes to being my girlfriend, but all that changes right now is our exclusivity. She still wants to keep our relationship private—for now.

Her not getting the scholarship puts a setback on us going public. It's not ideal. But if I can pine after Preston for years, I can wait one or two months for Sylvie to leave that jackass of an ex-boyfriend's apartment and start her new life. The best thing I can do for her is be supportive.

Speaking of Preston. I pick up my phone again, this time pulling up the chat I have with the boys.

Valentino:

So what do you think?

Speed answers immediately.

Speed:

That you're a wanton rogue.

That I'm sexually unrestrained? I gave her an orgasm in my car, but it's not like he knows that. Also, he's the one who was playfully hitting on my girlfriend tonight, the lustful scoundrel.

Valentino:

Goatish varlet.

Xander:

You took a while to text us back. I guess you were busy.

Oh, well, I can't refute that.

Valentino:

We messed around a little in the car when I dropped her off.

Preston:

You fucked in public? What if someone saw you?

Why does he immediately go there? All of Preston's negativity is getting on my nerves.

Valentino:

We didn't fuck. I don't want my first time with her to be in a car. And nobody saw us.

Preston:

You're being reckless.

Xander:

I think what Preston is poorly saying is that you're a public figure now, Val. Maybe exercise a little more caution?

It's hard to think of myself as a public figure when I'm still just me. Just a dude with a normal job and a girl he's falling in love with. Sure, I get recognized occasionally, but those instances are rare.

I change the topic.

Valentino:

What did you think of Sylvie?

Preston:

No comment.

That's a lie. He just doesn't want to say anything in the group chat.

Speed:

Thou art poison in my blood.

I laugh at the insult. Speed is just as fed up with Preston's bullshit as I am.

Speed:

Never have I laid my eyes upon a maiden so fine.

Me too, Speed.

Preston:

Xander agrees with me.

Is that true? I thought Xander and Sylvie got along just fine.

Xander:

Preston you're twisting my words.

Valentino:

Then what did you say?

My foot bounces as I wait for Xander's response.

Xander:

Sylvie is a sweet girl. She's everything you said. But she also seems to have a lot of baggage. I'm concerned that she's moving on too fast and that her heart isn't healed from her last relationship.

I can see how Preston could twist that to say Sylvie has too much baggage. Even if there wasn't a lot of time between when Sylvie broke up with Theo and when we had our first date, Sylvie had been over Theo for a while before their breakup.

Valentino:

She's been nothing but open and honest with me, and she wants to take things slow while she gets her life figured out. Plus, she's very protective of my image.

That's the whole reason she doesn't want to go public.

Valentino:

I offered my apartment to her, but she turned it down. She doesn't want to be dependent on someone.

Xander:

That's mature of her. I'd be more concerned if she jumped right into living with you.

Speed:

We support strong women.

Speed:

Except Preston.

I laugh out loud. I can always trust Speed to be honest.

Preston:

Not true. I support Julianna.

Speed:

She wouldn't be your girlfriend if you bit her head off like you did to Sylvie.

Preston:

I will admit that wasn't my best moment.

Xander:

So you will apologize to her?

Another good question. He absolutely should.

Preston:

I still meant what I said. And I still think you're making a mistake.

I shouldn't be surprised or hurt by what he said, but I am. I type and send my response without a second thought.

Valentino:

The only mistake I've made is thinking that you'd care about anyone other than yourself, Preston.

Xander:

That's not fair Val.

Preston:

Tell me how you really feel.

Fine, if that's what he wants. Furious, I start typing.

Valentino:

I think you're jealous that I'm dating someone else instead of pining after you. And that's the real reason you don't like Sylvie. I don't buy that you care about my *Mundo* sponsorship. Your life has been all about Julianna and you couldn't care less about your friends.

I hit send and storm into the bedroom, putting my phone on silent and setting it on the charger on my bedside table.

I'm sick of Preston and his holier-than-thou attitude. He wouldn't even give Sylvie a chance. And that's not the type of man I want to associate with.

It hurts because this Preston isn't the best friend I thought I knew. As our lives evolve, our friendship is drifting apart. Maybe this is my sign to stop trying to hold our friendship together.

Chapter 32
Sylvie

Every time I close my eyes I feel Val's hands on me, in me, driving my pleasure higher. Was it a little reckless to mess around in the car? Yes. But I had never done that before, and I have to admit, it was a little thrilling. He pleasured me without expecting anything in return. I wonder if he touched himself when he returned home—and to what?

Yet I open my eyes to a different reality—one where I still have to work with and do small things to placate Theo. Like continuing to go to church with him because his parents also pay our rent. That list of obligations we have to his parents includes a celebratory dinner for Theo's birthday.

They don't know Theo and I broke up. So far, we've kept up the charade that we're still together. I've gone along with it because I don't want to be kicked out of the apartment. Theo's gone along with it because he still has hopes I'll come back to him.

Is that confusing? Yes.

Is it fair to Val? No.

Do I have another choice? Not if I don't want to be evicted.

A part of me feels bad because the Griegos have been good to me, to us. Theo doesn't understand how good he's got it with his supportive parents.

Originally, the plan was for the four of us to go to dinner, and then Theo would bring me back to the apartment, drop me off, and go out with his friends.

That was before Val asked me to be with him, at his place during the second Odyssey. He's been so good to me and so understanding about my situation. When I saw the hurt in his eyes when I told him about the circumstances, I knew I had to make it right. I'd find a way to get out of going to dinner.

Which is how I ended up in the bathroom for the past fifteen minutes, applying subtle make-up to make it look like I'm sick. This is after I laid down for a "nap" because, as I told Theo, "I felt off."

I've never been good at lying, but I have to lie now, and lie convincingly.

I would find a way to give Valentino Santos anything he'd ask for.

"You ready to go?" Theo calls out.

Well, here goes nothing. I clean up the makeup, shoving it under the sink where it belongs.

"Theo, I'm not feeling well," I say as I step out of the bathroom.

Theo appears in the doorway, arms crossed. His blue eyes scrutinize my appearance.

I round my shoulders and school my features into a sad, pitiful expression. "I don't think I should go tonight."

Theo narrows his eyes and takes a step forward. He reaches out an arm and I think he's going to grab for me again. I retreat further into the bathroom. His eyes widen and he stops his advance.

"Sorry," he says, holding up his hands with his palms facing me. "I didn't mean to scare you. I was going to touch your forehead."

Breathe Sylvie, I tell myself. *He is not going to hurt you*, a little voice whispers in my ear. *He cares about you*. I shake the voice away and notice how trapped I am in the bathroom. There's no exit and Theo's in the doorway.

When he doesn't speak, I realize he's waiting for me to say something. "No thank you," I clearly state. "I don't want you to touch me."

The corner of his eye twitches. But he doesn't make another move toward me. He puts his hands down. I don't miss how they clench into fists at his sides. "What's wrong?"

"Headache, fatigue," I tell him. "I think the stress of school is getting to me."

"You stayed up late the last few nights," Theo agrees. He moves his head, searching my face. "And you look flushed. Maybe it's best if you stay home."

Hope blooms in my chest. Is this going to work?

"I'm sorry," I say, looking down.

Don't show him anything, I remind myself.

"It's okay," Theo says. "I know you wouldn't pretend to be sick just to ditch my birthday dinner with my parents."

Old Sylvie would go to the dinner sick because she felt obligated to. Today Sylvie will pretend to be sick to skip dinner. It's like a sucker punch to the gut. This doesn't make me a bad person though—right?

"Thanks for understanding," I mumble.

"Do you want me to pick anything up for you?"

My head shoots up. "What?"

"While I'm out? Do you need anything?"

The question takes me off guard. I can't remember the last time he asked me that. "No," I whisper, the bite gone from my voice. "I appreciate you asking. That's very thoughtful."

Theo nods. "I'll just go to the bar after dinner, then. I'll be back late."

"I'll be asleep."

"Take the bed." When I give him another confused look. "If you're not feeling well, it would be better to sleep there than on the couch in your office."

I want to accept. The mattress in the bedroom is so comfortable. But I don't want Theo to think it's an invitation to crawl into bed with me.

"And where are you going to sleep?" I ask.

"I'll crash on the living room couch."

"If you're sure." This feels too good to be true.

Theo nods and gives me a small smile that I return. It finally feels like we've reached a truce.

Maybe that's taking it too far. We are civil with one another and that's enough for me.

Theo takes a turn in the bathroom and I head to the kitchen to put on a production of a sick girl making chicken noodle soup.

Theo exits the bathroom and puts his boots on. "I hope you feel better."

"Send my apologies to your parents."

"I will," he says. Then adds, "I love you," and shuts the door behind him.

Holy shit. My lie worked. He bought it. He's going to dinner with his parent and leaving me home alone. I even get the nice bed tonight.

It's only after he leaves that I see the flaw in my plan. Theo's expecting me to be home when he gets home from the bar.

Which probably won't be until late, but it means I don't know how long I can stay at the after party, or if I can go at all.

That's not a bad thing. I can still make this work. The important part is that I'll be there for Val.

I wait twenty minutes before I shower and get dressed in a pair of jeans and an oversized sweater. I'm going for casually comfortable. Pulling my makeup bag back out, I do a natural makeup look so it doesn't seem like I'm trying too hard. But I want to look nice for Val, even if he'll be staring at a screen more than he will be at me.

Val's picking me up early because he has to set up and test his connections for the system.

It's been over a week since we've been able to see each other. When he gets out of the car, I all but run to him.

He scoops me up in his arms, and I plant my lips on his.

"I'd love a repeat of the park," Val says against my mouth. "But—"

"I know," I say, as he puts me down, dragging me along the hard planes of his body. Such a tease.

He opens the car door for me, then gets in on his side. "How is my Titaness today?"

"Better now."

"What excuse did you use?" he asks as we drive off.

"I told him I was sick."

"Classic." We both laugh.

Marviewburg is divided into seven distinct neighborhoods. I live in Yorke, an upscale neighborhood where a lot of families settle. There are boutique shops and charming restaurants.

To get to Val's place, we jump on the interstate and cross the Semath River into Warcester, like we're heading to 2Game but further south. Warcester is a diverse neighborhood with a lot of young blood and a strong sense of community. It's a hub for young professionals and the location of some of the best ethnic restaurants in town.

Val pulls into an apartment complex and parks in what I assume is his designated spot.

"Ready?"

"I'm excited to meet Annie," I say, getting out of the car.

I feel like this is a big step—me coming over to his house for the first time. We take the elevator to the third floor, then walk a short distance until we're in front of his door. He unlocks it and steps aside, letting me go first.

Val's apartment is smaller than mine, but he's also one person living alone. His kitchen is to the immediate right when we enter. The counter wraps around and he has two barstools set. Further into the apartment is the living room area. He has his computer station slash office space set up behind the couch to the right and a small television to the left.

On the couch is a pile of blankets and a beautiful tortoiseshell cat. "Is that Annie?" I ask nobody in particular. I'm completely focused on the majestic creature.

"The one and only," Val laughs under his breath. "Here." He hands me a cat squeezy treat. I beam, turning around to where Annie lounges.

When she sees the red tube she jumps down and pads over to me. I meet her about halfway into the apartment, bending down to let her sniff my hand. She does and gives me a head bump. Then I present her with the treat. Her attention completely focuses on the feline delicacy.

She eats it in little licks, like the classy lady she is.

Her tail stands up straight with a slight bend at the end. She purrs when I run my hand along her spine, scratching the spot right before her tail.

I think I'm in love.

"She's precious."

Val pulls something out of the oven and puts it on the stove. "She knows it too. I've been trying to introduce you two for a while now."

I grin sheepishly. I've been stalling about going to Val's house. Not because I don't trust him, but because I don't want to rush things with Val like I did with Theo. We moved in together within six months of dating.

Val is a very affectionate man too. The chemistry between us is off the charts and I know I'll end up with some clothes on the floor at some point. I want us to be in a space where we're ready for that step.

I don't know if we'll have sex today with the Odyssey and all, but I wouldn't mind if we did. If the car was just a sample of Val's talents, I want the whole damn platter.

Annie finishes the treat and I turn back to Val to ask him where his trash can is. He points to his left. I dispose of the wrapper, then wash my hands. When I'm done I'm greeted by the sight of him scooping two large helpings of pasta into bowls.

"Is that baked ziti?" I ask.

"I threw it in the oven before I picked you up."

That sounds like a fire hazard to me, but that's not the point.

Val made a meal for me.

I almost burst into tears as I slide onto a barstool. Val deposits a bowl in front of me. I see Val clocking my watery eyes, but he doesn't say anything. "I wanted to make sure you got something to eat before the Odyssey."

It amazes me that, even on a day about him, he's thinking about me. Taking care of me.

"Thank you," is all I can say before taking a bite.

Damn, that's good. It's hard to mess up ziti, but he has the perfect ratio of cheese to sauce to pasta. "This is delicious."

Val smiles and kisses my forehead before shoveling down his portion. "There'll be more here if you want some during the Odyssey. Drinks are in the fridge and the bathroom is right there." He points to the first of two doors to his left.

"And the other is your bedroom?"

"Curious already?" he flirts.

Heat rises to my cheeks. I can't say I haven't thought about it. "No," I lie.

"Have it your way," he jokes. He puts his bowl in the sink and washes it. "I'll get that." I come up next to him and add my bowl.

"You don't have to," he says.

"I want to. Let me take care of you, too. Go get ready for this Odyssey."

Val gives me a wink and goes to sit down at his computer. Once I finish washing the bowls, I move to the couch where Val has stacked every blanket he owns in a pile for me. He also placed a notebook on the coffee table with a marker.

"In case you need to talk to me while you watch," he says.

I don't know what I would say to him. He will be figuring things out in real time like everyone else, but I appreciate the thought.

"Can I get you anything?" I ask.

Val shakes his head. "Just sit down and get comfortable."

"I don't think there's enough blankets," I joke.

Val laughs. "You can have my comforter too."

That sounds excessive. Instead, I pile the blankets around me in a nest. When I'm done, Annie jumps up next to me, purring up a storm. I give her a few pets then pull my laptop and cheap headphones out of my bag so I can watch the Odyssey too.

Chapter 33

Valentino

Aurelius, Flickerfoot, Maverick, and Valen load into a sprawling expanse of dense forest. The canopy is thick enough to cast the forest floor in a perpetual twilight. The ground is covered in a thick layer of moss, fern, and fallen leaves. A single line of text flashes on my screen.

Quest: Retrieve the Song of Serenity

"Straightforward," I say.

"I doubt it," Dominic replies.

Well, he's grumpy. But that's normal for Dominic.

In the last Odyssey, all the teams loaded in the same area. This time, we seem to be alone. I wonder if the other teams are in their own woods? Or maybe they're just in a different part of this one? Maybe it's a race to the center of the woods to find this song—whatever that is.

Flickerfoot, Cameron's avatar, moves to fumble in a patch of ferns. Pushing them aside, he reveals glowing fungi illuminating the forest floor. "Are these new?"

I position Valen next to Flickerfoot on the screen, examining the fungus. My notebook has no information about this new plant. I pick a mushroom and get a message saying:

You've discovered the Green Pepe mushroom.

A spore cloud bursts from the underside of the mushroom cap and permeates the area. The word "poison" floats on the screen as I take five points of damage from the cloud it emits. I press the key to dash out of there. The others do the same.

Once we're all safe, I laugh and say, "Well, that's new to me."

I'm met with crickets. Nobody else laughs. Sure, my action cost us hit points, but it's only five and an innocent mistake.

"Let's not pick the plants we aren't familiar with," Bastian chides. "Some of us have less hit points than others."

I don't appreciate his tone. If I were playing with Speed or Xander, I'd tell them to chill. But right now, I'm live in front of millions of people, and I don't want to start a fight.

Instead, I ask, "How else are we supposed to learn about them? They could have been useful."

"Yeah, Bastian," Sylvie says softly so my mic doesn't pick it up.

My eyes flick up to her. She winks at me and then snuggles back into the blanket nest I made for her. She's watching the live stream with a headset on, Annie resting beside her.

Her presence helps settle my nerves.

Sylvie might have laughed, but nobody else did. Even Cameron has his serious face on. It must be the pressure. After the last Odyssey, people are expecting us to do something —incredible.

I don't know how we can top befriending a dragon.

A part of me understands the pressure, the nerves. I feel them too. But I remind myself we were chosen for this team for a reason. BGN liked the way we played *Mundo* as ourselves. The guys need to loosen up or we're going to look like fools.

The poisonous cloud disappears, and our avatars regroup. "New flora could also mean new Enkin," Bastian theorizes.

Dominic grunts in agreement. "We need to get moving."

"Then let's pick a direction and go," Cameron says.

That would be as bad as wandering around the desert with no direction.

"We need to find water," Dominic argues.

He's right. Life needs water. If we find water, we'll find something. Even if that something is an Enkin.

"Give me a minute to search the area," Dominic says. Maverick, his avatar, moves around my screen, searching the forest floor.

I don't like just waiting around, but Valen doesn't have the skills to track and navigate the woods like Maverick does. I am thankful to have a ranger on my team, though. Any team without a ranger is at a serious disadvantage.

While Dominic does his thing, I take another look at the forest. These trees are behemoths, with trunks so wide they could provide cover for a whole avatar, maybe two. They stand like proud guardians of the forest, their leaves rustling like whispers in the silence.

Wait... *silence*?

"There's no background noise playing," I say, wondering if the silence is significant.

Nobody answers me because Dominic calls, "Guys, I found footprints."

"Enkin?" Bastian asks.

"Humanoid." Dominic looks at each of us. "A single set. Big."

I shift in my seat. The idea of a large creature passing through here makes me uncomfortable, as is the idea of *following* those footsteps. But it's more direction than we had ten minutes ago.

"Sounds like a lead," I say reluctantly.

"Maverick lead the way, Valen watch our backs," Bastian orders.

Then Aurelius, Bastian's avatar, casts a spell allowing us to move more silently among the brush.

We fall in a single file line with Maverick leading, Flickerfoot next, Aurelius, then Valen. I move my camera left and right, looking for anything that might jump out at us. As we travel, we encounter a fog settling over the forest floor. It starts subtly as a light mist, but quickly becomes so dense that Maverick has to use one of his few ranger spells to continue following the tracks forward.

Something's not adding up here. First, there's no sound, and now the fog? I try to think back through my experiences about what could be the cause. But I come up with nothing. Whatever is going on in these woods, it's something new.

Cameron interrupts my thoughts. "Is that a house?"

I'm glad we found something. We're about twenty minutes into our two-hour-long quest with no leads to where the Song of Serenity could be.

The fog parts just enough for us to see a camouflaged house, built from the same type of weathered wood as the surrounding trees. Metallic netting drapes around the covered porch and windows. I spot a series of intricate, faintly glowing runes etched around the windows and door frame. Magical protections or wards, most likely. To keep something out—or someone in?

Unlike the vibrancy of the rest of the forest, this place feels barren. The garden is wilted, the ferns are brown and drooping, and the trees around the house are bare. It's like death scorched the area.

The door opens and an older man with a lean build, simple robes, and a long beard exits the house waving frantically at us. "What are you doing?" he cries, voice quivering.

"Great question," Cam comments.

"We've come seeking..." I start, but I'm cut off by battle music.

A cacophony of high-pitched cries fills the space and swarms of small black birds dive at us from the trees.

"Oh, shit!" Valen swings his swords at the birds, but he only makes contact with one, cutting it down. He takes hits from six of them. Individually, each hit is only a tiny amount of damage, but multiple hits from the swarm add up.

Dominic calls out, "They're sucking out our life force."

I glance up at my health bar. Am I reading this right? My total number of hit points has dropped to my current hit points after taking that hit.

This is a new life-draining type of effect.

"Has anyone seen this before?" I ask.

"Not me," Bastian says.

"Me neither," Cameron echoes.

Then this is a new type of condition from a new Enkin. These agile little creatures are dominating the space between the canopy and the ground. They gather and dive at us again.

"We need cover," I say.

"No shit," Dominic retorts.

The old man cries out again, "Quick, inside. Before they attack again!"

I don't know if we should trust this old man we just met, but his house is fortified, and I don't want my hit points diminished further. Valen dashes for the man's house. One by one, we cross into the protective enclosure. Some birds chase us, smacking against the barrier, and dropping dead. Others pull back, content to wait another day for their prey.

Once inside the man's hut, I take a moment to assess my surroundings. The walls are lined with shelves, each filled with an assortment of objects: jars of herbs, dried flowers, mysterious vials of liquid, and other mystical-looking items I can't quite make out in the penumbra.

This guy's got to be some sort of druidic master.

In the center of the hut is a wooden table. On one side is a bed covered in animal furs. Opposite the bed is a stone fireplace, its flames full and dancing. Next to that is a wooden ladder, which seems to be leading to a loft.

"Come, come, sit, sit." The man gestures to the stools around the table.

Now that we're closer to him, I can see his weathered skin and the deep wrinkles etched around his eyes and mouth. But his eyes are a bright, striking green that bounce around to all of us, alight with intelligence. He has pouches and tools attached to the many belts on his waist. His hair is unkempt and tangled.

Hesitantly, the four of us interact with a chair and sit at his table. Meanwhile, the man hobbles over to his shelves and removes four cups, a mortar and pestle, and some dried herbs. We watch as he grinds the herbs and sprinkles them into each cup. Then he retrieves a kettle from over the fire and pours water over the contents.

"Drink."

My gaze flicks to my teammates on my screen. Nobody wants to take the first drink.

When we don't do as he wants, he repeats himself, "Drink. Drink. Feel better."

I use Valen's medicine talent to examine the liquid. The result is not fully conclusive, but it shows one plant I recognize in his concoction. It's a medicinal one I'd use myself in a health potion.

"It's a recovery potion," I say. "It might fix our hit points."

I don't tell them that I'm not one hundred percent sure, but we're at an impasse.

"Why don't I drink first, just to make sure?" I suggest. I can take one for the team. I briefly glance at Sylvie, who rewards me with a beaming smile.

"We'll all drink it," says Cameron quickly, probably wishing he'd thought to be the selfless one.

Each of us interacts with the potion, causing our avatars to drink. I see my health restore, and my hit points return to normal. I need to get the recipe for this.

The man claps. "Good. Good!"

Looking at the druid, I notice I can lock onto him and talk to him like I can some other NPCs. I target him and say, "Thanks. You saved us back there."

"Birdkin are nasty creatures," he says. "Nasty."

A notification pops up on my screen. A Birdkin entry has been added to my notebook. Skimming the information, it says they are vampiric creatures that can siphon your hit points. Birdkin cluster together and attack a creature until it cannot heal itself anymore.

"How long have these Birdkin been here?" I ask.

"Too many days," he answers. "Too many."

"What's your name?" Cameron asks.

That's a better first question than mine, which is fine. Cameron probably needs that for his ego.

"Erlin," the man says, standing a little straighter.

"Do you live here?" I ask. When Erlin nods, I ask, "For how long?"

"Since before the song died."

That gets my attention. Our objective is to retrieve the Song of Serenity.

Dominic presses, "What's the song?"

Erlin's eyes go wide and he shakes his head. "I've said too much." He shuffles around his tiny hut as best he can with four visitors. "Too much."

"Erlin," Bastian tries, in a much calmer tone, "We seek the Song of Serenity. Do you know anything about it?"

"Take. Take. Only take," he mumbles. "Use for bad."

He's not giving up any information. I feel like we just lost our only lead. Out of the corner of my eye, I catch Sylvie waving her arms. I make eye contact with her and she holds up a notebook with the word "*Guardian*" written across the page.

Duh Val, I think, wanting to slap myself in the forehead. Erlin is the guardian of the song. He's not just going to give it to anyone unless we prove we're here for the right reasons.

"We're not planning on using it for evil," I say, choosing my words carefully. "We seek to save the song from those who would bring harm."

Bastian stops moving his game. "Val, what are you doing?"

I disconnect from Erlin so the NPC doesn't think I'm talking to him. "The dude lives alone in the woods. He's some sort of guardian- protecting whatever the song is."

"Val's right Bas," Cameron echoes. He and Dominic also paused their screens. "He's not going to just hand it over."

"We could ransack the place and take it from him," Dominic suggests.

"That's if the song is here," I counter. It's also kind of an asshole move.

"Are we assuming the song is an artifact and not an actual song?" Cameron asks.

"We don't know," Bastian answers. "But this guy is the only one who does."

"So, no ransacking his home," I say, eyes on Dominic, who scowls but doesn't respond.

I retarget Erlin again. "What can we do to prove that we want to do good?"

Erlin paces in contemplation. "You defeat birds, I show you song."

Damnit. I had hoped he would want a simple trade. Fighting those birds is going to take time, effort, and hit points in the best-case scenario. From the guardian's perspective, it makes sense. Those Birdkin are preventing him from leaving his cottage and it looks like their presence is sucking the life from the land.

"Deal," Dominic agrees for us.

"Good. Good!" Erlin exclaims. "Go fight." He shoos us out onto the protected front porch.

Once we're all out on the porch, he says, "Good luck," and shuts his front door.

"Time for a plan," Cameron says. "Rally Forthright?"

I smile at the phrase I coined last Odyssey. But my smile quickly fades as I think about the upcoming fight. Both Valen and Flickerfoot have a disadvantage when fighting swarms. They attack as a group with multiple hits while we can only target one part of the swarm at a time.

Aurelius, with his ability to cast spells, is our best weapon. "What area of effect spells do you have in your back pocket?" I ask Bastian.

"Fireball," he answers, in a deadpan that makes the rest of us laugh. Because Fireball might catch the entire woods on fire and burn everything down.

"I also have an Air Surge spell," Bastian adds.

"That could work," Cameron says. "Blast the birds away from us."

"I could use my Arrow Storm special to attack then," Dominic says. "But I need someone to distract them."

"I can do that," I say. I usually have a more active role in fights, but I can't do much in this situation, so I'll pull my weight any way I can.

"Okay, the plan is that, Aurelius blows them back, hopefully stunning them against the trees. Then Maverick uses his special attack to hit them. Finally, Valen and I run in to take out the rest with our daggers and swords," Cameron says.

I can get behind that.

"Ready to play bodyguard, Cam?" I ask.

"I think you mean bait," he answers with a laugh.

I can't disagree with that.

My heart races as I move Valen forward, out of the protection of the porch and into the decaying garden. Flickerfoot follows with his daggers out. Together, we inch our avatars forward into the clearing until the battle music begins anew.

This time we're ready for the pandemonium of bird calls as clusters of those tiny, vampiric creatures take flight. Moving my camera up, I see three distinct flocks: two positioning to attack Valen, while the other prepares to attack Flickerfoot.

"Bas?" I ask, a touch of warning in my voice. One hit from all of those Birdkin will cut Valen's health in half.

"Duck!" Bastian orders.

Valen crouches down. It's not enough. When Aurelius casts his Air Surge, Valen gets knocked over too and tumbles into a tree. Thankfully, he doesn't take damage from Aurelius's attack.

The spell hits the Birdkin attacking Flickerfoot and one swarm attacking Valen. Unfortunately, the second swarm begins their assault during the time it takes for Valen to recover. All those hits siphon away my hit points. Fast. Valen stands, and I dash towards some of the Birdkin struggling on the ground. He finishes the Enkin with his swords.

The plan is working.

I just hope Erlin can make another one of those potions for me. It's one thing to be a team player, but I want to be there to win the game.

"They're swarming again," Cameron warns.

"Incoming," Dominic calls before he unleashes his special attack. Valen dodges out of the way as the barrage of ethereal arrows rain down from—well, the canopy, because we can't see the sky.

Valen rolls toward a tree, where I can watch as the arrows take care of the bulk of the Birdkin. After Maverick's attack, Flickerfoot and Valen run in to finish off the Birdkin that are still alive. We both take a few more hits, but Aurelius and Maverick remain mostly untouched.

With our enemy defeated, we regroup on Erlin's protected porch.

"Good job guys," Bastian says. "We couldn't have done it without you."

I appreciate the recognition, because I feel like Valen was just a punching bag back there.

Erlin sticks his head out of the door. "You do it? You kill them?"

"Yeah, they're gone," Dominic says.

"Yah-ho!" Erlin exclaims, running outside and into his garden. He squats down and mumbles something to the dead and dying plants.

Just then, rays of sunlight break through the canopy, shining down upon the area. I hadn't noticed how the fog had disappeared until now.

I swear I see tears on Erlin's face.

"I think this meant more to him than we knew," I say. The boys nod in agreement. I feel something shift. I think we've just bonded.

In that moment, I'm reminded of how a video game can be so much more than just a story.

Chapter 34
Valentino

After returning to the house, I ask, "Hey Erlin, do you have any more of those potions?"

Erlin shakes his head. "No more herbs."

Damn. I can't restore my total hit points to normal. That could mean I'll have issues if we get into another fight. I could take the one health potion I have, but I'd rather save that in case there's a dire situation.

"Will you take us to the Song now?" Dominic impatiently asks Erlin.

His gaze sweeps over the corpse-ridden ground, then back at us. "You take care of birds. I show you grove. That is deal. We go now."

Wait a minute, a grove? My eyebrows pull together. I don't remember anything about a grove. Maybe that's where the song is?

Erlin waves his hand and a walking stick appears. He exits his house, circles to the back, and follows a small path we didn't see before. "Follow. Follow!"

With half my hit points and an hour remaining, we follow Erlin, hoping he will lead us to the Song of Serenity. As we move away from Erlin's house, the gnarled trees and decaying leaves transform into dense thickets and overgrown paths. Erlin may be the Guardian of the Song, but he must not visit it often. Or maybe he couldn't because of the Birdkin.

Sylvie waves her hands again, holding up the notebook with the word "*footprints*" written on it.

Oh shit, I forgot about them. The large humanoid footprints Dominic followed to Erlin's house. The hermit is the size of Flickerfoot, so his footprints don't match. Unless he's a shapeshifter. Then we're screwed. Hopefully, that's not the case. But if he's not, then where did those tracks come from?

For the second time during this Odyssey, I'm thankful Sylvie could be here. Her clues have helped me navigate the nuances of this mission.

I make a mental note to thank her properly.

"Dom," I start. "You said those tracks were humanoid?"

"Yeah—why?" Dominic asks.

"It didn't seem like Erlin's has left his house for a while."

Bastian concludes, "So you're wondering who made those tracks?"

"Hey, Erlin?" Cameron asks. "How long were you trapped in your house?"

"Long, long time," Erlin repeats.

"Like days or weeks?"

"Weeks," Erlin says.

"Those tracks were fresh," Dominic confirms what we're all thinking. Either Erlin is lying about who he is, or something could be waiting for us when we get to this grove.

With my luck, it will be the second scenario.

As we travel, Cameron continues to ask Erlin a string of questions. My guess is he's the type of player who likes to talk to every NPC to gather information. It's such a Cabbala thing to do. Some players just want to get to fighting the bad guy. Generally, those players choose to join the Machiava faction.

But Erlin gives us some good information. He tells us we're in the Whispering Woods. He came here as a young adventurer seeking the glory of the Song of Serenity. When he located the grove and encountered the artifact, he was given a vision.

"What was the vision?" Cam asks.

"The truth of power, yes," Erlin mutters.

Well, that's specific.

"Which was what?" Dominic asks.

"Song is balance," Erlin says.

That's cryptic. I guess we're not getting much more.

As we progress towards this mysterious grove, the oppressive feeling of the darker forest lifts. The trees grow taller and the canopy thins, allowing more light to filter through. Our path has fewer obstructions and is lined with green moss.

The music also shifts. The distant, melodious sound of running water replaces the silence.

"That's it!" Erlin exclaims, jumping and skipping towards a willow tree. Erlin runs his hands along the tendrils. As he does, a faint shimmer appears and ripples along a dome-shaped magical barrier.

"You must bare your heart to enter the grove," he explains, before walking through the barrier.

"What the fuck does that mean?" Dominic asks.

"That we have to bare our hearts to get past the barrier," I reiterate. Dominic gives me a look and I smirk.

"Is this another voice-activated thing?" Bastian asks.

"I don't think so," I say. "The game can't know if we're honestly baring our heart."

"Thank goodness," Dominic says.

"Aw, Dom," Cameron coos. "I want to know what's in that heart of yours."

Cameron, Bastian, and I all laugh, and Dominic cracks a smile. It feels good to laugh with them. It's like we're finally loosening up. This Odyssey has been much more serious than our last one.

"So, thoughts on what we have to do?"

"Strip," Cameron says, like it's the simplest answer. I watch as Flickerfoot's armor disappears. "You guys haven't been paying attention to him. Erlin went in au-natural, with no armor."

Unarmored, Flickerfoot steps up to the willow tree barrier, interacts with it, and walks right through it, just as Erlin did.

"I don't like this," I tell them. "Flickerfoot and Valen are already at half health and we're getting rid of our defenses?"

"We each have a health potion, and we're a team Val," Bastian says. "We got your back."

He's right. I have to trust that my teammates won't let me fall.

The three of us follow Cameron's lead, unequipping our armor and stepping up to the willow tree's magical barrier.

I command Valen to interact with the willow branches. He does and walks through the barrier, pushing aside the branches and moving into a serene sanctuary that transcends the boundaries of the willow tree. It's like we've been transported into another world.

Sunlight filters through the leaves, casting dappled patterns on the lush carpet of moss and wildflowers below. Ahead, a small waterfall cascades with a melodic rush into a crystalline pool, its water shimmering under the gentle caress of the light.

I'm so overwhelmed by the natural beauty and its contrast to the death and decay at Erlin's house, that, at first glance, I first miss the towering, muscular humanoid figure next to the pool of water.

The creature's skin is an unnerving shade of white. Its face, fierce with wide, menacing pale blue eyes stares us down, and sharp, tusk-like fangs, jut from its jaw. Two large, curling horns frame its head while unkempt silver hair falls to the middle of its back. In one hand, it holds a spiked club, and like us, it is free of any armor, wearing only a loincloth.

This is a Giantkin. Red Giantkin can be ferocious demons with extreme strength and constitution. White Giantkin, like the one in front of us, are accomplished sorcerers.

"He has Erlin," Cameron says. Flickerfoot has his daggers out, ready to fight.

My gaze flicks to the wounded hermit lying at the feet of the Giantkin.

"Do not interfere," the Giantkin growls at us.

Briefly, I wonder how the Giantkin could find this grove without Erlin. What knowledge does he possess, and will he share it with us?

But before we can explore that option, Cameron decides for us. "Fuck that," Cameron says, and Flickerfoot rushes the Giantkin. The three of us are left scrambling in his wake.

"Damnit Cameron," Dominic curses.

"We need to get Erlin," Bastian says as Aurelius readies a spell.

"I'm on it," I call, commanding Valen to run toward Erlin. "Dom, cover me."

I need to trust that my teammates will take care of me.

Maverick pulls his bow and moves away from Aurelius. Good. It will be harder to hit us all at once if we're spread out.

The Giantkin swings its spiked club at Flickerfoot, who dodges out of the way. Aurelius shoots an ice spell at the club, freezing it in midair. Maverick sticks the Giantkin in the shoulder with an arrow.

It's just enough of an opening for Valen to slide in to grab Erlin and drag him away from the Giantkin. I press the letter "I" to bring up Valen's inventory, select my only health potion, and give it to Erlin.

I let out the breath I was holding as I see his wounds disappear.

"Val!" Dominic cries.

I look over just in time to see the Giantkin cast a lightning spell that splits off in different directions, hitting all four of us.

Valen seizes with electrical energy and I watch in silent horror as my health bar depletes. Then I breathe a sigh of relief when it stops at a little under a quarter health.

Thank my lucky stars.

I can't rest though. As I look around the battlefield, I notice Flickerfoot is facedown.

"I can't take another hit guys." Cameron says. "A little help, please."

A part of me wants to chide him for recklessly running into battle but now's not the time. Unfortunately, I can't help him. "I gave my health potion to Erlin."

Thankfully, Maverick and Aurelius are still standing. "I got him." Dominic calls. "Val, distract the thing."

"I could go down in one hit," I tell them. Valen seems to be in better condition than Flickerfoot, but it's still a possibility.

"Then don't get hit," Bastian advises.

Says the guy whose avatar is standing furthest away from the Gianttkin.

But we have to get to Flickerfoot. If he dies, we could fail this mission. Leaving Erlin behind, Valen charges the Giantkin. It makes a large swing with its spiked club. At the height of the swing, I press my combo of keys to dodge the attack. Then, I left-click to attack, getting a few good hits in before Valen rolls away again.

I repeat the process, as Aurelius hurls spells at the beast. Slowly, we chip away at its health bar.

With Valen and Aurelius distracting the Giantkin, Maverick reaches Flickerfoot.

"Not again," the Giantkin growls, and shoots out another lightning bolt, but this time only at Maverick.

Luckily, Aurelius throws up a shield around Maverick, protecting him from the hit. The Giantkin roars in frustration, swinging his club in a wide circle. Flickerfoot and Valen both dodge, but Maverick is hit and knocked down.

"I'm okay," Dominic says. "But I can't take another hit like that."

Fuck, this is looking grim. We wouldn't be this vulnerable if we had our armor. Or if Valen and Flickerfoot had all their hit points. It's a bad day when the spellcaster has the most health.

Speaking of spellcasters, from the corner of my screen I see Erlin stand up and raise his arms to the sky. "Evil will not prevail in this sacred place," he says.

Thick roots burst from the ground, twisting around the Giantkin's feet. They wrap around his legs, body, and arms, restraining him.

Without thinking, I right-click on the Giantkin to do Valen's special attack. Valen runs up the roots, using them as footholds to get to the Giantkin's back before he plunges both swords into its neck.

"Val jump," Bastian yells.

I do, just in time to dodge the fireball hurtling toward the Giantkin. Upon impact, the roots catch fire and we watch as the Giantkin not only takes the damage from the spell, but continues to burn as he's engulfed by the roots also set ablaze. When his health bar is finally depleted, he falls into the pool of water behind him, extinguishing the flames.

For the next few moments, the four of us just breathe, trying to return our heart rates to normal after that intense fight.

When I feel like mine's under control, and I'm not shaking, I say, "Hey Cam?"

"I know—" Cameron's head falls. "Rally before just running in."

"Thanks, man," Bastian finishes.

"Contamination!" Erlin cries. He frantically jumps around at the edge of the pool.

"We should get the body out of the sacred pool of water," Cameron guesses.

Together, we pull the Giantkin's body out of the pool, which calms Erlin down.

"I'll harvest the body," Dominic says.

I leave Maverick to harvest what we can from the Giantkin and move Valen to the edge of the water. Erlin hobbles over to join me.

"You healed me."

"Of course," I nod.

Erlin goes to pat Valen on the shoulder. Then he points to the waterfall. "The song," he says.

An item under the water catches the light. The water is so clear I can make out a metallic object at the base of the waterfall.

Is that the song?

Valen jumps in the water and swims towards the object. I have to use my stamina to fight the current, but I eventually reach the spot right above the artifact. I interact with it and Valen dives to retrieve the item. I stop fighting the stream and let it carry Valen to the shore. He lands right before he runs out of stamina.

"What do you have there?" Bastian asks.

In Valen's hand is a small rain drum. I examine the it my notebook reveals the item is called "Serenity" and is etched with water motifs and runes. It can call forth water when used in battle.

"Mission accomplished," Dominic says, leaning back in his chair.

Except there's no text flashing across our screens saying we've accomplished our task.

I shake my head. "We're missing something."

I purse my lips, trying to think. What hasn't come full circle yet in this adventure? The silence and the decay around Erlin's house. The music of the game returned the closer we got to this grove. Closer to this artifact.

Maybe Cameron is right and The Song of Serenity is actually a song that needs to be played on this rain drum.

I turn to Erlin and ask, "Do you know how to play the song?"

Erlin nods.

Relief washes through me. It's a good thing we saved him.

"Will you play it for us?"

He holds out his hands. I pull up my inventory and pass the rain drum to Erlin.

He places the instrument on the ground and hovers his wooden staff above it. After muttering an incantation, small drops seep out from the wood and drip onto the rain drum. Each drop fills the area with the melody of a soft rainstorm. Except there's no water, just a sense of calm. The air ripples like water.

"It's healing us too," Cameron says.

Indeed, our health bars are replenishing, even the hit points stolen by the Birdkin.

The Song of Serenity brings everything back into balance and restores full health.

Once finished, Erlin goes to hand the artifact back to Valen. "No, you keep it safe," I tell him. Erlin smiles and text flashes across our screen.

Quest Complete: Retrieve the Song of Serenity

Chapter 35
Sylvie

With the mission complete, Val bids farewell to his teammates, logs off, and then rounds the desk to gather me in his arms. It's my new favorite place to be. I loop my arms around his neck, holding him too close. Val tightens his grip, his mouth right next to my ear. "You're brilliant."

My heart skips, no it soars. I don't feel like I did much, but it's clear that being here means the world to him. I'm so glad I ditched that dinner. He releases me, but cups both sides of my face in his hands. He smells so good, all citrus and sandalwood.

"Thank you for being here," he says and kisses me with all his excitement, adrenaline, and dopamine still coursing through him. I take it all, and everything else he has to give me.

It amazes me that he wants to credit me for his accomplishment. He's the one playing *Mundo* at an elite level with a sponsorship.

I break the kiss to whisper, "I'm glad I could be here for you," against his lips.

He's wearing his hair up in a bun, the shaved sides from his undercut visible. He wears his team jersey and a comfortable pair of joggers. And his whiskey-colored eyes stare down at me with such happiness and adoration that I can't look away.

I can't believe this man is mine, and I can't get enough of it.

I fist my hands into his jersey and pull him in for another kiss. He meets me with the same enthusiasm as before. His hands leave my face and trace my body down to my ass, where he grabs a handful, pulling me closer.

I catch his full lower lip between my teeth and gently nibble on it. He moans and it reverberates through my body right down to my core. Val's mouth moves to my neck, his facial hair tickling the sensitive skin there. One of his hands leaves my ass and travels up my torso to palm my breast. I can feel my nipples begin to harden while my body heats.

I didn't come here with the intention of sleeping with Val, but I can't deny the tension building between us, the passion we haven't been able to control. He's so goddamn beautiful. It feels like the gods carved this man in their image.

Val abruptly pulls back, his hands leaving my body. "I'm sorry, I got caught up in the moment."

I mourn the loss of his heat, and I close the distance between us again. "How long until we have to be at the party?" I ask, putting my hands on his chest.

Val's hands come to rest at my waist. His eyes flick to my mouth, his eyebrows pulling together suspiciously. "Why?"

A blush rises in my cheeks. Val's usually the one who initiates—*anything* in our relationship. He invited me to play *Mundo* together, gave me his number, and talked me into meeting in the park after the last Odyssey.

All good decisions.

But now, I'm in a position to lead and let Val know I'm ready for this next step.

With my stomach churning in nervous knots, I take a step back from him, grab the hem of my sweater, and pull it over my head. I watch Val's blazing brown eyes roam my body as I stand in my bra and leggings before him. I might as well be naked for the heat building between us.

"I was thinking you could show me your bedroom?"

Val's eyebrows raise before a smirk appears on his face. He pulls me back toward him and leans down, putting his mouth next to my ear. "And what will we do there?" His voice is hot and needy.

Oh lord. My heart pounds in my stomach. I've definitely forgotten how to flirt. How did I get this man to date me?

"Sylvie," Val says.

Oh, that's my name.

Hesitantly, I place my hand on his chest, turning my head to place a kiss on his neck. I let my hand slide down the plans of his chest, his abdomen, and cup him through the soft fabric of his sweatpants. I can feel him growing harder under my touch.

Val's head drops to my shoulders as he groans. "Don't play Rhea,"

But I want to play. I want to be the object of his desires.

"I want you, Val. I want to feel your skin against mine. All of you."

Val slips a hand into my hair, gripping me at the base of my neck, and turns my head to capture my mouth.

This kiss feels different, deeper, and more intense. It's the answer to my request.

Pulling away, he trails his hand down my neck, shoulder, and arm before grabbing my hand. Stepping away from the couch, and Annie, he leads me toward the door I have yet to explore.

"This is my bedroom," he says, as he opens the door.

I walk into the space, making a show of looking around. It's sparsely decorated. The apartment walls are off-white, and I spy a walnut dresser he's probably had since childhood, as well as a dark blue comforter with matching pillows on his bed.

After my inspection, I look at Val over my shoulder. He's leaning against the door, gaze locked onto me while his eyes peruse my body. He wants me. Wants every dip and swell, every scar inside and out. Val looks at me like I'm the most precious thing in the world. I want him more than I've ever wanted anything else in my life.

Emboldened, I reach around to the clasp of my bra, popping it open. I let the garment fall to the floor in front of me before turning to face him.

Val wastes no time crossing the room, squeezing my bare breast, and giving me another deep kiss before turning his attention to my neck.

"I'm going to worship your body." His smooth tenor is right in my ear, his breath hot on the skin he just kissed.

Shivers run through me and my core pulses with need.

He maneuvers me back until my knees hit the edge of the bed. "I'm going to strip you naked and pay homage to every inch of your luscious body with my hands, my mouth, and my tongue until you're crying out my name, coming on my fingers and face."

Oh gods. His words send tingles all over my body, right to my core it feels like the floodgates have opened. My hands grip him like he's my only anchor in a sea of building pleasure.

When did he get a mouth like that?

I want him to say more.

"If you're not okay with that," Val growls against my neck, his nose dragging up so he can look me in the eyes. "If you don't want that too, tell me now."

How could a girl say no?

"Yes," I tell him, my voice no louder than a breath. "I want that. I want you."

With a gentle push, he encourages me to lay back on his bed. I hit the comforter and I'm enveloped in his scent. I watch as Val grips the edge of his shirt, lifting it over his body, revealing inches of glorious warm, toned skin. His body is a work of art.

Val goes to the gym most days before work. The years of hard work and dedication are evident in the ripples of muscles he reveals. He's not broad-shouldered, but fit and sculpted with a body built for agility.

I'd be lying if I didn't say I feel a little self-conscious, like we don't fit together. Me all curves and him planes of well-defined muscles.

But then Val presses kisses over the supple roundness of my stomach. He knows exactly what I look like and is still attracted to me.

He still wants me.

Each touch of his lips to my skin is a spark sending shivers down my spine, right to my core, driving my body wild with need.

When he reaches my breast, he latches onto my right nipple, tongue swirling around the hardened peak. I arch my back as I feel his other hand on my left breast, kneading and teasing.

I let out another moan as his teeth scrape against the sensitive bud.

"Your body is perfect," Val says before he switches his attention to my left breast, giving it the same treatment.

And right now it's acutely attuned to every ounce of attention Val ravishes upon me. He's not in any hurry, as he takes his time with my breasts. I sink my hands into his hair. I love the feel of the silky strands sliding between my fingers. It's been so long since someone's paid attention to my body, to my needs, like this. I feel like I've been wandering the desert, parched, and he's my oasis.

Val releases my breasts as his hands run along my body, gripping handfuls of my hips, stomach, and ass. Then his fingers dance at the waistband of my leggings, as he makes eye contact with me. A silent question. I lift my hips in answer and he peels off the fabric.

"Spread these gorgeous legs for me," Val says, running his hands up my thick thighs.

He's looking at me like I'm a feast laid out before him. I'm more than willing to be devoured.

Val presses gentle kisses to the inside of my thigh before he uses his thumbs to spread me open. I feel a single finger running along my slit, circling my clit then repeating the process.

He's teasing me, going slow. Some unrecognizable noise escapes me, a mixture of frustration and pleasure.

"Let me know if I do something you don't like," he says.

I don't think that's possible. Everything this man does is perfection. Even if my body wants more, I trust my pleasure in his capable hands.

Then his mouth is on my core, his tongue moving in languid strokes up my slit. When he reaches my clit, he swirls the tip of his tongue around the sensitive nerves. I arch my back, hands flying to the sheets for an anchor as my body wants to fly away.

He inserts one finger, slowly thrusting before curling it ever so slightly.

"There," I gasp as he finds that spot that drives me wild.

Val growls in acknowledgment and slips in a second finger while his tongue continues its delicious dance around my clit. I toss my head back, loving the feeling of being full of him. The waves of pleasure build inside me. Each swipe of his tongue, each curl of his finger, brings me closer to release.

He's unrelenting in his pursuit of my pleasure and my hips rock in time with each stroke, riding his face as my pussy greedily takes everything he has to give. He's winding me up, sending me higher into the clouds.

"Yes," I cry out. "Right there, don't stop."

The world could end, and Val wouldn't stop.

And then I'm there, cresting over the peak into my climax. "Oh fuck, oh yes." I sink my hands into his hair as I ride out the waves rolling through me. Val licks me through it, lapping up everything as I ride his face.

When I still, basking in bliss, Val removes his fingers from me and stands. He dips them into his mouth, slowly sucking off the juices there.

Damn, that's sexy.

I watch his eyes close in delight as he pulls the fingers from his mouth. "I love the way you taste," he groans.

"That was amazing," I say, leaning up to press a kiss in the middle of his bare chest.

I feel Val chuckle underneath me as he bends and kisses the top of my head. I look down and see the outline of his erection through his sweatpants.

"You're wearing too many clothes," I tease.

He quickly rids himself of his pants and underwear.

Then Val's standing naked before me.

I lick my lips.

My gaze travels over his body, appreciating each dip of muscle and the hard planes of his fine masculine form. Then there's his cock. long and hard jutting out from his body.

He smirks. "Like what you see?"

Like is too weak a word for what I feel towards his man.

"Oh gods, Val," I say, reaching out toward him.

I feel the bed shift under his weight, then he's pushing me to lay on my back, straddling my thighs. He reaches above me, his torso stretching. I press another kiss to the center of his chest, over his heart.

"Raise your hips," he commands. I do so, and he slips a pillow under me.

Well, this is new, and should give him the perfect angle to hit that sweet spot inside of me. I hear the crinkle of the condom wrapper. I look down at his long, hard length as he rolls the condom down.

"I'm on birth control too," I feel the need to blurt out.

Val makes eye contact with me and smiles. "Good, can't be too safe."

He arches over me, placing a forearm next to my head to hold his weight. His loose black hair falls around us, creating a pocket dimension where time and space are completely ours.

"My Titaness," he whispers in my ear.

I preen at the compliment. "I want you," I echo my words from earlier. "Fill me up.

He teases me by sliding the head of his cock through my folds. Running it along the seam and my swollen clit. Then slowly, oh so slowly, he flexes his hips and begins to sink into me.

The stretch feels amazing. And the angle—oh gods—it's hitting the same spot he was teasing with his fingers before.

"Oh fuck," he groans, his forehead falling to mine. "Sylvie."

I know what he means. There are no words for how good it feels as he's filling me up. Once he's sheathed himself fully, he pauses, giving me time to adjust. But I don't want that. I give a little roll of my hips.

"Look at you," Val says, withdrawing slowly. "Grinding your needy pussy against my cock."

I didn't think Val would be a dirty talker, but I love it.

The words must have escaped my lips because Val responds, "You bring it out of me."

He pulls back, deliberately going slow so I feel every inch of his withdrawal. With a snap of his hips, he thrusts back inside me, filling me up. Val repeats the process again and again.

He's not worried about going fast

"Val, you feel—" I ramble, lost in rolling waves of pure bliss.

"I know baby," he groans, like he's holding back.

I don't want him holding back.

"More... please," I whine.

"Tell me what you want," Val demands, leisurely pulling out.

"Harder... and faster," I say, breathless. More of him.

He straightens, his weight on his knees. Then he rearranges my legs so they're braced on his shoulders. He thrusts into me at an unrelenting pace.

"You're going to come on this cock." He punctuates each word with a snap of his hips.

"Yes, Val." That's exactly what I want. The exquisite pressure building in my core again, coiling tight, ready to unleash another wave of pleasure through me.

Val holds onto my legs with one hand, and with the other, he reaches down to find my clit, just above where our bodies are joined. His thumb rubs my swollen nerves shooting electric bolts of bliss through me.

"Give me another one. Let me see you fall apart again."

And then I'm there, crying out his name as another orgasm rips through me, more intense than the first one.

Before I can recover, Val flips me over, face down in the bed, a pillow beneath my hips. I feel his still-hard cock pound into me as his fingers sink into my hips.

Val's stamina is on another level. Over and over, he pounds into me. I'm at his mercy, unable to do anything more than take what he gives me. I can give him that control because I know he cares for me. He would never intentionally hurt me. We haven't said "I love you" but I know, at this moment I'm falling for this man.

He lets out another string of praises. How good I feel. How well I'm taking his cock, until he's right there, falling over the edge.

Val pulls out and collapses next to me, breathing heavily. We're both sticky with sweat and shaking in the aftermath.

"Stay here," he says, kissing my shoulder. Then he rolls off the bed and heads out of the room. I snuggle into the comforter knowing I can enjoy a few moments of afterglow cuddles before I use the restroom.

When he returns, he surprises me with a warm cloth and cleans me up. Still naked, Val slips back into bed, gathering me in his arms and pulling me to his chest. I lay there content and thoroughly worshiped, listening to the steady beat of his heart, calling out to mine.

I'm not sure what this feeling is—but some might call it love.

Chapter 36
Sylvie

I don't know how long Val holds me in the aftermath of our lovemaking. I don't care. At this moment, I feel safe, cherished, and loved.

"You know," he starts. "We could just skip the party and stay here."

The suggestion sounds divine. Spending the night in his arms, waking up to his smile. I could cook him breakfast in the morning while he checks what the news outlets are saying about the second Odyssey.

But I can't be selfish. Val has friends and fans waiting for him at the after party. I glance at the clock next to his bed. Ten thirty, he's already thirty minutes late. I don't know how long the party will last, but I think it might be better if I just head home. Not that I don't want to go to the party—I do. I just need to ensure I'm back home by the time Theo gets home.

He senses my answer, the hope disappearing from his eyes before I shake my head.

"I'm sorry," I say, like it makes a difference.

Everything is still so complicated.

Val pulls me closer and kisses me softly. "Don't be," he says against my lips. "I'm happy you could be here with me."

"Your adoring fans are waiting for you," I say.

"I'll tell Speed you said that."

We both laugh and rise from the bed to find our clothes. I still feel pangs of guilt as we dress. I head to the living room to get my shirt, then make a quick trip to the bathroom.

"Do you want me to drop you off at the park?" he asks when I emerge.

"How can I refuse such an offer?"

Dressed and ready for the evening, Val drives me back to the park. He gets out of the car to open my door. Saying goodbye is hard, especially when we don't know when we will get time together again. But this feels different. Like there's been a shift in our relationship tonight.

It's then that I realize I've fallen in love with this man. I wrap my arms around him and bury my face into his chest, listening to his heartbeat.

"Let me know when you get home safe," he says.

"I will," I promise.

He kisses me again, drinking from me like I'm the only thing that can sustain him.

"See you soon Rhea." He whispers, then tears himself away from me. He gets back in his car and drives off. I watch his taillights disappear into the night before I turn and walk toward the apartment.

I check my phone. It's past eleven but I don't see any sign of Theo's car. Looking up at our outward-facing window, the lights are off too. All good signs that I'm home before he is.

As I climb the stairs, I remember his offer, he'd sleep on the couch and give me the bed. But after tonight's events and my realization about my feelings towards Val, it feels like a betrayal to Val to sleep in what was my bed with Theo.

Even if it is more comfortable than the day bed.

I slide my key into the lock, turn the knob, and open the door into a dark apartment. My hand reaches to the wall, searching for the switch. When I find it and the lights come on, I'm surprised to see Theo sitting on the living room couch, his feet propped up on the coffee table, staring at me with a vindictive gleam in his eyes.

"Welcome back." His voice is eerily calm. "Did you have a good time?

My brain short circuits. I don't know how to process what's going on. What's Theo doing home?

I take in his stiff posture, the tension in his jaw, and the intense, unblinking stare. He's still in the same clothes from the dinner with his parents. Did he not go out with his friends? He doesn't seem to be intoxicated. But his calm is a mask for something darker. I can count on one hand the number of times I've seen him like this.

And none of those times have gone well for me.

Shutting the door behind me, I ask, "Theo, what are you-"

"I'm asking the questions right now." The snap in his voice makes my spine straighten. "And you owe me an answer."

Oh god, what does he know? Did he find out about my secret bank account? Or my plans to move out? But I can't assume anything, and I don't want to give away my secrets. "Theo, I don't know—"

He cuts me off again. "I knew you were dumb, Sylvie, but this is next level."

I feel my defenses rising, my mind slipping back into the safe space it goes to when Theo is angry.

He stands and methodically crosses the room toward me. I cringe, making myself small. He puts a hand beside my head, against the door, using his body to block me in.

It's one of his intimidation tactics.

"I know where you've been," Theo growls in my ear.

What? Where I've been? How could he know?

"I have your location," he says as if he's reading my mind. "Remember? I can see everywhere you go."

My eyes go wide as my jaw drops. *Oh fuck.*

It's been years since I've shared my location with him. He'd use it to make sure I was safe traveling to and from school. How could I forget? He's known all this time, everywhere I've gone.

"Your pathetic performance about being sick tonight tipped me off you were up to no good. And lo and behold, you've been at his house all night. Did you have a good ride on his dick?"

I ball my fists and say, "That's not fair—"

"I knew you were ungrateful. But I never thought my beloved girlfriend would be a cheater too."

"We're broken up," I remind him. Why can't he get that through his thick skull?

"No!" Theo yells, slamming his fist on the door. The deep thud causes my heart to skip. I turn my head to the side, closing my eyes and pursing my lips, bracing for whatever comes next.

He takes a few deep breaths, calming himself. Then, through gritted teeth, he says. "You're mine, Sylvie. You're just confused right now."

Val's baked ziti threatens to come back up. I'm not confused.

I dare to look at him. "Theo, you're scaring me."

In the past Theo's broken me mentally and emotionally. But today I'm afraid things might cross into the physical. With the anger radiating off of him now, I wouldn't put it past him. I need to get out of this situation, or at least put space between us.

Theo caresses my cheek with the back of his hand. I flinch at the touch.

"I'm glad you're afraid," he says. He leans in closer, pressing his larger body against mine. "It's the least you deserve after cheating on me."

I go to say something, then stop. There's no use arguing, Theo's not in his right mind and he won't listen to me. As calmly as I can, I say, "If you back up and let me sit down, I'll tell you anything you want to know."

He's quiet for a second, then straightens, backs away from me, and motions to the couch. "Why don't you have a seat, my love?"

With careful steps, I slip past Theo, cross the living room, and gingerly sink onto the edge of the couch. Once I'm perched, Theo crosses the room to sit beside me.

"I'm going to show you something," he says, pulling out his phone.

He opens up his gallery and clicks play on a video. It shows someplace dimly lit by street lamps. I can make out some general shapes like shrubs and trees. The camera pans to a familiar car, parked all alone in a lot.

My whole body tenses as I recognize the car.

Recognize the two people making out.

He filmed Val and me in the car.

This is bad. If he uploads this online it could be the end of Val's career with BGN. And I have no idea how it could affect my internship.

My heart pounds in my chest. "Okay Theo," I say cautiously. "What do you want?"

Theo grins and his chest expands. "I want my girlfriend back." He reaches out to caress my face. "My perfect, obedient girlfriend."

I pull away from his touch. "That's not going to happen," I state firmly. I shouldn't contradict him right now, but I won't feed into his delusions either.

I can't go back to the shell of a human I was with him.

His smile broadens, like the Cheshire cat's smile. "Yes, it is. Do you know how I know?"

"How?" I pull my mouth into a thin line, hoping that he won't say what I think he's going to.

"Because if you don't, I will leak this video and the other images, along with a heartbreaking story about how BGN's golden boy is nothing but a lying homewrecker. How he slid into my girlfriend's DMs intending to steal her away."

We both know it's a lie. But it doesn't matter. The media won't care about the truth. They'll gobble up this juicy story and spin whatever version they want. I can see the headlines now.

Saint or Stalker

The Saint Who Would Steal Your Woman

Valentino is Mr. Steal Your Girl

Tears build up behind my eyes. I squeeze them shut. I can't let Theo see me cry.

Shaking my head I turn to him. "You wouldn't do that to your reputation."

Theo barks out a laugh. "I'll skyrocket in popularity in one night."

I press my hand to my chest. I feel like I can't breathe.

He continues, "But because I love you, I'm going to give you the chance to save him. Are you going to be a good girl and cooperate?"

Despite my best efforts, I can't stop the tears from sliding down my face. My head falls to my hands as I sob.

I don't have a choice. If I don't, and Theo releases the video, Val's reputation will crash. It will be the end of our relationship. No, I can't do that to him. I love him too much to put him in a situation where he could have everything he's earned stripped away from him.

Theo doesn't wait for me to answer. "This is how things are going to go, Sylvie. You're not going back to campus for class. You're going to give me your phone, your laptop, and all your passwords to your social accounts. And you are never going to talk to Valentino Santos again. Do I make myself clear?"

He holds out his hand for my phone. I take it out of my jacket pocket and place it in his hand, then collapse to the floor. I can't answer him. I can't breathe, no matter how deeply I inhale. My knees give out and I crumple to the floor.

I wish I'd known that my goodbye to Val wasn't a "see you later" or "until next time." Because if Theo has his way, I'll never be able to see or talk to Valentino Santos ever again.

Chapter 37
Valentino

I wake to an incessant meow and two paws kneading my chest.

"Okay, okay, I'm up," I grumble at Annie.

Satisfied, she jumps off of me and I roll over to look at my phone. It's ten a.m. No wonder Annie is demanding to be fed. I usually feed her around eight.

Then I notice the dozens of unread texts and missed calls from Speed, Xander, and even Preston. They must be congratulatory texts. I scroll through the notifications looking for the "home safe" text from Sylvie.

But it's not there.

I bite my lip. It's not like her to not text me. Anxiety creeps in. Is she okay? Did something happen with Theo?

I pull up Sylvie's text thread.

Valentino:

Good morning beautiful. <3

From the doorway, Annie meows again, more demanding this time.

"Yes, I'm coming, princess."

Setting my phone down, I make a mental note to call Sylvie later. I yawn, stretch, and roll to the other side of the bed where Sylvie would have slept if she spent the night with me.

She didn't come to the after party either. She had to get home before Theo returned.

Fucking Theo.

I tell myself it didn't hurt that she left. Tell myself it didn't hurt that she didn't attend the after party. But it does.

Speed and Xander asked about her. Preston didn't ask—because he wasn't there. He probably was doing something with Julianna. Whatever, I don't care.

Reluctantly, I leave my bed and drag my feet toward the kitchen to make coffee. Once it's brewing, I feed Annie and start making myself some eggs and bacon.

My ringtone cuts through the silence of my apartment. I ignore it, opting to plate my food and pour my coffee. I need both to face the world today.

How many interviews does Paula have scheduled? Three? Four? I'll need to check my calendar.

I inhale my breakfast and put the dirty plate in the dishwasher. When I return to my bedroom to dress for the day, my phone rings again. Speed's name flashes on the screen.

"Who's dying?" I ask when I pick up.

"Your reputation." It's the tone of his voice that catches me off guard. My playful friend Speed isn't on the other end of this call. It's lawyer Speed. "Dude, what the honest fuck were you thinking?"

"What are you talking about?" I ask defensively.

"Have you not looked at any social?" he asks. "Or read any of your messages?"

"I just woke up," I say, taking a sip.

"You've gone viral. And not in a good way."

My eyebrows pull together. What is he talking about? Did someone pick apart my Odyssey performance? "What does that mean?"

"You're gonna want to sit down for this," Speed says.

I put Speed on speakerphone, leave my bedroom, and sit at my computer in the living room. Setting my mug down, I do a quick internet search for my name.

The results explode with gossip headlines, pixelated enhanced photos, and videos.

SaintVal, the smooth-talking rake.

SaintVal, the rogue, caught stealing hearts.

SaintVal spurs frenzied affairs in love games.

What the hell is all of this?

I click on one and read: *In a twist that nobody saw coming, Valentino Santos finds himself at the center of controversy. He was photographed at a public park at night with a mysterious woman alleged to be in a relationship with another streamer.*

My mouth goes dry and my stomach drops. "The fuck?"

"That's what I said." Speed's tone switches from concerned friend to legal counsel. "Is this you? Did you get frisky with Sylvie in the parking lot of a local park?"

"We were in a car!" It was supposed to be private.

Speed goes silent. I don't need a video chat to see him pinching the bridge of his nose. After a beat, he says, "Cars still have windows."

"Clearly," I say, clicking on the several photos of Sylvie and me.

The photographer had to zoom in to get the shot, but there's no doubt it's me. It's my car. That's my face, my long hair. Sylvie is less discernible, but it's enough for someone who knows her to identify her.

There are photos of me leaning over the center console to kiss her. Of me climbing on top of her. One that highlights where my concealed hand would be.

A storm of emotions blows through me. Disbelief in this situation, rage that someone would drag Sylvie into this, and worry about what this means for my streaming career.

I doubt BGN will want me to continue on their team, not with a scandal like this. They want their players to stay clean and out of controversy. This puts me directly in the middle of one—painting me as the bad guy.

Then a thought occurs to me: does Sylvie know? Is this why she didn't text me back? Sylvie told me again and again how she wasn't comfortable with us going public because her situation was too messy—and I pushed her to give more.

And now look where that got us.

"Santos!" Speed is all business. "I'd advise you not to talk to anyone before you talk to BGN."

Dejected, I ask, "Are you my lawyer now?"

"Consider this your free consultation," Speed says. "You couldn't afford me otherwise."

Despite everything, that makes me laugh. "Thanks," I mumble, still staring at the headlines. At the videos people uploaded within hours of the news breaking.

Which makes me wonder: which was the first video? Who broke this news?

Scrolling back to the top of the page, my gaze stops at one particular video. At the face staring back at me. At the headline: *SaintVal is no Saint.* My blood runs cold. If I could shoot lasers from my eyes, there would be a hole in my computer screen.

"You know I'm here if you need me." Speed says. I hear the sincerity in his voice.

"Yeah. I know. Thanks." I tell him before promptly hanging up.

I move my mouse over the video and click on Theo's face. He's sitting in his gaming setup. His face is grim and he puts on a good show, weaving this sob story about the villainous SaintVal and how I stole his girl.

Conveniently, he leaves out the parts when he's made Sylvie feel unsafe in her own home, and how he undervalues and belittles her. Of course, there would be nothing about the abuse he put her through.

He paints himself as the victim.

I pick up my phone and dial Sylvie. The phone rings and rings.

And rings.

And rings.

Then her voicemail picks up. "Hi, you've reached Sylvie. Leave a message."

"Hey babe, it's me. Call me back when you get this." I end the call and then shoot her another text saying the same thing:

Valentino:

Call me when you get this babe.

I lean back in my chair, exhaling deeply, fighting the welling behind my eyes.

That fucker Theo. How did he know where we were that night?

It doesn't matter. The damage is done.

My phone rings again and my heart skips a beat, hoping it's Sylvie. The name isn't hers but it's just as shocking.

Preston.

Is he calling to offer an olive branch? Or is he calling to say "I told you so"? On the fourth ring, I swipe to answer his call because there's only one way to find out.

"Hey," I say, my voice morose.

"From the sound of your voice, I'm guessing you know."

"Just got off the phone with Speed."

"How are you doing?"

What a stupid question. How does he think I'm doing? My streaming career is basically over. My girlfriend isn't calling or texting me back. But I can't say that. "Overwhelmed. I'm shutting down."

"Do you need me to come over?"

Nervous energy builds through my body. I don't like the idea of waiting around. I need to do something. "Actually, can I come to you?"

"Yeah man. Whatever you need, the door is open."

I stand up from the computer. "Leaving in ten."

I hang up the phone and debate putting it on silent, but decide against it. I want to hear if Sylvie calls or texts.

I shoot a text off to Speed and Xander.

Valentino:

Thanks for the support. I'm going to Preston's to cool off.

Unsurprisingly, Xander's the first to text back.

Xander:

Are you two good?

I think we've buried the proverbial hatchet for now. This feels bigger than our petty squabbles.

Valentino:

Guess I'll find out.

Annie rubs up on my leg. I'd like to think she's offering her silent support. I pick her up and cuddle her in my arms for a moment. Then I deposit her on the couch, in the still-present pile of blankets I made for Sylvie.

I get dressed and leave my apartment, wondering if this is even something that can be fixed.

Chapter 38
Valentino

Preston lives twenty minutes away on the other side of 2Game in Warcester. I'm shaking in my seat, but not because of the traffic. My streaming career could be over.

As well as my relationship with Sylvie.

I try to put on Prospero's podcast as a distraction. They released an episode with their thoughts on the second Odyssey. But every worst-case scenario is running through my head. All I get from the podcast is that Prospero wasn't thrilled with anyone's performance.

"The BGN team gave a valiant, albeit lackluster performance," Prospero comments. "I expected more out of them. I guess their sudden rise to fame after the first Odyssey got to their heads."

I squeeze the steering wheel. They're not wrong. We didn't play the best game we could have, because we weren't being ourselves. Well, I was trying, but the others weren't giving me much to work with.

"The real shining star of this Odyssey was the Outlaws..."

A change of subject. That's good. At least they don't address the photos, Theo's video, or any other related media. They keep to the game and how the teams played. But maybe it's a matter of time. Prospero probably recorded this podcast before Theo posted his video.

I pull into Preston's complex, parking at the designated guest spot. Walking up to Preston's door, I knock twice. The door opens revealing a shirtless Preston.

It should be a criminal offense to look as effortlessly sexy as Preston does in the morning. A pair of joggers slung low on his hips, his hair tousled.

No, wait, backup. Why is Preston shirtless? I told him I was coming over.

Did he do this on purpose?

Whatever, it's his home.

"Hey man, come in." Preston steps aside and I walk in, catching a whiff of his favorite cologne that I used to love so much.

We walk down the short hallway that opens into his living room. A couch faces a TV mounted on the wall to my left. To the right is a half wall separating the living room from the kitchen. Past that is another hallway going back to his bedroom.

I blow past Preston and immediately start pacing the living room. Now that I'm here, I have no idea what to say.

Preston leans against the couch. "Listen, Val, about last night."

I bark out a laugh. "Honestly, you not being at the party is the least of my concerns right now." I don't mean to be short with him, but I didn't come over here to talk about him.

So why did I come to him? Because I'm lost. I'm floating in a sea of unknown outcomes and need my best friend. But can I even call him that anymore?

"Okay. How can I help? What do you need?" Preston asks.

I need to know if Sylvie is okay.

I need to know if BGN is going to kick me out.

My phone vibrates in my pocket, making my heart race. I stop pacing as a kernel of hope blooms in my chest. Maybe Sylvie texted me back.

But when I check I'm disappointed to see that it's just a social media post. I've been tagged in something. Again. I put my phone back in my pocket.

"Who was that?"

"Social media. People are relentlessly tagging me. I'd turn it off, but I'm waiting for a call, text, or something from Sylvie."

"People want you to respond," he says.

I note how he doesn't comment about Sylvie.

"Speed says I should talk to BGN first."

"He's right," Preston nods. "Have you heard from BGN?"

"No." I wish they'd call already.

"What about your teammates?"

"One text from Cameron saying he doesn't believe the rumors." They're keeping their distance from me. I don't blame them. The last thing they need is to get involved in this too.

I flop down on his couch, resting my elbows on my knees and my head in my hands. "I just want to talk to her."

That voice in the back of my head tells me she'll never talk to me again. This is her biggest fear realized. She warned me again and again but I dismissed her. I didn't think something like this could happen to me.

Then Preston says the worst possible thing. "I told you something like this could happen. That she was bad news."

Did he really just say that? I told you so? Like we're kids?

I turn my head to look at him, mouth open, eyebrows furrowed. "Do you want to say that again?"

Preston holds up his hands. "All I'm saying is maybe this is for the best."

Best for who? Because nothing about this scenario is the best for me. I doubt it's best for Sylvie either. Her name is being dragged through the mud too—by her ex-boyfriend no less.

Then I'm standing and closing the distance between Preston and me. "Are you kidding me?" I say, voice raised. "You're supposed to be my best-fucking-friend, and this is your response?"

"Do you want me to lie to you?" Preston asks.

"There's a difference between lying and having compassion."

Xander was right, it was a mistake coming here. Preston and I are never going to see eye to eye about Sylvie. He's had it out for her since he first heard about her.

"What is your problem with her anyway?" I ask. "Or was I right? You're jealous."

"Of course I'm jealous!" Preston explodes throwing his hands up in the air.

I'm taken aback by his reaction, the anger and frustration I hear in his voice. I take in his blue eyes, blown wide, the twitch in his jaw.

He's desperate, but for what?

I don't know what else to say, so I ask, "Why?"

As in, why does he care if he has Julianna?

Preston steps closer so his bare chest is right up against mine. "Because she's taking you away from me," Preston cups my face. "And you're more than just my best friend Val. It just took me almost losing you to realize it."

And he crushes his mouth to mine.

My body freezes in shock. I'm too stunned to do anything other than let Preston continue the kiss.

I used to dream of this moment, of tasting Preston's mouth. Of when the built-up tension between us finally broke and we would be consumed by the inferno of lust between us.

I didn't expect it to feel so—wrong. There's no fire, no heat, no spark in this kiss. Whatever attraction was between us—it's gone. Because Sylvie came into my life and rocked my world. Preston no longer ignites my heart the way she does.

And she's my girlfriend.

I place my hands on Preston's chest and push him away. I watch the lust in his eyes fade. The color drains from his face and his eyes widen. His gaze searches my face, for any indication I feel the same way.

I take a step back, putting distance between us as I shake my head.

Maybe Preston and I could have been together at some point. But he's not the person I'm meant to be with.

Then a feminine voice says, "What the fuck?"

Chapter 39
Valentino

Our heads whip towards the doorway to see Julianna Sinclair standing there in a matching loungewear set, hair tossed up in a messy bun, and her phone in her hand. I'm not sure how she got in. Either Preston left the door unlocked or she has a key to his apartment.

Her skin is flushed, her nostrils flared and the fire of the nine hells burns behind her eyes.

"Jules," Preston gasps. He takes a step towards her. "It's not what you think."

"Don't fucking gaslight me," Julianna yells, shouldering past me, placing two hands on Preston's bare chest and shoving him. Her breathing is labored and she's shaking with rage.

I take two steps away.

Thrusting a finger in Preston's direction, Julianna continues, "I know exactly what I saw. You're bare-chested, making out with the guy you said is only your best friend? You two-timing son of a bitch. How could you do this to me."

"Baby, it didn't mean—" Preston tries.

"Don't you dare 'baby' me," she shrieks, cutting him off.

The kiss didn't mean anything to him, I finish in my head. Good to know. The bastard doesn't want to share me with anyone else, but doesn't want me for himself either. Not that I want him.

I just want to know that Sylvie's alright.

Then, unexpectedly, Julianna turns her anger towards me. "And you."

What did I do? I'm a victim in this situation. The kiss wasn't mutual. Preston kissed me.

"I thought you were one of the good guys," her voice drops to something dark and menacing.

"What are you talking about?" I ask, honestly confused.

"Sylvie is a saint and has been through enough. She deserves more than someone who isn't going to put her first."

My face contorts, my mouth hangs open, and my eyebrows pull together. First of all, that's exactly what I want to do for Sylvie. She's been through enough in her life and deserves the world. I want to be the man who gives it to her. But, second of all, "How do you know my girlfriend?"

"Please," Julianna huffs. "I find it hard to believe Sylvie never told you she was working for me."

I feel like slapping my forehead. All the pieces were there. I should have put them together. "No, she didn't. All she said was she was working for an influencer."

"I'm supposed to believe that? When you're standing here kissing my shirtless," she turns to look at Preston briefly, "*ex*-boyfriend."

Her gaze meets mine again, and her next five words crush my soul.

"You're no better than Theo," she seethes.

Where the fuck does this girl get off saying that to me? Theo is a piece of shit who doesn't appreciate Sylvie for the goddess that she is.

"You have this all twisted around," I don't hide the irritation in my voice. Then another thought crosses my mind. "How the hell do you know Theo?"

She barks out a laugh, crossing her arms over her chest. "I dated Theo in high school."

"I thought you went to high school with Preston?" I look at the man in question.

"Theo was a year ahead of us. He was the guy Julia was dating."

So Theo, Preston, and Julia all went to school together. What a small fucking world.

My reality begins to spin as an uncomfortable truth washes over me. Preston wasn't at my party last night.

Sylvie said Theo was going to a bar Saturday night with friends.

My gaze flicks up to Preston who now looks as pale as a sparkly vampire. Or maybe a sweaty vampire.

"Where were you last night?" I ask tension in my voice.

He doesn't say anything. That's all the confirmation I need.

"Really, Val?" Julianna says. "Really? He was out with you last night."

I shake my head. I get that she's mad but she's already got a narrative in her head and she's not thinking clearly. "No, he wasn't. Ask anyone. He never showed at the after party."

Julianna throws her arms out, "So there are more lies?"

"You went out with him didn't you?" I accuse, venom in my voice. "Did you tell him about Sylvie and me?"

I see Preston's throat bob as he shifts on his feet.

"Preston," Julianna yells. "Answer the damn question."

"I didn't mean to!" Preston explodes. Now we're all yelling at each other. "Theo already knew something was up. He was tracking her phone. He asked me what was up and I said that Val was bringing a girl to his apartment. He put the rest together himself."

Anger boils through me as I pace the length of the room, my pulse pounding like a war drum. How could Preston do this to me? To Sylvie? Sure, Preston and I weren't in the best of places, but I would never do something vindictive to harm him or a person he cared about.

Because Preston told Theo about Sylvie and me, Theo went home and released the video that went viral and probably will get me kicked off of BGN's Odyssey team. And gods only know what Theo's said or done to Sylvie.

I force myself to take a breath, audibly exhaling. "Did you know about the video?"

"What video?" Julianna chimes in.

Her question goes ignored. "Hell no," Preston says, outraged. "I can't believe you think I'd do that."

"I didn't think you'd tell Theo about Sylvie and me, but here we are. And because of what you told him, Theo released that video. I'm going to get kicked off of BGN's team and who knows what has happened to Sylvie?"

"What the fuck are you guys talking about?" Julianna asks.

Feeling like it's best to just show her, I pull my phone out of my pocket and do a quick search for the video. I play the video that turned my world upside down.

Recognition passes over Julia's face as Theo appears and starts to speak. He explains a distorted narrative about how SaintVal slid into his girl's DMs and whispered sweet words in her ear, making her false promises of fame. He talks about how many other girls SaintVal has done this to. Then it shows the damning dark, gritty cell phone footage of us in my car.

Still seething with rage, Julianna pinches her eyebrows and paces the length of the living room. "So not only are you a cheating bastard, but you put Sylvie in danger too?"

"I had nothing to do with that video, I swear it."

"Like you swore there were no romantic feelings between you and Valentino." Julia throws her hand in my direction.

"I told you it—it's not what you think," Preston tries.

Julianna is having none of his excuses. I honestly wouldn't either. I'd be on team Julianna here if she wasn't dragging my good name down too.

I'll deal with her in a moment.

I stalk towards Preston and push him up against the wall. "You might not have recorded, but Theo posted it vindictively because of the information you gave him. I could look past your part in ruining my contract with BGN, but Sylvie could be in danger right now because of you."

And I can't forgive that.

Years of friendship—gone. All because Preston couldn't stand to see me happy with someone else.

"Why do you care so much?" Julianna challenges me, arms crossed over her chest. "You're in here kissing *my* ex-boyfriend."

Preston opens his mouth to answer, but Julianna cuts him off. "No, you don't get to speak right now. You have no idea what you've done."

I release Preston to run my hands through my hair. "He kissed me," I say through gritted teeth. "I would never cheat on Sylvie. I'm in love with her."

"That's a convenient excuse," Julianna says, her expression pulled tight.

"Just like it's convenient for you not to listen," I snap back.

But yelling isn't getting us anywhere. I steeple my hands in front of my mouth, trying to calm myself down. When I feel like I can talk normally again, I say, "Believe me or not, I don't care. I know what's in my heart and it's not Preston. It's a woman that's stuck in an apartment with a narcissistic asshole who I don't know how to help."

Julianna's eyes flick over me. I can tell she doesn't believe me, but it seems like she's willing to hear me out. She takes a seat on the edge of the couch and pats the spot next to her.

Who knew Julianna was so bossy? Maybe Preston likes that about her.

After a moment's hesitation, I join her.

She takes a calming breath and wipes the tears from her face. "If I'm right, then Theo's isolating Sylvie so she can't talk to you. She probably doesn't even know he posted that video."

Strangely, I'm relieved to hear that. At least Sylvie isn't ignoring me. But I'm still furious. "Theo's a piece of shit," I say.

"I'm not totally sold that you're not.," Julianna gives me a fake smile.

"Can you drop the attitude for ten minutes?"

Julianna purses her lips. She doesn't like that.

"Do you care more about Sylvie than your streaming career?" she asks.

It was never my goal to make streaming my career. I have a regular nine-to-five to pay my bills. Would it have been cool? Yes. But my fame isn't worth losing

Sylvie. At this point, I'm waiting on a phone call from Paula saying I'm off the team anyway.

"She's my everything," I say.

Julianna nods. "Then I have an idea. And unfortunately, it involves him." She points to Preston.

He drops to his knees before us. "Anything. I'll do anything to show you how sorry I am. I know I messed up."

Julianna and I exchange a look. She may not believe me but at least we're both on the same page now.

Operation: Help Sylvie is on.

Chapter 40
Sylvie

I barely sleep Saturday night. Theo guides me to bed, and I balance on the edge of the mattress, as far away from him as I can get.

After I do manage to fall asleep, I'm forced awake by the *shing* of curtains being pushed aside. Sunshine bathes the room in an obnoxiously bright light so jarring, I almost fall out of bed.

I hear Theo shuffling around the room, leaving briefly. When he returns, he's carrying some of my clothing. "I think you'll look great in this."

I want to rip the saccharine grin off his face, like I want to shred those clothes he wants me to wear.

But I don't know the new rules. When Theo and I were together, there were unspoken rules and boundaries. I knew how to behave so Theo didn't get mad. Or, if he did, I knew what to say to placate him.

Those rules don't apply now with Theo holding this video over my head.

So I bite my tongue, put on a counterfeit smile, and say, "Thank you," as I pick up the clothes and go into the bathroom.

Dressing in jeans and a blouse is like putting on a straight jacket.

I move into the bathroom to do my business and wash my face. I'm brushing my teeth when two sharp knocks sound and the door is ripped open.

"I'm feeling eggs and sausage for breakfast. Then we need to go shopping. Make a grocery list. You know what I like to eat."

Pursing my lips, I give him a tight smile. His eyes narrow but he doesn't say anything before disappearing into the living room.

I'm beginning to understand his vision for our relationship. He doesn't want a partner; he wants someone he can order around according to his whims without objection.

After finishing in the bathroom, I go to the kitchen and pull out a frying pan and eggs. Out of habit, my hand reaches into my back pocket for my phone—a device that's not there. Because Theo took it, along with my laptop.

Normally, when I cook, I listen to music or a podcast. Prospero probably released an episode with his thoughts about the second Odyssey.

"Theo?"

"Yes, love?" he answers.

I throw up a little in the back of my mouth. "Can I have my phone to listen to a podcast while I cook?"

He considers me for a moment. "I don't want to listen to that piece of shit Prospero and his thoughts on the Odyssey. I'll put on some music for you." He turns on *his* favorite playlist—a mixture of heavy metal and rap, not what I want to listen to in the morning.

But what choice do I have? If I push back or make him angry, then he could release that video and Val's streaming career will be over. I can't have that black mark on my heart. So I'll do whatever I need to do to make sure I don't ruin Valentino's career while he's in the Odyssey.

When his sponsorship with BGN is done in December, I'll leave Theo for good. Even if Theo releases the video then, it will be old news, and hopefully, Val will have built up his reputation enough to survive the scandal.

He'll probably never want to see me again, though. Not that he's trying very hard to contact me. My phone, which Theo has out on his desk, hasn't rung.

You would think he'd be more insistent on getting ahold of his girlfriend, especially with his insecurities about being ghosted.

Maybe he's not up yet, I reason. He had a late night at the afterparty.

I finish cooking breakfast and serve it at the table. Theo rambles while we both eat. He leaves his dirty dishes for me to clean up.

At the grocery store, Theo keeps a hand on my lower back as we walk through the aisles together. We grab food to make all his favorite things. When we return to the apartment, he tasks me with putting everything away and making lunch.

I'm assembling a sandwich for him when I hear my phone ring. Theo looks at the screen, mumbles, "Go to hell," and rejects the call.

A message soon follows.

I don't ask who it is. By Theo's reaction, I know it's Val calling to check-in.

I expect him to call again after that rejection, but the phone remains silent.

What is he thinking? I don't know how long this deviceless sentence is going to last, but when it's over, I hope Val will let me explain what happened. That I couldn't text him back even if I wanted to.

That I'm trying to protect him.

The rest of the day passes similarly. I cook, clean, and watch Theo stream as I read a manga to pass the time.

I don't sleep well Sunday night either.

Monday after breakfast, Theo hands me my laptop and watches as I compose an email to Dr. Winters and my professor, asking for an exemption. I need to finish the rest of my course online. As soon as I hit send, he takes the laptop away.

He puts it on his desk right next to my phone. Doubt creeps back into my head,—into my heart. Val hasn't tried contacting me again. The voice tells me he's given up on me, that Val's better off without me.

My life is too complicated. I told him something like this could happen, but he didn't listen.

Around lunch, my phone rings again. The seed of hope in me waits to hear Theo curse, a sign that it's Val calling.

Instead, he looks at the phone, and swipes to answer the call. "Hello?... Who?... I've never heard of you. What do you want with her? You can just tell me. She's here, she's just busy." I can tell he's growing irritated with whoever is on the other end of the call.

After another pause, he huffs and says, "Fine."

He holds the phone out to me. I wipe my hand on a towel and bring him his sandwich. Sitting the food down on his desk, I take the phone.

"Put it on speaker," Theo demands. He shifts in his seat while staring at me.

He's acting weird, but I don't want to push him. I put the call on speakerphone.

"Hello?" I say.

"Sylvie Rivera?" a feminine voice asks.

"Speaking."

"Sylvie, this is Karen. I'm calling about your apartment application."

I swallow and school my features, not daring to look at Theo. He doesn't know that last week I put in an application to a shady studio apartment in the Umberwoods, near my internship.

That was before Theo could hold the threat of the video over my head.

I don't know what I'm going to do if I'm accepted.

"I'm listening," I say, hoping my voice isn't shaking.

"I'm sorry to inform you that we cannot accept your application at this time."

Any hope I had comes crashing down. My heart feels like it's going to cave in. I put my hand to my chest as I try to breathe. My eyes flick to Theo, who leans back in his chair, smirking. I'm stuck with him and he knows it. Every time I try to get away from him, something gets in my way. But I don't understand why they can't accept me. I submitted all their required financial documentation. Nothing was wrong with my application.

A knot forms in my stomach. "Can you tell me why?"

"Your credit report came back with some questionable history. Specifically, a credit card in default," Karen answers.

My brows furrow as Theo's eyes widen. Then he looks away, rubbing his jaw.

"But that's not possible. I don't have a credit card." My voice is tight and clipped. Karen may be on the phone, but I'm looking right at Theo, demanding the answer.

Theo reaches for the phone, but I back away out of his reach. I need to hear what Karen says next.

"According to your credit report, you do, Ms. Rivera," she says. "I suggest looking into it with the credit bureau if you think it's a mistake. But at this time, we cannot accept your application."

"Thank you," I say meekly.

"Best of luck Ms. Rivera." Karen hangs up the phone and Theo snatches it from my grasp again.

My mind falls into a daze as I spiral into a deep, dark abyss. Theo is in my face, trying to talk to me, but he's speaking Dothraki for all I understand.

I didn't take out a credit card in my name. Theo's the only other person with access to my personal information. I doubt my father or stepmother still remember my social security number. And Theo was strapped for money because he quit his job.

"You took out a credit card in my name, and then didn't pay it," I seethe.

I feel my fists clench as I stand toe to toe with Theo. Anger courses through me, my limbs shaking with all the pent-up energy. I want to throw something. I want to scream and shake something.

Theo freezes and it confirms my suspicions.

"You piece of shit," I growl at him.

Before the video, an apartment was supposed to be my way out.

New apartment.

Dream internship.

Fresh start.

All steps towards an improved Sylvie.

But this—a defaulted credit card in my name—means Theo tanked my credit. No apartment in the area will accept me. I'm fucked. I have nowhere else to live.

Recovering, Theo says, "That's crazy. Do you really think I'd do that to the woman I love?"

There was a time I thought Theo wouldn't do anything to hurt me. I thought he was my blonde knight, my Viking savior, coming to rescue me from my evil stepmother.

Now I know better.

"You're the one who quit your cozy job, you're the one who was strapped for cash when your streaming career wasn't taking off. You're the one who thought buying flashy new pieces for your gaming set-up would get you more viewers."

I rarely questioned how Theo spent his money. He'd get angry if I did. I should have seen that for what it was: a deflection, a distraction, so I didn't probe any further.

I see the anger flash on his face and I know I'm right.

"Admit it, you took a credit card out in my name—"

"I did what I had to do to support you!" Theo explodes in my face.

It's just like him to spin this back on me. Just like him to blow up in anger to scare me.

I'm not scared. I see Theo for the pathetic excuse of a human he is.

"You made a choice!" I yell back.

"Watch your tone with me," Theo growls.

I cross my arms over my chest and purse my lips. I'm not running away from him, I'm not backing down, but he still has the threat of the video over my head.

"My credit is fucked because of you," I say through gritted teeth.

"That's just temporary, baby. It can be fixed."

"Was that your justification?"

"You're the one trying to move away from me."

"Theo, I broke up with you. We're not good for each other. Why can't you see that?"

"Because we love each other!"

"This is your definition of love?" I ask incredulously. "Love means we support each other. But you shit all over my dreams and beat me down to make yours happen. You're trying to fit me into a box that I don't belong in, Theo."

"You're just trying to paint me as the bad guy."

"Good guys don't take out a credit card in their girlfriend's name and then not pay it."

"Glad you're calling yourself my girlfriend again," Theo says. Of course, that would be the thing that he grabs onto. Not the "you don't support my dreams" part.

"Why did you do it?"

"I don't have to answer your questions, Sylvie." Theo slumps back in his chair. "I'm done talking to you. Sit on the couch and read your picture book. Don't speak to me again unless you're in a better mood."

I know that tone. Theo's done talking and doesn't want to answer any more of my questions. He doesn't know what to do with me because I'm not running scared.

With nothing else to do, I turn my back on him, curling up in my spot on the couch as Theo sits down at his desk and fiddles with something on his computer.

We sit together in angry silence and I've never felt so hopeless in my life. Even after my mother died, I at least had my father and a family —in some capacity.

He's isolated me from my friends, family, and the outside world.

Now, there's only Theo.

Chapter 41
Valentino

Monday at eight-o-three in the morning, I'm sitting at my desk to start work, a cup of coffee steaming next to me, when my phone rings.

I've been expecting her call. But that doesn't make it any easier. It'd be so easy to not answer the phone. Ignore the consequences in hopes they'll go away.

I answer sullenly, "Hey Paula."

"Mr. Santos," Paula greets. I knew this call was coming, but that doesn't make it easier to hear. "I have some unfortunate news."

"I'm let go?"

"BGN feels like it is best to terminate your contract, yes," Paula says. "For damage to their reputation."

For violating the morality clause.

I can tell by the clipped way she speaks that she's unhappy about this decision. She's using third person, "They" instead of "We."

"Do they care at all about my side of the story?" I ask.

It's a long shot, but it's the only chip with which I have to bargain. I kept silent for a reason, and this is it right here.

Paula hesitates before answering. "No. BGN is not a gossip network. They don't care about the petty internet squabbles between influencers. "

Damnit. I have nothing else to say. "Okay. Thank you for the opportunity."

"BGN will release a statement soon, saying you parted ways on amicable terms."

Well, that was nice of them.

"I get it."

The line goes silent for a heartbeat. Two.

"Val?" Paula says.

"Yeah?"

"You only get to tell your side once. You get one chance to clear your name. Be selective in how you do it."

I have the feeling she's telling me this off the record. "Thanks. I'll consider that."

"I hope to work with you in the future, Mr. Santos. Goodbye." Paula hangs up without another word.

Leaning back in my chair, I let it spin around in circles as I stare at the ceiling.

People are still giving commentary, reactions, and opinions about the video days later. They're trying to get as many views, clicks, and likes as they can before the new hot topic of the week blows up.

I don't blame them for doing that. We're all trying to work the algorithms to score that one viral video.

My follower count dropped to below pre-Odyssey levels.

When you imagine your rise to fame, you never picture your fall. You don't imagine yourself in the middle of a scandal.

Not that I think being with Sylvie is scandalous. Sure, maybe making her come with my fingers in the car wasn't the best idea. But the way Theo's painted the tale, the way the gossip channels are inferring fallacies into an already twisted narrative, it's all wrong.

Of course, they don't know the complete story. They don't know how Theo treats Sylvie. They don't know she left him, that she was trying to get away from him. How hard she's studying in school while working almost full-time to save up enough money to leave.

Gods, how I miss her. I pick up my phone and pull up her contact information. I've thought about calling or texting her again and again. But there's no point. Julia told me Theo probably has her phone and is screening my calls.

I wonder what would happen if he picked up the phone. What would I say to him? I know it won't help Sylvie. Nothing good can come of a conversation between Theo and me.

It still blows my mind she was working for Julia this whole time. How did I not put that together? What a small world.

Preston and I haven't spoken since Sunday at his apartment. He groveled at our feet while Julia and I discussed how we can best support Sylvie. Julianna's idea was to use Preston's connection to Theo. I don't like that the plan depends on Preston, but he seems willing to do whatever it takes to get back into our good graces—even pretend to be Theo's friend.

Still, I want nothing to do with him. If he wants redemption, then he needs to make things right with Sylvie. I can look past what he did to me, but his actions left my girl in a vulnerable position. And that's not acceptable.

I pull up the text thread I started with Speed and Xander.

Valentino:

Got the call. BGN booted me.

Xander:

That sucks man. I'm sorry, Val.

Speed:

Their loss. Want to sue them?

That's a terrible idea, that contract was ironclad. But the thought makes me smile.

Xander:

They didn't want to hear your side of the story?

Valentino:

They weren't interested. Said they weren't a gossip channel.

Speed:

Fuck nuggets.

Valentino:

But she did tell me to be careful about how and with whom I share my side of the story.

Xander:

It's good advice. You get to control your narrative now.

Sure, but the issue is part of the narrative isn't my story to tell.

Speed:

What was Paula like on the phone?

Valentino:

She kept saying "BGN thinks" instead of "I think."

Speed:

Sounds like she was trying to make it clear it wasn't her sentiment.

Xander:

Maybe she was advocating for you and that's why it took so long for them to get back to you.

I didn't think of that.

Valentino:

She did end by saying she hopes we work together in the future.

Speed:

Sounds like she's making moves.

Xander:

Sounds like you need to get your narrative together and decide how you want to present your side to the world.

He's right. I just don't know how to do that yet. I could make a video from my own channel and watch the fire spread from there. Or I could contact one of the several channels that have reached out to me for an exclusive interview, using their channel and reach to go further than my channel could.

I don't know which one is the right answer.

Speed:

And Sylvie?

I told them what happened on Sunday at Preston's.

Valentino:

The pirate plan is in motion for Thursday.

Breathing a sigh of relief, I put my phone to the side. It's almost nine a.m. and my daily meeting is about to start.

I lose myself in work over the next four hours. It feels good to just be Val, the IT guy, instead of SaintVal the *Mundo* streamer.

At lunchtime, I reheat my meal and have a seat at the counter. I scroll through my notifications for the latest videos or posts I'm tagged in. Call me a masochist, but at least I'm feeling something.

Everyone has something to say about the scandal.

Everyone except for Prospero, I think.

Then pause, an idea forming in my head. Prospero usually isn't one for gossip, but they do value truth.

I move back to my computer where Annie has taken my warm seat. I lift her up and set her on my lap as I pull up SaintVal's email. Shifting through my old emails, I find Prospero's contact information from way back when they first emailed me.

The message I compose is simple: *I have yet to speak, but my truth is yours, if you'll have me.*

Five minutes later, Prospero responds: *I'm available whenever you need.*

After work, we video chat and I tell them everything—from the first swing of her battleaxes to the night she walked out of my life.

Chapter 42
Sylvie

Over the next three days, I cook every meal, deep clean the apartment, and do whatever else I can to distract myself so I don't have to interact with the bane of my existence.

To say things are tense between us is an understatement. But Theo doesn't like leaving me alone. He'll ignore me while I'm sitting next to him but demand to know where I'm going the moment I stand up. Anytime he needs to leave the house, I have to go with him.

The only time I get to myself is when either of us uses the bathroom.

My professor gave me a week's absence from classes, but to be excused from the rest of the semester I'll need to provide documentation.

Theo told me to drop out.

I've been neglecting to do that, arguing to at least finish the semester.

He monitors my computer use. Usually, he's playing some video game and while I work right next to him. Sometimes he has me in the background of his videos while I read through source material—something he's never done before.

He's like a child with a trophy.

I cringe at his commentary and the way he talks to his teammates and others. It's nothing like Val, who was calm and collected when I sat and watched him play the second Odyssey.

Tears pool behind my eyes as I think about Val. He must be so hurt that I ghosted him. Then I think about how he never called or texted again after that Sunday. That hurt more than I was expecting. Especially after we were being intimate with each other. I expected... I don't know, more effort to try to get in touch with me.

I conjured a scene in my head where he called and bitched out Theo—a scene that never came to pass.

My heart may be hurting, but I hope Val understands I did this to protect him.

Thursday during breakfast, Theo says, "I've invited a friend over to hang out tonight."

Theo rarely has friends over to the apartment. He usually meets them out somewhere.

At least he did when he wasn't policing my every shit.

After another bite Theo continues, "You'll wear something nice and cook us a good dinner."

Do I push back? No, this isn't the time. Better to appease the beast. "Is chicken alfredo still alright?"

"Are you making the sauce from scratch?"

I don't want to. Still, I nod my head.

"Good," he says shoving the rest of his egg sandwich into his mouth. "I'm going to edit some videos.

"May I take a shower?"

He appraises me while he finishes chewing. "Sure. Put on some makeup after. I'll pick out your outfit."

"Of course," I say with a fake smile.

I feel like I'm in a sitcom. One of the old ones where it seems like the husband and wife are dysfunctional and barely tolerate each other.

I clean up breakfast, do the dishes, and then head to the bathroom. Stripping off my clothes is like shedding this facade. It's like my skin can breathe again.

In the shower's solidarity, I review my escape plan. I'm going to go to a shelter. My backpack is now my go bag. Just the essentials: a toiletries bag with a change of clothes, my interview outfit, a sweatshirt, a blanket. I can go to the library and use their computers. I might even stop by 2Game to log in to *Mundo* so I can message my friends and let them know I'm okay.

All I need to do is to survive until after the last Odyssey.

I close my eyes as the warm water falls over my skin, remembering the way Val's hands felt on my body the night of the second Odyssey. How it felt when he ran his tongue along my center.

The way he filled me and commanded my body.

Twenty-three more days.

Two sharp knocks on the door remind me I've been in here too long for Theo's liking. "Clothes are on the bed," comes his muffled voice.

Returning to the bedroom, I see that Theo has laid out a sundress for me. It's one I used to wear to church. Cooking alfredo in a sundress, how very 1950s.

I change and go back into the bathroom to put on minimal makeup before going to sit in the living room with Theo. He's editing his videos at his desk.

"You could wear more make-up."

I give him my fake smile. "I was going for natural beauty so I don't sweat it off slaving over the stove."

His mouth pulls into a thin line, but he doesn't say anything.

It's a small win but I'll take it.

Our guest arrives at five o'clock sharp. Theo opens the door, greeting them with the standard bro shake and half hug before ushering them into the apartment. They walk into the living room, and if my jaw could drop to the floor, it would.

Preston is in my apartment.

As in Val's best friend, Preston.

Granted, he's dressed very casually in a hoodie and jeans, but what the fuck is he doing here? And how does he know Theo?

"Sylvie," Theo snaps his fingers. I stop dicing the garlic and remove my apron to go "meet" Theo's friend.

"Preston, this is my girlfriend," Theo puts his arm around me. I note how I'm his "girlfriend" not "Sylvie".

I stare at Preston, not knowing what to do. I already know him, but does Theo know I met him? Is this a type of test?

"Nice to meet you," he says, offering his hand.

He's greeting me like he doesn't know me. So Theo doesn't know we've met. That still doesn't tell me how Theo and Preston know each other.

"Same," I take his hand.

If Theo notices the tension between us, he doesn't say anything.

"Nice dress," Preston says.

"Thanks," I say. Then, with a venom-laced compliment, I say, "Theo picked it out. He has great tastes."

Theo grunts in agreement, placing a kiss on the side of my head. I school my features so as not to grimace as shivers run down my spine.

"Thanks for coming for dinner. My girl here is a great cook."

"I'm not one to turn down a home-cooked meal," Preston laughs. "I need to get myself a stay-at-home girlfriend."

Theo thinks that's the funniest thing in the world. "Dude, it's the best. I feel like a king."

Theo releases me with a swat on the butt. "Grab us some beers, okay?"

This time, I can't stop the face I make. Thankfully, Theo doesn't see, but Preston does. I give him a skeptical look as I fetch the alcohol for them.

They have a seat on the couch and I hear Theo ask, "So you've been dating Julianna Sinclair?"

Wait, that's my boss. Preston's been dating my boss? Valentino told me he was obsessed with this girl since high school.

I hand them the drinks as Preston answers, "We broke up."

Theo cracks the beer and tosses the cap on the coffee table. "She's a prude."

I have to bite my tongue to correct him.

"You know we used to fuck when we were in high school, right?" Theo says like it's a badge of honor. A notch on his bedpost.

I turn my back on them so they don't see my eyebrows furrow as I start putting this puzzle together. Theo and Julia dated in high school. Preston and Julia went to high school together. Does that mean all three of them went to the same high school?

It's hard to hear the rest of their conversation while I make dinner. Preston sits with his back to me and I don't want Theo to see that I'm trying to read his lips.

Half an hour later, I finish making dinner and serve the two boys at our small table. Theo pulls his fancy streaming chair over to the table while Preston and I take the two kitchen chairs.

Preston keeps trying to make eye contact with me like he's trying to pass along a message, but I can't figure out what it is.

I'm still reeling from the revelation that he knows Theo. Is that why he said I looked familiar? Did he remember me from Theo's social media?

As they eat, Preston exclaims how good the food is. I think he's laying it on thick, but Theo eats it up. Like it's him who did the work instead of me.

The two mostly ignore me. Theo reminisces about the good old high school days and asks if Preston knows what this or that person is up to.

When he's almost finished, Theo says, "Well that went right through me. Be right back, got to take a shit. Watch my girl for me." He pats Preston on the back and then walks back toward the bathroom.

There's a moment of silence as both of us watch Preston and wait for him to close the door.

"What are you doing here?" I whisper hiss at him.

"No time," he whispers. He reaches into the front pocket of his hoodie. "Take this."

He produces a burner phone and shoves it in my hand.

My first thought is that this is a trap, that Preston's in cahoots with Theo now. That this is another way for Theo to "test" my loyalty. "I don't want anything from you," I say, dropping the phone.

"It's from Julia."

I'm stunned.

Preston continues. "Her number and Val's are programmed into it. The passcode is ten, zero, six.

The day Val and I met.

"I can't—" At the sound of the toilet flush, I glance down the hallway.

Preston looks confused. "What do you mean?"

"He'll release the video—"

But then I think about how this could be my chance to talk to Julia and Val. To explain what happened.

I hear the bathroom door open. I need to make a decision.

My hands shake as I slip the phone into my apron pocket. My heart pounds with every heavy footfall Theo takes as he walks down the hallway. He's going to know, the voice tells me. No, he won't, I try to convince myself.

I bet the only reason Preston came over today was so he could give me the phone from Julia.

As Theo approaches, Preston stands and hands his plate to me. "Thanks again, Sylvie. The alfrado was great."

I take a breath, putting on my fake smile, and nod before taking the plate and turning toward the sink. I don't trust my voice right now not to shake. I turn on the water and try to focus on washing the plate. The phone practically burns a hole through my clothes.

He's going to know, my inner voice cries.

No, he's not.

"Hey, how about we play some *Obsidian* and you guest on my channel?" Theo says to Preston.

"Sure man, I'd love to. Your numbers have spiked recently."

"It's finally my turn," Theo states proudly. Then he turns to me. "Once you're done with that, go to your office and read a book or something quiet."

I smile and nod.

Theo goes back to whatever game he's playing with Preston. When I'm sure he's not paying attention to me, I slip the phone from my apron into my bra. Damn dress doesn't have any pockets.

It's a small smartphone, probably a pre-paid phone of some sort, and fits comfortably between my bra and boob.

I owe Julia so much.

Then, I grab the manga I was reading from the coffee table and head back to my office with my lifeline snuggled close to my chest.

Chapter 43
Sylvie

Retreating to my sanctuary, I settle into my daybed, and pull my favorite blanket around me. I keep the door open because Theo would find it suspicious if I closed it, but I keep the phone under the blanket to help block out any light. I turn on the phone and do my best to muffle the start-up sounds.

When the lock screen appears, I enter one, zero, zero, six.

The phone unlocks and I feel a weight lift from my chest as I breathe a sigh of relief.

The first thing I do is turn down the screen brightness and set the phone to silent. Next, I pull up the messages. There's already a text.

Julia:

> Sylvie, when you get this, please text me. This is a prepaid phone with one month of unlimited data. I've downloaded your banking app and others I thought you might need. She even texted the phone's number, so I have it.

With shaking hands, I respond.

Sylvie:

Julia, is this really you?

Julia:

OMG, he got you the phone.

Sylvie:

It was a deep covert espionage operation.

Julia:

Lol.

Julia:

Now tell me what's going on.

Sylvie:

Theo recorded Val and me messing around in a car. He threatened to release it unless I took him back and never talked to Val again.

Sylvie:

He also took my laptop and phone, so I haven't been able to text anyone.

Julia:

Wait, he's been holding the video over your head?

Sylvie:

Yes, and threatening to release it if I'm not his perfect girlfriend.

Julia:

Sylvie, the video's already out there. Val showed it to me.

I feel like I'm going to be sick. My head shakes and my hands tremble. I bury my mouth in my elbow to stop from screaming. I stay like that for, I don't know how long, trying to control my silent sobs.

For the past five days, I've suffered through Theo's every indulgence for nothing. The video's already out there.

For nothing.

The video is already out there.

But how? Did Theo release it on Monday after our fight? Did Val release the video? That makes no sense. It would negatively affect his career. He wouldn't do that to himself—to us.

Right?

It makes more sense for Theo to have posted it. But when?

Sylvie:

Who posted it? How long has it been out?

As I wait for her response, I wonder how Val could tell Julia about the video. They had only met once, briefly, at his first after-party. Maybe through Preston? The last I heard, Val and Preston weren't talking.

Julia:

Theo did on Saturday night.

Julia:

[link]

I click the link and open a video with a thumbnail of Theo's face. I don't play it, I can't risk the video making noise. Besides, I already know what's on it. Instead, I look at the time stamp. Saturday at eleven ten. The same day as the second Odyssey.

Theo posted it before I got home. Like a fool, I believed him. I close my eyes and clench the blanket in my hand. My body feels heavy, like I could collapse in the fetal position and stay there indefinitely. But I can't stay like this. I owe it to myself to act.

Sylvie:

What happened to Val?

Julia:

BGN released a statement and they parted ways.

I screw my eyes shut. Val must be devastated. He worked so hard for this. Having BGN as a sponsor was supposed to be his big break. Now he's probably getting dragged on the internet.

And it's all my fault.

Sylvie:

Has he released a statement?

Julia:

No, not yet.

I close my eyes and bite my bottom lip to keep from crying. My tears won't help him now. Apparently, I can't do anything to help him.

Sylvie:

I don't know what to say... or do.

Julia:

Can I add Vyola to this chat?

Sylvie:

How do you know Vyola?

Julia:

I'll explain in a moment.

How many people in my life are connected that I didn't know about?

Another text message pops up. This time it's a group chat with Julia, Vyola, and me.

Julia:

Operation Smugglers deployed.

Vyola:

OMG, the plan worked.

I stare at her message, unable to put the pieces together.

Sylvie:

You know Julia? How?

Vyola:

Yes. No. Kind of? Hold on to your tits. I thought she was joking at first.

There's so much mystery around this. Why are they dragging this on? Why can't they just tell me? Still, there's something familiar in the way Julia interacts with Vyola.

Julia:

Honey, I'm Sebastian.

Shut. The. Fuck. Up.

Julia is Sebastian, as in my best friend Sebastian. But I've known Sebastian for months. They're supposed to be my best friend. Why hide this from me?

I don't think my heart can take any more revelations tonight.

Sylvie:

Why didn't you tell us earlier?

Julia:

I should have. And I'm sorry I didn't.

Julia:

At first, I was protecting my brand. And I liked just being Sebastian. You ladies didn't treat me any differently.

I'm still salty she didn't tell me, but I can understand that. Even in the short time I've been working for Julia, I know she's protective of her brand and what little privacy she has. Being Sebastian allows her to slip off the influencer shoes and not worry about anything else.

Vyola:

I was freaking out when she told me.

Vyola:

Mind blown.

I'm kind of jealous Vyola knew before me.

Suddenly, I hear footsteps coming down the hall. I clutch the phone between my legs and pick up my manga. Theo sticks his head in the doorway.

I look up and give him my best smile, "How's it going?

"You being good?" he asks.

No. "I'm just reading." I give my manga a small jerk to emphasize my point.

He nods his head and then dips into the bathroom. I skim the pages of the manga while I wait to hear his retreating footsteps.

When I dare to look at the phone again, Julia fills Vyola in on my situation.

Vyola:

If I was in the state, I'd be busting down your apartment door.

She must be traveling for work again.

Sylvie:

Lol I love you girl.

I've known Vyola since we worked together in the coffee shop when I was nineteen. She's been my friend longer than I've been with Theo.

Sylvie:

Vy, can I come live with you? I could take care of your apartment while you're traveling.

And I can sleep on the couch when she's not there.

Vyola:

Absolutely.

Sylvie:

Are you serious?

Vyola:

Yes, I'm serious.

I could live a thousand years and not find someone as steadfast as Vyola Jones. It means so much that she would open her home to me. For a moment, the nasty voice in my head creeps in and says I don't deserve to have friends like them. This time, I silence it and change the narrative.

I deserve to have good things and loyal friends.

Julia:

Vyola, when do you come back?

Vyola:

Tuesday the 13th.

Julia:

I'll see if Preston can get Theo out of the house that day.

Julia:

If not, we'll think of something.

Vyola:

So we can swoop in and extract the treasure.

I want to cry, these women are amazing.

Julia:

Sylvie, can you hang on until then?

I've done six years with Theo. I've survived five days of trying to be his perfect girlfriend with the threat of the video hanging over me. There's no doubt I can survive the next few days knowing the video's already out there in the world.

Sylvie:

Absolutely.

I'm a survivor.

Vyola:

Alright, now run off and text that man of yours.

Briefly, I feel bad I didn't text Val first. But this conversation with the girls needed to happen. They've been my support system, even if I didn't know Julia was Sebastian. I feel like I have a direction and renewed hope in life. I'm going to get away from Theo. I'm going to fix my credit. And I'm going to graduate and start living my life for me, not anyone else.

Hopefully, Val will understand why I stopped talking to him. I was protecting him from Theo—or trying to.

I'm about to pull up his contact information when another text from Julia makes me pause.

Julia:

Before you do that...

My eyebrows pull together. What else do we have to talk about? Unless she has something else to tell me about Val.

Vyola:

Well that doesn't sound good.

Words taken right from my mouth. I don't know if my heart can take any more life-changing news.

Julia:

I have to tell you something.

Julia:

And I take no pleasure in saying this.

Just say it, I think to myself.

Julia:

But if the roles were reversed, I'd want someone to tell me.

That sounds ominous.

What could have possibly happened?

Julia:

I walked into Preston's apartment to find him and Val kissing. That's why we broke up.

My heart stops. I reread the text and forget how to breathe. I feel like my universe stops spinning. This has to be a joke. But what reason does Julia/Sebastian have to lie to me about this? She gains nothing.

Val kissed Preston. He told me he had been crushing on Preston for years.

My mind flashes back to us in the top level of Potions and Pages, where Val first told me about his history with Preston. And I told him that if he ever wanted to leave our complicated relationship to be with Preston, I would understand. My tears come and, this time, I do nothing to stop them from falling.

Theo released the video on Saturday night. I got one call and one text from Val on Sunday. My mind jumps to the most logical conclusion: He was calling to end things so he could be with Preston. Because I'm a liability to his career.

My heart squeezes and I shatter into a million tiny pieces. My whirlwind romance with Valentino Santos is over. And as my heart breaks, I know the truth—I love him. It wouldn't hurt this much otherwise.

Vyola:

That two-timing scoundrel.

Julia:

Val said he was an unwilling participant.

Julia:

But I know what I saw. And they were in full lip lock.

My heart can't take any more. I turn the phone off and slip the phone between the cushions. I don't bother hiding it. It doesn't matter—nothing matters anymore.

Chapter 44
Valentino

Thursday comes and goes with no text from Sylvie. If Preston had smuggled the phone to her, she should have texted me by now, right?

Since I don't have her phone number I send her a message on *Mundo*.

SaintVal: Hey Rhea, I miss you. Please let me know everything is alright.

I try to keep myself busy, but there's no response. Does she not want to send one or is Theo watching her so closely that she can't?

I try her social media.

SantVal:

Hey Rhea, please let me know if you're okay. I'm here for you.

I wake up Friday morning to no response. What is going on?

I float through my day on autopilot. I feel like a wraith, passing through work requirements, attached to my phone, hoping and praying she will text me.

Nothing.

Something's gone wrong. I can't think of any other explanation.

Being without her feels like a death sentence.

I did not realize how hard I had fallen for her Sylvie she was ripped away from me. Being exiled from the ones we love is like being separated from a part of ourselves.

My mind begins to catastrophize what all could have happened between then and now. Has Theo cut off all of her communication? Does she not want to speak to me? But why wouldn't she? Unless...

Did Julia tell her about Preston kissing me?

My notification pings. I pick up my phone, but instead of a text or missed call from Sylvie, there's another message on my social media.

WildKat wants to send you a message

Hmm, the gamertag looks familiar, but I don't recall anyone by that name.

Probably someone else reaching out asking to have me on their channel to talk about the scandal.

I open my social media app and then go into my pending messages.

WildKat:

Hello Valentino, my name is Kat from the Outlaws Odyssey team. We have a proposition for you. Please respond at your earliest convenience.

I remember Prospero talking about the Outlaws. So I know they are a legit Odyssey team. But is this WildKat a part of it?

To the internet.

My fingers fly over the keyboard as I search for the name.

The first results that pop up confirm that WildKat, or Kat, is a part of the Guildmaster's Odyssey group called The Outlaws. Through a haze of emotion, I remember Prospero praising the group for doing well in the second Odyssey.

Scrolling further down the results, her streaming channel comes up. I click on it and review her content. She started her streaming career by playing first-person shooters like *Call of Duty*. That's a tough space for women with all the misogyny. I can't imagine how many times she was asked to go make a sandwich by other players.

She did some RPG "Let's Plays" before she started streaming *Mundo*. Like me, being part of the Guildmaster's Odyssey seems to be the height of her career.

The next search results are some gossip articles about her with scathing headlines.

WildKat or Wild Mouth.

WildKat's wild temper strikes again.

Unmatched wit and will, WildKat's rise against misogyny

So she's temperamental. Crushed a few men's egos. Big deal.

The next article catches my eye. *Padua Gaming parts ways with two members on the Outlaws team despite the success of Second Odyssey.*

Somehow this story got buried among my scandal. Two of the Outlaws quietly left the team due to differences with another player. I bet that player is Kat.

My pulse quickens, because that means the Outlaws have an open spot on their Odyssey team. Is she contacting me because she wants me to join?

I pull up her message again.

SaintVal:

Hey Kat, thanks for reaching out. What's the proposition?

That doesn't sound too eager, does it?

I don't have to wait long for Kat to respond.

WildKat:

Thanks for getting back to me. I'll cut to the chase. Because of unfortunate circumstances, the Outlaws have two openings on our Odyssey team we need to fill. Would you be interested in filling one of them?

I jump out of my seat, scaring Annie from her spot lounging on the couch. I chase after her to give her apology pets.

"Can this be real?" I ask her. How lucky am I to get not one, but two offers to play in The Guildmaster's Odyssey?

So why don't I feel more excited?

Annie purrs and arches into my hand before returning to her spot on the couch.

I run my hand through my hair, unable to contain my smile. I'm still worried about Sylvie, but I know she'd be thrilled for me and this new opportunity.

Calm down Val, be cool, I tell myself, returning to my seat. This is my chance at redemption, but I have to know.

SaintVal:

Are you aware of why I was let go from BGN's team?

WildKat:

Yes. And if I'm being honest, I couldn't care less about some grainy videos of you in a car with a girl. If anything, it will bring more media attention to our team.

I wish more people had her mindset, even if she is brutally honest. Negative media attention is still attention, and my name has been in the gossip sites a lot. If she doesn't have an issue with me and my new reputation, then who am I to say no?

SaintVal:

Okay, I'm in. What do you need me to do?

WildKat:

We know your play style but we'd like to do a test stream next Tuesday, as a trial run.

Thank goodness they're okay with playing together before the next Odyssey. That's one rule I didn't like BGN imposing on my previous team.

SaintVal:

Sounds like a good time.

WildKat:

Fantastic.

SaintVal:

Do you have someone else in mind for the last spot?

WildKat:

My teammate, Mia or TinyTitan, is reaching out to a couple of people but there are no takers.

Probably because they don't want to work with Kat.

I know one person who would be up for the challenge. But before I make the recommendation I shoot off a text to him.

Valentino:

Hey, you doing anything next Tuesday?

Speed:

I could be, depending on your offer.

Valentino:

An audition to play in The Guildmaster's Odyssey.

Speed:

Are you serious?

Speed:

Fuck yeah.

Valentino:

Possibly. I'm going to throw your name out there.

Speed:

You're the best.

In truth, he *is* the best. Speed's been there for me in a way Preston hasn't been. And he's never asked me for anything in return. So if I can get him this opportunity to play in something like The Guildmaster's Odyssey, I'll do it.

I switch back to my conversation with Kat.

WildKat:

Why do you ask?

SaintVal:

My friend, Speed is free and willing to play. We've got good synergy together.

I stare at my phone as I wait for Kat to respond.

WildKat:

What does he play?

SaintVal:

Half-demon illusionist rogue.

WildKat:

A support character, that's fine with me.

Well, that didn't take much negotiating.

WildKat:

Here's my number. Text me your details and I'll get everything set up. I'm looking forward to playing with you both.

I pull up Speed's text to see a message waiting.

Speed:

Well?

Valentino:

You're in!

Speed:

Valentino Santos, you are the literal best.

Valentino:

No, you're the best. Thanks for everything man.

I set my phone down and lean back in my chair. While I still haven't heard from Sylvie, my heart feels slightly lighter. Like I'm almost through the storm and starting to emerge on the other side. I have another chance.

Now, time to find Sylvie. Maybe if I drive around her campus I'll see her.

Chapter 45
Sylvie

When Tuesday comes, I make my favorite french toast breakfast with fresh strawberries. I'm celebrating. Today is the day I leave forever.

I've survived.

It helped knowing I could push back against Theo. I knew his threats were empty. He has nothing to hold over me anymore.

After I sit down to eat, Theo appears, grumbling something about too many carbs as he makes a plate and sits down at the table. He takes a bite, then says, "I'm going to help my parents with a few things later today."

Sure you are, I think. The truth is he's planning on having dinner with Julia at a new restaurant over forty-five minutes from the apartment. I'm hoping that will give us at least two hours to get my stuff out before he returns.

But I still have a couple of hours left, and I can't give Theo any indication that something is off.

I finish chewing. "Okay, when are we leaving?"

"You're staying here," he answers, a little too quickly.

It's funny how he can go have dinner with his ex and doesn't consider it cheating, but wouldn't accept that I broke up with him.

I fight myself from smiling. Schooling my features, I play along like I have no idea he's planning on meeting up with Julia. Keeping my eyes downcast I ask, "Oh, did I do something wrong?"

"No, it's just family business." Another lie.

I nod like I believe him.

"I'm leaving your cell phone here." He puts the phone on the table in front of him. "Do I have to remind you of the rules?"

"Contact you in an emergency or 911. No social media. No *Mundo*," I recite.

"That's my girl," Theo says. "I'll check it when I get back."

He can try. But I won't be here.

We finish our food in silence, and Theo goes about his business playing games and editing videos.

The following hours pass incredibly slowly. It's like I'm watching grains of sand fall from an hourglass, or waiting for flowers to wilt. I keep to myself and don't say much. I'm afraid that if I say something he'll see through me, somehow read my mind, find out the plan, and stop me.

My eyes skim the pages of a manga but I don't comprehend the words. Instead, I focus on my breathing and steadying keeping my shaking hands.

"Alright," he says around dinner time. He gets up from his desk and moves toward the door. This is it.

He slips on his jacket, then shoes. "You're leaving now?" I ask, hoping I don't sound too excited.

"Yeah, don't want to keep the ball and chain waiting," Theo says, referring to his mother.

Great way to describe the human who funds your entire lifestyle.

"When will you be back?" I ask.

"A few hours."

I nod. "Try to have fun."

He comes over to kiss me on my head. "Be my good little girlfriend."

"Of course." I fake a smile, knowing it will be the last one I ever give him.

Then Theo walks out the door—and out of my life.

Closing my eyes, I count to ten. I don't want to move too fast, in case he comes back to the apartment because he forgot something or changed his mind.

When he doesn't return, I break out into a fit of laughter and tears.

I'm free.

Finally free.

I feel like I'm floating as I move down the hallway to the spare bedroom, retrieving the burner phone from its hiding place in a shoe in the closet.

When the phone turns on, I get a notification that I have waiting messages from Vyola and Julia.

Vyola:

The house is cleaned and ready to go.

Julia:

Theo confirmed he's on his way.

Maybe I should be hurt by the fact he left me, his perfect girlfriend, to have dinner with Julia—his ex-girlfriend. But I'm past caring at this point.

He's no better than the scum on the bottom of my shoe.

Plus, she won't be there. So he'll suffer the embarrassment of being stood up.

Sylvie:

He just left.

Vyola:

Alright, leaving my house in 5.

Warmth fills my chest and I can't stop smiling. I'm getting out today because of the support of these two amazing women.

Now, time to get ready to leave. Theo might have a forty-five-minute commute there and back, but there's no way for us to predict how long it will take him to figure out that he's been stood up. We only have a guaranteed hour and a half. I have to be out of here by then.

My first step is to get contacts from my other phone. Burner phone in hand, I walk back to the kitchen and unlock the old phone. I copy my father's number and my half-siblings'.

I'm staring at the single page of contacts in my phone when it truly hits me how much Theo has isolated me. I knew my circle was small, but to see it whittled down to half a dozen people is disheartening.

When was the last time I talked to my family?

On a whim, I send a text to Dad and my siblings, Mason, and Randy.

Sylvie:

Hey, this is Sylvie. New phone. I'm leaving Theo.

Nobody responds immediately, but I don't expect them to.

Next, I go to the kitchen to grab some trash bags. My burner phone pings.

Vyola:

I'm on my way.

Julia:

Same!

It will take them a little bit to get here and I don't want to pack in silence. I tap the virtual assistant on the phone and say, "Play Prospero's latest podcast."

They have to have some commentary on the second Odyssey by now.

"Playing Isle of Insights," it says.

I'm walking back to my office as the familiar intro music plays and Prospero's synthesized voice says, "Today's episode of *Tempest Loading* goes off the charted path. SaintVal is back to break his silence and speak his truth."

My body freezes in the middle of removing a shirt from the hanger.

Prospero said Val's breaking his silence. It's been over a week since the video was released. I find it hard to believe that Val wouldn't have said anything, not even defended himself during that time. But the way Prospero is framing the conversation says otherwise.

"Well Val," Prospero says. "When I imagined talking to you again, I didn't think it'd be about a scandal."

Val gives a small laugh. "You and me both."

The sound is full and deep. I miss his laugh. The way his face lights up. How his smile seems to touch both his ears. It's hard going from talking to someone every day to being completely cut off from them.

I close my eyes and see an image of Val and Preston kissing. Julia said that Val claimed the kiss wasn't mutual, and that he didn't want it. My mind doesn't know how to process that. Because how could it not be mutual? Preston is better for Val than me.

I look at the time, only fifteen minutes have passed since Theo left. I shake my head, I think I have to keep moving. I stuff things in my

Prospero continues, "You haven't publicly shared your side of what happened yet. Why is that?"

"I'm afraid for her," Val says.

"The girl in the video?"

"Yeah, she's my girlfriend. Or at least, I hope she still is." I feel my cheeks flush.

I keep listening as I methodically remove my clothes from their hangers and shove them in the bag.

"That seems like a loaded statement," Prospero says. "But first, how can we refer to her?"

"I call her Rhea."

My heart tugs at the nickname. At the memory of the man who lit my soul on fire.

"That works. Let's start from the beginning. Is that you in the car?" Prospero asks.

"It is, but that's not the beginning of our story," Val corrects.

"Okay, when did this all start?"

I move on to the second bag as Val continues the story, detailing how we met during the *Mundo* update. "She has an exceptional build and went through the archeology talent to get Starwrath," Val praises.

I can't help but smile. That was how we first connected, over Celestina's build.

"Few people do that," Prospero notes.

Does Prospero sound impressed?

Val goes on to explain how we played *Mundo* together, and how through some social stalking, he figured out that we live in the same city.

"And was she in a relationship?" Prospero clarifies.

"At that time, yes," Val admits. "Theo, the guy who posted the first video, is very controlling. He doesn't like her talking to strangers, and he's manipulating her with money."

"So, financial abuse?" Prospero asks.

"Yes."

I stop packing my third bag to reflect on those words. I've never considered what Theo was doing to me—manipulating me with money as a form of abuse. But it makes sense the more I think about it. Somehow it makes me feel both better and worse.

A new wave of rage toward Theo swirls inside me.

Then I hear Val's voice again. "But Rhea gathered the strength to break up with him all on her own."

That's right. I did. I decided that I loved myself more than I loved Theo and I broke up with him.

I look over to the daybed, my safe space. I wish I could take it with me, but Theo bought it and would fight me for it.

Instead, I take my favorite blanket and fold it up before shoving it in a bag too.

Val continues to explain our first time meeting in person. "The night of the first Odyssey, we meet up at a neutral location."

"The park?" Prospero asks.

"Yeah," Val says. "It kinda became our place, you know? Anyway, I was stunned."

I have to bite my lips to keep from crying.

I get a text message shortly followed by a sharp knock on the door.

Vyola:

I'm here.

"Pause," I tell the virtual assistant.

I take a deep breath as I walk to the front door—trying to pull myself together. I don't want Vyola to see me holding back tears and think something bad happened.

Opening the door, I see Vyola standing there in athleisure wear and a bright smile.

"Hey girl," Vyola says. Then she sees my face and immediately wraps me up in a hug. "What's wrong Sylvie? You're not having second thoughts are you?"

The moment I'm in her arms the tears come. I do my best to shake my head and blubber out a "no."

"What's wrong?"

It takes me another couple of breaths to calm myself before I can manage to say, "Play podcast."

Prospero continues, "What was this first meeting like?"

"We were nervous, but we sat on the swings together and talked. I had only ever heard her voice before, so it was jarring trying to get used to seeing the human behind the voice."

"And Rhea had broken up with Theo at this point."

"Yes," Val states.

"You didn't kiss her?"

"The biggest regret of my life."

"When did you two start dating?"

"Soon after," Val answers. "Although I didn't ask her to be my girlfriend until closer to the second Odyssey."

"Pause," Vyola says and the podcast stops.

"Did you know?" I ask her, eyes hopeful that she would have told me.

"It just came out," Vyola said. "I was going to show you later when you were settled in."

She's right about that. I feel so emotionally drained right now.

"We have an hour to finish packing your things," Vyola says. "Do you want to keep listening to it?"

I know I'll be an emotional wreck but I don't think I could stop now. "Yes," I say.

Vyola grabs a bag and hands it to me, "Why don't you pack up your shoes."

They move on to talk about the video. Val was very careful when he talked about my living situation. "Going to her place wasn't an option, and she wasn't comfortable going to mine yet."

Val always went out of his way to accommodate me and make me feel comfortable. It's one of the things I love about him.

"Props to you Val, you're a good guy."

He really is. I've never met a man so patient and kind.

"It seems like the car was about as private as you could get at the moment," Prospero says.

"At the time? Yes." Then Val admits, "Now, I understand that was a bad decision."

"Did you have any idea you were being filmed?"

"No." Val firmly states. "I was focused on my connection with Rhea."

I can hear the blush in his tone. Looking at Vyola, I see her giving me the side eye and a smirk.

"Did you have any idea Theo would release a video and the footage?" Prospero asks.

"No. But Rhea was very conscious about her situation and how it could reflect on me. Rhea was afraid that someone would find out about her relationship with her ex, and then spin up a story that would paint me in a negative light and cause me to lose my sponsorship."

"Would it be fair to say that Theo is pushing a false narrative?" Prospero asks.

"I think that's a nice way of putting it," Val says.

"Well Val, I think we've captured your side of this story. Is there anything else you'd like to say to us or anyone listening?"

I stand still, waiting for his response. "Rhea, I love you, and I'm not giving up."

Sitting back, I put my hand over my heart and close my eyes. He's been waiting for me all this time and I thought he had moved on.

Vyola puts her hand on my back. "What are you thinking?" she asks.

"That I miss him," I say, the tears threatening to fall again. I'm grateful to be on the floor.

"Honey," she says sitting next to me. "You're obviously still on his mind. Have you texted him yet?"

I shake my head.

"Do you want to?"

Yes. My heart wants to connect with him again. It wanted to before, but my mind convinced me otherwise. I don't know everything that happened with that kiss, but Val still wants me.

I nod.

"Then text him," Vyola says. "But we do need to get moving. We have forty-five minutes"

She's right. I pull out my phone and text Val,

Sylvie:

It's Rhea. I don't want to give up on us either.

Then I put my phone away and get back to packing.

Chapter 46
Valentino

Days have passed since I spoke to Prospero and I feel like I'm going out of my mind waiting for Sylvie to text me back. I'm a desperate man and I don't know what else to do as I repeatedly check my phone, hoping for something, —*anything*, from her. I even resort to driving to her campus to see if she's there.

My work has been suffering. I'm not creating content. I haven't streamed. And I still haven't played *Mundo*.

Tuesday comes and I do my best to dive into work, trying to keep my brain distracted. I don't want to think about playing with The Outlaws in a matter of hours, or how Prospero released my episode.

Am I ever going to hear from Sylvie again? I'm more certain now that Julia told her about the kiss with Preston and I can't reach her to defend myself.

When five o'clock rolls around I let out a sigh. I heave myself from my desk and trudge to the kitchen to feed Annie who is patiently waiting by her bowl. She nudges my calves with her head and I reach down to give her a few scratches.

Five minutes later, there's a knock at my door. Annie briefly lifts her head in curiosity before returning to her bowl.

When I open the door, Speed struts in like he lives here. Backpack and all.

"Ready to do this?" he asks, excitement in his voice.

I wish I could match his energy.

"Hell yeah," I say, but it's forced.

It feels good to have Speed here doing this with me. Not that I regret playing with Bastian, Dominic, and Cameron. They're good guys. But playing *Mundo* with one of my best friends feels like my life is finding equilibrium again.

I'm still playing with two new people, and that's fine. I've been researching WildKat and TinyTitan.

Speed flops down on the couch, pulling his backpack around. "So what do you think of our possible future teammates?"

"TinyTitan, Mia, seems cool."

"I believe the word you're looking for is stubborn," Speed says between bites of pizza.

I wouldn't go that far. From what I've seen, Mia digs her heels in when she thinks the team should do something, but she's not unreasonable.

"Not in comparison to Kat," I say.

Speed's face lights up at the mention of our fourth teammate. I catch the sparkle of mischief in his eyes. "Now she's a spitfire."

He almost looks too excited. Speed likes a challenge, and Kat—at least from the videos I've watched—is easily provoked.

"What are you planning?" I ask, my eyes narrowing at him. I don't need him causing trouble. This is my last shot at getting back in the Odyssey.

"Are you suggesting that I," Speed dramatically places a hand on his heart, "would cause issues?"

"Yes." I deadpan.

"Slander!"

"Then why don't I believe you?" I look at him skeptically.

Speed shrugs and finishes his slice of pizza. "You've got trust issues."

I shake my head. "Just set up and get ready to play."

Speed smiles again, brown eyes still sparkling. He fetches his backpack and pulls out his laptop, headset, and a stand. He sets both up on the coffee table. He won't be streaming with us; he's just playing.

I return to my computer and go through the motions of getting my stream ready. Sliding on my headphones, I log into *Mundo* and start my stream. There are already subscribers waiting for me. My total number of subscribers has fallen drastically since the whole ordeal, but seeing viewers still waiting for me warms my heart.

I put on my SaintVal mask. "Hey Saints, thanks for joining me tonight. I have Speed with me and we'll be playing some *Mundo* with WildKat and TinyTitan from The Outlaw's team."

The chat fills with emotes of swords for Valen and a purple sparkly lute for Nix, Speed's bard. Then the questions about Rhea start.

Have you heard from Rhea?

Theo's an □.

Justice for Rhea!

They must have listened to Prospero's latest episode. But I can't think about Sylvie too much or I'll get distracted.

After all the vitriol I experienced following Theo's video, I didn't expect the overflow of warmth. I mean... I hoped for it. But actually seeing it feels different.

I can't help but smile as I say, "I know everyone has dozens of questions for me, especially if you listened to Prospero's latest episode. But today's stream is about collaborating with new friends. So those questions will have to wait. Ready Speed?"

I look at my friend set up on the couch, his headphones on. "Whenever you are."

"Then let's get questing," I say and launch *Mundo*.

Valen and Nix load into the Junta faction tavern. "We're meeting up with WildKat and TinyTitan outside of Anorev," I move Valen out of the tavern and travel towards the city gates. Nix follows close behind.

That's when I get two notifications.

WildKat wants to join your party.

TinyTitan wants to join your party.

I accept both invitations and find the two avatars waiting for us just outside the gates.

Video windows for both women pop up on my screen. Kat's warm, reddish-brown hair is pulled back in a braid and she wears dark makeup to highlight her striking features and olive-toned skin. Her avatar is Reyna, a warrior human using a sword and shield. She's a tank—her character is built to take hits and keep swinging.

On the other screen is Mia, or TinyTitan. Her long, dark hair is styled in waves framing her oval face and almond-shaped, bright brown eyes glow with excitement. She plays Elyndra, an elven cleric and healer-type character.

"Good evening *ladies*," Speed says. I can't help but roll my eyes at the emphasis he puts on the word.

"Thanks for joining us. Ready to get adventuring?" Kat asks, completely ignoring Speed. As she speaks I notice there is a small gap between her upper two front teeth.

I flick my eyes up to his video window to see my friend biting his lip. He doesn't like being ignored.

"We're excited to be playing with you today," Mia's tone is lighter than her counterpart's.

"Same, What did you—"

Suddenly, there's a sharp knock at my door. "Val, open up!" I recognize Xander's muffled voice.

Off-screen Speed and I make eye contact for a moment, then I nod. He removes his headphones, gets up, and scrambles across the room to open the door.

"What's going on?" Kat asks.

"One of our friends is knocking at the door," I explain. "Sorry for the interruption. I'm sure this will only take a moment."

"It better," Kat grumbles.

"Kat," Mia says, a warning in her tone. Then she adds, "I hope everything's okay."

Speed opens the door and Xander walks in, Pixel at his side.

And Preston is behind him.

Anger flares in my veins. Whatever this is, it's not going to take a few minutes. Staring at Preston I say to my stream, "I'm going to need to take a five-minute break. Thanks for understanding."

Then I pause my stream. Unplugging my headphones, I stand up, and approach Preston, "What the fuck are you doing in my house?"

If he didn't kiss me, if Julia hadn't seen it, I might be talking to Sylvie right now.

"Who's in your house?" I hear Mia ask. My stream may be paused but Kat and Mia are still on the group call. "It's not Theo is it?"

Thankfully it's not Theo, but I don't know if Preston interrupting my stream is any better. I grab the front of his shirt.

Preston holds his hands out to the side, "Val, I know you're still mad. But you need to listen. Julia texted. They're moving Sylvie right now. Do you want to help her?"

The anger I felt building in my chest stops and my body goes rigid. He said the only thing that could keep me from blowing up at him.

"Sylvie," I repeat, letting go of his shirt. I could see her. He knows where she is right now.

Preston nods.

My eyes go wide and I feel my heart in my throat. Of course I want to help her. Even if it's just to see she's okay before she sends me away. But leaving now means abandoning Speed, Kat, and Mia. Leaving means giving up on my last shot at finishing the Odyssey.

"Who's Sylvie?" I hear Kat ask.

Speed answers, "Rhea."

"Wait, Rhea as in your hopefully-still-girlfriend?" Mia asks, intrigued. She must have listened to the podcast.

"Yes," I say, still trying to process my options.

"What do you want to do?" Xander prompts.

"Val you need to make a choice. Either go get your girl or play with us to see if our styles mess well for The Third Guildmasters Odyssey." Kat says.

"No need to get jealous little dove, this is important," Speed says.

"Do. Not. Call. Me. Little. Dove," Kat snaps at Speed, but it sounds like a threat of bodily harm.

"Enough you two," Mia snaps. "Val, if Rhea needs you then you, should go to her."

"Make your choice Val?" Kat asks.

"Do you always take this attitude toward love?" Speed asks.

"Val," Preston prompts again. "Do you want to go?"

I have a choice to make: Show up for Rhea or my streaming career.

Except it's not really a choice at all. Sure this is a second-in-a-lifetime opportunity, but Sylvie is my future.

"I have to go to her."

"Then get moving," Xander says, then he takes my place at my desk.

"Mia, Kat, this is Xander. I'll be subbing in for Val while he goes to get his girl."

I can't hear what they say in response, but Pixel lays her head in Xander's lap and he absently pets her. He starts the stream up again. "Good evening Saints, this is PixelatedStone filling in for SaintVal while he goes to get his girl. We're going to do some questing with our new friends today and I'll tell you everything I know about this love story."

Well, I guess my subscribers will get what they want after all. No idea how that's going to go. I've never had someone take over my stream before.

But I'm going to get my girl and I don't regret it.

I give Xander a fist bump off camera and mouth "thank you" as I turn on my heels to face Preston.

"Do you know where she lives?" I ask.

Preston nods. "I'll text you the address."

This must be his way of apologizing, by trying to help get us back together.

I'm about to walk out the door when I get a text message from an unknown number.

Unknown:

It's Rhea. I don't want to give up on us either.

I almost fall over. That's the line I said on Prospero's podcast, when he asked me if there was anything else I wanted to say.

She listened to it.

Valentino:

I'm here for you.

Hold on Rhea, I think. Then I walk out my apartment door.

Chapter 47
Sylvie

I was thirteen years old when my mother died. I clearly remember packing up my life with the things I would bring to my dad's house. My entire life was condensed into two rolling suitcases and a backpack.

Now, at twenty-five, I'm stuffing my life into garbage bags and leaving behind the last six years of my life. There has to be a metaphor for that.

Vyola picks up a bag and carries it out the door. Julia does the same but pauses in the doorway. "Hey, Sylvie."

"Yeah?" I say as I look around the living room.

There are so many things I'm leaving behind. Things with memories attached to them that won't serve me in my next steps of life. And things I can't take with me or Theo would pitch a fit. He still might be pissed that I took things that are clearly mine, like my blanket. At this point, I feel numb.

"Hey," Julia puts her hand on my shoulder. "Everything okay?"

Oh, she said something to me. I must have missed it. "It's just a lot," I say. I don't know how I'm supposed to feel.

I'm lamenting leaving a place I called home. I'm saying goodbye to the good times I had and the love I shared with Theo once upon a time. I wish I could take my daybed and other little comforts. But I'm also angry with myself for letting the abuse go on for as long as it did, for not reaching out to my support system sooner.

And I long for Val to hold me on the third floor of Potions and Pages again.

Julia embraces me and I cling to her, crying for what feels like the thousandth time in the past hour.

"You're not second-guessing leaving are you?" Julia asks, letting me go.

I shake my head. I'm absolutely leaving. There's nothing left in this relationship for me anymore.

"How about you do one last sweep of the house, and then there's a surprise for you outside," Julia says.

I don't know if I can take any more surprises today, but I trust Julia.

I walk through the apartment one last time, looking in all the nooks where I stored my things, drifting through the spaces that kept me safe.

When I get back to the living room, Julia isn't there. She must have gone outside, taking the last bag of stuff with her. The only thing that remains is my emergency backpack. I swing it over my shoulder, the weight feeling heavier than usual, then I turn to head out the door.

Right before I close it, my old phone buzzes. Curiosity damn me, but I'm compelled to take a look.

Theo:

On my way home.

Fear spikes, but I remember that he's still a bit away—or at least I hope so. Besides, at this point, all my stuff is out of the house, and my friends are here to back me up. I'm leaving and nothing can stop me. There's nothing more he can do to me.

I'll have to change important account passwords when I get to Vyola's house. And I'll have to do something about the credit card fraud too. But right now, all I have to do is leave this place.

I walk out into the fading light of the evening sun, closing the apartment door behind me for the last time.

I wonder what the surprise is that Julia mentioned. I hope it's pizza. I don't want to cook tonight.

With a new lightness in my step, I take the stairs down to street level where four cars are parked in front of the complex. For a brief moment, I panic thinking one might belong Theo, but none of the cars are his. Julia, Vyola, and Preston—of all people—stand by one car. Is Preston the surprise? I do owe him a thank you for smuggling me the phone.

But then my eyes drift to the fourth figure, leaning against his car. He's dressed in a tight-fitting *Mundo* t-shirt and dark-washed jeans. He smiles at me, face beaming like the sun.

And the way he looks at me, like he cannot believe I'm real, takes my breath away.

"Hey Rhea," Val says, taking a step forward.

Val.

He's here.

My heart swells and my body begins to shake. I drop the backpack and run to him, throwing my arms around his torso. Val pulls me close, enclosing us into a space that is solely our own.

"You're here," I say into his chest—his heart.

"I'm here," he echoes.

Then his hand cups my jaw, tilting my head up to his.

Val captures my mouth and kisses me deeply, unhurriedly, but still scorchingly hot. He takes his time, drinking from me like we have all the time in the world.

I'm breathless when we pull away from each other.

"How did you know?" I ask.

Val glances up and over at Preston who is looking down at the ground, my backpack in his hand.

I hold onto Val's hand as we walk over to Preston. I don't want to let him go.

"Thank you," I say.

"It's the least I could do," Preston says. "You two belong together."

"Guys, we may have a problem," Vyola says right as a car flies around the corner and parks behind Val.

It's Theo.

He throws open the door and storms towards me. "Sylvie," he yells. "What the fuck do your think you're doing?"

But Val steps between us, stopping Theo from advancing any closer to me.

"Just walk away man," Val says, his voice calm and neutral. "Don't make a scene."

"I'm filming you asshole," Vyola says, holding her phone up.

"Get the fuck off my property," Theo snarls, even though it's his parents' property, not his. And we're standing on a public sidewalk.

Theo's doing his best to intimidate Val. I worry for a moment, he's taller by an inch or two, but Val doesn't seem afraid in the slightest. He crosses his arms and plants his feet firmly between us.

I have to stop this now.

"It's over, Theo," I say. "I'm leaving."

"Hi Theodore," Julia chooses that moment to speak up. His head snaps in her direction. She smiles and waves at him.

I see when our plan clicks in his head. "You set me up," he hisses.

"Yes. And you're the sad boy who left his perfect girlfriend to meet another woman for dinner."

"How do you even know her?" Theo turns to ask me.

"*Mundo,*" Julia and I say at the same time, then exchange a small smile.

Julia continues, "I couldn't sit back and watch you destroy another woman the way you did to me."

All the pieces fall into place. Julia said she had dated Theo in high school, and she also had a controlling ex. Theo was that boyfriend.

"You bitch," Theo steps threateningly towards Julia. She pulls out pepper spray, aiming it at him and Preston takes a step forward.

"I dare you to try something," Vyola says, phone still in her hand, filming.

Preston shakes his head. "Just go to your apartment, man."

"Not unless Sylvie comes with me," Theo says.

"That's not going to happen," I state firmly, squaring my shoulders.

Theo turns to glare at me. "I'll release the video—"

"You already did," Val says from beside me.

"Your phone," Theo tries—grasping for any control he has over me.

"It's inside waiting for you," I say.

I can see his brain turning, trying to find a way, anyway he can control me. "Sylvie you have three seconds," Theo orders me like I'm a dog who needs to come to heel.

"Or what, Theo?" I challenge. "What are you going to do? Freeze my bank account?" I take a step forward, Val still at my back, holding my hand. I appreciate the four of them being here, but I don't need them speaking for me.

"I am leaving you, Theo," I say again, definitively. "My things are packed. I'm moving out. And I will never speak to you again unless it's in court."

"Excuse me?" Theo asks, incredulously.

"You think you can take a credit card out in my name, destroy my credit, and get away with it?"

Val squeezes my hand. He's letting me speak, but is still right there, supporting me.

"You're throwing away everything we have together, everything we've built, for what?" Theo gestures towards Val, "For him?"

"No," I shake my head. "Theo, you threw away our love. Our story was over long before either of us realized it. You're not happy. I'm not happy. And I'm starting a new story."

I look back at Valentino. "My story."

Val smiles.

"Let's get out of here," I say.

Val nods and puts his hand on the small of my back as he leads me to his car and opens the door for me.

Theo shouts something incoherent but I don't care.

Val slips in the driver seat and takes my hand, placing a kiss on the back of it. "You did great. I'm so proud of you."

"Yeah, well, I'm shaking."

"That's okay," he says. "You're still one of the strongest people I know."

I relax into the seat with our hands intertwined, and together we drive off to start my new life.

Chapter 48
Sylvie

Five people is a lot for Vyola's one-bedroom apartment, but the extra hands are helpful with bringing my things up three flights of stairs.

When everything is in the apartment, Julia asks, "Anyone have objections to pizza?"

I shake my head, no objections here. "With extra cheese?"

"Done," Val says. Julia goes to get her purse, presumably to get some money, but Val holds up his hand. I got this." He then turns to Preston, "Let's get the ladies some food."

I catch Preston's gaze lingering on Julia, who has her back turned to him. "Alright."

When the boys leave, Vyola puts her arm around me. "Welcome home, roomie!" she says. "Let me give you a tour."

The space is self-explanatory, but Vyola takes me through it anyway. The kitchen is small and there's a U-shaped counter and bar stools for the dining area. Vyola has a couch—my bed—TV, a coffee table, and a desk against the wall shared with the bedroom and a single bathroom.

"And this is the closet," Vyola slides open one of the doors revealing an empty space. Two people could fit inside with the door closed. And she's doubled the racks to have more hanger space.

I start to tear up and throw my arms around my friend. She made room for my things. "Thank you."

"You're welcome."

Collecting myself I pull away from her and return to the living room to fetch a bag of clothing.

Julia sits on the couch with my backpack. "We should change your passwords," she reminds me.

Oh, yeah I should probably do that before Theo hacks into something.

I turn back to Vyola, "Can you start hanging stuff up while I work on the passwords?"

She gives me a thumbs up. "You got it."

I sit next to Julia on the couch and pull out my laptop from my backpack. First I log into my email and change that password, followed by my social media accounts. Then I change the password on my banking app just to be safe.

As I finish up, there's a knock at the door. Vyola answers and Val walks in with the pizza.

"Where's Preston?" Julia asks.

"He decided to go home to give Sylvie some space."

I make a mental note to thank him again later for his help. He may have kissed my man, but he was also there for me in my time of need. And he brought Val to me.

"Oh," Julia says. Is that a tinge of concern in her voice? With everything going on I haven't checked in with her about Preston.

We grab our food, move to the living room to eat, and put on some *Big Bang Theory* reruns. I'm in the middle of Julia and Vyola on the couch, while Val sits to the side of the coffee table on the floor.

As we eat in silence, I feel compelled to say something.

"Thank you," I start. "All of you. I don't think I would have found the strength to leave him without you."

Julia takes my hand. "Sylvie you found that strength all on your own."

"The way you told him off today," Vyola says. "I'm so proud of you."

"We're all proud of you," Val adds. He's still looking at me like I'm his whole world. I want nothing more than to curl up into him. To tell him that I love him. But I know now isn't the right time.

The sun has long since set when Julia says, "Sylvie, are you okay if I take off?"

There's nothing else for me to do tonight but finish unpacking my things. I shake my head. "Thank you for everything."

We embrace, and then Julia hugs Vyola and shakes Val's hand. I see something pass between them. An unspoken moment of gratitude, or maybe an apology.

After Julia leaves, Val says, "I should probably get going too."

I know he's right, but I don't want him to leave just yet. There's so much I haven't gotten the chance to say to him.

"I'll walk you out."

We leave the apartment and walk down to his car, hand in hand. When we reach the curb he says, "Come here you," and folds me into a hug.

I wrap my arms around his torso and breathe him in.

"Thank you," I say into his heart.

"For what?"

"For being here."

"I'll always be here for you."

He has. He's shown up for me in ways I didn't even know I needed.

We stand there like that, locked in an embrace until I feel the cold air nipping at my skin.

"I don't want to let you go."

"You don't have to," he says. "I can sleep on the floor."

But I have to let him go. As much as I want him here with me, I need to spend this night alone. Well, —alone with Vyola.

I shake my head. "I have to do this on my own."

He takes my chin between his thumb and forefinger. "I'm so proud of you, Sylvie. You're a survivor."

He kisses me.

"I'm sorry for ghosting you," I murmur.

"That wasn't your fault."

"I thought you didn't want me,"

"Sylvie I—"

"Later," I cut him off and pull him down for another kiss.

I don't want to talk about Preston right now, I just want this moment to be perfect for us.

"Whenever you're ready." And I know he means that. It could be tomorrow or next month, but I know when Val puts something on my timeline, he will wait for me until I'm ready.

Damn if I don't love this man. He respects my boundaries and my needs.

I pull away just enough so I can look him in the eyes. "Text me when you get home?"

He kisses me again, softly this time. "Of course."

I want to tell him I love him, but now isn't the time. Instead, I reluctantly withdraw from his embrace and watch him walk to his car and drive off into the night.

When I return to the apartment, Vyola is waiting with ice cream and *The Princess Bride*. "Girls night?"

"Hell yes."

It's exactly what I needed.

Chapter 49

Sylvie

The first two weeks after I left Theo feel strange. I wouldn't say I missed him, but rather I missed the intimacy between two people who lived together for so long. I hate to say it, but he probably knows me better than most.

He just didn't want to accept me for who I am.

Now I'm surrounding myself with people who see me. Julia, Vyola, and Valentino. I don't know how I got lucky enough to find him. Out of the millions of people to run into that day playing *Mundo*, by some twist of fate, he and I found each other. He supports me as I pursue my dreams, like my internship with Arino Family Practice, which starts in a few weeks. For now, the plan is still to work for Julia while living with Vyola and save as much money as I can.

I started attending classes again, catching up on my homework as best I can with finals looming.

It took a week before I finally had the bandwidth to sit down with Val and talk about everything that happened.

We had been texting every day and he'd call me to ask about my day and to say goodnight, but we hadn't talked about everything that happened.

We met at Potions and Pages, our spot, and talked for hours while sitting on the third-floor chaise. He told me about the kiss with Preston—how it didn't mean anything to him, that he was only concerned about me. I told him about Theo's blackmail and how I couldn't contact him—and then chose not to after Julia told me about the kiss. After all that, Val explained how he was supposed to audition with The Outlaws for The Third Guildmaster's Odyssey when Preston came knocking on his door.

Be still my heart. He gave up the chance to play in the Odyssey—for me.

With everything out in the open, we fall into each other's arms and make out until we heard someone's footsteps on the stairs.

Before we part for the night, he asks me to be his date to his family's Thanksgiving. I have to decline because Julia already invited me over.

I can see the pain from the rejection in his eyes, so I suggested going to 2Game to watch Speed and Xander play in the third Odyssey together.

Today's our second official date. It's been a little over two weeks since I moved out.

Val's picking me up any minute, and I'm cooking my stuffed shells to take to the potluck at 2Game. My eyes drift to the door again. I've been impatiently waiting for him to arrive and my heart won't stop racing. Because today's the day I will tell Valentino Santos that I love him.

The timer for the stuffed shells goes off. I pull them from the oven and set them on the counter to cool when a sharp knock comes from the door.

That's got to be him. My heart jumps to my throat and my body shakes. I take a calming breath smooth out my shirt and walk to the door.

On the other side, I find Val dressed in his dark wash jeans and BGN Odyssey jersey, long wavey hair flowing around his face.

How is he so gorgeous?

He smiles and says, "Hey Rhea," before producing a bouquet of chrysanthemums and white tulips from behind his back.

I fight to keep the tears at bay. "Are these for me?"

Val nods.

And I remember what he said on our first date—how he didn't get me flowers then because I'd have nowhere to put them. But now I do.

"Let me put these in water," I say, taking them. Val follows me into the apartment, shutting the door behind us. I find a vase in the cabinet under the sink, fill it with water, and trim the stems before arranging them in the vase.

"They're beautiful," I say, turning to him, my arms out in a silent request.

Val quickly envelops me, pulling me tight against his chest. I relax into his hold. Why did I wait over a week to see him again?

"I've missed you," he whispers against my ear.

The timber of his voice sends shivers down my spine. Val presses kisses along my neck. I indulge, turning my head so our lips meet, and dig my hands into his hair. Val pulls me in closer, and I feel his passion straight to my core.

I have to rip myself away from his kiss, or else we won't be going anywhere tonight. Plus, there's always later.

"What can I help with?" Val asks.

I shake my head. "Nothing. I just have to put foil on the dish I'm bringing."

Val peers around my shoulders to look at what I made. "Are those your infamous handmade stuffed shells?"

"The very same."

"I can't wait to taste them. Everyone else will have to fight me for them."

"As long as you save some for me."

"Of course, why wouldn't I?"

I want to say something but decide to save the story for later. Fuck Theo. I refuse to let a bad memory ruin this moment.

After packing up the food in a heat-safe container, Val leads me down the three flights of stairs. When we get to his car, he opens both door, for the food, and the front one for me. Once I'm seated, he shuts the door, gets in, starts the car, and takes my hand. It's like he wants the constant reassurance that I'm here.

"How has your day been?" Val asks, when we're on our way.

"You'll never guess who texted me," I say, excitedly.

"It's not Theo is it?" Val asks.

"Hell no," I say with a laugh. It's a joke. Val knows the only communication we have is through our lawyers. Speed thinks we have a good case against him.

The journal I kept will help because it documents the abuse and when Theo started buying new things for him, not for us.

"Good, because I will kick his ass."

I know he's telling the truth. Val almost went after Theo the day I moved out. "He's not worth it."

"You are," Val says.

But Val's reputation has already taken enough of a hit for me. After Prospero's podcast, Val's subscriber count increased again, but it's nowhere near the same numbers he had at the height of his career with BGN.

"Who messaged you?" Val asked.

"My sister."

"Miranda," Val says, then corrects himself. "Wait, she goes by Randy, right?"

"Yep," I say, popping the "p". "She wants to go to Marviewburg University and asked me to show her around campus. She's coming to visit with Dad and Mason."

"Are you going to meet with them?"

"I think so. And I'd like it if you met them too."

Val's smile stretches the width of his face. "I'm great with parents." Of course, he is. "Does that mean you'll meet my parents too?"

Now that makes me nervous. Val's mom is a huge support system for him, and she's been waiting for him to bring home someone for a while. "If you think you're ready for that," I say.

Our relationship has been non-traditional and messy from the start. So we're trying to take things slow-ish now that we have a clean slate. But we're like two magnets constantly being pulled towards each other. Nobody gets to define our relationship but us. And if it feels right to meet our families, then so be it. Nobody else can judge us.

We find a parking spot near 2Game, walk into the shop, and are greeted by Theseus. Technically, this is a members-only event, but Theseus made an exception for me if I brought food.

"Are those stuffed shells?" he asks as I pull out the dish.

"Hand stuffed," Val says.

Suddenly I have a ravenous swarm of men surrounding the table.

"Gentlemen, manners," Theseus scolds, and the men form a single-file line behind me. They wait patiently as a few other women and I get our food first.

The stream doesn't start for another hour, so we have plenty of time to play and chat.

At nearly eight p.m., Preston walks through the door. He's carrying a cookie platter and sets it on the table. "Sorry, I'm late."

Val tenses next to me and I put a hand on his thigh. His eyes meet mine. "You good?" I ask.

He nods. "We're good."

I know they weren't speaking for a while, but I trust Val to tell me if something is wrong.

Preston takes his time, talking to a few of the regulars before grabbing a plate of food and approaching our table.

"This seat taken?" he asks, indicating the one across from Val.

"All yours," Val says, leaning back.

"Are you excited to watch Speed and Xander?" I ask, trying to break the tension. "I'm guessing the tryout went well if they're playing together."

Preston laughs, almost spitting out his food. "Xander said it was a shit show. He and Mia banded together to leave Speed and Kat at each other's throats."

My eyebrows pull together. "Why are they still playing together?"

"That stream broke all The Outlaw's previous viewer records," Val says.

"Always for the views," Preston says.

Val pulls me closer and kisses the top of my head. "Not always," he whispers.

My heart swells at everything he's not saying. Val left that opportunity for me. I could easily be watching him play with The Outlaws, but Valentino Santos chose me. He was there for *me*. If that's not love, I don't know what is.

"How have you been?" Preston asks.

"Good. Things are picking back up with the stream."

"I've noticed," he says. "I'm happy for you."

"How are things with Julia?" Val asks.

I take a bite of my food. I know they met up for coffee to talk things over, but she's been very tight-lipped about her relationship with Preston.

"She's giving me the chance to prove myself."

"What does that mean?"

"It's not enough for me to just say I'm sorry. I hurt her and broke her trust. So we're slowly rebuilding it. I went to therapy a couple of times with her."

"The things we do for those we love," Valentino nods.

A couple more regulars join us and we theorize about what the third Odyssey will be like until it's time to start the stream. We move into the theatre room where several couches and chairs have been arranged in front of the projector.

Val chooses a couch and sits down, stretching his arm across the back. I snuggle into his side and his arm falls over me, pulling me in close. As the stream starts and the lights go down, it's almost the same feeling as when we were alone on the third floor of Potions and Pages. But it doesn't matter where we are, because as long as I'm in his arms, I'm exactly where I belong.

"Hey Val," I whisper.

"Yeah, babe?"

"I love you."

His eyes snap to mine, his mind processing what I just said. Then he gets on the floor in front of me, taking both of my hands in his. "Say it again." he demands.

There's some grumbling about love birds down in the front but Val ignores them, keeping his gaze pinned on me.

I blush and purse my lips before I repeat, "I'm in love with you, Valentino Santos."

Val surges forward, capturing my mouth in a searing kiss, earning more commentary from the gallery.

"I'm in love with you too, Sylvie Rivera."

Then he stands up and shoves a fist into the air yelling, "She loves me!"

There are hoots and hollers along with some "we knows" before Val settles back down on the couch next to me, pulling me in tight and kissing the top of my head.

"No funny business," Theseus warns.

My face is on fire from embarrassment, but it feels right to have told him. Everything with Valentino Santos feels right, because Val taught me what true love is.

Love is not only about the passion between two people. It's about respect and honesty. Val is a partner who will stand beside me, even in the face of opposition. Val and I have faced that opposition and come out of it even stronger than before. He will protect and nurture my heart just as I will his.

With Val, my heart and soul have finally found peace.

The End

Epilogue

Six Months Later

Sylvie

"Val, babe, we're going to be late," I say in between moans as Val's tongue runs up my core, circling it around my clit.

Jolts of pleasure shoot through me like lightning arcing across the sky, electrifying every nerve and leaving a trail of heat in its wake. I love my boyfriend's tongue and the way he knows exactly how much pressure to—

"Ah!" I throw my arms out to my sides, digging my fingers into the comforter.

When I gave Val a key to my studio apartment, I didn't expect to come home from work to find him naked, holding a bouquet of flowers over one of my favorite views. I barely got two steps inside before he was on me, pinning me against the door, capturing my mouth in a heated kiss, stripping me down, and navigating me to the bed.

And that's where I've been for the past—actually, I don't know how long it's been since Val's been devouring me.

"We've got plenty of time before we meet your father," Val purrs from between my legs. Then he sucks my clit into his mouth and my back bows off the bed. "Or I could just stop."

"Don't you dare. Finish what you started." I slip my hands into his hair, holding him to my core as I grind myself against his tongue.

"Yes," Val groans. "That's it baby."

I ride his mouth, chasing my climax until he slips two fingers inside me, curling them at just the right angle to hit the perfect spot.

"Give it to me Rhea, give me your orgasm," he commands.

My body tenses, then melts as ecstasy overtakes me. Val's talented tongue continued to work me through the waves until I am begging him to stop.

Val stands, grabs a condom, and slides it over his length before pulling me to the edge of my bed. My hips balance on the edge while I hook my legs around his neck. He slides inside me with a single snap of his hips.

"Perfect, every time," he groans, thrusting into me again.

He sets a rapid pace, hips pounding into me. This is not about making love to me. That would come later, probably after dinner. Right now he is satisfying the carnal desire we have for each other. I'm more than okay with that. Val always makes sure I am taken care of before he gets his release.

"You take every inch of this cock so well." Val wraps his arms around my legs, holding me as he continues to slam into me at his relentless pace. And I love every inch of his cock, every inch of him. I want to reach up and run my hands over his beautiful tawny skin, but my body feels like jello, cooked pasta, or something else without structural integrity. It's all I can do to curl my fingers into my comforter as he drives my pleasure higher again.

"Please Val," I say.

"One more, give it to me."

Each drive of his length into me pushes me higher until the tight coils of pleasure snap, and I'm floating over the edge of my second orgasm.

"That's it. Good girl," Val praises.

A few more thrusts and Val buries himself deep, a low moan rumbling through his chest as he finds his release. Still supporting my legs, he leans forward to place a kiss on my lips.

"Welcome home love," he says.

I laugh and kiss him again. "A girl could get used to this."

He withdraws and takes care of the condom. "Can you stand or do you need a minute?"

"I need a minute that I don't think we have," I say. Rolling over I pat around the comforter looking for my phone. I swear he tossed it on my bed, but maybe it's with the rest of my clothes.

"It's six thirty four," Val informs me.

Only four minutes behind schedule.

Reluctantly, I shimmy off my bed and tentatively test my weight on my noodle legs. Val moves behind me, wrapping his arms around my generous mid section, steadying me. His lips find the skin at the nape of my neck.

I take a moment to close my eyes, relishing in his affection before stepping out of his embrace. I grab his pants from the floor and toss them in his direction. "Clothes, now."

Val grabs them easily out of the air. "Fine," he pouts but gathers the rest of his clothes and dresses in a dark blue henley and dark wash jeans.

Leaving my work clothes on the floor, I cross the small space between my bed and dresser to pull out my favorite pair of jeans and a floral blouse.

Now dressed, Val plops down onto my hand-me-down couch Vyola gave me when I moved out last month. I'm still in a legal battle with Theo over credit card fraud, so my credit is still shot. Thankfully, my boss, Erik Arino, knew a guy who knew a guy who was renting out his studio apartment and was willing to take a chance on me.

So, for the first time in my life, I have an apartment I can call my own. And I have a gorgeous man I get to call mine. I'm lucky, but I also deserve to have good things in life. Took some time and therapy of my own to help me come to terms with that. Some days are still harder than others.

I make a quick trip to the bathroom, and then I'm ready to go.

"What's your dad in town for again?" Val asks as we leave.

I shut and lock the door. "He said something about a corporate summit. I'm just surprised he came back so soon.

It seems like he's been finding more excuses to come visit me. He first visited with my sister Randy, as she was touring Marviewburg University. She'll be going there in the fall. Dad, Randy, and Mason all came out for my graduation a few weeks ago, and now this.

"How do you feel about that?" Val asks.

"What are you, my therapist?" I tease.

"That could be a new role play." Val opens the car door for me.

I laugh and shake my head. "That one's a little too close to home."

While he gets in and starts the car, I pull up my text thread with my father. It's thirty minutes to the restaurant. I shoot my dad a text saying we're running ten minutes behind because of traffic.

I put my phone between my thighs and take Val's outstretched palm. "I feel like he's genuinely trying to reconnect. And I appreciate that."

Val squeezes my hand, giving me his silent understanding and support. I squeeze back.

"So how did you spend your Friday off? Besides waiting naked for me to come home?" I ask.

He tosses a grin in my direction. "Played *Mundo* with Mason."

"Not naked I hope," I tease.

Val sends me a wink. "That's only for you."

"I feel like you play with Mason more than you play with me."

"Not true."

"I love that you want to get to know my siblings."

Val gives me a look like he's holding a secret behind those eyes. "Mason's a good kid. Wicked smart. Loves his big sisters."

Both Mason and Randy are good kids. Somehow, against the odds of dealing with their evil mother, they're good people.

Looking out the window, I watch the Umberwoods neighborhood pass by as we sit in comfortable silence. *Epic*, the musical, playing in the background. My current obsession.

"What are you thinking, love?" Val asks.

I turn to look at him, his beautiful tawny skin, dark eyes, the facial hair accentuating his jawline. My boyfriend is a work of art.

"Just that I have everything I could have ever wanted," I say. My internship turned into a job opportunity. I have my own apartment, I have awesome friends and this amazing man in my corner supporting me.

I couldn't ask for anything more.

Valentino

I offer my hand to Sylvie, helping her exit my car and we walk hand in hand towards Vellum & Vine, an upscale dining establishment in the Umberwoods. Her father, John Davis, is already waiting for us in a booth, sipping on his whiskey.

John is a handsome, rugged type with masculine charm. He's tall with a lean build, salt and pepper hair, and a beard. I see the similarities between he and his daughter. They have the same eyes, and the same jawline. When he sees us, he sets down his glass and stands with arms outstretched. Sylvie releases my hand to fold herself into her father's embrace.

I'm filled with a sense of awe for my girlfriend, as she can still open her heart to her father, even after the man left her behind with her shitty ex. I have many choice words for both her father and her ex. I save them for Speed and Xander.

Releasing his daughter, he turns to me. "Good to see you Val," he says, extending a hand. Grasping it, I prepare for the tight squeeze, making sure I return the appropriate pressure.

"Good to see you too, John."

We slide into the booth and the server comes over to take our drink orders. John orders a whiskey neat, Sylvie orders a margarita, and I stick with water since I'm driving.

"How was work today?" John asks Sylvie.

"Good." She has to be careful what she says, patiently confidentiality and all that. "I've been seeing some of the same clients for a few months now and I think we're making real progress."

"That's great to hear." John turns to me. "And you're with an IT company?"

I don't stop the smile that overtakes my face. "Not anymore."

"So you quit your job?" A look of confusion crosses his face. This could be a delicate conversation, but I've prepared for it.

"I started a media company called Rogues of Revelry with one of my former Odyssey teammates, Bastian Hawthorne."

There's a spark of recognition in John's eyes at my mention of Bastian's last name. Yeah man, he's one of those Hawthornes. He quickly recovers and continues to grill me on my business plan. I don't mind. Considering what happened with Theo, John wants to know that his daughter is dating a responsible man.

"What type of media?" he asks.

"We'll focus on gaming, digital storytelling, and modern media culture."

"Do you have any sponsors?"

"We have two, including Prospero. Bastian's working on a few more leads. I'm developing content right now."

Sylvie whips her head around to look at me. "Prospero? Are you serious?"

I simply nod.

She throws her arms around me as best she can while sitting next to me in the booth. "Valentino Santos, how dare you keep this a secret from me?"

A small laugh escapes. "It just happened today."

"We should celebrate!"

The look I give her reminds her exactly how we celebrated already. The blush on her cheeks is adorable.

John clears his throat. "Do you have studio space?"

I nod. "In Hawthorne Towers. Equipment should be here next week."

The server returns with our drinks and asks for our orders. John Orders a filet mignon. Sylvie decides on the wild mushroom risotto, while I have my eye on a shrimp scampi.

Conversation flows easily throughout the rest of the meal. John and Sylvie do most of the talking and I don't mind. They need this time together to heal the wounds between them.

As we're finishing up our food, Sylvie leans over to me and asks, "Let me out?"

I slip out of the booth and then hold out my hand for her. She takes it, stands, and heads toward the restroom. I retake my seat across from John.

This is the moment I've been waiting for. There is an important question I need to ask him tonight because I don't know the next time he will be in town.

"You seem to have a solid plan for your business," he says.

"Thank you, we gave it a lot of thought. Pitched it to sponsors. I also have six months worth of savings." I need John to understand that I didn't just decide to quit my job one day and become a streamer. I'm more responsible than that.

John regards me as he takes a sip of his whiskey. He's staring like he's trying to see into me, searching for a deception. "How long have you and Sylvie been together?"

"Going on eight months."

"I was scared when I heard she was dating someone so soon after breaking up with Theo."

I nod in understanding. "He's sorting mail at his father's company last I heard."

"Fucker deserves so much worse." John swirls his whiskey. I raise my water glass to cheers him. That much we can agree on.

Enough of Theo, I thought. I have to steer the conversation toward a different topic.

"I love your daughter, sir."

"It scares a father when he hears that from a young man."

I don't know what to say to that, so I keep my gaze steady on him while I wait for him to elaborate.

John surprises me by saying, "You must think I'm a horrible person."

Yes, but I don't say that. "I don't presume to know what it's like to have a child."

"You're never ready. Those nine months are not enough time to prepare you for the moment you hold your child in your arms for the first time."

"Mhm," I say and take a drink of water. This conversation has deviated and I need to get it back on track. Maybe the direct route is best. "She's not a little girl anymore, John."

He takes a drink of whiskey. "I know."

"I want you to know that I intend to marry her."

John's eyes go wide as he almost chokes on his drink. He takes a minute to collect himself, coughing and clearing his throat. "I'm sorry that was a bad reaction."

"I hope it doesn't reflect how you feel about the idea."

I'm not asking him because I feel like I need permission. Sylvie's opinion is the only one that matters. But I want John to know that I'm serious about Sylvie, that she's the best thing to ever happen to me, and I want to be a part of her entire life, including her family.

"I knew you were serious, but you said it's only been eight months. Are you sure?"

"Never been more sure about anything in my life. I'm not going to pop the question anytime soon. She's settling into her new life. But I want you to know how serious I am about Sylvie."

John's gaze is steady, measuring me with the scrutiny of a craftsman inspecting something of great value—evaluating my strength, resolve, or something else. He let the silence stretch between us as he comes to his decision.

"I couldn't ask for a better man to take care of my daughter." John holds his hand out to me.

A faint smile crosses my lips as I take his hand and we shake.

The love of my life reappears at the table. "Sorry about that... is everything okay?"

John looks at her with tears in his eyes. "Yes, sweetheart."

"Your dad tried to choke on his whiskey," I say smoothly.

Sylvie laughs and slides into the booth again.

That night, as I hold my sleeping titaness to my chest, I study her features wondering what gods blessed me with such a creature. And, as I pull her closer, I imagine how I will happily spend the rest of my life showing her exactly how much I love her.

Acknowledgements

This novel has been a labor of love and many years in the making. *Games of Tangled Hearts* was born out of the idea of adapting the Shakespeare play, *Two Gentlemen of Verona*, into a gamer novel. I knew it was ambitious even from the start, but I didn't realize how ambitious until I was into the weeds. I poured so much of myself into setting up these characters, and this world that I hope you enjoyed it.

As much as I put myself into this novel, I was not alone, and I could not have done it without the support of many.

First, thank you first to my husband who has faithfully supported my efforts to pursue my dreams and also to make him a stay-at-home cat dad.

Thank you to my dad and family for rooting me on, even if they didn't always understand.

This novel wouldn't be possible without Katelynn, Keara, Lauren, Linette, Rose & Sami reminding me that I have a story worth telling.

Thank you to Karena, my writing coach. My editor Jessica, thank you for all your support and polishing this gem. To Kateryna for working with me to create the gorgeous cover. And to Kailey who helped me feel beautiful in my own skin.

And to you, for reading this. Your support means more to me than you would ever know.

Your first novel is a labor of love and lots of lessons learned, but I would want it to be any other way. *Games of Tangled Hearts* is exactly the story I needed to tell.

About the Author

Kelsey Winton writes nerdy love stories for readers who believe that romance is just as epic as any adventure. With a deep love for gaming, *Dungeons & Dragons*, and modern relationships, she blends heart, humor, and a little bit of chaos into every story. She lives with her partner and four feline overlords, who graciously allow her to write—when they're not demanding attention.

Games of Tangled Hearts is her debut novel, bringing together the best of geek culture, friendship, and a love that's worth the grind.

Connect with Kelsey on social media @authorkelseywinton or her website.

Bonus Chapter

Speed

Well this turned into a cluster fuck of an evening. It started when Val invited me to join him in auditioning with Kat and Mia from The Outlaws, a team in The Guildmaster's Odyssey. They need two more players for their team because, from what I've seen in their video footage, their previous two teammates got fed up with Kat's combative nature and quit after the second Odyssey.

As a divorce lawyer, I'm used to being in high tension situations, so I knew Kat wouldn't be anything I couldn't handle. Especially if teaming up with The Outlaws means I get to play Mundo in The Guildmaster's Odyssey. The third and final Odyssey is in a little over two weeks. Besides, her bold and striking beauty continually draws my eye to her video window.

The four of us are just about to start playing when our other two friends, Preston and Xander, all but knock down the door saying Val's true love, Sylvie, needs his help. So he had to make a choice, either audition for their team or go get the girl.

True to his namesake, he left. Not that I blame him. Val deserves happiness with someone who doesn't put him second—cough cough Preston. Sylvie deserves love too. The two of them together are sickeningly sweet together.

That leaves Xander and me alone in Val's apartment with Kat and Mia and down one spot to audition.

"Hello new person," Mia says.

Kat is not so kind. "Who the hell are you supposed to be?"

Xander's head whips toward me as if to ask, *what the fuck?*

A slow smile spreads across my face. He wasn't expecting her barbed tongue. From my extensive research, I knew Kat would be fun to play with.

"WildKat, TinyTitan, this is PixelatedStone. He'll be auditioning for the Odyssey instead of Val," I say.

"Nice to meet you," Xander says to Mia and Kat, but he raises one eyebrow at me.

Pixel, Xander's service dog, lays her head in Xander's lap and he absently pets her. Restarting SaintVal's stream, Xander says, "Good evening Saints. This is PixelatedStone filling in for SaintVal while he's on his quest for true love. But I'm going to log in as Luciento and we're going to quest with WildKat and TinyTitan while I tell you everything I know about this love story."

I'm sure the Saints are going to love that. But in all honesty, Val was tight-lipped about Sylvie. Of course, I know about them because I am his right hand man. One might even say I'm the one who brought them together—not that I'll get a thank you. But I doubt Val told much about Sylvie to Xander and even less to Preston.

"The Saints are asking how Val and Rhea met," Xander reads from Val's chat.

I know this one. "Easy. They met playing *Mundo.*"

"Are you serious? That's adorable," Mia responds.

"Val said they fought a Windkin together. She swooped in and saved him with that fancy axe of hers."

"Sounds like a woman after my own heart. Now if we're done playing matchmaker, are we actually going to play?" Her tongue was as sharp as her eyeliner.

If someone didn't know Xander as well as I do, they'd miss the way the corner of his mouth twitches at Kat's words. It's a nervous tick.

"What do you want to do?" Xander asks. He's trying to placate her.

"We found something on our way over here," Mia says, her voice bright and happy in comparison to Kat.

"Follow me," Kat orders, turning her avatar, a human warrior named Reyna, around and going back east towards Emor.

I think it's presumptuous that she thinks we're automatically going to follow her. But we are trying to get along so she'll invite us to join The Outlaws. Maybe her stream doesn't want to hear about Val's love life. Either way, I navigate Nix, my half-demon bard, after her.

"You sure you know where you're going?" I can't help but push her buttons a little bit.

For three long seconds, there's a heavy silence over the mics. "Your project is unwarranted. Not all of us are incompetent."

Mia cuts in. "We found the quest in Hearthglen. It's between Anerov and Emor."

"Which one of you is Machiava?"

"I am," Kat says.

"Oh that makes sense."

On video, I see Kat's eyebrows pull together. She goes to say something but Mia cuts in. "I'm in Junta."

"Awesome, us too," Xander says. "We'll get some bonus experience for working together then."

I know the two of them are trying to turn the conversation away from the thorny moments between Kat and me. Unfortunately for them, I'm not done trying to figure out what makes her tick.

"So Kat," I draw out her name. "What made you choose Machiava?"

"If my selection of faction is logical, I assume you would have figured it out by now."

"Humor me."

"No thank you."

"How about you tell me then?" Xander asks.

Kat audibly exhales. "To dissolve the patriarchy—obviously."

Ah, she's one of those types of gamers. I shouldn't be surprised given her background. "Been burned one too many times little dove?"

I watch with joy as her face contorts, shriveling up with disgust at the nickname.

"Are you dense?" She asks.

"Not at all. Why would you assume that? Is it because I'm a man? That's not very feminist of you."

Xander cuts in. "Saints want to know where Val took Rhea on their first date."

That one, I don't know. "SaintVal was stingy with that information."

"He didn't tell you?"

I shake my head. "No, and I'm very offended he didn't."

"Since we don't know, let's guess. Where would you take a first date?" Mia suggests.

"Dinner," I answer. It's classic and classy, and I can tell a lot about my date from how they sit down in their chair, to if they want dessert at the end of the night.

"Boring," Kat criticizes.

Excuse me? Boring? A dinner date is anything but boring. "Only if you can't carry a conversation."

"You assume your company is desired."

"If the person is on a date with me then, yes, I do assume."

"I think a first date should depend on the person," Mia interrupts.

"Or the time of year," Xander adds.

Dating is hard for him. Women are into the war veteran thing, but not so much the PTSD, service dog thing. Anytime he tries to be vulnerable with them, it's like their tough guy illusion of him is broken and they're no longer interested.

"So where are we going?" Xander asks.

"Hearthglen. It's a large town built on an estuary, lots of wooden bridges connecting everything," Mia answers.

"I don't think I've been there yet."

"I've been told it's better to build bridges than burn them," I say. Of course, I'm making a not-so-subtle jab at Kat.

"That's only if you care about building a bridge," Kat responds.

I'm about to say something when Xander pipes up, "Look at that!"

We emerge from the forests around Anerov to a bustling settlement where land and water meet. The village is nestled along the curved edge of an estuary. Cobblestone streets lead down to wooden docks and bustling marketplaces, where fishers, traders, and craftsmen offer their goods to locals and adventurers alike. A network of wooden bridges crosses the small inlet, connecting different parts of the village to create a system of walkways sprawling across both banks and estuary. Colorful boats rest in the shallow waters bobbing gently with the waves.

"This is gorgeous. I've never been here before," Xander says.

"Right!" Mia agrees.

Kat leads us to the local tavern so we can get the waypoint. That way if our characters were to die, we can fast travel to this point.

"The quest is by the docks," Mia explains as Reyna leads the group toward the docks to a man who is looking out over the water.

A text bubble floats above his head reading, "Oh no, what am I going to do?"

Kat approaches the man. She uses the voice-activated feature and asks, "Sir, do you need help?"

The NPC turns around looking delighted that someone asked. "Yes, oh I don't know what to do. I was fishing this morning out on the ocean when suddenly this woman popped her head out of the water. She had big green eyes that were staring up at me. Next thing I know, she cut my fishing line, taking off with my favorite bobber!"

Quest: The One that Got Away

Not his favorite bobber—seriously, who thought of this? Sometimes these small side quests are ridiculous.

"We can help you," Kat says, then moves Reyna away from the man and off the docks.

Quest Accepted: The One that Got Away.

"Wait a moment. You didn't ask about that woman," Xander says, following after Reyna.

"Why waste my breath? It's a Wavekin," Kat says.

I glance at Xander. His hand runs along Pixel's head. I purse my lips. He doesn't know how to handle someone like Kat who competes with him for the leader position.

The thing is, Kat's probably right. But we can't inflate her ego.

"Wavekin?" Xander asks.

"They are like fish people. They like to collect things from humans and are forever looking for the one thing that will satisfy the sorcerer who cursed them."

In all my time playing Mundo, I think I've battled a Wavekin once. Anorev, my faction Junta's home city, is landlocked. We don't encounter saltwater Enkin much.

"Thanks. It's nice to work with all the information," I say pointedly.

"I wasn't done, but if that's all you want." Kat shrugs.

"Kat," Mia warns.

She lets out a sigh. "They're nearly invisible in water."

"Can we lure them out with something?" Xander asks.

"Why would you do that?" Kat responds. Looking at her video box I see her face is twisted up in confusion. It's kind of cute.

Fighting can't be the only way we deal with them," I dare to say.

"It's the fastest."

"Fast doesn't always mean it's the best way little dove."

At the mention of my nickname, I'm rewarded by the sight of Kat's hackles rising. Her anger is like two eldritch blasts burning holes in the screen.

"Your incompetence is baffling. Feel free to walk, Nix off of the nearest cliff."

"And miss staring at your ass?"

"Now it makes sense, virtual is all you can get."

Mia's voice cuts off my verbal spar with Kat. "Guys The Outlaw's channel just gained one hundred subs in the last five minutes."

"Some more Saints have joined as well." I pull up SaintVal's stream on my tablet. Nix's emote, a purple sparkly lute, fills the feed.

"Thank you so much everyone!" Mia says. "Now come on, we have to find this Wavekin."

Mia's character, a gnome cleric named Elyndra, leads us down to the waterline along the docks.

We stand, weapons drawn, in the shallows, as waves gently lap at our feet. Elyndra takes a step forward. "I want to make a deal," Mia calls out.

A humanoid woman with bluish-green skin and purple hair emerges from the water. Her head is just visible above the surface. Big green eyes, a petite nose, and a tiny mouth. She looks ethereal, and graceful until she smiles a mouthful of sharp teeth.

"Deal?" her voice sounds like shoes stepping on glass.

"I thought you said the only way to deal with them was to fight them?" I ask Kat.

She bites her lower lip. "It's the most effective way."

"Hush you two. Let Mia talk," Xander scolds.

Mia gives him a nod of thanks. She returns to addressing the Wavekin. "I want to make a trade."

"Trade," the Wavekin grumbles in a way that makes it seem like she is less interested in a trade than making a deal.

"You took a fisherman's bobber."

"Tsh," the Wavekin hissed. "Found. Not steal."

"We mean no offense," I step in and cover for Mia's bumble. "We want to *trade* for the fisherman's bobber you found."

The Wavekin seems to ponder that. "Offer?"

"Anyone got any ideas?" Mia asks.

"I have this very shiny gold piece," I offer.

Kat barks out a laugh. "Gold, that's your offer?"

I shrug, "Women like gold."

"Money isn't everything..." Kat trails off like there's something more there. But now is not the time to dig deeper into it.

I've seen enough divorces to know that's not entirely true.

"I'm not sure if gold will be enough," Mia says.

"Enough of this," Kat says with a huff. Reyna, her avatar, draws her weapon and storms into the water.

"Fight," it hisses before diving back into the water.

Battle music begins playing. "Spread out. Look at the water," Kat orders.

Reluctantly, I do what I'm told, moving Nix away from the party to cover more ground. My eyes dash around the lapping waves, looking for any sort of movement. I catch it too late. The Wavekin jumps from the water, limbs extended, and rakes its claws across Nix's chest. As quickly as she appears, the Wavekin disappears back in the water. Literally, because she turns invisible in the water. Nix scrambles to get out of the water and back to the safety of shore.

My eyes flick to Kat's video window, a smug smile on her face.

Reyna splashes out into the water, sword raised. "Come at me salty harpy!"

The Wavekin leaps from the water to attack Reyna.

"Not a harpy," I say. They look more like nymphs or mermaids than harpies.

"Not the time," she retorts.

Before the Wavekin can slash at Reyna, Nix casts a spell, holding the Wavekin in place midair. That causes Kat's attack timing to be off. She swings when she expects the Enkin to be in range.

"You idiot! I just wasted my special attack on that swing," Kat cries out.

How was I supposed to know what she was doing when she didn't communicate that?

I may have messed up Kat's hit, but Xander wastes little time moving Valen forward, jumping in the air, and bringing both swords down on the creature. Mia also blasts it using one of Elyndra's magic spells.

It dies in two hits, leaving Reyna and Valen standing above the corpse of the creature.

"I got the bobber," Xander says. "Let's get back to the man."

Valen leads us back toward land and onto the docks. The man is elated that we've located his lucky bober. He clutches it to his chest and we're rewarded with a small sum of money and XP.

Quest Completed: The One that Got Away

"Well that was fun," I say as our avatars are gathered in a group on the docks.

"You said that with a straight face."

I do have a good poker face, but I don't appreciate her insinuating that I'm a liar on the internet.

"You can't tell me you don't want to play with me again," I say just to push her buttons.

"In no world would I ever–"

Mia cuts her off. "Kat, we've set records tonight. We absolutely want to play with them again."

Kat goes silent. I see her biting her lip in her video window. She's warring with herself. They need two more people and we just broke their highest record of viewers.

"I was just filling in for Val," Xander says.

"But we worked together so well."

Xander mouth pulls into a thin line as he looks down at Pixel. I understand he's torn. He was just here to be a placeholder because Val left. He never had any intention on being invited to play in The Guildmaster's Odyssey. What I don't understand is why he would turn down the opportunity.

With a shrug, I say, "Come on man, this is the chance of a lifetime."

After a few more moments of deliberation, Xander nods. "Okay, I'll play, if you'll have us."

Now my fate rests in Kat's rough hands. I look at the screen and watch her pick at the ends of her braid.

"Fine, they can play," she says through gritted teeth like a lioness snarling because someone took away her food.

"You won't regret it," I say, all smiles.

"I already do," Kat says, her hands rubbing her temples. She signs off abruptly leaving Mia, Xander, and me hanging out in *Mundo*.

"I'm happy to have you with us. I had a lot of fun today. We'll be in touch about the third Odyssey," Mia says, and then she signs off.

"Well, that went better than expected," I say, leaning back on the couch.

"You poked the bear."

"One of my favorite pastimes."

Xander shakes his head, hand stroking Pixel's head. "I don't know, Speed. She went toe to toe with you. I think you might have met your match.

I scoff. "Yeah, right."

There's not a woman on this earth that could bring me to heel.

Made in the USA
Middletown, DE
16 September 2025

13424498R00219